Also by Kainat Azhar

Journey to Hidaya

PEN DU LUM

KAINAT AZHAR

Merrinore Press
ISBN 979-8-9880164-2-7
Cover design by Maryna Arsenieva
Interior design by Lorna Reid
First edition September 2025
kainatazharchughtai.com

Trigger Warning

This novel deals with themes such as the death of a sibling, depression, and anxiety. Please read at your own discretion.

"How lucky I am to have something that makes saying goodbye so hard."

—Winnie the Pooh

Prologue

Fascinating, isn't it? How a pendulum swings back and forth, back and forth endlessly—unless stopped by air resistance or an external force.

Does the concept not give you pause? If not for the laws of physics, a pendulum could swing forever, oscillating back and forth until the end of time.

But to shatter your illusion as mine was shattered, know this—outside forces do exist.

And that's what happened to my family.

We were perfect—painfully, joyfully perfect. The corporate, nine-to-five dad. The loving, homemaker mom. The oldest brother, studying medicine and making us all proud. The middle one, who lived to make us all laugh.

And me—the youngest.

The only daughter. Prized beyond measure.

We lived in a house with a terrace garden. Siblings who bantered and fought but loved each other fiercely. Brothers who doubled as guardians and friends to their little sister. Parents who still went on date nights into their fifties and laughed into the night.

Our happiness swung back and forth like the bobs of a pendulum. Seemingly endless.

But like I said, there are always external forces. And one day, it struck.

Sudden. Sharp. Cruel. It broke the motion. Snapped the string. Stilled the joy.

And then, we were no longer the perfect family. No more banter between siblings. No more date nights for my parents. No more laughter or happiness or even the barest hint of contentment.

Because our pendulum had stopped swinging. And it had no intention of ever starting up again.

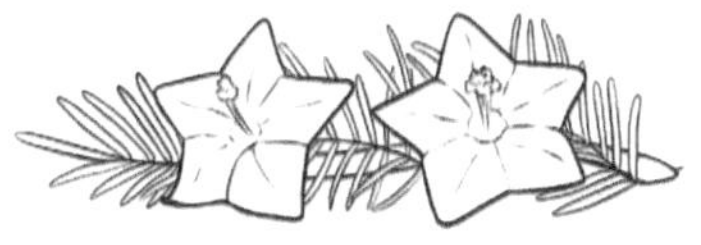

One

Cypress: Death, mourning

MY OLDEST BROTHER DIED at the age of twenty-four. And the world stopped spinning on its axis.

Two

Azalea: Fragility

I TRAIL UP THE stairs to my mom's room, carrying a tray of food and a bottle of DayQuil. Nudging the door open with the tray, I clear my throat to let her know I'm here.

The room is submerged in darkness save for a sliver of sunlight peeking through heavy curtains. My mom lies wrapped in blankets—a product of her perpetually feeling cold now—with her hair tied in a loose bun. She turns slightly, fixing me with a tired gaze.

"Hey, Mama," I say softly, setting the tray down on her bedside table and opening the curtains so sunlight floods in. She squints, shielding her face with one hand, then lowers herself back onto the pillow.

"What did the doctor say, hmm?" I murmur. "Soak in as much sun as you can."

She ignores me and croaks, "Is Arafat home yet?"

I still briefly at the sound of his name, heart hammering against my ribcage.

Mama continues as if she doesn't expect a response. "Let me know when he gets home. I'll cook him dinner."

I remain frozen for a few moments, trying to shove away the

heaviness settling like a suffocating cloud over me. I can't bend beneath its weight right now. I can only let myself succumb to it when I'm alone.

I take a deep breath and sit down on the bed beside my mom, placing the tray in my lap. I gently brush strands of hair from her eyes and nudge her. "Sit up, Mama. You have to eat."

It takes her more effort than it should to lift herself and rest against the headboard.

I smile and gesture to the tray. "I made chicken soup today. Your favorite."

She smiles weakly. "Did everyone else eat?"

I resist the tears pricking at the corners of my eyes. My dad is at work. So *everyone else* only consists of my brother Ihsaan, who's working from home. But we don't talk like that anymore.

I nod anyway and begin feeding her.

She sips slowly, pausing occasionally to glance around the room or run her fingers over a frayed patch in her clothes, as if seeing it all for the first time.

When she's done and has taken a spoonful of DayQuil, she snuggles back into her blanket and closes her eyes. "Wake me up when it's Asr time," she mumbles.

I nod, leaning down to kiss her forehead. "Okay, Mama."

I head downstairs with the tray. Lost in thought, I trip over the last stair and pitch forward, the tray crashing to the floor and its contents clanging loudly through the silence of the house.

I bend quickly, silently thanking God I used steel dishes instead of glass.

Footsteps rush towards me. When I look up, Ihsaan is bending down and murmurs, "Are you okay?"

I still briefly at his question. We haven't had a proper conversation in a long time, and just hearing the brotherly concern in his voice brings the ache surging back to my heart.

"Yes," I whisper, watching as he collects the dishes and sets them back on the tray. He rises with it and I mimic him, standing awkwardly in the hope he has something else to say.

But all he says is "be careful" before placing the tray in the kitchen and retreating to his home office.

I shouldn't be surprised. That's how it is between us now. Minimal words, necessary conversations. Carefully avoiding anything real. We're no longer the brother and sister who bantered and playfully fought so often that Arafat had to intervene. Not the Ihsaan and Hayat who called each other funny names and swapped sugar for salt in each other's coffee, racing to see who would complain to Arafat first.

Because I lost one brother to death. But the other—while he breathes—I've lost just the same.

Three

Marigold: Grief

WHEN I HEAD OUT for my morning walk earlier than usual, the sun is rising and the birds chirp cheerfully. Puffy clouds float across the multihued sky like sailboats drifting in the ocean. Vibrant green leaves coat the branches of the trees, preparing to change colors for the next season.

Everything is changing. Time is marching forward relentlessly, merciless and unforgiving. As if nothing has happened. As if the world hasn't collapsed on the shoulders of a once-happy family.

I fight off the tears threatening to climb up my throat.

Just keep walking. Just keep walking and it'll all go away.

All it takes is five minutes, though. A single leaf fluttering off a branch—that's what undoes me.

I press a hand against my stomach and begin to sob. Rough sobs that shake through my core and leave me unhinged.

Sometimes the pain is so unbearable, it becomes hard to breathe. Sometimes all it takes is one word, one image, one tiny memory for me to fall apart. Sometimes it can be as trivial as putting five plates on the dinner table before remembering the fifth isn't needed anymore. And then everything comes crashing down all at once, and the pain feels as fresh as it did two months ago.

"Hayat?"

My breath hitches. Holding back tears thickens the air in my throat. I roughly swipe at my eyes and blot my nose with the corner of my shirt, just as someone emerges in front of me.

Oh, no. It's Mikaal.

I avoid his gaze immediately and take a shaky breath. I forgot he takes walks early in the morning. Next time I'll have to leave later, at my usual time, so I don't risk encountering him again. I could do without his kind eyes and empathetic smile.

He looks so different now. I used to see him all the time—when he and Arafat studied together, or when he'd come over to hang out with my brothers. Then, when Things Went Downhill, everything changed. I saw him at the funeral and a couple times afterward, when his family brought food and kept checking in on us. But even then, he was quieter than usual. Rubbing his eyes with the kind of fatigue sleep can't fix and gazing mournfully around the house like he was searching for someone.

It's been days since I've seen him, though he lives just a few houses down from me. And now, he looks so...*tired.* Dark eye bags, scruffy stubble, hunched shoulders. So rough around the edges, frayed at the seams. As if he's trying desperately to hold himself together.

"Are you okay?" Mikaal asks, clearly witnessing my *not* okay-ness but still having the courtesy to ask.

I manage a nod, rubbing my watery eyes.

Mikaal searches his pockets and pulls out a tissue, handing it to me.

"Thanks," I mumble, voice soaked with tears.

He hesitates for a moment and I make the mistake of looking into his eyes. Immediately, I regret it—the grief pooling in them is almost too much.

After a moment, he says quietly—as if he doesn't believe his own words—"It'll get better."

I laugh scornfully. Everyone always says that. Everyone's been saying it from the beginning. At the funeral. At the gathering his university held. At the university hospital where he shadowed doctors. Weeks later, when people visited us and we were still crying as if it had happened only yesterday.

"Trust me, it will," Mikaal continues, sadness lacing every word. After a pause, he murmurs, "He was my best friend, too."

Something in his voice breaks me apart. I begin to sob uncontrollably, hands pressed to my face, blinking rapidly as I attempt to stem the flow of tears—trying to quiet the body that refuses to obey.

Mikaal looks stricken. "I'm so sorry, Hayat, I didn't mean to—"

I shake my head repeatedly. It's not his fault.

He sighs. "Look, keep making du'aa for him. I can't say not to cry or not to grieve— we're human, and it's natural. But…take care of yourself, okay? And trust that Allah will heal your heart with time."

I take deep, shaky breaths to reorient myself. Using the tissue Mikaal gave me, I blot my eyes and wipe my nose. Somewhere between the heartache and the tears, I register I must look nothing short of a complete, disheveled mess.

At the thought, I begin to laugh uncontrollably.

Mikaal throws me a quizzical look, and I simply shake my head. "I'm sorry," I say. "I'm so sorry."

"You have nothing to be sorry for," he replies automatically, the surprised lilt in his voice indicating how absurd he thinks my apology is.

"Well, I'm gonna—" I gesture behind me. "Thank you for the—" I hold up the used tissue, then feel stupid for doing so.

He nods, clearly understanding what I don't say. I back away quickly, wanting nothing more than to escape the sadness in his gaze.

When I'm a couple feet away, I think I hear him sigh. A long, loud sigh.

When I return home, my dad is sitting at the kitchen table with a cup of tea and toast, reading the news on his phone.

He was never an early riser. He'd pray Fajr, crawl back into bed, and struggle to wake up again for work. Most mornings, we had to hurry him out of his room, still yawning and rubbing his eyes, half-asleep.

But Arafat's departure has changed us all.

Seeing the breakfast in front of my dad, guilt prickles in my chest. "Salaam, Papa," I say, taking off my shoes.

He looks up and for a moment I catch the exhaustion in his face—before it splits into a wide grin. "Shehzaadi! Wa 'Alaikum Salaam." He locks his phone and stands to embrace me, pressing a kiss to my forehead. "Good morning."

"Good morning. Why didn't you wait for me? I would've made you breakfast."

He waves me off. "It's no big deal. How was your walk? You left early today."

I hesitate. "Same old."

He scrutinizes my face a little too carefully. "You okay?"

"Yes, of course." I turn away, tracing a finger along the place mat.

I think he senses he's treading dangerous waters, so he shifts gears. "That soup you made yesterday was so good. I was dreaming about it."

I laugh, some of the tension in my shoulders easing. "Really? I'll make some more if you want."

He shakes his head. "You tire yourself too much. We'll order food today."

"Are you sure? I don't mind cooking something."

"Yes, I'm sure. What are you in the mood for?"

I shrug. "Whatever you guys want."

"But what do *you* want?"

I mull over the question, tentatively voicing my opinion. "How about we go out to eat today?"

Papa's expression falters. "Beta…" he starts. "I'm not sure that's the best idea. You know how your Mama would feel…"

I nod quickly. "You're right, I'm sorry. I just thought…maybe it would be nice after some time."

He sighs. "It would. But you know…Layla. I'm not sure she could handle that right now."

"You're right, you're right. It's fine. We can just order pizza or something."

"Pizza?" Papa stands and begins washing the dishes in the sink despite my protests. "A world of possibilities and you want pizza?"

I widen my eyes innocently. "What's wrong with pizza?"

He bops my nose. "Nothing at all. Text me the order. I'll have Ihsaan pick it up on his way back from work. I need to head out early today—IT demands—but I'll be back sooner than usual."

"Okay. Wait—don't leave yet." I rush to the fridge. "Let me get your lunch."

Papa sighs, and for a moment, the playful smile slips off his face. I glimpse something he rarely lets us see: sadness. "My studious Shehzaadi, valedictorian daughter, obsessed with school and assignments and academics…you grew up so suddenly," he whispers, smoothing my hair back as he takes the lunch container from me.

I hug him fiercely and watch as he leaves and gets in his Civic. As always, I don't look at the car parked at the back of the driveway. In fact, I very purposefully keep my eyes away from it as I watch my father drive off.

For the next hour and a half, I busy myself by cleaning the house, checking on my mom, and organizing the pantry. Then I open my laptop at the kitchen table and spend the usual ten minutes staring at the Princeton admissions letter on the screen—a familiar ache piercing through my chest—before moving on to other work.

By the time I finish, it's 8:30 A.M., and Ihsaan is coming down the stairs.

Shoot. Seeing him reminds me: I forgot to ask Papa to Zelle me money for my Rutgers application. I bite my lip, anxiety coursing through me.

I could text him now. But he just left for work—I don't want to add to his list of worries. I haven't been able to find my wallet either, so using any of my cards is out of the question (I should probably be more concerned about this, but a lot of things don't seem to hold my attention the way they used to).

The sound of footsteps descending the stairs jars me out of my thoughts.

"Morning," Ihsaan murmurs, sparing me a little wave.

"Morning," I wave back. "Do you want me to make you something?"

He shakes his head. "I'll eat later at work."

"You won't have breakfast?"

Ihsaan peeks inside the fridge. "No."

I check my watch. "How much time do you have before you need to leave?"

"Ten minutes."

I close my laptop. "I'll make you something."

"It's fine, honestly. I'll grab a granola bar and coffee at work."

I shake my head. "Just wait a couple minutes."

Ihsaan reluctantly nods and heads back upstairs to change and say goodbye to Mama.

I move fast. I whisk an egg with diced veggies, fry the omelet, toast bread, and spread cream cheese on it. Then I layer the omelet on the bread, cut the sandwich in half, and wrap it tightly in foil just as the scent of Ihsaan's perfume wafts down the stairs.

"Thank you," he says, genuinely grateful as I hand him the wrapped sandwich. "Papa told me to pick up pizza after work. Text me the order."

I nod as he grabs his car keys and rushes out the door, revving his Yaris. Again, I do not look at the parked car ahead of his. I keep my gaze fixed only on Ihsaan as he drives away.

After an anxiety-riddled moment, I sigh and head back into the kitchen to wash the dishes.

Later that afternoon, with Ihsaan back from work, a memory catches me off guard as I head towards his room.

I skip down the stairs and singsong, "Mount Arafaa-at!"

As soon as I reach the kitchen, Ihsaan—who's sitting at the table— exchanges a glance with Arafat—who's boiling pasta on the stove.

"Uh oh," Ihsaan says. "She pulled out the nickname."

I roll my eyes at him and turn to a smiling Arafat. "Bhai?" I bat my lashes, feigning innocence.

"Oh, no, not the 'bhai.' What do you think she needs?" Ihsaan teases. "Wait, let me guess. Money? Or maybe..." He taps his chin theatrically, furrowing his brows. "Money? Or perhaps... hmm... money?"

"Ihsaan!" I groan, turning dramatically to Arafat. "Bhai, look what he's saying!"

Arafat turns to me with a placatory smile. "Acha, acha. Ignore him, you know he's an idiot. Tell me what you wanted to say."

"By the way," Ihsaan interrupts, looking up from his laptop, "we're both your older brothers, but only Arafat gets the 'bhai.' Why don't you call me 'bhai,' huh?"

I stick my tongue out at him. "Because you don't deserve the respect."

"Ah." He rolls his eyes and turns back to his screen.

"Arafat," I whisper, darting a quick glance at Ihsaan. "I need some money for food. My friends and I are going out."

Ihsaan beams triumphantly.

"How much?" Arafat asks, laughing.

"Fifty dollars."

"Astaghfirullah," Ihsaan hollers. "What restaurant is charging you fifty dollars for a meal? And how did the academic mastermind miraculously take time away from her books and assignments to grace the outside world with her unwelcome presence? Enlighten me, dear sister."

"Ihsaan!" I protest, folding my arms.

Arafat tugs at my arms. "I told you to ignore him, didn't I?"

"Yeah, ignore the living, breathing human being next to you. Arafat, I'm telling you, we should start tracking how much money she asks us for. She'll be indebted to us forever—especially to you. Med school is making you broke, bro."

Arafat pulls me in for a hug, resting his chin on my head. "Our baby sister, indebted to us? Have some shame, yaar."

With my head pressed against Arafat's chest, I stick my tongue out at Ihsaan, who rolls his eyes.

I shake myself out of the memory as I reach Ihsaan's room. It feels like a dream now.

His door is open, but I knock anyway. Ihsaan looks up from his laptop, fatigue etched into his face. Under the glow of the desk lamp, his eye bags are darker than ever—bruised purple, like shadows that won't fade.

"Hi," I say. "Can I come in?"

He nods, gesturing to his bed and closing his laptop.

I don't come in here often, so it still surprises me to see how organized his room is now. Mama used to have to scold him endlessly about acting his age and cleaning up after himself.

I sit on his bed and purse my lips, unsure how to voice my request.

"Everything okay?" Ihsaan asks.

"Yeah, um…I just…" I fumble with words.

He stares at me expectantly. A beat passes, then he prompts, "Yeah?"

"I need some money," I blurt out.

"Okay. How much?"

"A hundred dollars."

He nods and reaches back for his wallet, flipping it open and handing me a credit card.

I take it slowly, watching him carefully. "You're not gonna ask me what it's for?" *Or why I'm not just using my own card?*

He shrugs. "I know you're responsible and will use it wisely."

The compliment feels ironically like a punch to the throat. I smile weakly and thank him, exiting the room.

Four

Belladonna: Silence

ONCE AGAIN, I SIT and simply stare at the college application.

Before, back when everything was okay, I vowed I would never be one of those students who applied to Rutgers University. Living in Piscataway, one of the many densely Muslim/South Asian-populated towns in the tristate area, Rutgers is the college *every* brown person goes to. Because it's *right there,* practically in our backyards. Despite the fact that the university is one of the top public universities in the country, we all seem to take it for granted—because again—it's *right there.*

But now, I know I don't have another choice. After the way everything went down, it isn't feasible for me to be away from home for college.

Even if it means closing the tab on my Princeton University acceptance letter and sealing that chapter forever.

Four years of cutthroat AP classes and drowning in assignments. Four years of joining every club possible and participating in as many extracurriculars as my schedule would allow. Four years of wrestling with my GPA to become valedictorian. Four years of honing myself into an academic weapon.

None of it matters anymore.

I never told anyone in my family about my acceptance into Princeton. I know they would have gone crazy with delight—my parents would've thrown the party of the year, my brothers would've taken me out to celebrate. They'd have boasted to everyone within a six-foot radius that I'd be attending one of the most prestigious universities in the world.

But I never got to tell them.

I had planned to surprise my family with the news closer to graduation, and hiding the acceptance for two whole months had been the most difficult feat of my life, especially with my then chatterbox best friend Abeer Khan (who was always on the verge of blurting the surprise to my family). But when June dawned and I was finally preparing the grand reveal, my mom received The Phone Call.

The Phone Call that ended all our lives.

After that, academic weapon and Princeton-bound Hayat Amanullah didn't want to go to college at all. She didn't want to study. She didn't want to make friends. She didn't want to do *anything*.

But two weeks ago, in early August, my dad sat me down and begged me to start anew. Even though I refused to tell him where I'd been accepted, he still encouraged me to take a gap semester in the fall and start studying in the spring. He said he couldn't bear to see me so burdened with responsibilities when I was supposed to be pursuing my dreams and enjoying my life.

I hate it when he says stuff like that. He makes me seem like some amazing person doing my family a *favor*. God, if only he knew how badly the grief drowns me every single day, my arms flailing helplessly above the water. If only he knew how desperately I just want my family back. Radiant, cheerful mom. Jokester, prankster Ihsaan. Maybe even studious, happy-go-lucky Hayat.

But that Hayat is gone. She died the day her brother did.

So now, with everything that's changed, I have no choice but to apply to Rutgers—the place I irrationally promised myself I'd never step foot in.

After thoroughly browsing Rutgers' programs and admissions process, I was surprised to discover Rutgers seems…lively. All the organizations, clubs, extracurriculars—everything is so colorful and vibrant and full of life I actually found myself eager to apply. I'd been somewhat familiar with Rutgers from when my brothers attended, but seeing it all in detail was something else.

I finished the application a week ago. The only thing remaining—which gives me pause each time I open it—is the personal essay question.

When I applied to Princeton, the essay prompt asked me to describe an interest that was deeply meaningful to me. So I wrote about my flowers. My garden on the backyard terrace. My love for cultivating something beautiful from something as minuscule and seemingly insignificant as a seed.

But I can't even answer that question anymore.

The flowers in my garden have all wilted. The seed packets are scattered somewhere in a nook of the storage shed. The watering cans lie forgotten on their sides.

Instead, I stare at this new essay question that seems to scream at me.

The lessons we take from obstacles we encounter can be fundamental to later success. Recount a time when you faced a challenge, setback, or failure. How did it affect you, and what did you learn from the experience?

I shut the laptop lid and let out a deep sigh.

⌒

Later that night, at 2:47 AM, sleeplessness clings to me like a second skin. I tiptoe downstairs to grab a glass of water. The house is dark and eerily quiet—both dangerous conditions because they force memories down my throat like scalding hot water.

As I enter the kitchen, flashes of images surge behind my eyelids, and I squeeze them shut, failing to suppress the grief clawing its way up my throat. Sitting at the dinner table and laughing. My parents teasing each other. My brothers treating me like royalty for the smallest accomplishments.

Arafat.

My eyes fly open just as a noise from upstairs breaks the heavy silence. Drink forgotten, I follow the noise and tiptoe up the stairs towards Ihsaan's ajar bedroom door, heart hammering in my chest.

I swallow and take a deep breath before pushing the door wide open.

Ihsaan is sitting upright in tangled sheets, head buried in his hands as he takes loud, heaving breaths. His shoulders quake, his posture collapsed inward, small whimpers escaping from him.

I step forward slowly and a floorboard creaks.

Ihsaan's head snaps up, eyes bloodshot and watery. I hesitate, startled by the haunted look in his eyes.

Silly Hayat, a voice whispers in my head. *It's Ihsaan.*

"Are you okay?" I ask, moving closer and hovering uncertainly at the edge of the bed.

He swallows, Adam's apple bobbing up and down, before nodding shakily. Of course, it's a complete lie. He's still shuddering, sweat beading at his forehead.

I hesitantly perch on the edge of the bed and hand him a glass of water from his bedside table. "Did you have a nightmare?"

He takes the water and sips it carefully before nodding. He must see the concern in my eyes because he croaks out, "Don't worry. Happens sometimes." Before I can question him further he asks, "Why are you up?"

"Couldn't sleep."

He nods as if he understands. A pause, then, "Can you do me a favor? There's a medicine bottle in that drawer over there. Can you give it to me?"

I stand to retrieve the medicine and hand it to him, surprised that the neatness of his space extends to his drawers.

He shakes a pill out and downs it with water. I frown, realizing I never read the label on the bottle. "What is that for?"

"Anxiety."

My eyebrows shoot up. "Shouldn't you not be taking anti-anxiety medication that isn't prescribed to you?"

He caps the bottle and sets it on his bedside table. "It *is* prescribed."

He says it so casually, like it's nothing. I widen my eyes in disbelief. "What? Since when?"

"A month."

"Ihsaan, you've been taking anti-anxiety meds for a month?"

No reply. Just tired eyes and slow rubbing at his temples.

"Why didn't you tell anyone?" I whisper. *Why didn't you tell me?*

He looks up at the shift in my voice and sighs deeply. Then he reaches out and takes my hand. Just a squeeze, but the uncharacteristic gesture steals the air from my lungs.

"I didn't want anyone to worry about the meds or…the therapy. Everyone's already going through so much…" He trails off at the look in my eyes, tentatively rubbing soothing circles against my palm. "Relax, Hayat. Don't worry about it."

Don't worry about it? God, we used to know everything about each other. We used to bother and tease each other so much, it was impossible *not* to know all the crucial details of each other's lives. And I'm only now discovering, after a month, that he takes anti-anxiety medication and attends therapy?

I back away quickly, unable to mask the hurt on my face. He raises his gaze to mine and opens his mouth as if he wants to say something but thinks better of it. "Go to bed, Hayat. It's late. Get some sleep."

Without another word, I turn on my heel and walk out of my brother's room to trudge back down the hall to my own. All the while trying to tamp down the ache that has grown considerably heavier in my broken heart.

Five

White periwinkle: Memories

I END UP BEING a coward and submit the Rutgers application using my old essay about flowers, tweaking it to better fit the question.

When I read through it once more before hitting submit, I scoff in disbelief. The girl in the essay is nothing like me. She's curious, excited, full of life. Her passion oozes through every word.

So contradictory to today's Hayat Amanullah.

Once I'm finally relieved of this application burden, I shut the laptop lid and rub my eyes. My gaze falls to the window overlooking the terrace, sunlight streaming across the wooden planks.

Before I have time to overthink it, I slide open the door and step out onto the terrace.

Then I remember why I avoid coming here.

It's a graveyard now. Wilted flowers, cracked plant pots, scattered tools. The plants in the miniature greenhouse have lost all their color, drooping with neglect. The wicker lawn chairs are cracked in some areas, threatening to collapse.

I fold my arms and sigh.

Once, every morning began out here. After brushing my teeth and praying Fajr, right before breakfast. I'd skip outside and tend to my garden. Sometimes sweat beaded my forehead, and I'd have to tie my too-long hair into a bandana. I'd wipe the back of my hand along my brows and keep going.

Because those plants? Those flowers? They were my lifeline. My pride. My comfort. My slip of sanity between crazed study days and sleepless nights.

I always carefully watered them, refreshed the soil, bought new pots when I needed a change. I hung cute little frames of flowers all over the terrace. I even clipped corny gardening Post-It notes to the clothesline, stretching from the entrance to the far end of the terrace.

And since I insisted on taking care of the garden all on my own, sometimes during a trial and error phase flowers died. But unless they posed a health or environmental risk, I never threw them away. I kept them—mostly in journals and books—so that every time I opened one, I would be reminded of the hard work I'd put in, and it would bring a smile to my face.

God, I was so damn proud of that garden. Everyone—even if they knew nothing else about me—knew that.

That's why, Ihsaan used to sneak out to the terrace and scribble nonsense on my Post-Its or mess with the plants. Cue my shrieks of protest and Arafat's scoldings. But God, Ihsaan loved getting under my skin. The more I protested, the brighter his eyes lit up with mischief. And the more Arafat tried to coax us into not ripping each other's heads off.

Thinking of that Ihsaan now brings a searing ache to my chest so sharp I'm forced to clutch it.

Ihsaan was the most goofy, irresponsible person I knew. Arafat was the med student, the one on track to becoming a doctor. So Ihsaan always teased him for being the family favorite ("after crazy academic Hayat"). It was all a joke—because they were close, and my parents never compared us, regardless of what we decided for our professional careers. But Ihsaan made it his mission to be the family clown. The son who whispered jokes in my parents' ears. The brother who made Arafat and me gang up against him—or choke on our laughter.

But this Ihsaan? This quiet, secretive Ihsaan who doesn't want anyone to worry, who cleans his bedroom, who takes everything so seriously?

I don't know who he is anymore.

Six

Rosemary: Remembrance

I RECEIVE A BIRTHDAY party invitation from my old best friend, Abeer. The flier is all vibrant and pink—so like her—and her long, excited slew of texts begins with: please, please come. i miss you so much. and it'll be so nice to hang out before the semester starts. I ignore the rest of the rant and scroll through all the similar texts I never read or responded to.

Normally people would feel upset at the thought that all their friends will begin and likely end college at the same time without them—especially when they were known as "Harvard-bound" in high school and were the valedictorian.

I used to dress like it, too. *"Harvard-bound."* Patterned skirts, preppy sweaters, bows in my hair, and patent leather Mary Janes.

But I've succumbed to the numbness that pulls me under every day. Nothing matters anymore. I don't care that the people I used to be friends with will be starting their semester in the fall while I'd be lucky to start five months later in spring. I can't even remember why I spent countless sleepless nights studying for tests and enrolling in cutthroat AP classes. I don't remember why I wanted to go to college in the first place.

God, I don't even think I have friends anymore. After the

funeral, they all looked at me with such intense pity in their eyes it became unbearable to be around them for too long. Because once you're the girl who lost her brother, you're always going to be the girl who lost her brother.

So many of them tried reconnecting with me afterward. But I couldn't bear the thought of pretending everything was normal—that I was studious, happy-go-lucky Hayat again. Too much had changed. And letting go of them?

It didn't really hurt.

After Arafat's death, nothing hurt the same way anymore. It was just his loss—every day—tearing open my already gaping wounds. Ripping apart my insides and rendering me numb, powerless, speechless.

That's the only hurt I know now.

Besides "Harvard-bound," I used to be somewhat popular. I befriended every girl in sight, linked arms through the school hallways, chatted about makeup trends, new hairstyles, and the teachers we couldn't stand. I can't say they were all *real* friends. It was more like our relationships carried the superficial, shallow nature of high school. But I still enjoyed spending time with them.

But then my brother died and Things Went Downhill, and none of those friends mattered anymore. *Nothing* mattered.

God, I don't know how I even get out of bed most days when my legs tremble with the truth that hits me harder every day:

Arafat is *dead*.

Gone forever and never coming back. Buried six feet under and never returning. No more rushing to him when Ihsaan teased me senseless. No more asking him for money he gave without hesitation. No more being wrapped in his frequent hugs which irked Ihsaan, who found our affection for each other "cringey as hell." No more car rides and—

Car rides.

God, every time I think of his death, my brain conjures the image—so vivid, as if I'd witnessed it.

How much pain did he endure? What was going through his

mind when he merged too quickly—when his car flipped over and crashed into the embankment? Did he know that was the last day he'd see his family? Fist bump his brother? Muss his sister's hair? Did he know that was the last day he'd sit in class or shadow a physician at the hospital?

Did he know that was the last day his family would ever be whole, happy?

Dwelling on it breaks me all over again. Nobody tells you this—grieving is shattering yourself into pieces only to attempt rebuilding the next day. Then shatter. Then rebuild. Then shatter. Then rebuild. A horrible, agonizing cycle.

So forgive me. Forgive me if I don't give a damn about college, birthday party invitations, or speaking more than a few necessary words. Forgive me if I don't want to get rid of the dead, wilted plants on the terrace or drive the car my brothers gifted me the week Arafat died.

Forgive me if I don't give a damn about anything anymore.

Seven

Love-in-a-Mist: Perplexity

MY DAD ENDS UP stumbling across Abeer's invitation when I leave my laptop open on the dining table. When he brings it up during dinner, I know I'm doomed.

"Why don't you go?" he says cheerfully. "You and Abeer were such good friends. Joined at the hip."

I offer a noncommittal shrug, then instantly feel guilty. "I don't know, Papa. Just not in the mood."

He pauses, seemingly choosing his words carefully, "We should start getting in the habit of doing our old activities again, right? Busying ourselves and…" He trails off.

I sigh inwardly. I don't want to see anyone who's not sitting at this table. I'm sure my dad is well aware of this fact.

But looking at the desperate hope on his face, I can see how hard he's trying to keep it together for all of us. How hard he's trying to keep *us* together.

"What do you think, Layla?" Papa turns to Mama. "Shouldn't Hayat go?"

My mom pushes the food around on her plate as usual, eyes glazed and unfocused. She startles when my dad says her name, then clears her throat and murmurs, "What, Aman?"

Papa takes a deep breath. "Shouldn't Hayat go to Abeer's birthday party?"

Mama nods absently and returns to pushing rice around her plate.

Papa turns to my brother. "Ihsaan? What do you think?"

Ihsaan's gaze flicks to me before he nods. "I think she should go."

I think she *should go.* God, we're talking about each other in the third person now.

"Well, that's settled then." My dad beams. And despite my desire to protest, the innocent triumph on his face wrecks all my resolve.

"Okay," I murmur.

"Ihsaan can drop you off," Papa adds in a too-bright voice.

And despite everything—my resistance, Mama's radio silence, Ihsaan's distance—the satisfied smile on my father's lips swallows all those feelings whole.

⌒

I kiss my mom's temple and bid her goodbye before heading to Ihsaan's car. He's already inside, fingers absentmindedly tapping against the steering wheel.

"Sorry," I mutter as I rush in. "Did you wait long?"

He shakes his head. "No, you're all good." He gives my sage green dress a once-over and smiles tentatively, though it clashes with the dullness in his eyes and the pallor of his face. "You look nice."

Arafat whistles as I descend the stairs, twirling around in my dress before taking a bow. "Who's this beauty?"

Ihsaan glances up from his laptop. "You look like the churail in The Conjuring. *"*

I shake off the memory and return a small smile. "Thank you." I try not to think about the weight of all the things he's kept from me—the panic attacks, the anti-anxiety meds, the therapy.

The drive is quiet. We pass by various stores and shopping plazas. It's then that I abruptly remember something and gasp, slapping my forehead.

Ihsaan flinches, eyes wide as he turns to me. "What? What happened?"

"Oh my God, I forgot to get Abeer a gift." I laugh, embarrassed. I shake my head at my own forgetfulness. It's been too long since I've attended something like this.

My brother's shoulders relax. "It's okay. We can buy one right now."

He makes a U-turn, heading back towards Burlington. But as we pull into the parking lot, I notice something's off. Although his posture has relaxed, his fingers are trembling against the wheel.

I need to be gentler, more mindful of how suddenly things overwhelm him. He flinches at anything on the road—the honk of a horn, unexpected movements or sounds.

When we park in front of Burlington he asks, "Do you need money?"

"No, I found my wallet yesterday. I'll be right back."

I'm about to unbuckle my seat belt when Ihsaan's hand clamps down on my arm. I jolt back in surprise and search his eyes for the cause of his behavior.

He's staring straight ahead, shoulders tense and jaw clenched. I follow his gaze and find a Muslim girl just a couple years older than me walking towards Burlington, battling with the wind tugging at her hijab. She wears a white lab coat, a stethoscope dangling around her neck—like she's popped in between hospital shifts.

There's something familiar about her. I can't name it, but I feel like I've seen her before. It's New Jersey; she could be any of the fellow Muslims I see around. But I have the distinct impression that I know her…or at least my brother does. Her name might start with an A…Or maybe she was at the funeral?

I turn back to Ihsaan, an indent forming between my brows. "Ihsaan?"

He releases his iron grip on my hand, murmuring a hasty "sorry" before restarting the car and backing out of the parking space.

I give him a bewildered look. "Um, what are you doing? I need to go inside."

"I'll take you somewhere else to get the gift."

"What? But Burlington's right here—"

"I'll take you somewhere else."

The tone of his voice—so curt, so uncharacteristic—has me shrinking back into my seat. I study his clenched jaw and shaking hands all the way to Marshall's and eventually Abeer's house.

He parks and turns to me, opening his mouth as if he wants to say something. Maybe to address the weirdness back at Burlington. But then he shakes his head and says, "Have a good time. Call when you're ready to get picked up."

I stare at him, dumbfounded. How much longer will this go on? How long will he keep treating me like a stranger, like I'm not still his annoying little sister?

I huff angrily and mash the seatbelt button, but it jams. I close my eyes and breathe out a deep sigh.

The soft click of my seatbelt releasing causes me to open my eyes. Ihsaan watches me—guilt marring his features—before he turns away.

I grab Abeer's gift and exit the car, slamming the door behind me with more force than necessary.

It takes all of ten steps before I'm turning back around with panic dredging up my throat. I rush towards Ihsaan, heart pounding.

What if I had let him drive off like that? What if—God forbid—something happened to him or me and that icy moment was our last?

Ihsaan rolls down the window, brows scrunched in concern. "Are you okay?"

"I'm sorry," I say, voice trembling. I lean down, practically clawing at the door handle. "I'm so sorry."

"Hayat," he starts, scanning my face. "What's wrong?"

"I just—I'm so sorry." I cover my face, fighting off unwelcome tears.

I hear the click of Ihsaan's seatbelt as he opens the door and hurries to my side. "Seriously, what's wrong? Are you okay?"

I uncover my face and nod quickly. "Yeah, yeah. I just—" I

sigh, taking a deep breath and swallowing the tears in my throat. "I didn't want it to be…I didn't want you to leave like…" I gesture helplessly between us, words barely forming.

Understanding finally dawns on his face. He steps forward and, before I know what's happening, pulls me into a tight embrace. I freeze at the gesture, something he used to avoid like the plague.

And it's all I can do not to fall apart at the touch I've missed so much. At the comfort I've come to ache for.

Ihsaan steps back after a second, and he says very quietly, "I need you to know that some things are an amanah…not mine to tell. And sometimes it's better to…leave them in the past."

I nod, though confusion still lingers. Still, I head towards Abeer's house, waving to my brother and whispering a silent du'aa as he drives away.

It's a mixed party.

I should have gauged as much—Abeer and her brother Rameez are twins, after all. But since I've known her, they've always celebrated separately, so it didn't even register that they might have a party together. I should've paid more attention to the invitation.

As soon as I step inside Abeer's unlocked door, however, it becomes clear from the vibrant purple decorations that it's only her party. I glance back at her texts, and sure enough, she had cautioned me about the mixed crowd, knowing how I'd feel about it. I must've skimmed it too distractedly the first time.

Still, I'm thrown off instantly. Even though the guys are huddled on one side of the room and the girls on the other, I briefly consider calling Ihsaan to come get me. But I know leaving early will only worry my father, so I take a deep breath and muster whatever courage I can.

"Hayat!" someone squeals.

I turn halfway before I'm abruptly assaulted by bouncy curls and a perfumed hug that invades my nose. I cough and step back, meeting the warm, familiar eyes of my old best friend.

Abeer grabs my shoulders. "O-M-G, I can't believe you're *actually* here. You made my night!"

I smile, tentative but genuine. "I couldn't miss your birthday." *Although I had fully intended to.* I pass her the gift bag, and she squeals once more.

She shakes me like she still can't believe it, then pulls me in for another hug. "Oh my God, how *are* you? How's everything going? How's Ihsaan bhai? How are your parents? Tell me everything. O-M-G, your hair's even longer than before!"

I laugh at her endless stream of questions. "Everything's fine." I pause before teasing, "Won't you at least let me sit before interrogating me?"

"Oh gosh, I'm so sorry. Come on, let's go meet everyone."

She tugs me towards the living room, and I force myself past the rising nausea and nerves.

As we enter, the room goes silent. Heads turn. Conversations halt. And all eyes are on me.

I squirm, angling my head downwards to avoid the searing intensity of their stares. But who could blame them? The last time they saw me, I broke down onstage during my valedictorian speech. I had to be escorted aside to recover.

"Guys, look who's here!" Abeer announces.

I glance up briefly and spot some familiar faces greeting me with tentative smiles, easing my tension.

"Hayat?" Rumana, an old sort-of friend, stands to hug me. I awkwardly pat her back. When she pulls back, her pitying gaze reminds me how long it's been. "How are you?" she asks quietly.

"I'm okay," I reply. My eyes flit around the room—everyone is watching our interaction, silent and focused. I take a deep breath, wanting so badly for them to overlook the elephant in the room. "Hi, guys. How is everyone?"

And it's enough to start up the conversations again, albeit they're a little more hushed and awkward.

We talk, we eat, we laugh. I almost feel like a teenager again. Like the smart, popular high school girl everyone was dying to be friends with. Sure, I have to dodge questions about college, deflect condolences about my brother, and absorb the weight of their constant probing eyes. But like I said, once you're the girl who's lost her brother, you're always going to be the girl who's lost her brother.

In between lighthearted conversation, there are moments when I feel like an elephant trying to wear a turtle's skin. Too much has changed. And I know they're all probably thinking: "Harvard-bound" Hayat Amanullah is wasting her life away.

But for a few moments, it almost feels like *before*.

As I'm talking to the girls, I feel a bout of self-consciousness hit, as if someone's watching me. I turn and, sure enough, there he is.

Abeer's twin, Rameez Khan.

Our eyes meet briefly, and I catch the hint of a smile on his lips before I quickly turn away.

Oh, the things I could say about Rameez Khan. He wasn't boxed into the typical high school labels—jock, geek, popular—he fit into all of them. He was on the soccer team, admired by everyone, and he wasn't afraid of utilizing his intelligence. He single-handedly dismantled the social hierarchy of high school cafeterias for a senior project. He was genuinely *nice* to people, despite everyone vying for his attention. He'd utter a single word and everyone would erupt into rambunctious fits of laughter. The twitch of his lips could make a room full of girls swoon.

Abeer and Rameez's parents—Algerian mom, Pakistani dad—gave them striking features. Thick brows, full lips, sculpted noses, and curly hair to die for.

I know, I know—how cliché? But shoot me if when Rameez looks at me, my heart flutters. Just a little. Enough to notice. More movement than it's felt in months.

Throughout the night, I'm distracted, constantly aware of Rameez's eyes on me. And I don't reciprocate—not necessarily because I don't want to, but because I don't know how…or why.

Abeer and I became friends freshman year, but even after four years, I barely know Rameez—mostly because he's a guy. He was rarely around, always off playing soccer, doing something impossibly impressive, or working out at the gym. And when he *was* around, he'd greet me and try to make small talk. But then he'd be swept back into being The Coolest Person On The Planet. Always working hard, always achieving, always making his parents proud. And we would never get the chance to have an actual conversation.

When Ihsaan arrives to pick me up, I stand to say my goodbyes. Abeer hugs me tight, as if her life depends on it, and whispers in my ear, "Please don't let this be the last time we see each other for a while."

I nod shakily, unsettled by the emotion in her voice.

Rumana hugs me too. "Do you want us to walk you to your car?"

"Oh, no thank you. My brother is here to pick me up."

Comprehension dawns slowly in her eyes. "Oh. You don't drive anymore."

A thick, loaded silence hangs in the air until Abeer crushes me again. "I'm here, okay? I'm always here. Always."

This, coupled with her obnoxious curls tickling my nose, brings a smile to my face.

I head to the foyer and slip on my shoes just as someone approaches.

I look up and nearly trip forward. *Great.* That would be the single most unattractive thing to do—especially in front of *him.*

Rameez is standing in front of me, hands in his pockets, wearing a strange expression.

I stand quickly, smoothing my too-long hair where it's comically risen.

"Hi," he says, rubbing the back of his neck. "How are you?"

"Uh, good. I'm good," I splutter. A beat later—still trying to recover from the shock that *Rameez Khan* has approached me—I tack on, "How are *you?*"

He nods. "Good, thank you."

An awkward silence hangs in the air between us.

All of a sudden, I can't stand another moment of the quiet. This has all been too much. Ihsaan's weird attitude, the lively birthday party, seeing friends I feel like I don't know anymore, Rameez's constant stares. I sigh—long and loud.

"Look, just ask me what you wanna ask already. How am I doing after my oldest brother died? Great, thank you. Now this is the part where you tell me it's gonna be okay and to stay strong. Since I know all that already, can I go?"

He presses his full lips together. Those thick brows furrow. He looks genuinely upset, and a ripple of unease stirs in the pit of my stomach.

"I wasn't going to…I just wanted to ask how you were doing. Out of courtesy." Pause. "You seem different."

I'm surprised *Rameez Khan* even noticed me enough to notice I "seem different." The shock is enough to embolden me to ask, "A good different or a bad different?"

He shakes his head. "Not bad. Just…older."

To dispel the tension and silently apologize for my earlier rudeness, I joke, "Well, I *am* a couple months older since the last time you saw me. Whenever that was."

I know exactly when it was. I was a sobbing mess as we all threw our graduation caps in the air.

A smile lights up his face. And curse me for feeling that stupid flutter in my heart again.

Not good. This is not good. How cliché would it be to have a crush on *Rameez Khan,* for God's sake. Half the girls in this house probably do.

I catch Rumana darting a glance between us before she quickly turns away.

Correction: *all* the girls in this house probably do.

"Well, it was good to see you," Rameez says, giving me a small salute. I smile against my better judgment. "I hope I see you around more."

And then he turns and walks back into the living room.

For a couple moments, I stand motionlessly at the door, mind spiraling, heart too loud. And then I practically run from Abeer's house.

When I greet Ihsaan and buckle my seatbelt, he turns to me and says, "You're all red."

"What? Hello to you, too."

He shakes his head. "Sorry. Salaam. I was just saying…" He tilts his head and scrutinizes me. I squirm under his gaze. "You're blushing. Or something."

"What? You're crazy. Why would I be blushing?" My voice comes out too high.

He raises an eyebrow and switches the gear into drive. "You tell me, Sherlock."

Sherlock? A playful nickname?

I turn to him and level the same scrutiny he gave me. "Never mind me. You seem to be in a better mood."

He shrugs lightly. "My supervisor talked to me about a promotion. I just got my offer letter."

"What!" Too late, I remember my warning not to startle him while driving. He jumps slightly before taking a deep, calming breath. "Sorry. You got promoted so soon? That's amazing! Congratulations."

He nods dismissively.

"To what position?"

"From HR Assistant to HR Coordinator."

"Ihsaan, that's so amazing! It hasn't even been five months!" Still high on the strange interaction with Rameez and this rare moment with Ihsaan, I blurt out, "We should celebrate! Let's go get food. Cake. Flowers. Something."

Ihsaan furrows his brows. "No need."

"No need? Ihsaan, it's not every day that one of your brothers gets promoted. We should—" my voice dies mid-sentence as Ihsaan's shoulders tighten.

Brothers. I said brothers.

A beat of silence. Heavy.

"I think it's best if we go home," Ihsaan murmurs.

I nod wordlessly.

The rest of the drive is spent in strained silence.

Eight

Queen Anne's lace: Sanctuary

I DON'T KNOW HOW it happens and for a couple moments I have no idea where I am. But when I become consciously aware, I realize I'm in the middle of the road in my neighborhood, headlights of a honking car flooding my vision.

I gasp, cold dread filling my insides. My head whips wildly around the dimly lit streets. I look down at my bare feet and shaking hands, and a surprised sob escapes me.

A car door slams and I flinch, stumbling backwards.

"Hayat?"

I freeze in my tracks at the familiar voice. Too dazed to place who it is, I shield my eyes against the glare.

"Hayat, is that you?" A figure approaches, and I rub my eyes and begin to back away quickly. In my haste I trip over the hem of my pajamas and crash down, palms scraping against the asphalt.

"Hey, hey." The figure holds up both hands, slowly moving closer as if I'm a wild, wounded animal. He bends down, and the headlights finally illuminate his face.

Mikaal.

For the second time this week, he watches me with concern etched across his features.

"Hey," he says. "It's just me. Are you alright? You scared the hell out of me, running onto the road like that. What are you doing outside right now?"

Words fail me. I'm in my donut pajamas, barefoot, bleeding, and stretched out in the middle of the road.

Mikaal's gaze trails to my bare feet and slowly back up to my face, his eyes widening with renewed shock. "Oh God, Hayat, are you okay? You...you were sleepwalking?"

"I don't—I don't..." I lift my scraped, trembling hands and glance down at my appearance.

Then I burst into tears.

"Okay, okay. It's okay. Do you want me to call your brother? Or your parents?"

I shake my head with such force that Mikaal holds his hands up. "Okay, don't worry. I won't. Come on, let me take you home."

He stands and gestures for me to do the same. I stagger to my feet and mumble incomprehensible words through sobs. He nods or says "okay" in reply, each gesture laced with reassurance. He dashes to the trunk of his car and retrieves a pair of men's shoes, gesturing for me to slip them on. He keeps his distance but guides me towards the car, and I limp the few steps, hissing with each one.

Mikaal returns to the trunk again and comes back with a throw blanket. He begins to hand it to me, but I can't seem to lift my arms—all I can manage is to stare at him, unmoving and wide-eyed. He carefully drapes it around my shoulders without touching me.

That's when it hits me—I'm in *donut pajamas,* not remotely appropriate for being outside, much less standing beside a guy who's not Papa or Ihsaan. I clutch the blanket tightly around myself, trembling as I slide into the backseat.

Mikaal closes my door and gets in the driver's seat. "Oh man, Hayat, if I hadn't seen you..." The concern in his voice is unmistakable. I've known him for two and a half years, and I've never seen him this worried. "Are your feet okay? Sorry, I know it's kinda gross wearing someone else's shoes."

I nod wordlessly, unsure if he can even see me in the dark, too shaken to speak.

"I'm taking you to the hospital. To patch up your feet."

"No!" I all but shout. Then softer, breath shaking, "No. I don't want any trouble."

"Trouble? Hayat, your feet are—"

I shake my head vehemently.

"I'll do it myself if you don't want anyone to find out—"

"No, please," I whisper, lips trembling. "I just wanna go home."

He seems to want to say more but quiets at my insistence. Then his tone shifts. "How did you even…When did you realize you were sleepwalking outside?"

I inhale shakily. "When you honked."

Mikaal sucks in a sharp breath. "Oh, man. Was this the first time you've sleepwalked?"

I nod. I can hear the clinical shift in his tone—med student instincts kicking in. He and Arafat were both attending Rutgers RWJ med school together.

A few seconds later, Mikaal pulls into his driveway. I glance at him, confused.

"Give me a second," he says. "I'll be right back."

I wait quietly as he steps inside his house and disappears. I inhale slowly, steadying myself, then glance at the time on the dashboard.

1:17 AM.

God, I must've got out of bed, unlocked the house door, and wandered blocks away—without even knowing. It's never happened before. What would've happened if Mikaal hadn't driven by when he did? If he hadn't found me? Where would I be now?

My distressed thoughts are interrupted when Mikaal returns with a paper bag. "Sorry, I just needed to grab this." He pulls out and makes the two-minute drive to my house before switching off the engine.

For a moment, we're both completely silent before he observes, almost to himself, "The house door is open."

I look up and begin to cry all over again, although I'm not sure I ever stopped.

"Oh—hey, it's okay. I didn't mean to—" Mikaal shoves a hand through his hair and turns slightly towards me. "I'm just glad I came across you and that you're okay, Alhamdulillah. Can I—do you want me to call someone out to get you?"

"No." My voice cracks with desperation.

He's quiet for a moment before he says, "Okay. Let me walk you to your door then." He circles to my side and opens the car door. There's a brief, awkward moment as we both register that, because I can't walk properly, he will need to help me.

"Um, do you need—is it okay if I—" He gestures between us.

Mikaal Zaman is a practicing Muslim. He's not the kind of person who would touch a woman outside his family—out of respect to women, his upbringing, and his religious values. Perhaps that's why he keeps asking if I want to call someone from home to come get me: so he doesn't risk putting either of us in an awkward or compromising situation.

But he's a good man. And I trust him.

That, and I can't risk worrying my family any further by telling them I'd been sleepwalking around in the neighborhood.

I nod slowly and slip off the blanket.

"Keep it on," Mikaal insists, and I oblige. He reaches down and gently lifts my arm, placing it across his shoulders. A strange feeling shoots through me—this is the first time I'm touching a man who isn't my father or brothers. I'm not the most religious person, but physical boundaries have always been something I've adhered to.

Right now, though, I don't really have a choice, as my health calls for an exception.

Together we walk—well, I limp, and he walks while bearing my weight—towards my house.

Halfway there, Mikaal huffs. For a moment I wonder if it's because of my weight, but that fear is quickly dispelled when he says, in an uncharacteristically sharp tone, "This is stupid. You need to get checked at the hospital. You're clearly more hurt than you're letting on."

His words pierce me somewhere deep. I shake my head. "No, please. I don't want to worry anybody."

When we reach the porch, we step quickly away from one another. I brace myself against the door as Mikaal shakes his head angrily. "Taking care of yourself isn't worrying anybody."

I remain silent, unsure how to respond to this very un-Mikaal-like exasperation—so different from the gentle Mikaal I've always known. Sure, I'd seen glimpses of other moods when he was with my brothers, the way friends show different sides depending on the company. But to me, Mikaal has always been nothing but nice.

He rakes a hand through his hair and sighs."Arafat would've killed me if he knew…" He trails off into another sigh. "Wait here for a second."

Mikaal jogs back to his car as the weight of his words settles over me. Does he feel obligated to care for me simply because I'm the little sister his best friend left behind? I mean, I guess he's always sort of felt like a third brother to me.

As I watch him head to his car, my mind drifts to everything I know about Mikaal Zaman—everything I've learned over the past two and a half years.

Homeschooled, he breezed through high school and graduated at seventeen. Then, as if testing the limits of academic speed, he completed his undergrad in just two and a half years, graduating at the impressive age of nineteen. And as if that wasn't enough, he dove headfirst into med school and *thrived*. That's when he met Arafat, and the two became inseparable. Now twenty-two and in his third year of med school, Mikaal is the same age as Ihsaan, but he and Arafat were always closer. I suppose starting med school together forged something stronger.

Beyond his intellect and relentless drive, Mikaal is one of the most gentle and emotionally perceptive men I've ever known. I can see how that kind of compassion, along with many of his commendable characteristics, is invaluable in a profession like medicine.

My thoughts scatter as Mikaal reaches me, lifting the paper bag he'd retrieved from his house.

"As a med student, I completely disapprove of your stubbornness," he says, arching a stern brow. "But since I know you're dead set—here." He holds out the bag, and I accept it with knitted brows. "Wash your feet with mild soap and warm water. There's Neosporin and some non-stick gauze bandages in the bag. You probably already have those at home, but I figured just in case." He shrugs. "And wear thick socks at home until your feet heal. But look, if they get infected, you really need to go to the doctor. And please…" his voice dips, "Just rest. And Hayat…be careful, okay? Maybe sleep with your mom or lock your room door. God forbid anything like this happens again…" He sighs, backing away. "Well, I'm gonna head home now. Take care. Salaam."

Only when he's halfway to his car do I realize I've been standing silently the entire time he spoke. A panicked cry lodges in my throat—he can't leave without me expressing my gratitude.

"Mikaal!" I shout. He turns, and the porch light illuminates his face.

What I want to say is "thank you." But what tumbles out is, "What were you doing out right now?"

His expression shifts, becoming mournful. "I was…feeling restless and couldn't sleep so I went to the masjid."

"Oh."

He waits for a moment, like he knows there's something more I want to say. And I do. But the words won't come.

"Good night, Hayat." He turns and walks back to his car.

Only when Mikaal starts the engine and begins backing out of the driveway do I remember—I'm wearing his huge shoes and wrapped in his soft blanket.

And all I wanted was to say "thank you."

My phone pings with a text.

loved seeing you last night <333333333

btw you're still the most adorable squishy lovely human being and i want to see you again >_<

I stare at Abeer's texts for a moment before sighing and locking my phone screen. I'll reply later.

This morning, my dad looked at me weirdly when I shoved another pair of socks onto my already covered feet. "Cold?" he'd mused.

"Yeah," I nodded vigorously. "So cold nowadays."

He'd glanced outside at the August sun and regarded me for a careful moment. I held my breath until he murmured, "Well, okay then. Let me change the AC temperature."

Papa had been easy to deceive. Ihsaan, on the other hand, won't be.

That's why I prepare his breakfast while he's showering and have it set on the table before he's making his way downstairs.

"Good morning," he says, waving.

"Morning," I chirp a little too cheerfully from my spot on the dining table.

He eyes the food gratefully. "You really don't have to make me breakfast every day." He leans close to the plate and sniffs the omelet. "This smells amazing."

"I like to," I say truthfully, typing gibberish on my laptop.

"Did you eat already?" he asks in between chews.

"Yeah, I was hungry a little while ago. Had some cereal."

Ihsaan's eyes bore into mine as he eats, and I shift under his gaze. "When are you gonna eat real food?"

I scoff. "Cereal *is* 'real food.'"

"You know cereal just makes you hungrier afterwards, right?"

"Okay, *Dr.* Amanullah." I halt as soon as the words leave my mouth, eyes darting up quickly from my computer screen.

Ihsaan pauses mid-chew, unsaid words hanging between us.

That was Arafat's nickname. In a couple years, it would've become the way everyone addressed him.

For the next few minutes, Ihsaan eats quietly and I pretend to do work on my laptop. When he stands, I panic. I usually walk him to the door—or watch him leave from the window. If I don't do it now, he might think something is up.

I blurt out the first thing that comes to mind, "Ah, these cramps are *killing* me today."

Ihsaan shoots me a furtive glance before looking away. Ah, the bliss of male awkwardness regarding anything even remotely feminine.

"Maybe take a painkiller?" he says gruffly, busying himself with tying his shoes.

Despite myself, I hold back a bout of laughter. "Yeah, I think I might."

He grabs his car keys and is about to head out when I say, "Oh, I almost forgot! What do you want for dinner today?"

Ihsaan wraps and unwraps the lanyard of keys around his fingers. "Um, don't worry about it. I'll bring food home. Just get some rest."

I gather my hair in a claw clip. "I don't mind cooking."

He shakes his head. "Just relax. I'll take care of it."

I want to argue, but seeing the conviction on his face I backtrack. "Well, okay then." I contemplate my next words before daring to say them, "Have fun, Mr. HR Coordinator."

He cracks a smile, and warmth pools in my heart.

When Ihsaan leaves, I remove my socks and inspect the blisters. They look worse than last night, though they feel better after following Mikaal's instructions. But wounds usually get worse before they get better, right? Something like that.

For the next hour, I clean already-tidy areas of the house and check on my mom. She's awake, but confined to her bed as usual. I make her breakfast and force her to eat it. As I'm making my way back downstairs, my feet ache so badly I have to pause to catch my breath.

Then the weirdest thing happens. The doorbell rings.

I furrow my brows, trying to catch my bearings as I slowly descend the stairs. Who could it be? We don't usually have visitors. Not anymore.

The effort of carrying the tray to the kitchen has me gasping for breath. By the time I hobble to the door and pull it open, I'm in too much pain to greet the person standing in front of me.

"Hi!" Abeer chirps, wringing her hands. "I know this is probably weird, but I wasn't sure if you'd reply to my texts and I was so happy seeing you last night. I just wanted to stop by for a little bit. Hope that's okay."

Before I'm able to form a reply, I stumble against the door.

"Hayat! Oh my God, Hayat! Are you okay?" Abeer rushes forward and lifts me up, huffing. She manages to drag me to the sofa in the living room before heading back to shut the front door.

When she materializes at my side again, she presses hasty fingers to my forehead. "Are you sick? What's wrong?"

I shake my head. "Nothing. Anemia, you know? I just got dizzy," I lie. "I wasn't—"

"Is that…dried blood on your socks?" Abeer points to my feet and to my utter dismay, she's right. "What happened? Tell me what you need. Should I get you something?"

I want to cry in exasperation. Nobody was supposed to witness this. I bury my head in my hands.

A soft hand touches my arm. I look up into Abeer's worried eyes. "Please," she says. "Let me help you."

For a moment, I have the strongest urge to tell her to *help* me by going back home. But I'm too exhausted to deal with the repercussions, so I sigh instead. "There's a bucket in the bathroom. Can you fill it with warm water and bring it here, please?"

She nods and quickly obliges. While she's occupied, I remove my socks and examine the damage.

The blisters have gotten worse, and blood is escaping through the wounds. Not infected yet, but getting there. Maybe I shouldn't have resumed my chores as usual. Maybe I should've taken Mikaal's advice and actually rested.

Abeer returns, stumbling towards me with the bucket of water. She's breathless by the time she sets it in front of me, and my eyes prick with an unfamiliar warmth at her huffs and puffs.

"Thank you," I whisper, hissing as my foot makes contact with the water. Abeer watches helplessly, lips pressed together.

"Hayat," she finally says. "You wanna tell me what's going on?"

"It's nothing, I just—"

"Hayat."

At the curt tone of her voice, I raise my gaze to hers. My old best friend—a fierce lioness just as much as she's an adorable kitten.

"What did I tell you last night? I'm *here*, Hayat. Please don't push me away anymore. I'm here for you."

Our gazes are locked in a silent battle. Hers: resolute, unwavering. Mine: wary, reluctant.

Yet despite my hesitance, despite the tension coiling my insides, despite the dread that's settled permanently in the pit of my stomach—something in Abeer's eyes makes me let go. I lower my shield and drop all my weapons. Defenseless—but this time, it's of my own volition.

"I was sleepwalking."

Nine

Jasmine: Cheerfulness

ABEER STAYS FOR MUCH of the day and to my surprise, her presence doesn't bother me.

When I told her what happened last night she—naturally—freaked out. Told me I needed to buy deadbolts and put mouse traps on the floor next to my bed ("The benefits will outweigh the costs!" she squeaked when I gave her an appalled look). She advised me to inform someone in my house so they could keep an eye out if there is ever a next time, God forbid.

That last one is a definite no. Everyone already has enough to deal with. When I explained this, Abeer glared at me and said, "Fine. I'll just tell Ihsaan bhai myself."

I grabbed her arm in panic and half-shouted, "No!" Then, calmer, "No, Abeer, please. Ihsaan's the last person who needs to know. He has…too much going on."

"But he's your *brother*—"

"No," I repeated, firmer this time. She bit her lip but eventually nodded.

Now, to celebrate Ihsaan's promotion, we're baking him a cake. Well, Abeer's doing most of the work, since I can't move much without hissing in pain. She follows my instructions, mixing the ingredients together, all the while shaking her head and laughing.

"I just—I still can't believe it. You used to *hate* cooking. Baking. Anything that had to do with the kitchen."

I shrug. "People change."

"No, but like, the weirdest thing is, after trying your pasta I've discovered that you're actually *good* at cooking now. How did *that* happen?"

"Thanks," I reply dryly.

Abeer laughs, loud and consuming, filling the entire kitchen. For a moment, the tension in my shoulders eases and my heart fills with nothing but warmth. It's been a long time since I've heard laughter like that in my house.

Then come slow footsteps descending the stairs. Abeer's furrowed brows meet my equally startled gaze as my mom enters the kitchen.

Her hair's matted to one side—typical, since she seldom leaves her bed—and shadows sit heavy under her lifeless eyes.

"Auntie!" Abeer drops an egg into the batter, shell and all, and excitedly rushes to Mama. She carefully wraps her arms around her to avoid getting chocolatey hands in Mama's hair. "Salaam! How are you?"

For a brief moment, Mama stands motionless. Then her lifeless eyes spark and she wraps her arms around my old best friend.

"I'm good, beta," she croaks. "Aap kaisi ho? Rameez kaisa hai?"

I'm unhappy to admit that my heart jumps a little at the sound of his name.

Abeer pulls back and smiles. "Mai theek hun. Rameez is good, too."

I've always loved that Abeer's parents made it a point to teach their kids both Urdu and Arabic; to embrace a fusion of their cultures rather than pick sides.

My mom smoothes her hair back and adjusts her clothes. "Did you eat something, Abeer?"

"Yes! Hayat fed me pasta. It was *so good*. Auntie, who is this and what have you done with Hayat?"

Mama smiles, just for a moment. But then something shifts. Her gaze falters, and the light fades from her eyes, as if a thought passed through her and took joy with it.

Abeer notices the shift in atmosphere and returns to the kitchen island, fishing out the egg from the chocolatey goo. She shoots me a sheepish look.

"What are you girls doing?" Mama asks.

I turn to her in surprise. This is more conversation than she usually attempts.

"Baking a cake!" Abeer exclaims. "Hayat wanted to surprise Ihsaan bhai."

Mama's brows knit. "Surprise Ihsaan? For what?"

Abeer stumbles with the whisk in her hand, head shooting up. She tries to mask the astonishment on her face, but fails to do so before I catch it.

"Ihsaan got promoted," I murmur quietly.

Mama seems to digest this information, and Abeer quickly turns away. She tries to busy herself with mixing the contents of the bowl, but the shock still lingers on her face.

I can't blame her for her reaction. Of course she's surprised my mom doesn't know about something so important. Especially because Abeer knew Mama before—knew how she kept track of and celebrated even our smallest accomplishments.

The tension in the room is dispelled by the ring of the doorbell.

"I got it!" Abeer chirps, rushing to the door and leaving my mom and me in awkward silence.

"Are you hungry?" I ask her.

She shakes her head. "Not really. But let's wait for Ihsaan and your dad to come; we'll eat together. And we'll ask Abeer to stay, too."

My eyes widen. My mom—suggesting we eat together? That's new. I clear my throat and look away so she's not upset by my surprise.

Ihsaan enters the kitchen, followed at a distance by a chattering Abeer. He laughs at something she says as he reaches forward and absentmindedly kisses Mama's temple. He frees his hands of two large brown bags and sets them on the kitchen island, waving at me.

"I brought gyro platters," Ihsaan says. His eyes rove over the mess in the kitchen. "What's going on here?"

I laugh. "Abeer is baking."

Ihsaan clutches his chest in mock horror, and for a moment I catch a glimpse of the old Ihsaan: carefree, jokester Ihsaan. The sight brings back a flood of memories and warmth.

"Great!" Ihsaan exclaims with exaggerated horror. "So does someone have 911 on speed dial?"

"Ihsaan bhai, that's not nice!" Abeer folds her arms in mock anger as I silently giggle at the scene taking place before me.

"Kiddo, you and Hayat almost burned down the kitchen once. Can't blame me for wanting to stay alive."

Abeer rolls her eyes and returns to the contents of the bowl, pouring the mixture into a lined cake tin. Ihsaan turns to me and says, "I'm just gonna shower and be back."

I nod. "Papa will be home soon. We'll eat when he comes."

Later, when everyone is settled at the dining table, my dad is speaking animatedly with Abeer. He asks about her parents, her brother (heart flip), and the classes she plans on taking in college. Ihsaan butts in with the occasional joke, and even Mama is gazing fondly at Abeer.

Tonight we've gone back to using five dinner plates, and suddenly everything feels wholesome again. Which is why I'm already dreading Abeer's departure.

When she brings out the cake (I try not to stand too much— I'd rather not draw attention to my feet), Ihsaan looks at the chunky frosting spelling out *Congrats Mr. HR Coordinator* and turns to me, eyes shining with an unreadable emotion. He grabs the butter knife and slices the cake, earning a round of applause. He feeds a portion to our parents, then to me, and finally hands Abeer a slice on a plate.

As soon as Abeer leaves, the house quiets. My father kisses my forehead before bidding me goodnight, and my mother halfheartedly offers to wash the dishes, but I wave her off. Ihsaan has disappeared somewhere in the house.

Exhausted, I load the dishwasher and let it run while I clear the dining table. Abeer's laughter continues to ring in my head, and I find myself smiling as I clutch a dishrag in my hand.

Then I remember something and grab my phone to text her.

> hey, you're prob tired of hearing from me after today but i need a favor tomorrow, if you're free.

Her reply arrives before I even set my phone back on the table.

> never tired of you. what's up?

> can you take me to RWJ hospital tomorrow? i just need to drop something off and talk to someone.

> of course.

I let out a deep sigh of relief. It's been uncomfortable holding on to Mikaal's belongings, and I want to return them to him as soon as possible. But instead of walking over to his house and handing them to him—risking questions from his understandably confused parents—I figure showing up to his workplace will be safer.

I head to Arafat's bedroom, taking a couple deep breaths before entering.

And promptly freezing in place.

Ihsaan is sitting on the floor against the bed, head buried in one of Arafat's T-shirts. His shoulders are shaking, and he's murmuring something incomprehensible as he weeps.

My knees lock in place. I can't move, can't breathe. My mind won't let me reconcile the carefree, jokester Ihsaan at dinner just half an hour ago with the trembling version before me now.

My brother shakes his head back and forth, hands clutching the T-shirt with such intensity I fear he might tear the fabric.

"How could you leave me?" he whimpers, a stark contrast to the composed, professional tone he always carries now. Heck, I can't remember the last time I saw Ihsaan cry. "I—I wasn't ready for any of this. Can't do it without you."

I reach up to clutch my neck, as if I can stop the tears burning in my throat. I must make some sort of sound, though, because Ihsaan's head shoots up and his breath hitches.

"Hayat?" His voice comes out shaky. I try to look away, let him have the privacy he clearly needs. But my gaze locks onto his, and the grief spilling from his eyes pierces what's left of my heart.

"Sorry, I didn't—I didn't mean to—" I swallow, awkwardly standing in the doorway. When Ihsaan doesn't respond, I hesitate before stepping forward and shutting the door behind me.

I try to come to Arafat's room as little as possible. Because every time I walk in and don't see him typing on his laptop, ironing his white coat, or scribbling notes from his textbooks, a strange sensation grips me. As if someone has shoved their fingers into my chest, wrenched out my heart, and left my ribcage rattling.

It feels so *wrong* not to see Arafat in his room.

But I needed a place to store Mikaal's blanket and shoes until I returned them, and this seemed like the least suspicious place. I didn't think anyone else would come in here.

Ihsaan sniffs, wiping his nose on his sleeve. He angles his body away from me, and another stab pierces my heart. "Go," he says quietly. "I'm fine."

"You're not fine." I step forward gingerly, bending down to sit next to him.

He scoots even further away.

"Ihsaan." I reach up to touch his shoulder, but he flinches away from me. My fingers hover midair, sharpness pricking at my eyes.

"Seriously, Hayat." He doesn't meet my eyes. "I said I'm fine."

I quiet then, realizing he doesn't want to talk.

There's the difference between us, I guess. I wish I could talk about our collective pain, carve a path through it together.

Ihsaan, however, wants to become a locked door. One whose doorknob I may rattle and rattle but never be granted entry.

No wonder I haven't seen him cry since Arafat died. No wonder all that buried emotion has probably caused his panic attacks.

Ihsaan sniffs once more before standing. I follow, watching as he carefully folds Arafat's shirt and places it on the bed. As if Arafat is in the shower, and he'll come out any second to slip the shirt on.

It takes everything in me to rein in my tears.

When one of us is crying, the other must smile. When one of us is falling, the other must stand. And when one of us is teetering off a steep cliff, ready to dive, the other must rush forward and haul them back.

Because all we have is each other now.

Ihsaan and Hayat.

So I reach forward and grab my brother's arm, pulling him close. I wrap my arms around his torso and bury my head in his chest, focusing on his heartbeat.

Alive. Alive. Alive.

After a moment's hesitation, Ihsaan hugs me back and buries his face in my hair. My once-jokester older brother is trembling in my arms.

I'm about to rub his back soothingly when he pulls away and rushes out of the room. It happens so quickly my hands are still outstretched to hold him, my fingers tingling from the contact I've craved for so long. My tears remain stuck in my throat so I don't make things worse by breaking.

But none of it matters.

Because I've been reaching for the ghost of my living brother ever since the other one died.

Ten

A LOUD HONK STARTLES me as I'm tying my shoes. "Coming!" I yell out the open door to Abeer.

I head into the living room to kiss my mom goodbye. She's out of her room today and even went to the kitchen to make a cup of chai.

"Mama, are you sure you'll be fine?" I ask as I kiss her temple.

She waves me off and nods. "Yes, don't worry about me."

"I'll be back soon, okay? I just need to give something back to someone from school."

It doesn't feel good to lie—especially about something so arbitrary. But I can't risk the follow-up questions I'd receive if I told the truth: that I was sleepwalking through my neighborhood, and my dead brother's best friend prevented me from collapsing in a ditch somewhere, after which he gave me his blanket and shoes.

Yeah, I'll pass on the awkward questions.

I give my mom another kiss, grab the tote bag containing Mikaal's belongings, and rush out the door.

My feet are feeling much better today, and the blisters are morphing into faded scabs. I have Mikaal to thank for that.

But I woke up this morning facing a dilemma. I wasn't sure

how to express my gratitude to Mikaal. *Hey, thanks for showing up at the right time and making sure I didn't get run over* didn't seem appropriate. Neither did *I'm sorry I was wearing my donut pajamas when you luckily stumbled upon me and woke me from sleepwalking barefoot in our neighborhood.*

Initially, I thought maybe I could just hand over his belongings. But that seemed oddly anticlimactic and ungrateful.

Then I thought maybe I could get a thank you card or something. But that felt wildly inappropriate, given the serious circumstances under which he'd found me.

After much contemplation (which mostly just frustrated me above anything else), I decided to make him a plate of food. Rice, chicken, salad—the works. It seemed like the safest thing to do considering our moms often sent each other food.

That, and I still want to keep my boundaries intact.

It's ridiculous how much thought I've had to devote to something that should've been simple. I've never had to contemplate something so deeply when it came to Mikaal. The only real interactions we've had were when he hung out with my brothers or when I visited Arafat at RWJ. So it's exhausting having to think so much about an interaction that was once second nature.

I don't even know if he'll be there; I have no idea what his rotation schedule is like. I'm just traipsing in like I own the place and hoping I'll stumble across him.

I break out of my thoughts and huff out a "sorry" to Abeer as I reach her car. But then I stop abruptly when I spot her in the passenger seat before my gaze shifts to the driver.

Rameez.

Immediately my heart stutters, and I stumble out a surprised "Salaam."

He smiles, the gesture lighting up his eyes. "Hey."

"Sorry!" Abeer exclaims loudly as I sit in the backseat. "My idiot brother tagged along so we could run some errands together. Says I won't know *which yogurt* he specifically wants."

I laugh, glancing at Rameez in the rearview mirror. He flashes me another smile before mussing Abeer's hair. "Habibti," he says to her in a tone of mock endearment.

She shoves him, and I rein a bout of momentary panic at their antics while he's driving. "Badtameez," she hollers.

Rameez rolls his eyes. "How are you, Hayat?"

Don't panic don't freak out. Heart stop doing that.

"I'm okay. How are you?"

He nods. "I'm good."

Abeer's eyes dart between the two of us before she scrunches her face. "You guys are so awkward and weirdly formal."

I giggle nervously, heat rising to my cheeks, before looking out the window.

"So what's up? What are you doing at the hospital?" Abeer chirps.

I had planned on telling her the real reason, but with Rameez in the car, I stutter out a half-baked lie, "Just—I needed to, um…talk to some of Arafat's cohorts. They reached out. They had some…paperwork and stuff."

This lying thing is getting uncomfortable and disturbingly frequent. But luckily, mentioning someone dead always has amazing powers of shutting everyone up. Abeer and Rameez don't ask any more questions.

We drive in silence for a few minutes until Abeer says, "What are you doing? RWJ's that way."

Rameez darts a glance at her before his gaze flits to me in the rearview mirror. "This is the quicker route."

"No, it's not—"

He throws her a sharp, wide-eyed look, clearly meant to communicate something obvious. Abeer still looks confused, but she seems to realize—right as I do—that he's taking the local route to avoid the highway.

The site of The Car Crash.

Warmth pools in my heart, and sharp tears prick my eyes. A sensation equal to falling spreads throughout me.

I glance at Rameez in the rearview mirror, eyes roving over his curls, his thick brows, his strong jawline. My heart thuds out of tune as I watch him. I wrestle with the warmth in my chest, trying to tamp it down because having this dumb little crush on my old best friend's *brother* is going to be *awkward*. But as I watch him drive—his fingers tapping against the steering wheel, those curls falling against his forehead—I can't help it.

Beautiful, smart, *and* thoughtful.

He must sense my gaze because he glances up and meets my eyes through the rearview mirror. I startle, unsure whether to look away. But the corners of my lips lift of their own accord as I attempt to communicate how grateful I am for his thoughtfulness.

He smiles in return.

⌒

"I'll be done in like an hour, I think," I say as I shut the car door.

Abeer nods. "Sounds good." She regards me with soft eyes. "Will you be okay in there? Alone?"

I swallow the emotion rising in my throat. "Yeah, I'll be fine. Don't worry about me."

"You don't have to do it alone."

I smile at her. "I'll be fine. Really."

"Okay." She reaches forward and squeezes my hand. "We're gonna do some groceries, and then I'm swinging by Rumana's to help her do this dumb hairstyle she saw online and insists on trying out for a family dawat." She rolls her eyes.

I'm surprised by the flash of hurt in my chest. Of course Abeer still has other friends and things to do. And she's close enough to others now to regularly visit and be comfortable with their families. It's been a while since Abeer and I have spoken, and just because I've been stagnant for two and a half months doesn't mean she has. Just because I suddenly want her back in my life doesn't mean she paused hers for me.

Rameez ducks his head to see me from the driver's side. "Text Abeer when you're ready, okay?"

I'm flustered by the concern in his voice and still trying to recover from Abeer's comment, so I simply nod.

Abeer blows me an air kiss. I nod and back away, waving to the two of them. Rameez doesn't drive off until I'm inside the hospital, though, and it makes me want to melt into a puddle of goo.

I need to stop thinking like this.

I've known the twins for four years now. Abeer was my closest friend before everything happened. We clicked instantly in freshman year, despite being total opposites. And when I first met Rameez, I recognized the feeling in my heart all too well—the warmth, the stutters, the butterflies. I vowed to tamp it down because I didn't want to make things awkward with Abeer. It helped because I didn't see her brother much; he was always off being The Coolest Person On The Planet.

But after Abeer's birthday party and Rameez's sudden attention and care, the feeling I tried to bury is starting to break free.

I can't risk having a naive little crush on him again. It would make my friendship with Abeer complicated. Plus, there would be no point. *Everyone* likes Rameez. And there's nothing special about me.

"Hello, how can I help you?" A nasally, clinical voice interrupts my thoughts as I approach the reception desk. I blink at the man behind the counter and smile tentatively.

"Yes, hi, I just wanted to see Mikaal Zaman." I pause, realizing I don't know which unit he's begun rotations in. "Um, I just needed to give him something." I gesture to the bag I'm carrying.

The man watches me for a moment too long before saying, "ID, please."

I extract my license and hand it to him, waiting as he prints out a visitor badge. He hands me the sticker. "And you are?"

"I'm his..." I pause for longer than necessary as I stick the badge to my shirt. His eyebrows rise. "Family friend," I settle for.

He nods, and I blow out a breath I didn't realize I was holding. I frantically try to recall past snippets of conversation between Arafat and Mikaal that might hint at where Mikaal is doing rotations. I remember Arafat mentioning his cohort was talking about internal medicine, surgery, and pediatrics. Of course, it could be any one of those—or none at all. I don't know if I'll even be allowed into a unit if I'm not visiting a patient. I usually met Arafat in the cafeteria.

I decide to take my chances and go with my best guess—internal medicine—as I glance back at the receptionist sheepishly. "Um…I'm sorry, where's the…internal medicine unit?"

He seems to be holding back a smile as he points to the hallway on the left. "Go down that hallway and past the double doors, then take the elevator to the fourth floor."

I tap the counter, relieved he didn't ask more questions. "Thank you."

As I'm walking away, I swear I feel him smiling at my back. But I don't turn around; I'm already embarrassed enough.

I trudge through hallways, take the elevator, press buttons with shaky fingers. By the time I reach the internal medicine unit, my heart is pounding with the clinical smell of the halls, the familiar beeps and whirs of machinery, the chatter of patients and doctors and technicians.

I stumble against the wall, gripping a pole for support. My tote bag slips from my hands.

"Miss?" someone calls. Her voice sounds oddly far away. "Are you alright?"

And then another voice—this one familiar. "Hayat?"

I try to recall why it sounds familiar, but I'm too preoccupied with remembering how to breathe.

One, two, three.

My eyes glaze over the polished floor beneath me. So shiny. So clean.

Arafat probably walked on this floor.

"Hayat, are you okay?"

One, two, three.

I reach up to clutch my throat. Something is trying to claw its way out, and I need to stop it. Something tells me that if this feeling ever escapes, it will be impossible to rein in again.

A hand touches my shoulder softly and I flinch, looking up into two pairs of concerned eyes.

A woman is speaking, but her voice reaches me like it's behind warped glass. I look at the person next to her. *Mikaal.* Hands shoved in the pockets of his white coat, a crease between his brows.

That look shocks me back into reality.

Why does he always see me like this? Unstable. Teetering on the edge of a cliff.

He probably thinks I have some kind of malfunction.

I blink at the two of them and shake my head. "I'm sorry," I say, and my voice sounds really far away. "I got dizzy."

They look like they know I'm spewing a load of bull. "Are you sure?" the woman asks. I realize she's a resident and read her ID badge: Cheryl Hamada.

I nod. "Yes, I'm fine. Sorry to worry you."

She steps back and smiles. "No need to apologize. We just wanted to make sure you were okay. Are you visiting someone?"

My eyes dart from her to Mikaal, who's been oddly quiet throughout this encounter.

"Um, yes," I say. I gesture to Mikaal. "I came to see *him*, actually."

Cheryl lets out a surprised laugh. "Oh, okay. Well, I'll leave you to it, then." She touches my shoulder briefly. "Let us know if you need anything, okay?"

I smile warmly at her as she walks away. "Thank you."

I recollect myself and retrieve the tote bag before turning to face Mikaal. I raise my hand in an awkward wave. "Hi. Salaam."

His eyes are guarded as he reaches up to run a hand through his hair. "Wa 'Alaikum Salaam." He pauses, and I physically feel tension coiling in my shoulders.

There's something strange about meeting someone a couple days after they witnessed you sleepwalking the streets of your neighborhood at 1 A.M.

"Hayat, are you sure you're okay?" His hands are back in his pockets as he gives me a once-over.

I huff, annoyed by the amount of times I've been asked this question recently. "Yeah, yeah, I'm fine. I just—" I lift the tote bag and am about to explain the reason for my visit when my lips clamp shut.

This is so *awkward,* God. I've never had to personally interact this much with Mikaal. He's my brother's best friend, for God's sake. Why is this so weird?

"Hayat?" He breaks me out of my trance by waving a hand in front of my face. "You don't look so good to me. Why don't we sit down and talk?"

I nod as he leads me down the hall and into the break room, observing how he purposely leaves the door open so we're visible to everyone.

I settle down and he pulls open the fridge before finding what he's looking for. He pulls out a box of orange juice, slides it towards me, and leans against the wall with folded arms.

"Drink," he orders.

"I hate orange juice."

"Drink," he says again.

I sigh before reaching for the box and opening it, sipping an insignificant amount. His eyes bore into mine, and the intensity is so rattling that I take another few sips.

There is something very weird going on here. The dynamic between us has shifted since that night, and I don't like it. I don't like it at all. So I need to fulfill my purpose and get the hell out of here as soon as possible.

"How are you?" I ask.

He nods. "I'm good, Alhamdulillah. How are you? How are your feet? Are you feeling better?"

My cheeks redden. Ugh, so *embarrassing.* "I'm okay, yeah."

"Really? You're kind of limping."

I look up, surprised that he noticed. I've been trying to cover it as best as I can. I thought I was doing a good job.

"Yes, I'm fine."

He looks like he wants to say something else before he changes his mind. "So what brings you here today?"

I set the abomination called juice on the table and lift the tote bag. "I wanted to give these back to you."

He takes the bag from my outstretched hand and glances quizzically inside.

"The Neosporin and bandages are in the plastic bag. I laundered the blanket and shoes." His eyebrows rise, and I rush to explain. "Don't worry, I did some research. Your shoes are washer and dryer safe, and I didn't want to give them back to you just like that…" I trail off as he lifts the container of food from the bag and squints at the contents. "And that's just…I wanted to thank you. For the other night. If you hadn't been there…"

Unexpectedly, Mikaal breaks out into a fit of chuckles. He sets the container on the counter and touches his forehead, shoulders shaking.

"What?" I say, panicked. "What is it?"

He simply shakes his head and continues laughing. Abruptly I'm reminded of Rameez—the way his eyes light up and his curls bounce against his forehead when he laughs.

I fold my arms, unimpressed. "Is something wrong?"

He forces his laughter to subside at the look on my face and shakes his head. "No, no. Of course not. I just—Hayat, I really appreciate it, but you didn't need to launder my shoes."

I furrow my brows, miffed. "I looked it up. They're washer and dryer safe—"

He chuckles again, smile lingering. "No, no, I mean—it makes me feel bad. I don't like that you touched my gross shoes and laundered them. You didn't need to do that, really."

"Oh." My shoulders relax. "Oh, no, it's not a big deal. I just…I didn't wanna give them back to you just like that after I'd worn them."

"It's a big deal to me. I would rather you have done that than get your hands dirty." His smile fades. "But thank you, you went through the trouble. I appreciate it…" His gaze falls back to the container of food, brows creasing.

I'm surprised by his reaction. But I guess it makes sense. I mean, I would feel bad if someone washed my shoes, too.

"Did you make this?" He taps the container, and I hesitate before nodding.

He lifts the lid and peers inside, then holds it up to take a whiff. His eyes brighten. "This smells amazing."

I fluster. "Oh—I—yeah, I just—well, I've been experimenting with different dishes and…" I stop, holding my breath as he pulls a fork from the drawer and digs in. He chews slowly, eyes contemplative, then breaks into a grin.

I exhale.

"Amazing. Didn't know Arafat's sister cooked so well."

A laugh huffs out of me. I love it when people say I cook well. I used to be horrible at it, so every compliment feels like a little victory now.

Mikaal closes the container and places it back in the tote bag. "I'll eat this during my break. Thank you so much again."

"Oh." I realize belatedly that he wasn't on his break when he stumbled upon me. "I'm sorry. You have things to do, and I'm keeping you." I pocket my phone and stand.

"No, it's okay. Thanks for stopping by. Although next time, don't go through the trouble of coming all the way here. You can give whatever it is through Ihsaan." He looks up, briefly contemplating his next words. "I know it must be difficult for you to come here."

My breath hitches as I look away, strangely touched by his concern. "Well, I better let you get back to work. See you. Salaam."

I'm rushing out the door when Mikaal says, "Wait a second."

I squeeze my eyes shut. *Great.* When I open them, he's standing in front of me with the orange juice in his hand.

I look up and am weirdly floored by how tall he is. How did I never realize that I have to crane my neck to look at him? His head is, like, all the way up there.

I groan. "Please. I don't want it."

He shoves it forward and says sternly, "Finish it."

I take the juice just as someone arrives in the doorway.

"Mikaal," she says, somewhat breathlessly. I look up and freeze when I recognize her. "There you are. We're gonna do a round soon."

"Alright, I'm on my way." Mikaal turns back to me. "Thank you, Hayat. I really appreciate it. And…there's no need to feel indebted to me. I did what anyone would do." Pause. "I'll see you around, okay?" He backs out the door with the tote bag in hand. "Take care."

The girl steps back to make room for him to pass, and he disappears around the corner. She turns back to me, and her eyes widen. "Hayat?"

For a moment, I realize this is the second time Mikaal bid me goodbye and I gave him no response. But I don't have time to mull over that because the girl is standing in front of me as if she's met a friend after a very long time and is bursting with words.

It's the same girl from outside Burlington—the sight of whom caused Ihsaan to back out of the parking lot without explanation. The sight of whom stirred memories just out of reach.

"Oh my God, hi. Assalaamu 'Alaikum." She steps forward and grasps the end of her hijab with trembling fingers. She's also wearing a white coat with the university emblem and her name tag, and since she knew Mikaal, I assume she must be a med student too.

"Wa 'Alaikum Salaam," I pause, unsure of how to proceed since I don't actually know who she is.

"Oh, gosh." She brings a hand up to cover her mouth and chuckles. "I'm so sorry. You don't know me, do you?"

I watch her as she laughs, trying to find clues that would help me recognize her. She definitely looks familiar. I've probably seen her around RWJ and the masjid community—maybe even greeted her in passing. Other than that, I conclude only one thing with certainty— she's *gorgeous*. Like, drop-dead, jaw-droppingly gorgeous. Heart-shaped pink lips stand out against smooth cream skin. Bright brown eyes and a pert nose are set against a perfectly structured face. A smile that lights up her entire face grazes her lips.

"I—no, I'm so sorry. You look really familiar, but I…*should* I know you?" I ask sheepishly.

Her face falls for a moment before she resumes smiling. "No, I, uh…no, I guess I wouldn't expect you to." She steps forward and lifts her hands tentatively. "Can I hug you?"

"I—yeah, of course." My intrigue overpowers my surprise, and I meet her halfway as she wraps me in a tight hug. As if we've known each other forever.

When we pull back, she gazes at me for a moment before shaking her head. "I'm sorry, you probably think I'm crazy." She takes a deep breath. "I'm Aneela. Arafat and I studied together."

The smile vanishes from my face. Another person who knew my brother. "Oh," I say, suddenly very interested in the floor.

"Yeah, we were in the same cohort." I look up at the subdued tone of her voice. She quiets, then a bright grin adorns her face. "He used to talk about you in classes all the time. My baby sister this, my baby sister that. 'Hayat is such a smart and hardworking kid.' It was sweet. And impressive, considering you don't always see siblings like that." Aneela chuckles. "Trust me, I would know. I have three brothers and a sister."

"Oh, wow," I laugh. "That's amazing, Masha Allah." I swallow the emotion rising in my throat at the thought of Arafat talking about me with such pride.

So now I know where Arafat met this girl. But what about Ihsaan? Did he know her, too? And why was he so panicked when he saw her? She doesn't seem like she'd harm an ant, let alone elicit a reaction like that from a grown man.

It's an uncomfortable truth to grasp, that you don't know as much about your siblings as you thought you did. That they have an entire life that doesn't involve you.

"How are you holding up?" Aneela asks softly, touching my shoulder. "How's your family?"

I'm so exhausted with having to answer the same questions over and over. I know people mean well, asking out of genuine concern and courtesy. Since I'm slowly rejoining civilization after basically vanishing, it makes sense. But I'm so *tired* of being the poor, pitiful girl who lost her brother. It's hard enough already—everyone's well-intentioned concern only makes it harder to bear.

I force a smile for Aneela because despite everything, I realize I like her. "We're...better." *Except for the fact that the life I envisioned has crashed and burned. My mom barely leaves her room, my remaining brother only talks to me when he needs to, and my dad tries to keep us all together but it's mostly just a tough-guy dad act.*

"I know." She squeezes my shoulder. "I understand. But from what I've gathered, you're incredibly strong. You'll pull through. And if you ever need anything, I'm always here."

I remain silent, touched by her sincerity and her conviction in my strength.

"Well, I apologize for bombarding you like this. I wish we could've met under different circumstances." She laughs—I decide I really like the sound—and gestures to herself. "I was just viewing lab data on a patient with dangerously low hemoglobin levels. Not exactly ideal circumstances, but"—she shrugs and smiles—"I'll take what I can get."

I smile in return. "Don't worry about it. I'm glad I met you." I pause, flustered by the way she's looking at me, eyes shining with an emotion I can't decipher.

"Can we meet some other time? If you're free, that is." She extracts her phone from her coat. "Or...can I have your number, at least? I would love to get to know you better."

"Oh," I blink, shocked by the unexpected request. "Yeah. Yeah, of course." I type my number into her phone and she saves my contact.

"Well, I wish I could stay and chat, but I have to go." She touches my shoulder briefly. "I'll message you, okay? Loved meeting you. Assalaamu 'Alaikum." And with one last emotionally ridden glance, she turns and exits the break room.

I'm so confused.

How does Aneela seem to know so much about me already? Even if Arafat talked about me often, how much can you really gauge from hallway conversations and group projects? And it still doesn't explain why Ihsaan looked like he was going to break out into hives when he saw her.

I shake my head to clear my thoughts. This is all too mind-boggling. I need to think about it later, when I'm in bed and away from prying eyes.

I spend the next half hour taking a much-needed walk around the perimeter of the hospital. The bustle near the ER, the loud streets of New Brunswick—they're chaotic but welcome distractions from the noise in my head.

When Abeer texts me, I head to their car parked at the curb.

"Hel-*lo*, human," she hollers, extending an ice cream sundae to me.

I shake my head, a smile tugging at the corners of my mouth, and climb into the backseat. Rameez salutes me through the rearview mirror, and I grin.

"Sorry, we tried putting most of the stuff in the trunk so there'd be room for your legs but it might still be a tight squeeze. Anyways, how was your little trip?" Abeer asks, munching on her ice cream cone loudly.

I pause for a moment before realizing I won't have to lie. "Good, actually."

"Did you meet fellow *hoomans*?"

"Yes," I giggle. "I met fellow *hoomans*."

"Stop chewing like that, Abeer." Rameez wrinkles his nose, lightly shoving her. "Bidun akhlaq."

Abeer leans over and smacks loudly in his ear. I giggle silently at their antics, and when Rameez catches my eye in the rearview mirror, his eyes spark.

I forget how to chew.

When we reach my house, I invite them inside, but they decline—worried their groceries will get spoiled in the heat. I bid them goodbye, heart stuttering when Rameez throws me another one of his smiles, and head inside.

"Mama," I shout. "I'm home."

She emerges from the kitchen with a rare smile. "You took a while."

I freeze, instantly feeling guilty. "Yeah, I'm sorry. I just ran into some people and—"

She laughs. I blink. Then I notice her appearance: clean clothes, wet shower hair, the strong scent of perfume. She looks good. Normal. Healthy.

"Beta, I wasn't complaining. I'm glad you spent time with friends."

"Oh," I exhale, stepping forward to kiss her forehead. "What did you do at home?"

Mama gestures to the kitchen. "I cooked. I miss cooking."

"*Ooooh*," I stretch out the syllable, heading towards the smell. "What did you cook?"

"Chinese rice and teriyaki chicken."

"Oh my gosh, Mama!" I can't describe the feeling coursing through my veins, arresting my senses. Seeing my mom up and about like this makes me ecstatic.

She smiles softly. "It's almost done. We'll eat together when your dad gets home." She gestures behind her. "I'm going to use the bathroom."

"Okay." I'm breathless, stunned by the homey sight of my mother in the kitchen. Cooking. Smiling. Doing what she used to love.

Just then, footsteps thump down the stairs. Ihsaan appears, freshly showered, and waves at me.

I knit my brows. "You're home early."

He nods. I wait for him to provide an explanation, but he doesn't. He's busy buckling a watch around his wrist when he says, "I heard you hung out with your friends. Who dropped you off?"

"Rameez and Abeer."

He pauses. "You came with Rameez?"

"And Abeer."

Ihsaan abandons the watch, setting it down slowly on the kitchen island. His fingers tap the counter, a fissure appearing between his brows. "Just…um, try coming with just Abeer next time?"

I let out a surprised laugh. "What? Ihsaan, I've known them for like four years."

"I know, I know," he rushes to continue, still not meeting my eyes, "I just…We're older now, you know? I just want you to be careful with guys."

I laugh again, but this time it's laced with a hint of anger. I know I'm not necessarily the most cultural or religious person, but I know where my boundaries lie.

"Ihsaan, are you serious? You've never said anything about my friends before. What's the problem now?"

"I'm not saying anything about your friends." He blows out an exasperated breath. "Sorry, this is coming out wrong. Just…be alert, okay?"

"*Okay*," I snap mockingly.

I'm mad. I don't know why I'm so mad. Maybe because six out of seven days Ihsaan doesn't care what I'm doing—and suddenly he remembers he has a little sister?

He runs a hand through his hair. "Look, Hayat, I'm not trying to offend you. As your brother, I'd say this about *any* guy—and you could say the same to me about any girl. Keep your distance."

I start to imagine how strongly he'd react if he knew I was recently in Mikaal's car at 1 A.M.

I scoff in disbelief. "Okay, Ihsaan, okay."

"What?" he says.

"You just—you don't give a damn about me any other time. You barely even talk to me unless you need to. Or if it's small talk. Otherwise you keep pushing me away. But when it comes to some *guy*—who, by the way, I've known for all of high school—your overprotective brother vibe switches on?" I shake my head. "Save it, Ihsaan."

He's quiet, and it only makes me angrier. *Why am I so mad?*

I turn, ready to storm upstairs—and then I remember. "Oh, and another thing. I met someone at the hospital today."

He furrows his brows. "What were you doing at the hospital?"

"Not relevant. But I met someone." I pause, scrutinizing his reaction. I can tell he's trying his best not to betray any emotion. "She told me she knew Arafat. Her name was Aneela."

Suddenly, whatever defenses he's carefully constructed crumble. Panic mars his features, and his eyes widen.

I soften my tone. "You know her. Don't you, Ihsaan?"

There's a beat of silence—heavy, deliberate—before he slowly shakes his head and clears his throat. "No. I mean, I know *of* her. From Arafat. Just that they were in the same year and cohort."

I step forward and fold my arms. "You know you have a tell, right?" I gesture to his hands. "You always spin that around when you're nervous. Or lying."

Ihsaan glances down at his silver ring, startled, before pocketing his trembling hands.

"Seriously," he insists. "That's all I know about her."

I shake my head. "I don't know why you're lying to me, Ihsaan. But if you're not willing to talk to me about anything else or answer any of my questions, then you have no right to pretend to be the protective older brother."

I drop my arms and head upstairs, heart hammering with anger. Deep breaths. *One, two, three.*

I love my brother, I really do. But he has no right to ignore me and then suddenly decide to care when it comes to some *guy.*

When I'm in my room, my phone pings with a text.

It's Aneela. Save my number :)

Oh, I will. I sure will.

Eleven

Lily of the Valley: Return to happiness

I SLIDE OPEN THE door to the terrace and take a deep breath.

The place is in ruins. Wilted flowers, upended wicker chairs, cracked pots scattered across the wooden floor.

I'm holding one of my old gardening books that I stumbled across, turned to the first chapter. *Lily Of The Valley: The Flower That Prevails.* It gets its name from its resilience and its ability to survive almost any weather. It grows best in partial shade and has a crisp scent, a little like jasmine. It symbolizes love, purity, and a return to happiness. And it's often used in wedding bouquets.

Ironically, it also contains heart-active substances and is poisonous if consumed.

I'm startled out of my thoughts when a voice behind me says, "What are you doing?"

I turn to see Ihsaan standing awkwardly, hands buried in his pockets, and he's not meeting my eyes.

I turn away, last night's anger rising up my throat. "Nothing."

Silence. Then: "That doesn't look like nothing."

I snap the book shut and catch him flinch. "Do you need breakfast?"

He sighs. "Hayat, I can make my own breakfast."

"Okay," I shrug noncommittally, stepping forward onto the terrace.

Lily of the valley. Return to happiness.

My eyes rove over the wreckage of what once used to be my favorite hobby.

"Are you thinking of starting again?" Ihsaan murmurs, walking over to stand next to me.

"Even if I was, it's none of your concern," I snap, stepping around him to head back inside.

"Hayat." He grabs my arm. "Don't be like that."

I pull away, arms folding tight across my chest. "Don't be like what?"

He gestures between us, eyes trained to the floor. "Like…this. Cold. Distant. You and me…it's just us now."

"Oh, *now* you remember that it's just us?" My voice rises an octave, and his troubled eyes finally meet mine. My attempt at cool indifference fails; I scoff and shake my head angrily. "Where is this concern when you ignore me for weeks? When you only talk to me to ask if I *need* anything? When you lie and keep secrets like I don't matter? You lied straight to my face, and you expect me to be okay with it?"

Ihsaan's gaze drops back to the floor, his toe nudging the edge of an upturned flower pot. "That's not fair, Hayat," he says quietly.

"You know what else is not fair?" I'm breathing hard now. "Finding out *weeks later* that my brother takes anti-anxiety meds and goes to therapy. Having to extract major information out of him like his promotion—which he would otherwise never tell me himself. Knowing he's lying to me about some *girl* but not understanding why. *That's* not fair."

I start to head back inside, but Ihsaan's voice roots me in place. "I told you. Some things are an amanah."

I scoff. "Okay, Ihsaan."

"Please try to understand." He's standing helpless, hands outstretched.

"No. *You* need to understand *me*, Ihsaan. I've tried to be patient because I know you never asked for any of this. The responsibilities, the grief—I know it's hard. It's been hard for all of us." I exhale sharply. "But God, you don't even *talk* to me anymore. You're so subdued all the time, and even if I try to talk to you, you brush me off." I throw my hands in the air, fuming. "And then last night, when I'm driven home by people I've known for *years*, suddenly you wanna be the concerned big brother?" I shake my head. "You don't get to start caring about me now when you haven't for the past two and a half months."

"He was my brother, too!" Ihsaan shouts.

For a beat we're both absolutely silent, breathing hard and staring each other down.

Then, quieter, "He was *my* brother, too. And I lost him, too. You're not the only one who lost him." He breathes heavily, gaze searing into mine. "You *still* have a brother. I lost my only one. The only older sibling I had—and suddenly I'm supposed to fill his shoes."

Ihsaan laughs without mirth. "And I have really *big* shoes to fill, Hayat, do you realize that? He was going to be a *doctor*—the apple of everyone's eyes. And me? The joker? The guy who didn't take his classes seriously enough?"

He blows out a breath. "I'm *twenty-two*; don't you remember what I was always saying before I graduated college in May? That I was gonna *travel the world*." He scoffs. "I never even *dreamed* of becoming a corporate slave this early. I'm lucky I graduated and had enough prior experience to land a job so quickly, *and* get promoted later. But that was never the plan." He rubs a tired hand across his face. "The plan was always for Arafat to be the grown-up. The guy taking care of everything—you, Mama, our family—while I went and '*chased my dreams.*'"

He shakes his head and chuckles humorlessly. His shoulders sag. "I was the picture of immaturity. The definition of careless and reckless. So *forgive me*"—he pauses, breathes hard—"forgive me if I don't know how to do this, either."

He steps forward and shoves past me to head inside. I turn to watch him go, anger and grief and regret crawling up my throat all at once. His words nag at me, piercing me somewhere deep.

He was my *brother, too.*

You still *have a brother. I lost my only one.*

I have really big *shoes to fill, Hayat.*

I rub my face tiredly as my brother's anguished words echo in my mind. And I find myself thinking: *But you still have me, Ihsaan.*

Ihsaan and I don't speak for the rest of the day. And since he's working from home, it's even harder to pretend he isn't five feet away from me.

My mom is in the living room again today. My brother and I have silently but collectively decided to join her so that she doesn't retreat to her room.

My dad left for work about an hour ago, kissing each of our foreheads in turn. His eyes sparkled when he saw Mama on the sofa. That, despite everything, brought a smile to my face.

Mama's watching a Pakistani drama on TV now, occasionally chortling at the scenes. The first time she laughs, Ihsaan and I simultaneously gape at her. Our eyes automatically stray towards each other to exchange a shocked glance before we remember we're still mad at each other.

I'm on my laptop browsing through Rutgers University's majors and minors. I have absolutely no idea what degree I want to pursue. Environmental science used to be the obvious choice, but now…nothing feels the same. All those exams and sleepless nights and AP assignments and extracurriculars to get into Ivy League and academically pursue what I loved…all of that feels a lifetime away.

And I have…the oddest feeling that I'm supposed to be heading somewhere else—somewhere new after Arafat's death. So I'm hoping some extensive research will help me figure it out. That, and frantically texting Abeer my thoughts.

I'm mid-spiral, typing out a paragraph to her about my crisis, when another message pops up at the top of my screen:

Salaam. How are you?

I hesitate, eyes flicking up to Ihsaan. He's also on his laptop, face screwed up in concentration. His words from this morning replay in my mind: *I never even* dreamed *of becoming a corporate slave this early.*

I shake the thought from my head and return to my phone screen.

salaam, aneela, I type. **i'm great, how are you?**

Guilt gnaws at me as I put my phone down and glance back at Ihsaan.

Just then, he gets a call on Teams. Sighing, he slips in his AirPods and answers. "Hi, I'm good, thank you…No, no, don't worry about it. What's up?" Clicks echo as he works on his laptop, nodding along to the person on the other end of the call. "Yes, I see it. Okay, so the reason you can't view those files is because you don't have access to them. Since you're an intern, Ian has to grant you permission to transfer the CVs to the folder. I'll send in a work order so that you're able to view and transport those files." Pause. "Yeah, of course. Don't worry about it. Take care."

I hold my breath the entire time. I've never heard him speak like that—all businesslike and professional. It baffles me. I mean, I know he works in HR at a fancy company and was good enough to be promoted after only a few months, but I don't really know what he *does.* And I've never really bothered to ask.

The realization makes his words from this morning haunt me more.

Ihsaan catches me staring and offers a strained smile.

I look away quickly, not wanting him to think we're on good terms now.

Later in the afternoon, when Mama is taking a nap and Ihsaan is downstairs in the basement in the makeshift gym, the doorbell rings. I close the book I wasn't really reading and hurry to answer.

"Hey, girlie." Abeer steps inside, huffing as she hoists a bag of fertilizer and two plastic bags full of gardening supplies. I rush to take them off her hands, but she refuses my help. "I got it. Just tell me where to put them."

I quickly lead her to the terrace. She dumps everything onto the floor and leans down to catch her breath.

"Thank you," I whisper, guilt washing over me as I watch her. Abeer hates any form of physical exercise, so I know buying all this and lugging it to me must not have been easy for her.

She waves me off as she straightens. "What are friends for?"

"Seriously, I—"

"Oh, hush. Please don't do the whole formal 'thank you' thing." She bumps her hip against mine. "We're besties, aren't we?"

I bite my lower lip, trying to contain the emotions coursing through me at the word *besties*. I don't deserve friends like Abeer—not after ghosting her for months and then suddenly welcoming her back into my life. And she's trying so hard—

"Uh oh." Abeer tilts her head. "I know that look. You're overthinking. Please stop—it's just a couple things. It was really no big deal. Plus, I'm pretty much free for the rest of August, and there's nothing on earth I would rather do than hang with you."

I smile, blinking to fight the moisture in my eyes. "Where's the receipt? I'll Venmo you."

Abeer rolls her eyes. "Don't worry about it."

"Whoa, whoa. You promised. You said you'd let me pay you back."

"Pay her back for what?"

Both of us turn at the sound of Ihsaan's voice. He's wiping the sweat from his forehead with a hand towel and watching us quizzically.

"Salaam, Ihsaan bhai!" Abeer chirps. He responds to her greeting, then turns back to me, a question in his eyes.

I toe a nail on the wooden floorboards, refusing to meet his gaze. "Abeer bought some gardening supplies. I...asked her to."

It's so quiet for a few moments that I'm unable to resist looking up. I immediately wish I hadn't, though, because the crestfallen expression on Ihsaan's face is almost too much to bear.

"I asked you this morning—" He purses his lips, stopping himself. His eyes skim the supplies on the floor before settling on Abeer. "How much was everything?"

"Ihsaan bhai, it's—"

He pulls his phone out and types quickly. "Abeerxoxo, right? I think I have your username saved from the last couple of times."

Abeer nods quietly, eyes darting between the two of us. "Forty-eight dollars," she murmurs, relenting beneath the fierce emotion in Ihsaan's eyes.

"Sent. Let me know if you received it."

Abeer pulls out her phone and nods. Ihsaan throws me one last loaded look before heading back inside the house.

Guilt swirls in my chest.

Abeer turns to me, eyebrows raised. "Um, do you wanna explain what just happened?"

I shrug, bending to pick up the fertilizer. "Nothing."

"I'm pretty sure that was not *nothing*, ma'am."

"We're just not seeing eye to eye on some things." I pick up the plastic bags and begin pulling out the contents.

"I sensed a lot of…hurt," Abeer says slowly.

Lining up the gardening supplies on the ground, I shrug. I'm too hasty, though, and knock the watering cans over with a loud clang.

I close my trembling hands into fists.

Abeer leans down and gently places her hands over mine. "Hayat. Look at me." I try to blink away my tears but they escape, trailing down my cheeks.

"Hayat, what's wrong?" Abeer tucks a strand of hair behind my ear. "Please talk to me."

I shake my head. "Nothing, I just…" My voice cracks. "He's keeping secrets from me."

"And? That's not all, is it?"

"And I just…" I sniff. "I miss my brother, and I said some things I shouldn't have. I made him upset."

"Hayat, listen to me…" Abeer turns to the sky, huffing out a breath. "Your family…your family suffered an enormous loss. And you're all dealing with grief in your own ways. This is not the time to be hard on each other. This is the time you need each other the most."

"I'm trying!" I say indignantly, voice cracking. "I try with him *all the time.* It's like he doesn't care at all. He wants to keep things to himself. He just wants to be left alone."

She's quiet for a moment, lips pursed in contemplation. Finally she says, "Do you want my advice or do you just need to vent? Because I'm ready for anything—just tell me what you need."

My voice is quiet and reserved when I say, "Your…advice?"

Abeer squeezes my hand. "Like I said, everyone deals with grief in their own ways. You're suffering so much more than you're letting on, but so is your brother." She lets her words hang for a moment before continuing. "Think about it. Ihsaan bhai lost the only brother he had and is now suddenly the oldest child. And you know the responsibilities brothers carry in Pakistani families. He's…probably overwhelmed. Trying to juggle so many different things at once. Don't you think I've noticed it, too—how he's changed? Ihsaan bhai is a completely different person now."

I bite my lip. Abeer's words echo Ihsaan's from this morning—almost like a mirror. If even she, an outsider, saw it so clearly…have I just been selfish and unfair? Have I only been looking at things from my perspective, my grief?

Abeer wraps her arms around me and embraces me tightly. "Hayat," she whispers in my ear. "Don't let the pain of losing one brother push you away from the one who is still here and cares so much about you."

I squeeze my eyes shut at her words, unable to respond but finding comfort in her embrace nonetheless.

～

We're halfway through cleaning the terrace when Abeer gets a call from home and has to head out. She wraps me in a tight hug and whispers, "Love you, girl" before leaving.

My mom is just waking from her nap as I shut the front door. She rubs her eyes, blinking up at me. "Who was that?"

"Abeer. Did you sleep okay?"

She nods. "Did Abeer eat before she left?"

"Yeah, I fed her some rice."

"Good. Did you and Ihsaan eat?"

I hesitate. "I'm not sure where Ihsaan is, but I ate with Abeer."

Mama's brows furrow. "Not sure where Ihsaan is? What do you mean?"

"No, no, he's home," I quickly reassure her. "He was working out in the basement, so I think he's still down there."

Mama stands, rubbing her face tiredly. "Let me go see what my bacha is doing."

I startle at the endearing term as she heads downstairs.

My phone pings with a text, pulling me out of my thoughts about the subtle changes in my mom lately.

It's Aneela.

> I'm good, too, Alhamdulillah! How's your summer break going?

it's alright, I reply. just trying to figure out college things for the spring semester

> Oh, are you taking a break for the fall semester?

> > yeah if they accept me for the spring lol

> They'd be dumb not to. But it's great that you're taking a breather. I hope you're able to recharge and spend time with your family before college.

I rear back in shock. Excluding Abeer, anyone else who has heard of my gap semester has either wrinkled their noses or raised their eyebrows in a not-so-encouraging manner—something I witnessed firsthand at Abeer's party. As if "Harvard-bound" Hayat was doing everyone a disservice by choosing her own timeline.

> yeah. also just not sure what i wanna study or do at all anymore lol

> Ah, I remember those days. If you ever need advice or just wanna talk about anything, you can always reach out to me! Doesn't have to be college-related :)

I cock my head to the side, rubbing my chin. Not that I don't appreciate her friendliness, but her overly enthusiastic and seemingly random kindness is a little unsettling. I can't help but wonder if it's genuine or something else. And since Ihsaan refuses to tell me anything about her, I'll just have to take matters into my own hands and figure it out myself.

actually, I type. i hope you won't mind if i take you up on that offer. i really would appreciate the advice, preferably from someone already experienced.

Of course! she replies immediately. Want to talk on the phone or meet up in person?

I hesitate. meet in person, if that's okay. but i don't drive anymore and don't want to bother my brother when he's off of work. if you don't mind, can we meet at my place whenever you're free? i understand if you're unable to, tho.

Three dots appear, then disappear, then reappear. I can't help but feel it has something to do with my mention of Ihsaan.

Finally, Aneela replies, Of course. I'm free tomorrow after 3. Is that okay?

perfect, thank you so much. I pause, fingers hovering over my screen, before typing, looking forward to seeing you.

Likewise!

I should probably cook something nice. After all, I'm asking Aneela to take time out of her busy schedule to help me with college stuff…or pretending that's my reason when really I want to figure out what her connection to my family might be.

I get the feeling Ihsaan would probably flip out if he knew she was coming.

Just then, Mama and Ihsaan stroll into the kitchen. His arm wraps around her shoulders, and she's clinging to him with a smile. He says something, and her responding chuckle echoes through the house.

The sound warms my heart.

"Mama," I say. "I'm having a friend over tomorrow. She's helping me with some college stuff."

Ihsaan's eyes bore into mine. "Who's the friend?"

"Oh, just someone. You probably wouldn't know her."

He looks like he wants to press, but his attention quickly drifts to the terrace. "You guys cleaned up the terrace?"

I shrug. "Just a little bit. Still have a lot left to do."

Mama glances at me, her eyes sparking with something I haven't seen in a long time. "You're gardening?"

I look down, color rushing to my cheeks. "I'm trying to start again. Let's see how it goes."

"Do you want help?" Ihsaan murmurs.

I peek up at him, still embarrassed from our fight this morning and rattled by Abeer's words echoing in my mind. *Don't let the pain of losing one brother push you away from the one who is still here and cares so much about you.*

"Yeah," I whisper. "Sure."

For the next hour until Maghrib, Ihsaan and I work quietly on the terrace. He does the heavy lifting, I do the cleaning. I come across several scattered Post-Its—now moth-eaten and covered in dirt—and stash them into a box. I don't read them—I've cried enough today.

It's quiet as we work, but it's a companionable silence. Every time I look up, my brother is still there—present, steady, doing one thing or another. And every time he catches my gaze, he gives me a soft, tentative smile.

And for now, that's more than enough.

Twelve

Foxglove: Secrets

I END UP MAKING tacos before Aneela arrives, not wanting to go overboard but still wanting to make something substantial for her first visit.

She texts me after 3 P.M. to say she's on her way. I sit at the kitchen island with bated breath, too anxious to do anything but stare at the wall.

Should I ask her if she knows why Ihsaan is acting weird? I obviously wouldn't use that phrasing, but…is it appropriate to bring something like that up only the second time we're meeting? Maybe I should play it safe. Lay low. I wouldn't want to scare her off, not when we're just starting to get to know each other.

The sound of the doorbell jolts me from my thoughts. I slip off the stool and rush to the door, pausing for five seconds so she doesn't think I was waiting (which I was, but she doesn't need to know that).

As soon as I open the door and see Aneela's bright smile, I'm stunned by her beauty. She's practically *glowing*.

"Salaam!" she says warmly, leaning in to hug me. She smells like lavender and lilies—a sweet, comforting scent.

When she pulls away, she hands me a bouquet of roses. "I hope you like white ones."

For a second, I'm too stunned to speak. But when my silence elicits a concerned look, I shake my head and smile weakly. "Wa 'Alaikum Salaam. I'm sorry, please come in. I just wasn't expecting…" I gesture at the roses. "You really didn't have to."

Aneela smiles and steps inside. Her eyes scan the house with a softness that sharpens into something else, an emotion I can't quite decipher. When she turns back to me moments later, she seems a little shaken, but her next words distract me before I can ask about it.

"No, no, it's alright. I heard you're into flowers. And I didn't want to come empty-handed."

I do a double take, fingers tightening around the bouquet. "Wait—how did you know that?"

"Oh." She laughs nervously, bringing a hand up to cover her mouth. "I'm sorry, that must seem so stalker-ish. Just…I've heard Arafat mention it. He was always talking to his friends about your garden."

A lump the size of a tennis ball forms in my throat. I try hard to swallow it, blinking rapidly to get rid of the moisture that has formed in my eyes.

I take a deep breath before speaking. "What would you like to drink? Water? Juice? Coffee? Chai?"

If Aneela finds my deflection strange, she doesn't mention it. "Water is fine, thank you."

"Ah. My fault for offering a med student anything but water," I tease, trying to lighten the mood. I grab her a bottle of water from the fridge and lead her to the living room.

She laughs, settling on the couch. "Nah, we're just like everyone else. We're not *that* boring, I promise."

I know, I think, shaking away the image of Arafat munching on his favorite chips—heart-burning, eye-watering Takis.

"Is…your mom home?" Aneela asks after a moment.

Is that a waver in her voice? But why would there be? Maybe I'm just imagining it.

"She's…in her room—she's usually there. I think she's asleep."

Aneela nods in understanding, and again I think I see something flicker across her face—relief? Sadness? But it's gone before I can catch it.

I grab a vase and scissors and settle down beside her, trimming the rose stems. "So how was your day?"

She smiles. "It was good. I'm doing rotations in internal medicine right now, and it's going pretty well, Alhamdulillah."

"How are you liking it?"

"Oh, I love it," she says animatedly. "I'm probably doing pediatrics after this, and I have a feeling these two will be my favorite."

"Oh, yeah? What makes you think so?"

"Well, I think hospitals are generally the kinds of environments that remind you of God and all His miracles. But when I was studying pediatrics, especially the NICU, it was so…" She gazes into the distance, eyes bright with emotion. "Hayat, do you know how many risks newborn babies face? How many things could pose a threat to them? Subhan Allah, with the amount of things that could go wrong, for healthy babies to be delivered so regularly is just…Subhan Allah. I'm definitely looking forward to my rotations in pediatrics."

I halt in cutting the rose stems, mesmerized by the spark in her eyes. A smile blooms on my face. "And internal medicine?"

Aneela turns to me. "Kinda the same, to be honest. To *see* chronic conditions like diabetes, hypertension, heart disease— there's just *so much*. It's truly humbling, knowing how much could go wrong and being lucky enough to study it rather than experience it."

Her voice has grown quiet, gaze drifting somewhere far away. Then she blinks, sheepish. "I'm sorry. I did that thing where I talk about med school and the hospital all the time."

I chuckle. "No, no. I loved hearing you talk. You should've seen the look on your face. It was like a mom talking about her baby."

She laughs, and it's a tinkly little sound that only makes me like her more.

And adds to my confusion about why Ihsaan seems scared

soulless every time she's mentioned.

"Enough about me—tell me about you," Aneela interrupts my thoughts. "How's your family? How's everything going with you?"

"Oh, you know," I shrug. "My family's fine. I don't do much. I just…" I gesture vaguely at the house. "I cook meals, clean the house, take care of all that stuff."

Aneela furrows her brows. "Whoa, don't downplay yourself. Cooking meals and taking care of your house is a big deal. It's never *just* cooking meals and taking care of your house."

"No, I—" I clamp my lips shut, embarrassed because she's right. And because I hate when people my age wrinkle their noses at my current lifestyle, so doing the same to myself feels hypocritical. "I didn't mean it like that." I sigh. "Or maybe I did, I don't know. People just say dumb stuff sometimes, so…" I trail off, unsure of the point I was trying to make.

I snip off a stem a little too aggressively, and Aneela places her hand over mine. "Hey," she says softly. "Are you okay?"

I nod roughly. "Yeah, I just…" I put the scissors down and curl my trembling hands into fists. "I'm eighteen, and three months ago all I was thinking about was graduation and my valedictorian speech and studying at my dream college. Now everyone around me is doing big things like attending college and getting their first or second internships. And I'm here deciding what to cook for lunch every day and cleaning the rooms and cupboards and shelves that are already clean." I trace a thorn with my finger. "It's stupid, I know. I have no right to be bitter about it. This was, and still is, my *choice.*"

Whoa, where did all that come from?

My chest feels light, like I've tossed off a backpack I didn't realize I was carrying. And this is only our second meeting, yet I'm blabbering like I've known Aneela for a while.

"Hayat, sweetie," she lifts my chin, startling me with both the touch and the endearment. "You are so hard on yourself. Why are you comparing your journey with anyone else's?" She gestures around the house. "Do you think it's a normal feat for an eighteen-year-old girl to carry an entire household on her shoulders? You wake up every day—probably earlier than everyone else—you clean the house, you cook meals for your family, you take care of everyone…and you think that's not a big deal?"

I stay quiet, my eyes trained to the floor.

"First of all, you're doing more than most people your age could possibly do," Aneela says gently. "Everyone has their own capabilities and strengths—don't use anyone as a standard except a past version of yourself.

"Second, people will always have something to say about women, whether they're homemakers or working. Don't let their words dishearten you. And third, everyone runs on different timelines, all of which are planned by the perfect Planner. Why are you worried?" She tucks a strand of hair behind my ear, and once again I startle at the affectionate gesture. "Like you said, you chose this life, and don't let anyone convince you otherwise. College isn't going anywhere. What you're doing for your family right now matters. You're exactly where you're supposed to be, doing exactly what you're supposed to be doing."

I stay silent, unsure how to respond to that. Unsure how to describe the effect her words have on me. How do I explain that I've never felt the absence of an older sister until right now? That I've been craving my mom's touch and comfort for weeks and this is the closest I've felt to it?

Luckily, I'm saved from having to say anything as footsteps echo down the stairs, and my mom enters the living room.

"Mama!" I chirp a little too loudly, shooting up from my seat. Aneela follows suit, and I notice that her eyes widen the second she sees my mom. "This is the friend I told you about yesterday. Her name is Aneela."

There is pin drop silence as my mom's tired gaze flicks from me to Aneela. Immediately, her eyes widen as a spark of life emerges. The spark shifts to a burning, blazing flame, and pretty soon the emotion in her eyes is so intense I almost find it difficult to continue looking at her.

I turn my confused gaze to Aneela, and her eyes seem to reflect my mother's flames. They stare at each other, motionless. Wordless. And then, very slowly, my mom takes a wobbled step towards her, inhaling a shuddering breath.

What the hell is going on?

Aneela meets my mom halfway, and they seem to be communicating with their eyes before Aneela breaks the tense silence. "Salaam, Auntie," she says, almost breathless.

And I think I might faint when, instead of verbally replying, my mom steps forward and pulls Aneela into an embrace, eyes squeezed shut. They cling to each other like long-lost friends reuniting after years apart, and I just stand there, brows furrowed, chest tightening. Maybe I should ask Aneela to check my pulse—because whatever my heart's doing right now, it's *not* normal.

First Ihsaan acts all cagey about her, now Mama's acting extremely weird and affectionate. Clearly, this isn't their first meeting. Clearly, something is going on. And clearly, I'm losing my mind not knowing what.

My mom pulls back from Aneela, her eyes glassy. Then her gaze flicks to me, and she must see the bewildered expression I haven't even tried to hide because she steps back and clears her throat.

"How are you…beta?" she murmurs to Aneela.

"I'm good, Alhamdulillah. How are you, Auntie?"

Mama smiles weakly. "I'm good, too." Then she turns back to me. "Hayat, did you feed…your friend?"

It takes me a moment to find my voice. "I was just about to, Mama."

"Oh, no, no," Aneela says. "You really don't have to. It's alright."

"Of course we do," my mom says, yet again surprising me. "Come on."

I silently lead the way to the kitchen, heart beating rapidly the entire time.

So Ihsaan isn't the only one keeping secrets—apparently my

mom has a skeleton or two in her closet as well.

With trembling hands, I place the taco shells and ingredients on the kitchen island. Mama hastily makes her way to the cupboards, opening and closing two at a time.

"Mama, what do you need?"

"Hayat, where are those porcelain dishes?"

The serving spoon clatters from my hand to the counter. *Porcelain dishes? What the hell?*

"Oh, no, no, please, Auntie," Aneela says, stepping forward. "It's alright. Don't go through the trouble, please."

My mom's eyes dart around helplessly. She bites her bottom lip, and for a flash of a moment, her eyes are filled with such sadness that my breath stutters.

"Mama," I start slowly. "We packed those dishes away a while ago, remember?"

Aneela turns to me. "Please, Hayat. Don't worry about it. I really appreciate your hospitality and kindness, but there's really no need."

Mama is quiet for a moment before she gestures to the tacos. "Well, alright. But please eat, beta."

Aneela obliges and sets a taco shell on the regular, non-porcelain plates I set out. She eyes the ground beef next to the taco shells and smiles. "Did you cook this, Hayat?" she asks cheerfully. I can tell she's trying to diffuse the tension that has suddenly skyrocketed in the kitchen.

I nod, smiling tentatively.

"So talented," she murmurs as she fills her taco with meat.

My cheeks turn pink.

The sound of the front door opening and the jingle of keys catches our attention. I look up, darting a confused glance at my mom. "It's four," I say. "Papa and Ihsaan aren't off of work yet."

I'm halfway off my stool when Ihsaan enters, rubbing the back of his neck.

Oh. My. God.

Oh shoot oh shoot oh shoot.

My fight or flight response kicks in, and I don't even bother hiding my gasp. He usually gets off of work at five-thirty—what is he doing home so early?

Ihsaan looks up tiredly and opens his mouth to greet us when his eyes snag on the back of Aneela's hijab.

She turns around, and Ihsaan goes rigid. All traces of fatigue vanish from his body. His eyes widen as if he's thunderstruck, and a vein begins throbbing at his temple. Even from across the room, I hear his breath catch. There's fear in his gaze—fear and something else I can't quite name. Whatever it is, it's intense enough to keep me rooted in place, heart racing.

Okay, I've had enough of this. If somebody doesn't tell me what's going on *today*, I'm going to lose my mind.

Just as I open my mouth to demand answers, Mama speaks first. "Salaam, beta," she says. "You're home early. Is everything okay?"

My brother blinks, resuming motion just long enough to hug her from the side. But his shoulders are still tense, and his jaw is clenched so hard that I'm convinced if I listen close enough, I'll be able to hear his teeth grinding.

His panicked eyes flick to mine, and for a moment I feel guilty. I don't want him to think I'm going behind his back with this whole Aneela thing, which is why I agreed to meet her when he was at work. But it was just my luck that he showed up early today.

"Ihsaan?" Mama prompts. He turns to her, disoriented. "Are you okay?" she says worriedly.

"Yes," he whispers, clearing his throat. "Yes, we just finished a major project and Teresa gave everyone an early leave." He turns back to Aneela, who's smiling tentatively at him.

"Salaam, Ihsaan," she says warmly, oblivious to the tension escalating in the room. "How are you?"

So they *do* know each other. She'd heard of me, but she seems to be *familiar* with Ihsaan.

He flinches at the question, averting his eyes. "I'm alright, Aneela. And you?"

She nods. "I'm good, Alhamdulillah."

Ihsaan glances at me briefly, and for a moment his expression is unreadable. Something wild and fractured behind his eyes. Then he looks away.

"How's work?" Aneela prompts. I catch my mom throwing her an unnervingly fond glance. "You work in HR now, right?"

Now? My jaw tenses. Okay, what the hell? Who is this woman who seems to know my entire family when I've only just met her? Does Papa know her as well?

Ihsaan's gaze flicks to me again, and I can't tell whether his unease is tied to Aneela's presence or the fact that he knows I've caught him in his web of lies.

"Yes," he mumbles, rubbing the back of his neck again. "It's going well."

I have never seen my brother like this.

Aneela smiles. "Good to hear." She gestures towards me. "Hayat was kind enough to invite me over. We were gonna discuss some college stuff."

He nods wordlessly, looking everywhere but at her or me. The kitchen falls silent again, the tension in the air so palpable I could cut it with a knife.

I don't know why everyone is keeping secrets from me, but someone needs to tell me what's going on. Because I'm losing my mind by the minute.

I open my mouth to demand answers, but I'm interrupted yet again, this time by Ihsaan. "Well, I'm gonna…" He gestures vaguely towards the stairs. "…go." He kisses Mama's forehead and gives Aneela a tight nod, ignoring me altogether as he turns away.

"Nice seeing you," Aneela says with a smile, then turns back to her taco as if all's right in the world.

There's no way I'm letting my brother run away this time. I need answers, and I need them now.

"Excuse me, Aneela," I smile tightly at her. "I'll be right back, okay?"

She nods, chewing thoughtfully, and I dash upstairs after Ihsaan. His bedroom door is just swinging shut behind him when I shove it open. It slams against the wall, and Ihsaan flinches as he spins around, eyes wide.

"What the hell, Hayat?"

"Don't *what the hell, Hayat* me." I whisper-shout, realizing a little too late that we have a guest downstairs and I'm losing my chill. "Care to explain what's going on?"

Ihsaan groans, pure frustration etched across his face. "I don't know what you're talking about." He starts rifling through his dresser, pulling drawers open two at a time.

"Ihsaan, please cut your BS," I shut the door behind me so our voices don't travel. "I'm sick and tired of it."

"Like I said," he snaps back, slamming the drawers shut and pulling his closet doors open. "I have no idea what you're talking about."

I growl in anger—I actually *growl,* like a feral little thing. "Please stop," I beg. "Stop with the BS. *Stop* with your lies. *Enough,* Ihsaan, *enough.*"

He doesn't respond. Keeps tearing through the closet. His movements are erratic, his breathing shallow.

Something clicks in my brain.

"What are you looking for?"

"My medicine!" he chokes out, shutting his closet door and banging his head against it.

My stomach drops. *Oh, God.* How could I have forgotten?

He's having a panic attack.

I rush forward. "Okay, stop, stop, stop." I wedge my hand between the closet door and his forehead before he cracks his skull open. "Stop. Let me find it."

I ease him onto his bed, then scramble to find his medicine. I pull open every drawer in the room, rummage through the contents of his closet, and check the bathroom—finally catching sight of the bottle on the counter. I rush back to my brother and shake a pill onto my hand. Ihsaan takes it and downs it with a swig of water.

He's breathing hard, hands trembling in an alarming manner. I cover his hands with my own, rubbing soothing circles on his skin.

All my rage has dissipated, replaced by a spike of fear, guilt, and an overwhelming concern for my brother.

"You okay?" I ask after a few minutes.

He nods slowly, pulling his hands back to cradle his head.

I have no idea what to do, what to say. How could I have forgotten that the smallest things set him off now? Why did I think agreeing to meet Aneela here was a good idea?

More importantly, why does her presence affect him *this* much?

A couple seconds later, as if he can sense my thoughts, Ihsaan lifts his head and looks at me. His voice is riddled with exhaustion when he says, "You invited her to our *house*?"

Well, then. I wasn't going to bring it up until he calmed down, but since he's initiating it...

"Yes," I admit. Then I add, "But if you tell me why it's such a problem, maybe I won't next time."

His posture is rigid. Then, slowly, his shoulders sink. I can pinpoint the exact moment all the fight leaves him. The exact moment he gives up.

"Look, Hayat," he mumbles, a waver in his voice. "I don't think this is something I have the right to disclose, because it's not for me to tell. But the guy who was planning on telling you is...gone. And I thought we'd just be able to forget about it and put it behind us, but I don't think that's possible anymore."

"Ihsaan," I protest, my heartbeat quickening in anticipation. "You're not making much sense. If this is about Arafat, don't you think I have the right to know?"

Ihsaan flinches at our brother's name. "Normally, I would say yes. But he wanted to surprise you. And he never got the chance to." He hangs his head, rubbing the back of his neck. "Just know that I'm sorry. I wasn't purposely lying or keeping secrets from you. I just thought it was best to leave this in the past."

I grasp Ihsaan's arm desperately. "I know. I understand. But he was my brother, too," I murmur. "I think...I deserve to know what he was going to tell me."

Ihsaan nods, inhaling a shaky breath. "You do." After a

moment's pause, he turns to me, mouth opening and closing before he finally says, "Arafat and Aneela wanted to get married."

I gasp, hand flying to my mouth.

Oh, my God.

My chest caves inward.

Arafat…wanted to marry Aneela?

I'm hit with that familiar wave of grief when I think about how soon Arafat was taken from us—how many experiences he was robbed of. And then I'm hit by an even bigger wave of sadness that news this big was kept from me for so long.

"But why…" I whisper. "Why wouldn't Arafat want to tell me? You all clearly knew. Why keep it a secret from *me* only?"

Ihsaan shakes his head. "It's not that he deliberately wanted to keep it a secret from you. He just needed time. He needed to discuss it with Mama and Papa first, and he didn't want you getting attached if things didn't work out. After our parents gave him the green light, he asked me to reach out to Aneela and see if she was interested. Then they met once under my supervision. Nothing was final yet—they just wanted to talk and figure some things out before potentially moving forward. And he wanted to surprise you about it; he was really excited to tell you." Ihsaan sighs, running a shaky hand through his hair. "They really liked each other, that much was obvious. I'd always known it, too." His voice grows quiet. "They wanted to make it halal as soon as possible."

A sudden image flashes back to me: Aneela standing among the congregation during Arafat's janaza prayer. I had been too much of a mess to pay attention to anything that day, but I suddenly remember a hazy image of her standing there, red-eyed and crying.

I struggle to wrap my head around this groundbreaking news. How was I not aware of something so big in my own house? How am I only meeting Aneela now, when Arafat had known her well— enough to want to *marry* her? Even Ihsaan had been involved— acting as the middle man for their conversations about marriage.

And to think that Arafat delayed telling me just because he

didn't want me to be upset if it didn't work out for him.

It's always incredibly uncomfortable to discover that there are so many things you never knew about someone who is no longer with you. I'll never hear these words from Arafat himself, will never get to ask him the questions burning on my tongue now, will never get to nudge and tease him about Aneela.

I've realized that death causes you to forget the deceased's flaws. Sure, there were probably things about Arafat that irked me; but now those things feel muted, faded. Normally, I'd be more upset about being kept in the dark. But now, I remember him only in softness. Even his secrets were selfless.

I blink away the tears forming in my eyes and turn to Ihsaan. "There's still one thing I don't understand, though," I murmur. "Why do you act so *scared* every time I mention Aneela? And why did you pretend like you didn't know her?"

He sighs, dragging a hand down his face. "I didn't *mean* to pretend," he says, voice trembling. "It was just easier. I didn't want to explain this whole…thing. He's gone, Hayat. I didn't want to open another wound."

I bite my lower lip. "But why are you *scared* of her?"

Ihsaan averts his eyes, inhaling deeply. "I'm not *scared*," he mumbles, but the quiver in his voice is unmistakable. "And…you can invite whoever you want, whenever you want. It doesn't matter to me."

Taking note to return to this later, I shift gears. "Poor Aneela," I say. "I can't imagine how she must be feeling. To lose someone you never had the chance to be with and love fully…"

Ihsaan stands abruptly, setting the medicine bottle on his bedside table. "I need to take a shower. I'll see you downstairs later."

Not comprehending his behavior but understanding that I've been effectively dismissed, I stand. Part of me wants to continue questioning him, but another part of me realizes that I need to give him a break. He just had a panic attack, and I don't want to say or do anything that might send him over the edge again.

"Make sure to come downstairs for dinner," I say when I reach the door, hesitating before adding, "I'm sure Aneela will be gone by the time Papa's here, so you don't need to…worry."

Ihsaan's jaw clenches and unclenches. "I told you it doesn't matter to me. Seriously." He heads to the bathroom and shuts the door behind him.

I sigh, pinching the bridge of my nose between my thumb and forefinger.

I shouldn't be surprised—Ihsaan Amanullah does everything in his power to run away when things get complicated.

Thirteen

Snowdrop: Hope

I WAKE UP FEELING like my brain is splitting open.

I turn to my bedside table and register the glaring neon 3:47 A.M. Groaning, I push myself up into a sitting position, immediately massaging my head as the blood rushes to it. It feels like someone's cracked my skull open with a vise.

I shove the covers aside and stumble out of my room, steadying myself against the wall as I head downstairs. I have to pause multiple times to close my eyes, massage my temples, and take deep, heaving breaths to combat the headache.

Once I finally reach the kitchen, I rifle through the contents of the medicine basket and pull out migraine chewables. I've always had a very hard time swallowing pills (I think I've swallowed a grand total of two, and both took me way longer than they should've) so I have to resort to syrups, kids' medicines, and chewables. Not ideal, but beggars can't be choosers.

Arafat used to scold me for it all the time. He said crushing pills in water ruined their effectiveness, and that sooner or later I'd have to learn to swallow them. The two times I managed it had been purely because he sat me down for twenty minutes and held my hand. "Relax," he'd said. "I know you're scared because you think you'll choke, but you won't. I promise. We chew and swallow bigger things every day without any issue." He tapped my temple. "It's all in your head." Then he pointed at my throat. "There's no issue down here."

I used to tell him he'd be a big-shot doctor soon enough with an alternative figured out for me.

I sigh deeply, popping the pill in my mouth. I chew for a couple seconds, eyes roving around the dark kitchen.

The knowledge that Arafat and Aneela wanted to get married has shaken me to the core. On top of that, finding out only *after* his death—and never getting the chance to talk to him about it—kills me.

And the fact that he didn't get to surprise me himself…

The sound of an engine outside the house jars me. I move to the window just as a car drives past.

Isn't that…Mikaal's car?

I glance at the wall clock. It's 3:55 A.M. Did Mikaal *just* get home?

I don't know what that man does, but his schedule is crazy. Even when Arafat was alive, I would often hear them discussing how Mikaal juggles all his responsibilities. As if attending med school isn't exhausting enough, he works part-time at a car dealership. And if he miraculously has free time on top of all that, he spends it either with his family or by volunteering at the masjid.

Perhaps it's because he's trying to support his parents more since he's an only child? Or maybe there's just some incredibly ambitious goal he's trying to accomplish. Maybe he's trying to become the best doctor he can be.

So when does this man even sleep?

Oh, what do I care? He can be as busy as he wants, what is it to me?

Still…I wonder how his parents must feel when he returns home so late. I wonder if his mom waits up for him, if she falls asleep on the couch with a blanket haphazardly wrapped around her in anticipation of the jingle of his keys. I can't imagine how worried she must always be for her son. Even though he's a good, respectful Muslim guy, he's still her son. God knows how the woman does it—how she always waits and waits for him.

I shake my head, dispelling any thoughts of Mikaal or schedules or worried moms.

I trudge back to my bedroom, debating whether I should wait the hour until Fajr or sleep and wake up again to pray.

The migraine makes the decision for me—if I sleep now, I'll have a hard time waking up again. So I switch on my room light and extract a Qur'an from the bookshelf, settling at my table.

An hour later I pray Fajr, wake the rest of my family to pray, and stumble back into bed. The medicine finally kicks in, my eyelids droop, and just before I lose consciousness, I'm hit with the strangest scent—sandalwood and something clinical.

Arafat's scent.

I don't know if pulling it from memory because I'm suddenly sick and missing him or if it's somehow really there. Either way, it comforts me, and I drift peacefully to sleep.

I wake to Ihsaan roughly shaking me, panic lacing his voice as he calls my name.

"What?" I gasp, losing all traces of sleep. "What happened? Is Mama okay? Is Papa okay?"

Ihsaan sweeps my features, eyes full of anguish, before letting out a choked sound and enveloping me in a hug. "Oh, thank God," he breathes. "Thank God."

I return the embrace, but confusion knits my brows. "Ihsaan, is everything okay? What's wrong?"

He pulls back and squeezes my hand, and I startle at the affectionate touch. He used to hate being physically or verbally affectionate. He would pretend to gag every time Arafat hugged me or told me I was a cute little munchkin.

"You weren't awake," he gasps. "I thought...I thought something happened—" He stops abruptly, shaking his head.

I glance at the clock on my bedside table and my eyes widen. No wonder he thought something was wrong with me—it's 9 A.M. I almost never sleep past six anymore.

"Are you okay? I was about to head to work but when I didn't see you downstairs, I…" Once more, Ihsaan grows quiet.

I shake my head, reaching up to massage my temples. Although much better after the medicine and some rest, the aftereffects of the headache linger. "Yeah, I'm sorry. I just had a really bad headache last night and took some medicine. After I prayed and woke you guys up for Fajr, I went back to sleep."

"Oh." Ihsaan nods, relief seeping into his features. "Are you okay now?"

I nod. "Better. Sleeping it off helped."

"Do you need anything? Do you want me to get you something or…" Ihsaan's eyes trail around my room as if he's seeing it for the first time. They land on a picture frame of the three of our hands—mine, Ihsaan's, and Arafat's—with SpongeBob characters drawn on them. "No," I murmur. "I'm okay."

He hesitates, an indecipherable emotion in his eyes. "I'll be back in a bit."

"Aren't you supposed to be going to work?"

"I'll call out."

"Whoa." I grab his arm as he stands and turns away. "Don't use your PTO because of me. I'm fine, really. It was worse last night."

He shakes his head. "It's fine. I'll work from home today." Then he slowly tilts his head and throws me a hesitant smile. "Besides, who told you I'm staying home for you? You're not that special."

I rear back in shock at the playful tone of his voice. Ihsaan, joking?

I stare pointedly at his clothes, seeing as he's dressed for work. He follows my gaze and shrugs. "I like looking nice at home from time to time, you know."

I roll my eyes. "*Okay,* Ihsaan." Then I smack my forehead. "Oh my God, Papa must have left by now, right?"

Ihsaan nods.

"Oh no!" I drop my head against the headboard. "He probably didn't eat breakfast. Or take lunch."

"Don't worry. I saw dishes in the sink so he probably made something. If he needs anything else, he can get it from work or I'll order some food for him. Now you stay put," he says, backing out of my room. "I'm making you breakfast."

Before I can open my mouth to protest, he's gone. And for a while after, I blink at the empty doorway, smiling.

I'm half asleep when Ihsaan returns to my room, tray in one hand, thermometer in the other. I blink awake and try to sit up, rubbing my eyes.

He sets the tray on my bedside table. "Open wide," he says, inserting the thermometer under my tongue.

"I'b fide," I mumble around the thermometer.

He presses a hand to my forehead, and I flinch at his cool fingers. He stares pointedly at me. "Like hell you are."

The thermometer beeps and Ihsaan pulls it out, raising his eyebrows as he turns it to me, showcasing the glaring 102 degrees.

"Please don't skip work for me," I say.

Ihsaan groans. "Eat your breakfast, Hayat. You're not special enough to stay home for." He smirks. "I just felt like working from home today. Besides, I'm an HR Coordinator now, remember? *I* get to boss interns around."

Realizing that our argument is going nowhere, I turn to the tray of food. Omelet, pancakes, avocado toast, and orange juice are all set in the tray alongside a bottle of DayQuil.

"Oh my God, Ihsaan, is this all for me?" I squeak.

He settles on the bed by my feet and fidgets with his silver ring. "I didn't know what you'd be in the mood for."

I shake my head, warmth pooling in my chest. "There's no way I can finish all of this."

He sighs. "Just eat what you can. I'll finish the rest."

"No way. You can't eat my sick food. I don't want you to get sick, too."

He rolls his eyes. "Eat. Now. I'm going to get my laptop."

I'm about to protest and tell him to work in his home office, but he vanishes before I'm able to say a word.

I take a bite of the omelet. I'm not even hungry, but I close my eyes anyway and let the flavor settle in. Because *wow*, can my brother cook.

When Ihsaan returns and settles at the end of my bed, I raise my brows and gesture to my breakfast. "Who taught you how to do *this*?"

He rolls his eyes again. "I'm a grown man. Stop acting like I've never touched a stove."

I laugh. "I didn't say that. I know you're usually way too busy to be able to cook five-course meals. I just think…as a twenty-two-year-old Pakistani man, there's no way you cook like this unless someone special caught your eye."

The effect of my words is startlingly immediate—Ihsaan's cheeks redden, and he ducks his head closer to his laptop to avoid my gaze.

My jaw drops, the fork suspended midair halfway to my mouth. I slowly set it on the plate. "Oh, my God. There *is* someone!"

"No, there isn't," he says hastily, rubbing the back of his neck.

"Yes, there is! Look at you!" I giggle, pointing to his blushing face. "You're all *red*!"

"No, I'm not," he says indignantly, still refusing to meet my eyes. "Eat your food."

I cover my mouth to stifle my giggles, and Ihsaan finally meets my gaze and raises his brows. "Hayat," he says exasperatedly. "There is no woman who's caught my eye. Now eat your food before I shove it down your throat."

This feels so *nice*. Ihsaan speaking like his old self. Us bantering and laughing like we used to. No tension or cold silences, just warmth and ease.

I hold up both my hands in mock surrender. "Okay, I'll let it rest. For now."

His relief is immediate, which only makes me more convinced

there *is* someone. And now I'm dying to know who has my former jokester brother in such a tizzy, blushing like a rom-com lead.

When I'm done eating and have taken my medicine, I lie back down and close my eyes. "Wake me up for Dhuhr," I mumble, already drifting off.

Just as sleep begins to claim me, I swear I hear Ihsaan murmur—as if to himself—"There's no one who's caught my eye."

Fourteen

Purple lilac: The first emotions of love

IT TAKES ME THREE days to recover from my sickness. Turns out I got a beginning-of-September cold and it messed with my stomach and head.

All three days, Ihsaan works from home, loudly grumbling and constantly clarifying that he isn't doing it for my sake. But every day he works at the little table in my room. And every couple of hours he whips up something for me to eat and continuously reminds me to take my medicine. And every time he thinks I'm not looking, he throws me concerned glances.

Before my dad leaves for work each morning, he kisses my forehead and instructs Ihsaan to take good care of me; Ihsaan responds by scrunching his face and giving me the stank eye, but he always nods at my dad.

My mom, of course, mostly stays in her room.

You know when you're sick and you suddenly start to remember a million things that make you sad? Over those three days, I must've chewed Ihsaan's ears off. I rambled about our broken family, how terribly I miss Arafat, my wilted garden, my lost friends, the old "Harvard-bound" Hayat...and somewhere in that haze of delirium, I accidentally blurted something about my acceptance to Princeton University.

That jolted him. Ihsaan had been listening with a quiet, almost somber look—until the word *Princeton* left my lips. He sat up straight, eyebrows knitting.

"What did you say?" he asked. "You got into Princeton?"

Panic flared through me. "What?" I replied hastily. "I never said that."

"Hayat, you *just* said Princeton."

I shook my head, heart beginning to beat rapidly against my chest. "I just meant I really wanted to go there. I never said I got in."

Ihsaan tilted his head and scrutinized me with narrowed eyes. "But I *heard*—"

"Oh, my God, Ihsaan," I huffed, turning away and pulling the covers over my face, hoping he hadn't detected my alarm. "Stop eating my brain. I want to sleep."

After that, he didn't press. But I could feel the tension radiating off him, so I feigned sleep until he resumed typing on his laptop.

When I woke up yesterday feeling much better, I got a text from a random number.

> hey, abeer mentioned that you're sick. just wanted to check in and see how you're doing.

I furrowed my brows at the unfamiliar number and typed back, who is this?

Abeer had been texting me nonstop and even begged me to come visit. It took some serious convincing to stop her—I didn't want her catching anything now that the fall semester had begun. Still, I had no idea who she'd told about my condition to prompt that message.

Three dots appeared, then disappeared, then reappeared, until finally the response arrived. it's rameez.

My heart lurched, and my eyes widened. Rameez Khan? Texting me to ask how I was feeling? As my heart beat rapidly against my chest, I tried to formulate an appropriate response—

something polite but not overeager. Before I could hit send, another message popped up.

> admittedly, i'm a litttttle bit sad that you don't have my number saved after this many years, but i'll give you the benefit of the doubt ;)

Warmth pooled in my chest. What was I supposed to say? *Rameez Khan* texted me. God, how was I supposed to respond?

For a moment, I hesitated, a thought nagging at me. I never made it a habit to keep boys' contacts in my phone unless it was for school or other necessary things. My parents had always taught us—especially in line with Islamic values—to treat everyone respectfully but keep opposite genders at a polite distance unless we're immediately related. I'd always adhered to that, establishing my boundaries.

But something about Rameez always felt…different. Good. The blush that tinted my cheeks, the warmth that spread throughout me, the giddy, invincible feeling. Especially since he, like his sister, treated me like a normal person after Arafat died.

That couldn't be bad, right? People say to trust your gut, and mine was telling me that after everything my family had been through, Rameez seemed to be the light at the end of the tunnel. The glimmer of hope. The person who made me feel like a normal teen girl again.

One of the few things that remained before *and* after Arafat's death.

Plus, it wasn't like my intention was wrong, right? I was just being polite and courteous. So, with trembling fingers, I saved Rameez's contact.

i'm sorry, I replied to his text. i guess i just never got around to it.

> ah, no worries, i was just messing with you. how are you feeling now?

> much better, thank you.

He typed for a while, and I stared at my screen like I was starving—like his response was the only thing that could fill my appetite.

> if you need anything, don't hesitate to let abeer or me know. we are always at your service, ma'am :)

I stifled a giggle as heat bloomed in my cheeks.

"What are you giggling at?" came Ihsaan's voice, startling me.

I looked up to find him watching me with narrowed eyes, his fingers hovering above his keyboard. He never really looked at me like that anymore. My brother either looked at me with indifference or hurt, never really curiosity or skepticism. The expression seemed so foreign on his face that for a moment, I was taken aback.

I locked my phone and stuffed it beneath the covers. "N-Nothing." The last time I mentioned Rameez, Ihsaan basically did the whole alpha male "stay away from him" thing. I was *not* going to risk bringing a guy up again.

"Hmm," he said, tapping his chin. "When someone smiles maniacally at their phone, it usually means—"

"Oh, lay off, Ihsaan." I rolled my eyes to mask the rapid thumping of my heart. "Tell me more about your new responsibilities as HR Coordinator, *Mr.* Amanullah."

Ihsaan paused, his intense eyes searing into mine. I almost missed his usual indifference when I realized he was trying to unearth whatever I was hiding. I forced myself to meet his eyes for a few seconds before he finally looked away.

I know he probably wasn't convinced, but I breathed a sigh of relief anyway.

Now that I'm fully recovered, slipping back into my regular routine is proving harder than expected.

For a few days, I got used to being pampered and fussed over again. Everyone in my family gave me their undivided attention—something I haven't felt since Arafat passed away. My dad still tries, but he's buried in work as a way to avoid his grief. My mom hardly leaves her room anymore, completely consumed by hers. And Ihsaan? He's usually indifferent. Distant.

And I *understand* that. I understand their grief and hopelessness. I just didn't realize how much I missed being taken care of.

For the first time since Arafat died, Ihsaan bridged the distance between us and took care of me. He acted like I was the most colossal inconvenience—but still, he took care of me. His dramatic sighs and fake annoyance were his way of covering up the fact that he hates overt affection…but cares deeply.

It just felt so *good*, being taken care of instead of constantly taking care of everyone else. For three whole days, I didn't have to worry about whether everyone ate, whether my mom took her meds, whether my dad came home exhausted. As selfish as it sounds, I enjoyed not being the caretaker. Even if it was just for a little bit.

I shake these thoughts off and sigh, staring at the meal chart pinned to our fridge.

A few weeks ago, I created this list—seven columns, one for each day—organized by prep time, dietary preferences, and mood. It's pretty intricate, if I may say so myself. (You can take the girl out of the APs but you can't take the APs out of the girl). Plus, it makes my life a whole lot easier.

Today's pick: boiled rice and chicken tikka, with a side of salad and chutney.

As I measure out cups of rice, a memory hits me. The last time I made this dish was for Mikaal. I see his face in my mind—his surprised smile as he took a bite.

Amazing. Didn't know Arafat's sister cooked so well.

I pause, hand still buried in the bag of rice. Would it be weird to make some for him as well, since he seemed to enjoy it last time? I love when people enjoy my food. I was horrible at cooking and probably would've stayed horrible were it not for the sudden responsibility of feeding my family every day. So it's okay if I distribute some to others, right?

I decide not to overthink it and cook a little extra to give a plate to both Abeer and Mikaal—since Abeer complimented my food the other day (and she once gagged at my earlier attempts).

A couple hours later, once everything's wrapped up and ready, I text Abeer if she can swing by and pick hers up.

She responds half an hour later:

> awww thank you so much girlie <3333. i'm so sorry tho, i have classes until 8 today and then rumana and i have a club meeting until 10 :(okay if i pick it up tomorrow?

My heart sinks a little. Right. The semester has begun, and everyone is busy with their classes and their own lives.

My gaze falls on the wrapped plate of food, and I feel a strange pang in my chest.

Why am I upset? My life hit pause after Arafat died, but everyone else obviously still has things to do and places to be and friends to meet. I shouldn't expect anyone to be available at my beck and call.

I wish I could just drive again. That would solve half my problems.

I send her a thumbs-up, and her response comes almost immediately after:

> or i can ask rameez to drop by, if that's okay w you and your fam? his last class ends at 5.

My heart stutters. I bite my lip, contemplating a response. Rameez Khan at my house? Would that be weird? I wouldn't invite him inside, of course, but what if I say something stupid or make a fool of myself? I already feel like he's just texting me out of pity.

But...it would be so nice to be able to see him. It's been a couple days since I last saw him, and just the thought of his warm eyes and warm smile immediately brightens my day.

I text Abeer back with trembling fingers: that's fine.

Then I glance at Mikaal's plate. Abeer's busy, so she can't take me to the hospital again. Ihsaan's at work, and I wouldn't have asked him anyway—I'd have to explain why I made food for Mikaal in the first place. That would spiral into Mikaal catching me sleepwalking, and it would just be a whole mess.

I could just walk to Mikaal's house and drop it off; he's only two minutes away. But I hesitate—what if his parents are home?

I stop short at that last thought. So what if his parents are home? Why does the idea make me so uneasy—like I've crossed some invisible line? Is it guilt? Embarrassment? Or something I haven't admitted yet? I don't know. But suddenly, I can't help wondering if I *am* doing something wrong.

No, right? I'm just giving food to a fellow human being. Who I've known for years. Who also happens to be my deceased brother's best friend. Who also saved me from sleepwalking and ending up in a ditch somewhere.

I bury my face in my hands and groan. Why is this all so needlessly complicated?

Calm down, Hayat. You're overthinking it. You're just giving food to people. It's not a big deal.

I sigh and shake my head. I'll just drop the food off at Mikaal's house, and I'm never doing this again. I can't deal with this stress.

I text Ihsaan:

do you have mikaal's number?

Mikaal Zaman? is his response.

yes

Uh, yeah ??

can i have it pls

He sends me a confused face emoji.

i just need to ask him something about one of
arafat's classes

I feel guilty lying again, but the truth will just bring up too many unnecessary questions.

He sends me Mikaal's number, but for a moment I hesitate. This is the second guy whose number I'm saving—who isn't family or school-related.

But it's not like I'll be texting either of them regularly. I just need to know if Mikaal's home.

I must spend a whole minute biting my lip, adding and removing exclamation marks, and contemplating how best to word my text to Mikaal. Finally, I settle on:

Salaam. This is Hayat Amanullah. How are you?

I wait with bated breath for his response, knee bouncing up and down. I can't help but scrutinize my message—how I used capital letters as opposed to my usual lowercase, as if I subconsciously felt the need to be extra respectful. When five minutes pass and it becomes clear he's probably busy and won't respond anytime soon, I sigh and return to the kitchen to wash the dishes.

Later, I get lost in one of the gardening books I unearthed from my closet, and the doorbell rings.

I startle. 5:37 P.M.

Oh, my God. Rameez is here!

Oh shoot, oh shoot, oh shoot.

I look down at myself—at my unbound and tangled hair, at my sweater with masala stains—and go into full panic mode. I have absolutely zero time for damage control, so I simply smooth my hair into a bow clip, rub some color into my cheeks, take a deep breath, and rush to open the door.

Rameez is standing on the porch with one hand in his pocket and one running through his curly hair. He looks impeccable in a black tracksuit and white running shoes. He looks up, meets my eyes, and breaks into a smile.

My breath catches in my throat, and for a moment I forget how to speak.

This...this feeling. This exhilaration. This nervous energy...it's been foreign for the past three months. I forgot what it felt like to have a heart that beats without hurting.

Rameez breaks the silence with a casual "Hi."

"Hey." To my utter embarrassment, my voice comes out breathless. If he notices, he doesn't comment on it. "Thanks for coming," I add. "Sorry you had to take the time out."

"Of course, no problem. How are you?" He gazes at me with a quiet intensity that sets my heart racing.

"I'm—I'm good, thank you. How…how are you? How are your classes going?"

A corner of his lips lifts at my stuttering, and I want to melt into the ground.

Relax, Hayat.

"They're okay," he says, shrugging. "Might switch some around before add/drop period closes."

I nod slowly. There's a moment of loaded silence before I blurt out, "What are you studying again?"

"Business. Not sure what specifically yet, but that's the current plan." He chuckles, eyes crinkling at the corners, and the motion is so endearing that my heart stutters. "I'm trying to be less sporadic and indecisive. I can never figure out what I want."

I shake my head, and before I can process the words that come out of my mouth, I say, "Don't worry. You're good at everything you do."

My eyes widen just as he glances at me in surprise. I clear my throat, trying desperately to come off as casual and not portray how I'm obviously losing my chill. "Do you want water? Juice? Sorry, I would invite you inside, but it's just me and my mom, so—"

"Oh, no worries. I should probably get going soon, anyway." He smiles softly, and something in my chest shifts. Warms. As though sunlight has found a way through the fog and remembered where my heart lives.

This is *bad.* After all these years of knowing Rameez Khan and wrestling these complicated feelings—I'm exhausted. Abeer's party happened. Then the car ride. The texts. And suddenly, it's like someone turned up the volume on everything I've been trying to mute. I just don't know how to deal with this.

"You okay there?" Rameez's voice jars me out of my thoughts. I blink, refocusing on his concerned smile.

"Yes," I say. "I'm so sorry. I just—sorry about that. Wait here, I'll bring the food."

I leave the door open and rush into the kitchen, hiding from Rameez's view. I lay a hand against the heart beating persistently against my chest and press my forehead to the cool wall to reorient myself. "Breathe, Hayat," I whisper. "Breathe."

As I'm returning to the porch with the food, I spot a familiar car driving towards our house, and my footsteps falter. It's Ihsaan.

He's about to pull into the driveway when he sees Rameez's car blocking it. He parks at the curb and steps out, leaving the engine running.

Oh, shoot. I did *not* want Ihsaan to witness this exchange. He might get the wrong idea.

As he walks up to us, I smile nervously at Rameez. He beams back, seeming completely at ease, like we aren't on the verge of a family sitcom misunderstanding.

"What's up, man?" Rameez nods at my brother, holding out a hand to do the classic dude hug. My brother smiles, locking him in a brief embrace.

I feel it again when I see the two of them hug. That shift in my heart, that warmth.

"Salaam, Rameez. How are you, man?" Ihsaan says, shooting me a brief but loaded glance.

"I'm good, I'm good. How are you? How's everything?"

Ihsaan nods. "Great, Alhamdulillah." He glances at me again before turning back to Rameez. "What brings you here?"

Rameez gestures to me. "Your sister was kind enough to make some food for my sister, so I just came to pick it up. Abeer is busy all day," he says by way of explanation.

I'm so glad he made it clear that I prepared the food for Abeer, not him.

"Well, I better get going," Rameez continues. "Sorry I blocked your driveway."

Ihsaan shakes his head. "No worries. Do you wanna come in?

"No, I should probably head out. But thank you."

I quickly hand the food to Rameez. He gives me that award-winning smile again, and I have to force myself to remember how to breathe, especially since my brother seems to be subtly scrutinizing me.

"Thank you, Hayat. Take care," Rameez says. He holds my gaze for a fraction longer—something unspoken lingering—then heads back to his car. A small wave before he reverses out.

Ihsaan returns to his car and pulls into the spot that Rameez's car occupied seconds ago. When he comes back inside, for some reason my heart begins beating rapidly against my chest. Why do I feel as if I've been caught doing something wrong?

Ihsaan loosens his watch and slips it into his pocket. He bends down to remove his shoes, then stands and begins twirling his ring around his finger. *His nervous tell.* Before he can say anything, I blurt, "Abeer is busy all day. She doesn't have time to stop by, so she asked if her brother could get the food instead."

My brother nods. "Okay."

"Yeah, I didn't want to wait until tomorrow, and maybe she would've been busy tomorrow too, so I wasn't—I didn't—"

"Hayat," Ihsaan says, walking towards the sofa. I trail after him. "Breathe. I'm not interrogating you," he chuckles. "Why are you so nervous?"

I flinch. "I'm not, I'm just…I don't want you to think I invited him over or something."

Ihsaan sits down, blowing out a sigh and resting his head against the sofa. "Do you think I have such little faith in you that I would assume something like that?"

My breath catches in my throat. Instantly, I feel guilty. "No, I didn't mean that."

He straightens his head to look at me, and I squirm under his gaze. "Hayat, I just told you to be careful and keep your distance. Around any man, for that matter. I didn't say I thought you were doing something wrong." He scrunches his brows. "It makes me kinda sad that you assume that would be my first thought." He sits forward, hands clasped beneath his chin, weighing his words.

"Look, Hayat. I trust you. I'm sure you understand, though, that as your brother I'm just naturally concerned about any man that's in your life." He holds a hand up as I'm about to interrupt him. "Just like you women see something in other women that we men may not notice, we men also see something in other men that you may not notice."

Another sigh. He runs his fingers through his hair, frustration soft but present.

"Again, I'm not trying to interrogate you or anything like that. It's just…observation. I just wanna look out for you. There are…little things…like if he was just picking up a plate of food, he could've parked at the curb and left the engine running, since it wouldn't take long. Yet he chose to pull into the driveway, park, and turn the car off. Just to pick up a plate of food." He raises his eyes to mine slowly. "Doesn't that seem strange to you?"

I hadn't even thought of that. And I know Ihsaan means to warn me, but his words secretly excite me. That means Rameez parked his car because he was expecting to have a conversation with me—however short?

"I mean…" I begin slowly, trying to keep the smile off my face. "I guess you're right, but sometimes people don't like leaving the engine running. Like, for safety reasons. And I have never sensed any wrong intentions from him, ever. He's my best friend's brother, Ihsaan."

Ihsaan shakes his head. "No, no, I'm not saying he's a bad person or anything like that at all. I'm just saying"—he rubs a hand against his face, takes a deep breath—"just be conscious of things like that, okay?"

A surge of anger rises in me, but I swallow it down. He's trying. He's just looking out for me.

I nod. "Okay. I will. Papa's on his way—go freshen up, and I'll warm up the food."

He nods gratefully and starts to leave, then stops. Glances at me with furrowed brows. "By the way, what did you want Mikaal's number for?"

My breath hitches. Why is he so interested in my life these days? "I told you, remember? I just needed to ask him something about one of Arafat's classes."

Ihsaan waits for further explanation, but when it becomes clear that I'm offering none, he nods and treads up the stairs.

That reminds me...I wonder if Mikaal has replied to my text.

I head to the kitchen, turning the stove on under the food and grabbing my phone from the counter. The screen lights up at my face, showcasing a notification from Mikaal.

Wa 'Alaikum Salaam, Hayat. I'm good, Alhamdulillah. How are you?

I'm good, too, thank you for asking. Oh, God, I forgot to mention how I got his number. He probably thinks I'm a weird creep. I quickly type: **Ihsaan gave me your number. I just wanted to ask you something.** I bite my lip, trying to think of the least awkward way to say this. **Are you home right now? I wanted to give you something.**

Wanted? No, that sounds weird. I quickly edit the text to **I needed to give you something.**

There, that sounds less personal.

Three dots appear, then disappear, then reappear. For some strange reason, I'm holding my breath.

Yes, I'm home.

Okay, I need to get this over with quickly—while Ihsaan's still in the shower and before Papa gets home. No drama. No explanations.

I grab his food and slip into shoes, hastily rushing out of the house and down the block. I walk persistently and purposefully, and for some reason my heart is thumping against my chest.

When I reach Mikaal's house, I take a deep breath and ring his doorbell. I glance at the time on my phone as I'm waiting and do a double take when I see another notification from Mikaal, sent three minutes ago.

Everything alright? You could send it through Ihsaan, you don't have to go through the trouble.

Oh God. *Oh God, oh God, oh God.*

What the hell am I doing? He's being polite because that's just who he is, but he clearly thinks I'm a dumb, weird *creep* who has nothing better to do. And why wouldn't he? I'm his dead best friend's little sister. Practically family. Why would he care?

Oh God, I shouldn't be doing this.

The urge to flee hits hard. I spin around, desperate to make a clean escape, but the door creaks open behind me.

I squeeze my eyes shut and reopen them, turning back to the door sheepishly.

Mikaal is standing in the doorway in his white coat, eye bags indicating he just returned from a shift at the hospital. He smiles politely. "Salaam."

"Wa 'Alaikum Salaam," I say, a little breathless. I look down at the plate of food, cheeks flaming, feeling utterly stupid. "I just—I was just making some food and…and you seemed to like it the other day. Just…wanted to give you some as well. I made some for my friend, too," I rush to add, then realize how crazy I sound. I clamp my lips together to refrain from further embarrassing myself.

There's a moment of strained silence before Mikaal says, "Oh. Oh, that's very…that's really thoughtful of you. Thank you, Hayat, I appreciate it."

He reaches for the plate, and I practically shove it at him in my haste to get away.

Mikaal's smile begins to dim. He purses his lips, seeming to contemplate something. For a moment, I register how dark his eyes are. Much darker than Rameez's brown, but somehow just as warm, if not warmer.

Yet right now, they seem wary. Guarded, even. As if he's bracing himself for something.

"Is…everything okay?" I ask hesitantly, confused by his demeanor.

He nods. "Yeah, sorry, I just…" He glances at me for a moment, still seemingly lost in thought, before he decides to backtrack. "I'm so sorry, I'm just tired."

"Oh." I fumble with the sleeves of my dress. "Oh, of course. I'm sorry to keep you."

"No, my bad. That's not what I meant. I just…" Mikaal presses his lips together, contemplating.

Whatever he's about to say is interrupted by a voice from inside the house. "Mikaal? Who is it, beta?"

He turns and calls out, "It's Hayat, Mama."

Seconds later, his mom appears at the door, clad in vibrant shalwar kameez with a dupatta draped across her chest. She must be around forty-five to fifty years old, but she's always looked so *young*. A slim figure, well-maintained skin and hair, and bright eyes. I've always felt an odd, youthful sort of kinship with her. Behind the kind smile and sparkling eyes lies a free-spirited woman with flair.

She smiles warmly at me. I smile back hesitantly, trying to conceal the rapid ascent of my heart rate. I hope she doesn't think I'm weird for coming over to her house. We used to give each other food often and still occasionally do, but since my family shut ourselves in, things changed.

"Hayat?" She grasps my hand. "How are you, beta?"

"I'm good, Auntie, Alhamdulillah. Aap kaisi hain?"

"I'm good, too, beta. How's your family? Your mom?"

My smile falters and I shrug. "Fine. You know how it is."

She nods in understanding. My eyes dart to Mikaal, who has been strangely quiet throughout this exchange. There's a cleft between his brows, signaling he's deep in thought. For a moment, there's pin drop silence between the three of us. Then I rush to explain, "I was cooking and decided to drop by and give you some as well."

"That's so sweet of you. Thank you, beta." She smoothes my

head, a typical affectionate gesture Pakistani elders give to those younger than them.

"It's no problem. Chale, I should go." I glance at Mikaal once more, who throws me a polite but distracted smile.

"Arey, aise kaise?" Auntie's eyes soften. "At least come in, have something to drink."

I shake my head. "Next time." I dare to look at Mikaal one last time. He's working his jaw, and he seems to be lost in thought again. His eyes meet mine for a moment, and the smile he offers is diplomatic.

Weird.

I turn to Auntie and wave, backing away. Both of them wave back and say "Thank you" simultaneously.

On the walk home, an uneasy feeling settles in my chest. Is Mikaal mad at me or something? Because he was acting sort of strange. Maybe I said or did something that bothered him? But he's always been so nice to me.

Maybe he really was just tired. Or distracted. He seemed to have wanted to say something a couple times but stopped himself.

I shake the thoughts out of my head and take a deep breath. It's pointless to be plagued by these questions.

Like I said, I don't intend on doing this again.

Fifteen

Forget-me-not: Forget me not

THAT NIGHT, I DREAM of Arafat.

It's a memory, one from just a few days before his death.

He enters the house, something tucked behind his back, grinning at me and wagging his brows.

"Guess what's in my ha-and," he singsongs.

I stop chewing my food. "A grenade?"

"God, Hayat." Arafat shakes his head. "Seriously."

I gasp. "Strawberry cheesecake? Oh, my God, Arafat, you're the best."

He flinches. "Not strawberry cheesecake. But I'll get you that too sometime."

I pout. "What's better than strawberry cheesecake?"

I glance over at my parents, who are both sitting at the dining table and exchanging knowing smiles. My gaze then flits to Ihsaan, who's sitting across from them and fixing his broken Xbox controller. He glances up for a moment and rolls his eyes, muttering, "Drama queen."

Arafat approaches me and says, "Okay, close your eyes."

My eyes narrow, darting between both of my brothers. "Is this another one of your stupid pranks, Ihsaan?"

Ihsaan's jaw drops. He looks at my parents, raising his hands defensively. "See? You tell me to be nice to her, but she's mean to me all the time. I mean"—he gestures to himself—"look at this face. Itni masoom shakal hai meri. Does this look like the face of a prankster?"

Scoffing, I open my mouth to retaliate, but Arafat sighs, nudging my shoulder. "Ignore him." He leans closer and whispers, "Do you think I would be part of one of his dumb pranks?"

I giggle, and Ihsaan throws his hands up in mock anger, shaking his head. My mom chuckles and pats his hand affectionately.

"Okay," Arafat continues. "Now close your eyes."

I do as he says, and he grasps my arm. I sense him not-so-subtly whispering and rapidly gesturing towards my family members, and then their footsteps head for the front door.

"Bhai," I say. "What's going on?"

"You'll find out." Arafat lets go of my arm, using his hands to shield my eyes. "Just follow my directions and don't open your eyes until I tell you to, okay?"

"O-kay," I draw out, heart beating in anticipation.

The warm May air greets me as he guides me outside. Then Arafat removes his hands.

"Okay," he whispers. "Now open your eyes and take a look at your early graduation gift from me and Ihsaan."

I do as he says, and it takes me a moment to register what I'm seeing. Then realization hits—I scream in delight, bouncing up and down before spinning around and crushing Arafat in a hug.

"Oh, my God!" I yell. "You got me a Volkswagen Bug?"

Arafat beams. "Not just me." He nods behind me. "Ihsaan paid for half."

I turn back around and catch my parents beaming with pride, while Ihsaan sticks his tongue out at me.

"You too?" I say, bewildered.

"Yeah, yeah, only cause Arafat's basically a broke med student." He rolls his eyes in mock annoyance. "I still don't like you, so don't get the wrong idea."

"Oh my God," I whisper to Arafat, wide-eyed. "He's right, though. How did you manage this?"

"Don't worry about it." Arafat squeezes my shoulder. "I've been saving up for a while. So has Ihsaan."

I squeal, pulling Arafat with me and rushing to hug my parents. "Thank you, thank you, thank you!" I exclaim, kissing their cheeks.

My mom laughs incredulously, tucking a strand of hair behind my ear. "Beta, why are you thanking us? It was your brothers."

"Thank you for giving birth to my amazing brothers!" I yell, wrapping an arm around Arafat and attempting to hug Ihsaan, who scrunches his nose and ducks away.

My dad chuckles, his eyes lighting up. "It was Arafat's idea; he's been saving up for a very long time. Then Ihsaan found out and begged to pay half. They've been planning this for a while."

I stick my tongue out at Ihsaan. "You'll never admit it, but I'm actually your favorite sibling."

"God, no." Ihsaan's face twists in mock disgust. "You're literally a churail."

"Will you guys stop it for once?" Arafat says exasperatedly. He grabs my hand and nods towards the tiny yellow beauty in front of us, lips curving up in an eager smile. "Wanna give it a go?"

I wake to my heart thudding rapidly in my chest, as if it's attempting to escape the confines of my ribcage. I press a hand against it, taking deep breaths until the frantic rhythm slows.

Tears—dry and gritty—cling to my cheeks.

The clock on my bedside table reads 6:13 A.M. Even though I'm not praying today, I don't think I'll be able to go back to bed. Rubbing the sleep out of my eyes, I sit up and gaze outside the window.

The late September sky is slowly morphing from navy blue to light periwinkle. There is still some time before the sun is fully risen, but the birds are awake, chittering and chirping with relentless enthusiasm.

I shove the covers aside and trudge to the bathroom. After freshening up, I get dressed and head downstairs.

I pause briefly at the foot of the stairs—then resolve hardens in my chest, and I veer towards the front door. Grabbing the keys, I step outside and walk down the driveway to the car I've been avoiding for the past four months.

There's dust on the windows of the Volkswagen Bug, and bird poop litters the hood and windshield. Its vibrant yellow paint seems to have dulled. I run my hand along the driver's side window and observe the grime sticking to my fingertips.

Then I open the door, take a deep breath, and duck inside. Resting back against the seat, I close my eyes and simply inhale.

It smells like Arafat.

Of course it would; the last time this car was used was the day from my dream—the memory of when he and Ihsaan accompanied me for my first drive. We first went to get boba, then spontaneously headed to the movie theater.

We had a blast that night. I haven't had the heart to even look at this car since then—I still carpooled with Abeer to school, and Arafat passed away only days later.

I wipe away the fresh tears gathering at my jawline, inhaling slowly through my nose and exhaling from my mouth to regain my bearings.

I run my hands along the seats, the visors, the dashboard, the gear shift. As I'm exploring, my sleeve snags on something wedged between the center console and the passenger seat.

A pale envelope.

Curiously, I tug it out and flip it over to see who it's addressed to.

To Hayat.

My heart jolts with something close to alarm. I run shaky fingers along the two words written in that familiar handwriting, my breath beginning to come faster in short puffs.

The envelope is worn, the corners dog-eared. And there's a layer of dust. This was not put in here recently.

This is from Arafat.

A strangled sound escapes my throat, and I clutch it to dispel the sudden anxiety coursing rapidly through me.

With trembling hands, I open the envelope and pull out the contents.

It's a letter. The two pages fall into my lap, and I hesitantly unfold them.

As soon as I see Arafat's handwriting, tears rapidly well in my eyes and splatter the page. I press a hand to my chest, where my heart pounds so hard I swear I can hear it in my ears.

Hayat,

If you're reading this, you're gonna graduate high school soon and give your valedictorian speech, which makes you officially the coolest person on the planet. I'm so proud of you, kiddo. I think you already know that, but I have to keep saying it.

So you know I'm a bit of a sentimental guy. I like the little things. And I thought I should tell my baby sister all the reasons she's amazing in a letter. Plus, I've got some secrets to tell you, and a letter just feels more personal.

I wanted to give you this letter with the car, but by the time you get to the end of it, you might kill me for not telling you sooner, so I'm saving myself from your immediate wrath (call me selfish, but you're a little scary when you're mad). So I'll drop this in there a couple hours later.

But first, reasons why you're a sweetheart:

1) This isn't news to anyone who knows you, but you're crazy intelligent. Sometimes when you're talking about your classes or your schoolwork, I just get this warm, prideful feeling. You have a quick brain, and you're extremely observant. I'm often surprised by how

you're so young but so cognizant. You put us all to shame.

2) You're emotionally intelligent. To reiterate my last point, seeing and observing are two very different things, and you are always so conscious of what's happening around you, how people are feeling, and how you are asserting yourself.

3) You're passionate. Whatever you love, you give all of your heart to it. I love seeing the care and attention you give to your garden, how your eyes spark when you talk to someone about flowers, the way you throw yourself in academics. May your eyes always, always light up.

4) You're lively. Whatever room you walk into, you immediately transform the environment. You have a bright, consuming presence, one that puts a smile on anyone's face (and if it doesn't, they're either crazy or asleep).

5) You're funny. Seriously, you are the comic relief in our house (okay, fine, Ihsaan is pretty funny, too, but you win).

6) You're adorable. I just wanna squish your cheeks.

7) You have a carefree and youthful spirit. I hope it always remains that way.

8) Even though, as Ihsaan says, I'm a bit of a broke med student, I secretly love it when you ask me for money (don't tell Ihsaan). I've seen some pretty strained sibling relationships, and it comforts me that our bond is so strong that you don't mind asking me for things. May Allah always keep it that way.

9) You bring me Takis.

10) You are the best sister anyone could ever ask for.

I have to pause reading to contain the tremors racking throughout my body. Tears are now rapidly pooling down my cheeks, and my chest is aching. I take a deep, shuddering breath and summon some semblance of courage to read the next page.

Enough flattery. Now, on to the secrets.

In the first marking period of your freshman year, do you remember that day you came home crying and complaining about how you were failing biology and hated science and wanted to just give up? And then me, you, and Ihsaan sat down together and worked through what was troubling you, came up with a plan for you to better understand the concepts, and discussed getting extra help from your teacher? I never told you this, but ironically, ever since that day, I've had a secret wish.

I want you to become a doctor.

The way you changed after that day...it still astonishes me. Who would think that a crying girl would go on to become valedictorian of her school? Your passion, dedication, and intelligence is so valuable on its own, and even more valuable in an industry like medicine. Every time I look at you now, I cannot imagine your future without a white coat and a stethoscope around your neck. When you were crying that day, do you know what I saw? I saw a girl becoming a woman. I saw your pain and anger towards science as fuel for what would come after.

And what happened?

You not only passed the class, you did extremely well. And then, throughout high school, you excelled in all your classes, including science. I don't think you've ever realized how much that one day changed your life, and how you began to gravitate towards what you once found too difficult to handle.

My point is: when you put your mind to something, you don't simply complete the task, you give it everything that you have. In medicine, not only will you survive, you will thrive. You will give it everything you have, and you will be a force to be reckoned with.

If this is something you would even consider, I would be the happiest brother alive. But at the end of the day, it is, of course, entirely up to you. But I hope you think about it. Even for a little bit.

Secret #2 (which I think you might kill me for not telling you in person):

I don't want to make this letter about myself. But when I was thinking of how to tell you, this felt like the best way to break the ice. I can be a little shy sometimes, you know me.

Okay, here goes:

I like someone.

And I want to marry her.

She's one of the most amazing people I've ever had the pleasure of knowing. I knew of her in undergrad, and now we're at RWJ together. I can't help but feel like Allah is answering all my du'aas. This doesn't feel real, but it is. Alhamdulillah.

Okay, enough about me.

When you come rushing to me after you read this letter and demand me to give you more information, I'll tell you all about her.

Until then, much love.

Your (favorite) brother,

Arafat

By the time I finish reading the letter, I'm crying so hard I have a difficult time breathing. My body shakes with violent sobs, my throat is raw, and my chest refuses to expand. I press my forehead to the steering wheel, trying to contain the tremors, but they won't subside.

I push open the car door and stumble outside, gulping desperate mouthfuls of air to replenish my starved lungs. I stagger forward a few steps, then break into a run, wind whipping at my hair as I veer towards the bike trail. My eyes blur and burn as I run, but I don't stop. I can't stop.

Just as I reach the road before the trail, my legs falter. I stumble, knees crumpling on the asphalt. Coughing and spluttering, I wheeze for air, but it won't come. My lungs refuse to obey.

My head is spinning dangerously, my thoughts splintering into nothingness.

"Hayat?" A voice reaches me through the fog, and I manage to look up.

Mikaal's blurred face emerges in front of me, and he's repeatedly saying my name, but I can't gain my bearings enough to respond. He sits on the asphalt in front of me, holding both his hands up.

"Okay, listen to me," he instructs in a clinical voice. It's oddly comforting, and I focus on it with the barest slip of consciousness left in me. "Watch my fingers, okay? On the count of three, inhale." As he counts, he pulls his fingers down into his palm. "Good. Now exhale. Relax. Just focus on breathing, okay? And keep watching my fingers."

We repeat the process. Inhale. Exhale. Again. Eventually, the haze thins. My chest loosens. The spinning slows.

I blink slowly, registering Mikaal in a new light. He was out on his morning walk, hence the tracksuit. And he's still sitting on the asphalt in front of me, hands raised like I might collapse again at any second.

For some reason, the mere sight of him is enough to calm my racing heart.

"Okay," he says, exhaling hard. "Are you okay? Feeling better? Can you breathe alright now?"

I merely nod, lacking the energy to even speak. My eyes snag on the letter that has fallen to the ground in front of me, and my chin begins to tremble again.

"Are you sure?" Mikaal says.

"Yeah," I rasp.

He's silent for a few minutes, carefully monitoring me as I finally regain my bearings. Then he pulls out his phone and says, "Stay put for a moment."

"What are you doing?" I immediately panic, reaching forward as if to snatch his phone.

He stands and backs away. "I'm sorry, Hayat. I'm worried about you. I kept your secret last time because you asked me to, but your family—at least your brother—should be aware of this."

I scramble upright, swaying slightly before finding my footing. Alarm crawls up my throat. "There is no *this*, Mikaal. I'm fine. Please."

He runs a hand through his hair, eyes darkening. "So you're not having frequent panic attacks? You're not sleepwalking?" His eyebrows rise as he waits for my reply.

I'm silent for a moment before I mumble, "Please don't."

Mikaal shakes his head, dialing a number and pressing his

phone to his ear, eyes solemn. "I'm really worried about you, Hayat. I'm sorry."

I watch him helplessly as he waits for Ihsaan to pick up. "Hello?" he says moments later, and my heart jolts. "Yeah, Salaam, Ihsaan. Sorry to bother you at a time like this, but could you come outside your house real quick? Near the bike trail? It's..." He glances at me. "It's Hayat. It's kind of important. Yes, yes, everything's fine. Don't worry. Just come outside."

Ten minutes later, when an anxious Ihsaan has checked me for injuries and has quietly spoken with Mikaal, I'm standing in front of them—head down, heart thudding—as they both stand with their arms folded.

"Thank you, Mikaal. Seriously," Ihsaan says, throwing me a look warring between angry and pitiful. "God knows what could have happened if you weren't there every time."

"No, man, don't say thank you. I just thought..." Mikaal hesitates as I raise my sharp gaze to his. "You deserved to know."

Ihsaan nods, and the two of them do the dude handshake before Mikaal heads off, throwing one last unreadable glance in my direction.

My brother sighs, dragging a hand down his face. I open my mouth to say something, but he shakes his head. "Don't."

For a moment, I think of how Arafat would have reacted if he were here. He would have hugged and comforted me first and asked questions later.

But this is Ihsaan. He gets angry first and comforts later, if at all.

"Do you have any idea," he murmurs slowly. "What those two minutes were like? From when Mikaal called me to when I rushed here? Do you have any idea of the horrible thoughts that went through my head?"

"Ihsaan, I—"

"*Don't* apologize, Hayat," he snaps, voice uncharacteristically harsh. Ever since Arafat's death, his voice has been either exhausted or indifferent. Harshness, I am unaccustomed to.

Tears sting my eyes.

Ihsaan laughs bitterly. "I find out my sister is struggling—from someone else. I find out she's sleepwalking in the neighborhood past midnight, having panic attacks in the hospital and on the road—something could have happened to you if Mikaal wasn't there every time, Hayat." His voice rises an octave. "Something could have *happened* to you, do you understand me?"

"But it didn't," I mumble quietly. "I'm okay."

Ihsaan scoffs, taking a step back and splaying his hands out. "Do you even hear yourself right now? You're *lucky* Mikaal was there. And God knows what other stuff has happened that you've told no one about or that no one's been around for."

I remain quiet.

"Hayat." Ihsaan's eyes soften, but his stance remains stiff. Cold. "Why didn't you *tell* me you were struggling? Why didn't you *say* anything?" His voice breaks almost imperceptibly. "Why are you suffering alone?"

"Well, it's not like *you're* open to sharing everything," I shoot back, my voice rising. "You're apparently suffering so much you need meds and therapy, and you didn't tell me about your promotion until I extracted the news from you. Not to mention you have some secret fear of Aneela—and God knows what else. So don't be like that."

I hate this. I hate that our relationship progresses excruciatingly slowly and then crashes back down, crumbling. Every time I think we're past something, we end up back at square one.

Ihsaan is rapidly spinning the ring on his finger, lips pursed as he considers me. "That's different," he finally says, voice quiet. "I'm the oldest sibling now, whether we like it or not. And I need to..." he swallows, takes a deep breath, "I need to take care of you now."

There is pin-drop silence as the breeze blows between us, whispering secrets too soft for us to hear.

"I'm sorry," I finally whisper, tears welling up again.

After a charged moment, Ihsaan steps forward and wraps his arms around me. My face presses against his chest, and his chin rests on my head. "No, *I'm* sorry," he mumbles. "I should've been there for you. I should've known. I should've—"

I shake my head, my throat burning from holding back tears. "Stop. It's not your fault."

He pulls back after a couple seconds, and I sense that even though he's trying for me, physical affection is still something he shies away from.

"Can we talk about what happened?" he says, eyes darting down to the envelope and papers still clutched in my hands.

I hesitate, then lift the envelope to show him the handwriting on the outside. His eyes widen as recognition flits through them. "Is that…"

I nod, taking a deep breath. "A letter from Arafat. I found it in the Bug."

My brother stands absolutely still, absolutely speechless. Eyes roving hungrily over the letter as if it could somehow bring our brother back. He takes a shaky breath. "I'm sorry for getting mad at you."

I shake my head. "Stop saying sorry." My lips curve up hesitantly. "It doesn't suit you."

My attempt at a joke doesn't faze him, and he continues to eye the letter as if he's a drowning man and the sight of it is his first breath of air.

"He wanted me to be a doctor," I whisper, clutching the letter to my chest. "Did you know?"

Ihsaan's eyes flick to mine as comprehension dawns on his face. He looks away for a moment, the breeze blowing between us as the first rays of sunrise flash in his hair. Finally he murmurs, "Yes."

"Why didn't you tell me?"

He turns back to me. "Because he didn't want you to feel pressured into making a decision."

"Ihsaan…this is my dead brother's last wish for me." He flinches when I say the word *dead*.

As the morning sun warms me, I allow myself to think of Arafat fondly, without the constant ache. My sweet, loving oldest brother.

Who studied medicine and liked spicy Takis. Who laughed like laughs were limited and he was determined to use them all up. Who set his alarm fifteen minutes early every morning to carefully iron his white coat. Who mediated between me and Ihsaan every time we bickered. Who bought my parents flowers just because he felt like it.

Who loved like love was air, and he was desperate to breathe it all in.

I take a deep breath and bring the letter to my lips, pressing a tender kiss to it. My voice is low but firm. "I'm going to honor his wish."

Sixteen

Black dahlia: Betrayal

EVER SINCE I READ Arafat's letter, my life has been given a new purpose. I've been poring over pre-med programs at Rutgers University while I wait for their admissions decision. I spoke to my parents (my dad was ecstatic, my mom's eyes filled with tears as she trudged upstairs), and I even mustered up the courage to rifle through some of Arafat's old med school textbooks.

No wonder he still kept them. Whenever I asked him why he didn't sell or get rid of the ones he no longer needed, he would give me a cryptic smile and say, "You never know when you might need them again."

I decide to tell Aneela about my decision next. She responds with several excited texts, earnestly tells me to contact her if I need help with anything at all, and says, **Your brother would be so proud of you.**

I hold my phone to my chest, teary-eyed and warm.

When I tell Abeer, she reacts in classic Abeer fashion—calls me immediately and freaks out, squealing so loudly I have to yank my phone away from my ear to prevent possible ear damage.

I have the strongest, oddest urge to tell Mikaal Zaman as well, but I shoot the thought down immediately. There's no valid reason for me to contact him, and I don't want to make things weird between us.

Instead, I text Rameez. We've been texting more and more frequently over the past couple of days, and it's been a while since I've had exciting news to share, so I feel like telling everyone I care about.

I halt at the thought—*Everyone I care about?* Has Rameez fallen into this category as well?

I shake the thought off as I wait for his reply.

you're full of surprises, he says. **what brought on the decision?**

I hesitate, then decide to tell him the truth: **arafat wanted me to be a doctor. i only just found out.**

He begins typing, then stops, then resumes. Finally he says, **he'd be really proud of you.**

thank you.

med school will be lucky to have you. Then, seconds later, he sends a **<3.**

I startle, my eyes widening both at the compliment and the heart. *Oh, my God.* A heart? My hand instinctively presses to my chest, where the same little symbol is suddenly beating wildly.

A heart. What does it mean? Is it a friendly, platonic, you're-my-sister's-best-friend-and-I-support-you heart? Is it a we're-becoming-better-friends-and-I-appreciate-you heart?

Or could it possibly mean something else?

I don't know how to respond. Should I send one back? Leave him on read? Type something witty and pretend I didn't notice?

I bite my lip, staring at the little symbol. Maybe I shouldn't reply immediately so as to not look like a desperate attention-seeker. Yeah, I'll wait for a few minutes. Or hours.

I distract myself by opening the group chat Abeer added me to, where Rumana has sent a birthday party invitation. It's in one week, and apparently *everyone* is invited (many who are not in the chat as well). By everyone, I'm assuming a significant population of high school faces and college newbies will be there.

I don't want to go. Crowds make me anxious now. People ask too many questions, look at me with too much pity, are always too nice (in a faux, I-pity-you-so-I'm-being-nice-to-you kind of way). But I think Abeer really wants me there.

I'm not sure Rumana would even really care if I didn't show up. We were never *super* close—Abeer was the mutual link.

Just then, I get another text from Rameez:

btw, are you going to rumana's birthday party?

Oh, my God. Rameez is gonna be there? For a moment, a swooping excitement takes over me, before a thought gives me pause.

That means it's going to be a mixed party.

But also…Rameez.

After Arafat's death, I have not been truly happy until Rameez and I became reacquainted, and dare I say we're friends now. This is just a party, and there will be others around. Besides, it's not like we're hanging out alone, God forbid.

Don't I deserve to be happy?

I stare at Rameez's text for a moment before typing, **yes, i'll be there.** And then, after frantic lip biting and blushing, I send a :).

~

When deep cleaning the house, I stumble across a bottle of Ihsaan's anti-anxiety meds. It jolts me back into the memory of Mikaal telling Ihsaan everything, and Ihsaan demanding to know why I hadn't told him I was struggling.

The whole situation with Mikaal leaves me feeling hollow and weird. I feel as if I've somehow bothered him or burdened him. I can't shake the image of him—kneeling down in front of me on the asphalt, counting out breaths, steadying me like I was a patient he couldn't afford to lose. He didn't have to do any of it. But he always did.

Each time I've lost my composure, Mikaal has somehow been there. On the morning walk path. On the dim streets of our neighborhood at 1 A.M. In the hallway of RWJ. Near the bike trail.

And each time, despite stumbling across me by chance, he has been careful and clinical in handling me. As if I'm another one of his patients—but more than that, a reminder of his dead best friend. As if he feels responsible for me by association.

The entire ordeal gives me an unpleasant, nagging feeling. So I try to neutralize the situation the only way I know how.

I bake some brownies for him.

Cooking, I've begun to realize, is both a source of comfort and a tool of communication now. At first, I despised it. Then, when I was suddenly responsible for feeding four mouths, it became a responsibility. Then routine. Then habit. Now, it's become a tool for me to convey my feelings. With Abeer or my family members, a way to show affection. But with Mikaal, a way to apologize.

I know I said I wouldn't do this again because of the stress it put me through last time, but I can't help it. I feel weirdly indebted to Mikaal and don't know how else to shake off the feeling.

Last time, he told me I didn't have to go through the trouble and could send whatever it was through Ihsaan. Maybe he said it out of kindness. Or maybe I was bothering him. Either way, I need to do this in person. I need to personally apologize, even if it means potentially embarrassing myself.

I don't know why I'm so bothered by the idea of embarrassing myself in front of Mikaal Zaman. My brothers have known him for over two years now, hence *I've* known him for over two years. Even though our interactions were always minimal before, he's been a constant in the past couple years of my life. It's always been Arafat and Mikaal. And occasionally Ihsaan—although he had his own rowdy group of friends as well.

To make sure Mikaal is home so I can get this over with as soon as possible, I text him once the brownies are ready. Salaam! Hayat again. Just wondering if you're home? Wanted to drop off something.

Moments later, three dots appear, then disappear, then reappear. Finally he writes, Wa Alaikum Salaam, yes I'm home. Just about to head out.

Perfect. I lock my phone and shove it in my pocket, grabbing the house keys as I head outside.

During the two minute walk to Mikaal's house, I rehearse my lines. What I'll say if his parents open the door. What I'll say if *he* opens it.

He ends up opening the door, and I forget every word.

For a beat, I just stare. Mikaal is dressed in a black button down and black pants. His sleek black hair is combed to perfection, save for a single thick strand falling against his temple and brushing his lashes. His eyes are lightly smeared with kohl, a sight that gives me pause. *How many men wear kohl anymore?* It's a forgotten sunnah, but one I find mesmerizing.

I don't remember the last time I saw Mikaal like this.

With a pang, I realize the idea of him all dressed up and heading somewhere hurts me. God knows where he's going, but to see him like this—and to know that the places he once used to frequent with Arafat, he now frequents alone—pierces my heart.

"Salaam, Hayat." Mikaal clears his throat, interrupting my forlorn thoughts. "How are you?"

"I'm good, how are you?" I say, my words jumbling together too quickly.

He raises his brows at my flustered behavior, the ghost of a smile on his face. "I'm okay, Alhamdulillah. Sorry, I'd invite you inside, but I'm the only one home."

"Oh yeah, of course, I understand." I'm suddenly struck with déjà vu, having this conversation with Rameez the other day.

Mikaal's gaze flicks to the brownies in my hands, and for some reason his expression becomes cautious. I look down at the plate and thrust it towards him. He takes it slowly, eyeing it with some confusion.

"Oh yeah," I rush to say. "I just—I wanted to..." I pause, forgetting everything I'd rehearsed at home and on my way here, rendering me speechless.

Then the spool begins unwinding. The words come. Fast. Unfiltered.

"You've been…you've been so nice to me this whole time. And you, like, kept making sure I was okay every time I…had a panic attack or something. So…thank you. This is just a way for me to thank you." I cough, trying desperately not to embarrass myself. "You know, I obviously have not been okay for the past couple of months. But I felt like…I could count on you if I needed to. Like, you understand my pain because of how close you were to Arafat too, you know? It still feels so weird sometimes, when I see you and I don't see him standing next to you. It's like…it doesn't make sense, you know? Some things in life never add up. I think, for me, this will always be one of those things. I don't think I can ever look at you without imagining my brother standing next to you."

For a moment, there's pin drop silence. In my haste to blabber everything, I didn't notice I'd stepped forward. Or that I've been staring at my shoes.

Finally, I raise my head to look at Mikaal, trying to decipher the silence between us.

His lips are pressed together, and he's rubbing at the stubble on his jaw in contemplation. His kohl-lined eyes flick to mine, and he holds my gaze for a beat before lowering it to the ground.

"I know how you feel," he says quietly, voice thick with emotion. "Sometimes I see you or Ihsaan and have to do a double take. It feels wrong not to see Arafat with you guys. You were…" He reaches up to rub one of his eyes, slightly smearing the kohl in the process. I'm surprised at how endearing I find the motion. "You guys were inseparable. Everything—everyone's so different now."

Mikaal trails off, lost in thought. His gaze suddenly snags on the little note I attached to the plate of brownies. If his mom had opened the door, I probably would have discreetly ripped it off and crumpled it, but luckily Mikaal is the one to see it.

But his brows furrow as he reads the note, and my heart thuds in anticipation. *Why is he so quiet? What is he thinking?*

I just wanted to say a few nice words and wasn't sure if I'd be too embarrassed to say them out loud. So I wrote: *Thank you so much for being there for me the past couple of months, and the past couple of times I haven't been okay. I don't know what would have happened if you weren't there. I appreciate it so much. Please accept this small token of gratitude.*

Without warning, my cheeks heat in a combination of embarrassment and nerves. I take a deep breath to try to reorient myself.

Maybe the note was a mistake? Maybe I'm making things weird for us?

When Mikaal looks back at me, my thoughts halt abruptly. He seems to be studying me with guarded eyes. He balances the plate in one hand and rubs at the stubble on his jaw again, and discomfort settles in the pit of my stomach. I have a feeling what he's about to say is going to be unpleasant, especially since there was something…off about him the last time as well.

"Hayat, look…" His eyes dart around, looking everywhere but at me. "Please stop thanking me. Seriously, you're embarrassing me. I'm glad I happened to be there when I was. And I'm sorry if it initially upset you when I told Ihsaan; I was just worried for you. But I realized it maybe wasn't…the best way to handle things. So I really am sorry." His shoe scratches at the ground and he inhales sharply. "And while I really, really appreciate this gesture—and the last couple of times as well—I think…I think it's best if you do this through Ihsaan next time, if ever."

I raise my head, momentarily shocked. I thought he may have just been annoyed and inconvenienced by me, but this seems to be something else. Knitting my brows, I mumble, "What…um, what do you mean?"

Mikaal takes a deep breath, eyes focused somewhere above my head before finally settling on me. "I mean…let's both keep our boundaries in check, okay? Even though you're Arafat's sister, you're still…even though we know each other, we shouldn't…" He presses his lips together, seeming to war with himself. "We're not—we shouldn't get too…friendly. We should keep our distance."

For a moment, I'm so stunned I don't know what to say. Then

I raise my brows. "You think I'm trying to make a move on you or something?" I splutter.

Mikaal grimaces, a pained expression taking over his features. "No. God, no, that's not what I meant—"

"Then what did you mean?" I say, folding my arms and standing my ground despite feeling like I'm going to melt into it out of embarrassment. "I can only be nice to you if I'm apparently trying to make a move on you, right?"

Mikaal scrunches his brows. "What? No, of course not. That's not what I said—"

"I just wanted to be *nice*, Mikaal. I thought, 'Hey, how can I thank Mikaal for saving my sanity and dignity multiple times? Let me bake something and give it to him because he seemed to enjoy my food the last few times.' I won't do it again if it bothers you that much."

A bout of frustration takes over him, but he reigns it in with practiced control. "Look, Hayat, you're misunderstanding," he says. "That's not the point. It's not really about the food. I just meant that we should—both of us—should maintain a respectful distance. And only interact when necessary. I would say this to anyone of the opposite gender, not just you."

"But you didn't—you've never had a problem interacting before. What changed?"

"It's always been for a reason, Hayat," he says gently. "We've never interacted just for the sake of it. Before, it was always around your brothers, and just polite and courteous. And the last few times, we happened to cross paths and I…wanted to help out when you were in difficult situations. But…" He looks away, taking a deep breath. "I'm sorry, I don't mean to upset you, but I don't want to overstep any boundaries. I respect you a lot, and I respect my best friend's memory. And recently…this is starting to feel too…" He glances down at the plate of food and the note attached to it. "Personal."

I make a disgusted face, too put off by his words to register that he doesn't want to upset me, meaning I am indeed visibly upset.

"Personal? My brother *died*, Mikaal. Of course it's personal. And I've always thought of you as, like, my third *brother*. Are you serious?"

As soon as the words leave my mouth, I know they're not true. They haven't felt true for a while.

He gives me a meaningful look. "That's just it, though," he says, voice gentle but firm. "Even if you may feel like a sister to me and I may feel like a brother to you, you're *not* my sister. And I'm *not* your brother."

I step back, his words striking me somewhere deep. He looks as if he feels guilty for upsetting me (again, *why am I upset?*), but he doesn't look apologetic for his words.

"Well…" I swallow, tucking my hair behind my ear. "I'm sorry to have bothered you. I won't speak to you again."

Mikaal looks like he wants to say something else but clamps his mouth shut when I abruptly turn away.

I hear him sigh as I rush away from his house, cheeks flaming.

Seventeen

Crocus: Youthful glee

FOR THE REST OF the week, I'm in a sour mood.

The interaction with Mikaal has left a very unpleasant taste in my mouth, and I've been reevaluating every conversation I've had with him since Arafat's death. I didn't think I was being too "friendly," like he implied, I just thought I was being *nice*. But I guess people can't appreciate kindness without assuming an ulterior motive.

And the idea that maybe he felt I was trying to make a move on him or trying to get close to him or something? It's mortifying. I've been avoiding stepping outside for days just so I won't risk running into him. Cooking for him felt like a harmless act of appreciation. But every time I think of the discomfort that clouded his face when he read that note, I want to melt into the ground.

Thankfully, I have something to distract me from the entire ordeal: Rumana's birthday party.

Abeer is at my house, chattering away and applying makeup and twirling around in her dress the way normal teen girls do. She begged me to let her do my makeup, and even though most makeup tends to break me out, I relented when she gave me her puppy dog eyes ("I promise I'll only use the super necessary products! Your skin will be completely fine!").

Ihsaan comes home and drops by my room at the commotion, eyebrows rising at the dresses strewn across the floor and the makeup products littering the vanity. Abeer's eyes widen as if we've been caught doing something wrong, and she chirps out a greeting to my brother.

"Wa 'Alaikum Salaam, kiddo," he says in response, belatedly knocking on the door when he sees her there. "What's going on here?" Since Ihsaan's overprotective older brother comments and the embarrassing encounter with Mikaal, I've subconsciously been more observant of various gender interactions. I don't leave the house much, but I still take note of whatever I am able to. Like right now, how Ihsaan is not entering the room so as not to make Abeer uncomfortable, and how his gaze is mainly on me, despite his question being directed towards both of us.

"Birthday party!" Abeer squeaks happily, plugging in the straightener and parting my hair as it heats up.

Ihsaan gives me a once-over. "Wow. You *don't* look like a churail."

I scoff as Abeer laughs merrily. "It's the Abeer touch," she says, quickly adding, "Not that our gorgeous Hayat ever looks like a churail!" when I give her a dry look.

Ihsaan shakes his head, lips turning up in the ghost of a smile. Then he purses his lips and begins to fidget with the ring on his finger.

Abeer stops straightening my hair and scrutinizes Ihsaan, cocking her head to the side. "Is something wrong, Ihsaan bhai?"

"No, no, nothing's wrong." His gaze darts to me once before he quickly asks, "Whose birthday party is it?"

"Do you know our friend Rumana?" Abeer says before I'm able to respond.

"Sounds familiar."

"Yeah, hers. She invited, like, the whole world."

Ihsaan nods, fingering a patch of peeling paint on my door. He seems restless, and I don't think Abeer has answered the question he's truly asking.

"It's a mixed party," I say quietly, and his head snaps up at my voice. Our gazes lock, and there's an indecipherable question in his before he looks away.

Abeer glances between the two of us, raising her brows. "I feel like there's some secret sibling telepathy happening here." She turns to Ihsaan. "Are you okay with it being a mixed party?" The desperation leaks through her voice, signaling she really hopes my brother's answer will be in the affirmative. And I know Abeer is the kind of person who, even if she would be upset if Ihsaan discouraged me from going, would still respect our family's decisions and religious values. It's one of the many things I love about her.

Ihsaan's eyes seem to pierce through my skull. I hold my breath in anticipation. Part of me is hoping he'll express displeasure at it being a mixed party, which will give me a solid excuse not to go. But the other, more dominant part of me is hoping he'll be okay with it, because I really want to see Rameez.

Ihsaan takes a deep breath. "I trust you guys. Just be careful."

Abeer nods. "Never fear, Abeer is here. I will take such good care of your little sister." She tries to squish my cheeks as I duck away.

Ihsaan chuckles from the door. "I meant both of you take care of each other, kiddo. But anyways, have fun, guys. I'm gonna check on Mama. Don't get home too late." As he's turning away, our gazes lock for a single moment, and I detect a tiny, almost imperceptible flash of worry in his eyes.

But a flash all the same.

I wanna go home already.

This party is too loud, too chaotic, and there are way too many people. The only thing grounding me right now is the anticipation of Rameez's arrival. Without it, I'd be drowning in hushed conversations, prolonged pitied looks thrown my way, and overly enthusiastic smiles—like everyone's trying so hard not to make me feel left out that it only emphasizes how out of place I feel.

Am I being an inconsiderate brat? Possibly. But I'm just so sick of being treated like the girl who lost her brother. It haunts me every single day at home. All I want is to feel normal *somewhere.*

"Hi there," someone says from behind.

I startle, spinning around and placing a hand over my heart.

It's Rameez. Dressed in a black button down, jeans and black shoes, he looks like a knockout. His hair has been strategically gelled and styled to appear effortlessly perfect, and his wrist sports a sleek black watch that's simple but polished.

For some reason, I'm reminded of Mikaal's similar outfit during our last interaction, and immediately a sour taste crawls up my throat.

Rameez holds his hands up, lips turning up at the corners. "Sorry. I didn't mean to scare you."

I shake my head, removing my hand from my heart (which has started beating irregularly at the sight of Rameez Khan). Tucking my hair behind my ear, I laugh nervously. "No, no, it's okay. I was just lost in thought."

For a few moments, we simply stare at each other, taking each other in. His eyes rove over my face, settling on the eyeliner Abeer very carefully flicked at the corners, before moving to my straightened hair, styled in a high pony and accompanied by miniature sparkly black clips. I hastily brush my hands down my black dress, hoping I still look as presentable as I did when I left the house. At the motion, his eyes flick back to mine and he smiles almost shyly.

"We're matching," Rameez murmurs—so quietly I almost don't hear him over the noise of the party.

I smile, heart thudding against my chest. "What a coincidence."

"You look…really pretty." He rubs the back of his neck, eyes trained to the ground.

I'm momentarily stunned by his quiet demeanor, his

bashfulness. Then the compliment sinks in and my heart begins fluttering like crazy. "Thank you. You look great, too."

He chuckles, gently running a hand through his hair so as not to ruin the style. "Enjoying the party?"

I shrug noncommittally, gazing around us with something close to displeasure. When we first came in, the guys were in one room while the girls were in another. But at this point the guys and girls have begun to mingle, some playing Uno, some taking turns playing Forza Horizon on the Xbox, some munching on food at the dining table, and others laughing too loudly.

"I'm gonna take that as a no," Rameez says when my silence drags on for too long.

I cover my face with my hands and peek through my fingers. "I'm so sorry, I keep getting lost in thought."

"Don't worry about it. Where's my sister? Why are you here alone?"

I sigh, twirling a piece of hair around my finger. His eyes track the movement, and my breath stutters.

How do I explain that Abeer has barely left my side? That every time someone pulled her away—for pictures or gossip or party games—she made sure I was okay first. That she turned down half a dozen invites just so I wouldn't be left alone with strangers and condolences. She kept trying to convince me to join her, but I couldn't take another "sorry for your loss."

It took me an unhealthy amount of convincing to let her know I'd be fine and would mingle on my own (a lie), just so she could enjoy herself.

I turn to Rameez, plastering a smile on my face. "Abeer was with me the whole time. She just left—she's taking some pictures of the birthday girl."

He nods. "Did you eat something?"

I tilt my head, hesitating to utter my next words. My eyes focus on a place somewhere above his head as I say, "Abeer and I had some snacks. But...we were waiting to have dinner with you, actually."

When I muster the courage to look into his eyes, they've

become so warm that blood rushes to my cheeks. I don't think I've ever been looked at by a man this way, as if my words have shifted the ground beneath his feet.

Rameez smiles softly, then nods towards the dining room. "Let's go."

As we head to the dining table, I'm acutely aware of several pairs of eyes on me. I've been subtly gawked at since I arrived, but now the air has shifted. I'm no longer being looked at because I used to be the "Harvard-bound" girl or because I'm the dead brother's sister or because I broke down in tears during my valedictorian speech; I'm now being looked at because I'm accompanied by *Rameez Khan*.

The realization causes my breath to stutter. I give Rameez a sideways glance, and he seems either oblivious to the stares or completely at ease with them as we approach the dining table.

For a moment, a thought nags at me. Up until a couple weeks ago, I would have been entirely uncomfortable with the idea of attending a mixed party, let alone befriending and being accompanied by a guy. Abeer's party was a bit of an unpleasant surprise, and I think she wasn't expecting me to come at all because of my radio silence. At what point did the idea of texting Rameez until late at night and being excited to see him at parties become comfortable and normal to me?

I shake the thought out of my head, unwilling for it to disturb my night.

Rameez grabs plates for both of us, handing one to me first. I tuck my hair behind my ear shyly as he gestures for me to take food before him.

"There's my favorite gal!" Abeer shouts as she wraps me in a chokehold. She eyes the plate in my hands and shakes her head in mock anger. "And she didn't even wait for me to eat dinner."

I open my mouth to defend myself just as Rameez smirks at his twin. "She preferred someone else's company," he says, winking.

Abeer gapes between the two of us. "Not fair. My best friend and brother are ganging up against me."

My eyes light up. *Best friend.* Even though she's said it before, my heart always warms at the thought that she still considers me her best friend.

Then I start to protest on the topic at hand, "I'm not—"

Rameez nudges me casually, silently communicating for me to play along. But I'm suddenly too distracted by the touch to pay attention to anything going on.

My eyes trace the movement, and although he seems unfazed by it, my heart begins to beat rapidly. Are we comfortable now? So comfortable he can touch me casually and think nothing of it? Should I be worried?

Maybe.

But if I am, I'm also thrilled to the point that any trace of concern quickly evaporates.

Abeer's huff of protest jars me out of my thoughts. I turn to her as she folds her arms over her chest in mock anger, but I don't miss the way a spark of confusion lights her eyes as they dart between myself and her brother.

I haven't really told her that her brother and I text almost every day. I don't know why. Maybe admitting it out loud would force me to confront things I'm not ready for. Uncharacteristic decisions I've been making. Feelings that are starting to seem…serious.

I wonder if he's mentioned anything about me to her.

I'm once again jarred out of my distracted thoughts when Abeer throws an arm around me and says, "Whatever. We know Hayat loves me." She shakes me and says, "Are you having fun?"

"Yes," I say, only half-lying. Truthfully, not until Rameez showed up.

I'm saved from having to convince Abeer of my lie when Rumana heads over to us. She looks beautiful, clad in a Barbie pink dress and a white *Birthday Girl* sash, paired with matching white jewelry and a tiara perched proudly on her head.

"You look amazing," I say politely as she approaches.

She grins at me, the elation of being the birthday girl practically oozing off of her. "Thank you, Hayat. You look gorgeous yourself."

Others join us at the dining table, and everyone begins chatting as they pile their plates with food. My eyes light up when I see the mound of garlic knots. I squeal excitedly, then clamp my lips shut when Rameez throws me an amused smile.

"Sorry," I murmur. "I love garlic knots."

"Why are you saying sorry?" he chuckles, grabbing one himself.

"No, I just—" A smile blooms on my face. "My brother loves them too. It's kind of a sibling thing now. Ihsaan asks me to make them from time to time."

The soft smile Rameez is directing at me makes me blush from my head to my toes.

"Oh, that reminds me," I say, smacking my hand against my forehead. "He asked me to make lasagna the other day and it completely slipped my mind."

"You cook for your brother?" Rumana suddenly asks, cocking her head to the side.

I turn to her, perplexed by the tone of her voice. "Yes?" It comes out more like a question because I'm confused by the way her nose is scrunching in something close to disgust.

She laughs. "I would *never* cook for my brother."

I can't explain why, but it feels as if a rock has settled on my chest. I frown quizzically at Rumana, then look around at the others to see if anyone else is as struck by her words as I am. Only Abeer and Rameez are tuned into the conversation; everyone else is too busy getting food and mingling.

Rumana continues, "How come your brother doesn't just cook for himself?"

"Um…he does when he has the time and energy. But I like to cook for him because he works full-time and is tired when he gets home." My voice has dropped considerably.

Rumana's brows knit. She seems to want to say something else but catches the guarded expression on my face and rushes to say, "Oh, I don't mean to offend you, Hayat! Sorry. I just thought it was weird."

Abeer lightly smacks Rumana's arm. "Girl, what's wrong with that?"

"Nothing, it's just—"

"It's fine," I mumble in a low voice. My eyes are on my plate of food, and suddenly I don't have an appetite anymore. I'm about to set the plate down when Rameez catches my elbow.

My gaze darts to his sympathetic one, and he murmurs, "Do you want to eat on the terrace?"

I blink rapidly, horrified by the fact that tears have begun to pool in my eyes. "Okay," I whisper.

He continues to keep a firm grasp on my arm as he leads us to the terrace, as if he can sense I'm hanging by a delicate thread.

"Hayat?" Abeer says from behind us.

I turn to her, blinking to keep my tears at bay.

The expression on her face is a mix of confusion and sympathy. "Are you okay?"

I nod. "Just need some fresh air."

Her gaze zeroes in on where her brother is holding me, but she nods.

Rameez leads me outside, and once the cool October air hits my face, I feel a smidge better.

It's just the two of us here. We sit across from each other at the wooden table on one side of the terrace, and for a moment I just stare at the woodwork before a tear runs down my cheek, startling me.

"Hey," Rameez says, leaning forward to look into my eyes. "Talk to me, Hayat."

I sniff, grabbing the tissue under my plate and dabbing my face. "I'm sorry."

"Stop saying sorry. Tell me what's going on."

I'm quiet for so long that Rameez reaches forward and brushes soft fingers over my hand. I jolt, raising my gaze to his concerned one.

"Hayat," he says. "Talk to me, please."

I focus on his gentle voice to ground myself, taking a deep breath. "I just hate when people say stuff like that."

He nods for me to continue, wrapping his other hand over mine as well. I'm too upset by Rumana's words to feel any sort of excitement at this new development, but I do register a twinge of unease.

"Like, I know my life right now is probably very different from everyone else's at this party, but…I chose it. And I don't mind it. Four months ago, I could never have *imagined* that I would be here—not attending college and being a homemaker of sorts—but these are my circumstances and my choices now. How is that wrong?"

"People are stupid," Rameez says, squeezing my hand. "Your circumstances are different, therefore it only makes sense that your choices are different. And even if you didn't have, as you say, a 'different life,' you still have the right to choose how you want to live. If you wanna cook for your family, so be it. Screw everyone else; all that matters is what you think."

I quiet at his words. He's angry on *my* behalf, angry because someone made *me* cry. The realization causes warmth to spread through my chest and makes me feel considerably better.

I remove my hands from under his to dab my face with tissue. "Thank you," I say. "I wish everyone thought the way you did…but unfortunately, that's not the case. I see the way everyone here looks at me, and I know they're probably thinking the same as Rumana. The AP girl, the academic mastermind, the valedictorian, the"—I hold my hands up in air quotes—"Harvard-bound' girl…now a homemaker and caretaker."

He shakes his head angrily. "People always have something dumb to say. I'm sorry you have to hear that. It's unfair and uncalled for."

Before I realize it, I'm beaming at him, and he does a double take when he sees the expression on my face. "What?" he chuckles.

"Nothing. You're just…Thank you. I appreciate you."

His lips turn up at the corners. "I appreciate you, too, Hayat. Now eat." He nods at our plates. "Don't stress. Your life is perfect as it is."

Eighteen

Protea: Transformation

WHEN I GET HOME from the party, Ihsaan is hovering in my room and not-so-subtly scrutinizing me. He's been checking up on me every night since Mikaal spoke to him about my *incidents*, for lack of a better word.

Today, however, is different. I can tell he wants to ask me something, but because of the constantly fluctuating distance between us, he seems hesitant to upset me.

To distract him, I redirect the attention towards him. "So," I say as I wipe my face with a makeup remover. "I had fun tonight. Hanging out with old friends. Which reminds me—why don't you hang out with any of your friends anymore?"

Ihsaan flinches, the question catching him off guard. Then he shrugs, averting his gaze. "Don't really have the time to now."

I scrunch my brows as I unclip my hair. "That's not true. You're off on the weekends, you work from home for two days, and after your promotion you've had different work timings. You can make time if you want to. And I'm sure your friends have been trying to stay in touch with you."

His eyes slowly travel up to mine. For a few moments, there is only the sound of the bristles running through my hair as I brush it.

Then Ihsaan says—so quietly that I almost don't hear him—"It doesn't feel the same anymore."

I set the hairbrush down, trying not to show how eager I am that he's opening up. Alas, after rattling and rattling at the doorknob of Ihsaan Amanullah's heart, it has just opened a crack. "Because Arafat is…gone?"

He flinches again, rubbing a hand behind his neck. "Yeah."

"Do you think…" I start slowly, pressing my lips together to contemplate my next words. "Do you think it might help you to hang out with them? They might be able to understand."

He shakes his head. "I don't want anyone's pity. My pain is obviously very different from theirs. Even if they can understand me, they could never relate to me. They lost their friend; I lost my brother." His voice grows considerably quiet as pin drop silence settles between us. His words resonate deeply since I just experienced another gathering trying to escape from the sympathy in everyone's eyes.

Ihsaan breaks me out of my thoughts, his voice hesitant, "Besides, Arafat was…the glue. Now that he's gone, we've all kind of…" He brings his hands together and then blows them apart in a motion simulating an explosion. "Scattered."

My heart lurches at the despondent tone of his voice. I hate seeing him like this. I know we've had our issues over the past couple of months, but I want my brother to be happy. I want him to laugh and joke and be unserious again, like the old Ihsaan Amanullah used to be.

"I know what you mean," I whisper, and the room is so quiet that even my low voice carries. "But I think you should try to reconnect with them. Who knows?" I shrug. "Maybe they need your company just as much as you need theirs."

Ihsaan's eyes bore into mine as he contemplates something. "When did you get so old?" It's meant to be playful but it weirdly stings, and sharp tears prick my eyes.

"I'll think about it," he says eventually.

And those four words are enough to bring a smile to my face.

The next weekend Abeer comes over because she misses my "cute squishy face" and needs to rant. She doesn't bring up the weird incident at Rumana's house, and I don't broach the topic either.

I sense that even though Abeer and I have somewhat eased back into our old routine, she's grown much closer to Rumana over the past couple of months, and I don't want to put her in an awkward position where she feels like she has to choose between her best friend (?) and a close friend.

We're seated at the kitchen table, assembling chicken wraps, when she starts yapping away about one of her professors. She loves the guy, but the class bores her senseless. I listen with a bemused smile as she rants and breathes like it's cardio. When she finally pauses to refill her oxygen supply, I rest my chin in my hand and deadpan, "Drop out."

She clutches her chest and widens her eyes in mock horror. "Is this the same Hayat Amanullah who—just last week, might I add—told me she's going to become a doctor? The same Hayat who once burst into tears when she got a ninety-six in one of her AP classes instead of a hundred?"

I stick my tongue out at her. "I'm kidding."

She bops my nose. "I know you are. Speaking of which—not that I'm complaining—but you've been in a much better mood lately."

My thoughts immediately drift to the constant texting between Rameez and I since Rumana's birthday party, and a corner of my lips turns up. Two days ago he sent me a picture of his new shoes, and I was a bit surprised that he felt comfortable enough to do so. I proceeded to send him a picture of the book I was reading—one of Arafat's old med school textbooks—and we've been going back and forth with random pictures since.

It seems like a casual exchange, but behind every picture I send him is an almost imperceptible flicker of unease I'm not willing to observe too closely.

"Yeah, I was actually having a pretty bad week last week," I say. "But…certain things made it better."

She furrows her brows while adding chopped pickles to the wrap. "Why were you having a bad week, and why didn't you tell me you were having a bad week?"

I chop the chicken tenders into bite-sized pieces. "Because you were going crazy with assignments last week. I didn't wanna bother you."

She rolls her eyes. "Tell me now!"

I sigh, immediately grimacing as I remember. "It's nothing major, really. I just had…a very awkward and embarrassing encounter with someone, and it made me feel weird for days."

Abeer abandons her wrap and turns to me with wide eyes. "A guy?" I nod and she squeals, startling me. I set the knife down and narrow my eyes at her.

"Sorry!" she chirps, eyeing my finger. "Are you okay?"

"If I didn't stop cutting, your wrap would've been covered in blood, not ketchup!"

Abeer flinches and examines my hand, leaning back when she's satisfied. "I'm sorry! But who's the guy? Tell me, tell me, tell me, tell me—"

"Okay, okay," I say hastily, holding my hands up. I press my lips together, unsure of why I'm hesitating to tell her this. So far, I've only had to drown in my embarrassment alone. If I vocalize it, it will become too real. But it was my fault for hinting at it, and Abeer won't let it go until I tell her.

Breathing out a deep sigh, I murmur, "So you know Mikaal, right?"

She nods vigorously. "Yup. Arafat bhai's bestie. He found you when you were sleepwalking, right?"

I nod, then begin explaining the interactions we've had since Arafat's death, and the limited ones before that. When I get to the part where Mikaal told me we should keep our distance, I scowl. Abeer prompts me to continue, and I finish the story hastily without looking in her eyes. I feel oddly embarrassed about it all, as if I've revealed some deep, shameful secret.

Abeer presses her lips together, contemplating my words. Finally she says, "You might not like what I'm gonna say, but here goes…" She takes a deep breath. "Mikaal might be right."

I knit my brows, anger flaring up. I try to tamp it down as I say, "What do you mean?"

"Hayat, look." Abeer preoccupies herself with assembling her wrap so as not to look into my eyes. "I definitely have a *lot* to improve in terms of practicing my faith, but I know you, and I know what you were like before, too."

"What was I like?"

She sighs, raising her gaze to mine. "You weren't very comfortable interacting or being friendly with guys just for the sake of it. Sure, you interacted when it was about school or something, but you never really went beyond that. So if Mikaal got uncomfortable by your niceties, it was probably because he noticed that you were being different than before."

I grimace, guilt dredging up my throat. *She's right.* But hearing the truth causes an uncomfortable feeling to settle in the pit of my stomach.

"I don't think he told you to keep your distance to upset you. As your brother's best friend, he probably feels some kind of responsibility towards you and doesn't want you to compromise your values. Or maybe he doesn't want to compromise his values, either. I've only seen him around here and there—at the masjid or at community events or with your brothers—but from the little I know of him, I know he doesn't just mess around with people for the sake of it. I think all his interactions with women probably have a valid purpose."

I squirm at Abeer's words, discomfited by the idea that Mikaal potentially feels responsible for me. I don't want him to feel any sort of debt for me—his dead best friend's little sister. I want him to treat me like a regular person.

Abeer sets her chin in her hands and scrutinizes me. "Why are you so upset, though?"

"What?" I say quickly. "I'm not upset."

She raises her brows. "You're a terrible liar."

I avert my gaze. "Seriously, why the hell would I be upset?"

"You tell me."

"Fine," I huff, relenting. "Maybe I *am* a little upset. But that's just because I was surprised. I didn't think he felt that way, or that I was being weird."

Abeer ducks her head to look into my eyes. Then, suddenly, a slow smirk spreads across her face. "Hmm. Or is the cause of your distress something else? Is it what I think it is?"

"What?" I panic at the sly look in her eyes. "What do you mean?"

She wiggles her brows. "Is someone catching feelings?"

I gasp, standing so quickly that my chair falls backward. My eyes widen at the amused expression on Abeer's face. "What the hell?" My voice comes out too high, a hot spike of alarm zipping through me. "*No.* Oh, my God, no. Absolutely not."

"Why so panicked?" Abeer says, a smile spreading across her face.

"Because that's—because you're *crazy*, that's why. You're *crazy* for even thinking that. I mean—I know he kind of called me out on this, but I've always kind of seen Mikaal as a third...*brother?*" It comes out a question, as if my very tongue is rebelling against the statement. And my heart, to my utter dismay, has begun beating like helicopter blades.

My best friend cocks her head to the side, the smile still on her face. "But he's not your brother," she points out. "Like he said."

I huff. "Oh, my God, I *know* he's not my brother. I'm saying... he's always kinda felt like one, I guess?" *Liar, liar.* "I just... get that vibe from him?"

Abeer holds her hands up, pressing her lips together to contain her laughter at the anxious expression on my face. "Okay, okay. I'm just messing with you." She becomes serious again, but I'm not sure if she believed me. "So if you're *very* sure you don't have feelings, why are you upset?"

"I don't know, I just..." I trail off, frustrated for not having a proper response to her question.

"Do you think he's trying to be holier than thou? Are you offended by him setting boundaries? Like, what's the problem?" Abeer throws question after question at me, and each one feels like a physical blow.

Why can't I give her a proper answer?

I pick up my chair and hesitantly sit back down, playing around with my fingers and avoiding the scrutiny in her gaze. "I think... I feel like..." I take a deep breath, squeezing my eyes shut and reopening them. "His presence brings me comfort." I blow out an exhale. "There, I said it. Sometimes when I see him, I think of... before. I don't know, I just...I remember better times when I see him."

Abeer tilts her head. "I mean, it makes sense. But that can't be the only reason, can it?"

I squeeze my eyes shut, pressing my palms to my eyelids. "When Mikaal told me we should keep our distance, I felt weirdly...*heartbroken.* I guess it's because he's kind of been a constant in my life for the past two-ish years; I've always seen him around with my brothers and it felt like..." I remove my palms from my face and open my eyes, blinking blearily at Abeer. "It felt like I was losing someone else after Arafat's death."

Abeer pushes the cutting boards to the side and reaches across the table to grasp my hands. She squeezes them, her touch exuding warmth.

"Losing Arafat has wrecked me," I murmur. "I can't afford to lose more people that he knew. That's why I made it a point to befriend Aneela, even though Ihsaan is weird about her for some reason. I just...Arafat's not here, and I wanna be able to have a connection with every part of him that *was* here. And Mikaal...Mikaal was one of those things."

I quiet, focusing on the warmth of Abeer's hands to gain my

bearings. I can't believe I just said all that. I didn't even realize how I felt until the words left my mouth.

"I understand," Abeer says, sadness lacing her voice. "When you told me about Aneela, I was kind of confused about why you wanted to get to know her so badly—now, after everything. But I get it. And…weirdly, I understand both your position and Mikaal's position." She pauses, waiting for my reaction, but when I remain silent, she continues. "You feel connected to him not just because he's another living memory of Arafat bhai, but because being around him gives you a sense of sukoon. But Mikaal doesn't wanna make any compromises and wants to set boundaries, even if it means upsetting you in the process. I obviously don't think his goal is to upset you, but maybe he thinks it's better to potentially upset you than to cross any lines."

I watch Abeer's thumb as it strokes a comforting pattern across my knuckles. "I guess you're right," I finally say. "But I can't help but feel upset and angry."

She nods. "I know. But I also know you can accept and appreciate people's preferences and values. Speaking of which, can we talk about your…preferences?"

My gaze darts to hers. I scrunch my brows. "What preferences?"

She averts her eyes and presses her lips together in contemplation. When she opens her mouth again, I'm surprised by the words that come out of it. "There's something going on between you and my brother, right?"

Oh God. I never thought we'd actually be having this conversation. I assumed whatever is "going on" was sort of under the radar, but I should've known.

"Are you mad?" is the first thing I whisper. It feels like a confession.

"What?" She turns to me with knitted brows. "No, of course not. I'm just a little surprised, is all." Abeer hesitates. "Can I say something?"

"You know you can always talk to me about anything."

She nods, removing her hands from over mine and fidgeting

with them in her lap. "You're changing, Hayat. And look, after everything you and your family have been through, I want nothing but for you to be happy. You deserve it, *always*. You can't imagine what it was like for me to watch you from the sidelines as you spiraled and spiraled. I'm so, *so* glad you're coming back to yourself." Abeer hesitates, running her fingers through her tangled curls. "Again, I know I'm like, the least religious person, and I'm not sure I have a right to say this, but I think as your best friend, it's my duty to caution you.

"Like I was saying before, you didn't really do male-female friendships, let alone relationships. Remember how uncomfortable you were by the idea of mixed gatherings?" I don't reply, but Abeer barrels on anyway, guilt marring her features. "To be honest, I didn't expect you to show up to my birthday party…We hadn't hung out and I hadn't heard from you for like two months. And I know I really wanted you to come with me to Rumana's birthday party, but you know I'd never force you to attend something you're uncomfortable with, right? Only when you said it was okay with you did we make a plan to go."

She smiles sheepishly. "I was always the…'heathen' out of the two of us. I did things you wouldn't necessarily do, and you would always try to keep me in check. We were just talking about compromise in regards to Mikaal, but I think there were a lot of things you put your foot down on, too."

She sighs, her eyes traveling up to mine. "Trust me, I'm not doing the whole back-off-from-my-brother thing. I love Rameez, and I love you, and I want both of you to be happy. I just wanted to say…make sure you're not sacrificing Hayat Amanullah and her values in the long run. Just be careful, okay? Just…be sure you're coming back to *you*. To Hayat."

Abeer quiets then, tentative eyes probing my face for some kind of reaction.

I won't lie, her words unsettle me. Is it because they're true? Because I've been noticing a change in myself, too? There's no denying it: I've felt happier since starting…whatever this is with

Rameez Khan. Being with him fills me with both exhilaration as well as a nervous thrill at every new turn. So… am I quietly compromising my morals for the sake of our… friendship?

I shake the questions from my head and blow out a sigh. "Okay," I say, eager to steer this conversation in another direction. "Thank you for always looking out for me, I appreciate it. I think I'll be okay. I'm also glad you're not weirded out by all of it."

"Of course not." Abeer smiles at me, but it doesn't quite reach her eyes.

Nineteen

Purple coneflower: Healing

THE FRUSTRATING REALIZATION I'M starting to come to terms with is that pursuing medicine is going to be *difficult,* to say the least.

Ever since I shifted to this new lifestyle, a part of me has been…relieved. My days used to be filled with rigorous AP classes, hours of studying, restless sleep, and anxiety for the next exam or assignment. Despite the ache I feel at delaying my studies, I have to admit I've grown fond of this quiet life. Slow mornings, uneventful days, and silent nights. That's why, getting back into the groove of things with my decision to go the pre-med track has proven to be a bit challenging.

I've been talking to Aneela constantly, flipping through Arafat's old materials and textbooks, doing tons of research, and a plethora of other things to try to map out possibly the next few years of my life.

I find myself constantly wishing Arafat were here. I have so many questions that only he would have been able to answer. I tend to be in a constant state of missing him—that never really goes away and I don't think it ever will—but the feeling has been heightened lately.

But since I've been talking to Rameez more and more frequently, I've noticed that I feel…happy and at ease again, at least momentarily. It's foreign and kind of terrifying, but the fact that I'm able to feel something other than grief provides me with a sense of relief I didn't realize I was yearning for.

While doing my research one day, something prompts me to open my Princeton acceptance letter again. I simply stare at the screen for a few minutes, sharp tears pricking at my eyes.

I accepted the admission back in May, a month before Arafat's death, but I obviously cannot attend. It's about an hour's drive from my house, and that alone comes with a host of issues. One: I don't drive anymore, so someone in my family (probably Ihsaan) would constantly be burdened with chauffeuring me. Or I'd have to Uber, which would be an added cost. Two: An hour's drive means I would spend most of my day on campus, and I can't afford to leave my mom or the house for that long. Three: I technically got a full ride, but dorming is completely out of the question. I'm needed here.

In no world would attending Princeton work out for me.

My despondent thoughts are interrupted by the jingle of Ihsaan's keys as he enters the house. He makes his way to the kitchen and plops a bag of takeout on the island. His tired eyes rove over the mess on the kitchen table—my laptop, textbooks, and other materials—and his brows incline.

"Well, well. She's back. What's going on here?"

"Salaam to you, too," I huff, folding my arms.

"Sorry. Salaam. What are you doing?"

"Just figuring some college and pre-med stuff out. Um…Aneela's been helping me."

At the mention of Aneela, his shoulders immediately tense, but he reins back in emotions with calculated practice as he nods. "Sounds good. Do you wanna take a break and eat? I brought shrimp and rice."

I squeal, and Ihsaan's expression goes from tense to amused. "Thank you, thank you, thank you! Yes, let's eat. Papa's almost home. I'll get some juice from the pantry."

I make my way to the back of the kitchen while Ihsaan opens the takeout boxes. I rummage through the pantry for a couple minutes but am unable to find the carton of juice Ihsaan bought a couple days ago.

"Ihsaan!" I shout. "Where's the juice?" Silence. "Ihsaan?"

Still nothing. Uneasy, I return to the kitchen—and stop cold.

Ihsaan is standing in front of my laptop, eyes widened at the screen. His hands have tightened and his knuckles have begun to turn white. He raises his shocked gaze to mine, all traces of fatigue wiped away.

"You got into Princeton?" he whispers.

Oh, my God. I forgot to close my laptop lid. I open my mouth to deny it, to explain—to say *something*, but language fails me.

"Hayat," he says, voice low but carrying a groundbreaking intensity. "You got into Princeton University?"

There's no point hiding it anymore. The truth is right in front of him.

I nod slowly, averting my gaze.

Ihsaan makes a sound somewhere between a choked laugh and a gasp.

"I *knew* you said this the other day when you were sick, but you kept denying it. Back in March you said you were keeping the university a surprise until June but…why didn't you tell anyone?" He's back to whispering, as if the weight of the words is crushing it.

I play around with the ends of my hair. "Why do you think?"

"No, don't do that," Ihsaan says, continuously flexing and releasing his fists. "Answer my question."

I shrug. "It was going to be a surprise, like you said. But then…Arafat. And it's not possible for me to go anymore."

"What do you mean?"

I scoff, finally looking into his eyes. "What do you think will happen here if I leave?" I gesture around the house. "This place will go up in flames. Mama never leaves her room anymore, you and Papa are too busy at work, who else would have taken care of the house and Mama?"

Ihsaan's eyes are filled with a grief that seems to shatter upon my last question. "We would've figured things out together," he says quietly.

I laugh mirthlessly. "Yeah, right. There was no other option for us. I had to do what I had to do. So you have no right to be angry."

"I'm not"—Ihsaan sighs, rubs a hand along the length of his face—"I'm not angry *at* you, Hayat. I'm angry *for* you. I'm angry you didn't share this with anyone and buried it."

I shrug again. "Doesn't matter. Besides, this wasn't really a priority for me anymore. The week I was gonna surprise you guys, I got the most horrible news of my life. So I didn't really give a damn anymore."

"And now?" he says quietly, eyes flitting back to my laptop screen.

I'm silent, playing with the ends of my hair again. Finally I say, "I don't wanna talk about this. Can we just set the table?"

"But Hayat—"

"Please," I mumble, clasping my hands together.

Ihsaan presses his lips together, and even though I can tell he wants to say more, I proceed to set the table, and he mimics my actions quietly.

Dinners at the Amanullah house are usually quiet now—save for my dad trying to make conversation every now and then—but today is especially quiet. Papa's forehead is lined with work-related wrinkles, Mama is pushing food around her plate as usual, and Ihsaan is barely eating, eyes constantly darting to me before flitting away.

After dinner, I'm wrapped in my blanket and reading a gardening book when I hear voices from my parents' room.

I hold my breath, trying to eavesdrop on the louder-than-usual conversation.

I'm unable to hear what's being said, so I quietly make my way to their room, tiptoeing to a stop right outside their door. I arrive just in time to hear Ihsaan grit out, "Seriously, guys. Mama. *Enough.*"

I hold my breath as I wait for my mom's response to his uncharacteristically hostile tone, but it doesn't arrive. Ihsaan continues in a sharp voice, "We're all grieving, we're all hurting. But this needs to stop. If not for me or Papa or even yourself, then for the eighteen-year-old girl downstairs who is sacrificing everything to take care of this entire damn family."

My heart thuds against my chest. *What is Ihsaan doing?*

I hear the croak of my mom's voice as she says, "I lost my *son*, Ihsaan."

"I'm your son, too, and I'm still here!" Ihsaan shouts, causing me to flinch. "Your daughter is still here! Your husband is still here! We can never get rid of the pain of losing Arafat, but we can make sure we're still living for those who *are* here." His voice lowers, but it's still tense. "I *know* you're hurting, Mama. But Papa lost his son, too. Hayat and I lost our brother. But *enough* now. It's *October*; it's almost been *four months* and you don't speak, you don't eat, you don't leave your room, you don't take care of yourself *at all*. This needs to *stop*."

Silence, then my dad quietly says, "He's right, Layla."

All of a sudden, the sound of Mama's sobbing emerges from my parents' room. A cleft forms between my brows, and I have half a mind to barge inside, wrap her in a hug, and take all her worries away.

"Did you guys know," Ihsaan's voice softens a bit, "that your daughter downstairs, who cooks and cleans and takes care of all of our needs, who barely hangs out with her friends anymore, and who *never* complains, got into Princeton University?"

Something twists in my chest. I want to run in and stop him. But I don't.

"She chose not to go. Because she thought this house couldn't function without her. Because she grew up too fast. And she believed we needed her more than she needed herself." His voice breaks. "We've failed her. All three of us have failed her. Since June, we've been failing her over and over again. When she stepped up for all of us, we let it happen without question. When she silently decided she wouldn't go to college, we just accepted it. When she went from hating cooking to cooking two or three meals a day for us, we didn't step in to help. She's given up so much for us over the past few months, and we just let it happen."

I dare to peek through the crack in the door. Ihsaan sits at the edge of the bed, holding Mama and Papa's hands. "None of us will ever truly get over Arafat's death, but we have to *move on*. We have to keep *living*, if not for ourselves then for each other. Over time, Allah will heal our pain, Insha Allah. We just have to trust Him and trust each other. Please." His voice breaks again on the last word, and he leans down and kisses my parents' hands. "We need each other."

I watch as my dad pats Ihsaan's back, an unreadable emotion in his eyes as he gazes at his son. I watch as tears stream down Mama's cheeks as she pulls Ihsaan in for a hug and cries against his shoulder. I watch as the three of them grasp each other, crying and hurting and comforting one another.

I watch as my broken family becomes a little less broken.

Twenty

Orange tulip: A profound connection

THAT NIGHT, I DREAM of Arafat.

We're in a field of orange tulips, the sun's rays glittering across the vibrant flowers. I'm laughing as I run after him, hands outstretched to touch his shoulder.

"I'm gonna get you!" I shriek in delight as I chase him.

"It's too late!" he shouts back as he continues to run.

All of a sudden, he vanishes into specks of white dust. I stop short, leaning down to catch my breath as I squint around the field. I whip my head this way and that, a cleft forming between my brows.

"Arafat?" I shout as I stand straight. "Arafat, where are you?"

The breeze blows through the quiet field, ruffling the orange tulips. The only other sound is my heavy breathing as I come to the realization that I'm utterly alone.

My knees crumple as I fall to the ground. A searing ache forms in my heart, and I clutch my chest to try to stave off the pain.

"Arafat!" I shout as dark gray clouds begin rolling across the sky, hiding the bright sun. "Arafat, don't leave me!"

All of a sudden, the sky opens up and heavy rain falls, accompanied by cracks of thunder and sparks of lightning. I attempt to shield myself from the rain by holding my arms above my head, but my efforts are futile as rain pours mercilessly from the sky.

I wrap my arms around my shivering body, rainwater sliding down and soaking my clothes. "Arafat," I mumble inaudibly against the chaos of rain and thunder.

Then a hand taps me on the shoulder. I muster the strength to turn around and look up just as someone opens an umbrella above my head.

It's Ihsaan.

He's grinning at me the way he used to—mischievous and positively radiant. As he holds the umbrella with one hand, he reaches for me with the other.

"Come on, Hayat," he says. "Ready to go?"

I jolt awake, inhaling sharply in the darkness of my room. My breaths come short and fast as I clutch a hand against my chest, tears trailing down my cheeks. I turn to my bedside table to look at the time.

2:33 A.M.

I'm unable to sleep for the rest of the night.

My mom has started coming out of her room every day now.

She wakes up before Papa and Ihsaan leave for work, and we all eat breakfast together. This is such a shocking feat that for the first couple of days, I stare around at everyone in amazement, slowly chewing my food.

It's a bit awkward at first, admittedly. We all sit in silence for a couple minutes, so much to say, unsure how to start. But we're trying.

Yesterday, when I was looking at my food calendar on the fridge, Mama touched my arm and shook her head. "I'll cook today," she said quietly.

I scrunched my brows. "Are you sure?'

She nodded, pulling a pot out from the cabinet.

I sat at the kitchen table with Arafat's old premed materials as my mom cooked daal chawal, humming as she skipped around the kitchen. The warmth spreading through my chest at the sight of her out of bed distracted me from focusing on anything in front of me. I simply watched her with my chin in my hands and a smile on my face.

Ihsaan's outburst must've really gotten through to her—and honestly, it touched me too. Hearing my previously immature brother defend me so passionately sparked a wave of sisterly affection. I want to show him how much I appreciate it, but since I secretly overheard everything and he hates hugs (my go-to for affection), I've just been extra nice. He's probably a bit confused, but it's the best I can do for now.

After Ihsaan spoke to our parents, Mama's been asking me if I've applied to any colleges, if I've been hanging out with my friends, and if I want her help in restarting the terrace garden.

She doesn't broach the topic of Princeton, and neither do I.

Papa tried bringing it up, but I shifted topics so quickly he understood I didn't want to speak about it.

Mama's also been asking Ihsaan for updates regarding work and other things—whether he's happy with his job, whether he's still working on the travel bucket list he used to have.

She's been asking my dad what he would like to have for dinner every night, if he needs help with anything work-related, and if there's anything he wants to talk about.

Even Ihsaan and Papa have been conversing and trying to be more involved, as if renewed from the shift in Mama's behavior.

I've become so used to my mom's presence being in the background that I'm a little unused to all the care and attention. I'm definitely not complaining—watching her wake up with a smile every morning (even if it's just for our sake) warms my heart more than anything. Her effort to care for her health makes me want to jump for joy. And seeing her roam the house looking well put together, trying not to stay holed up in her room, never fails to bring a smile to my face.

She keeps encouraging me to hang out with my friends, and I almost feel bad, as she seems to be blaming herself. I don't want her to feel guilty about anything—she's been grieving her oldest child and a mother's pain is different from everyone else's. To make her happy, I tell her I'm going to be spending the day at a farm with Abeer.

When Abeer honks from the driveway, I kiss my mom's forehead and dash outside, eager to hang out with my best friend. But as I approach the car, my excitement falters—Rumana's sitting in the passenger seat.

"Hi!" Rumana chirps. "I hope you don't mind that I crashed last minute; I was bored."

I plaster on a smile as I get in the backseat. "Of course not!" I exclaim. "Good to see you."

Abeer gives me a side hug from the front seat and ruffles my hair, but I notice she's avoiding my eyes. We were supposed to hang out like old times—just the two of us. Rumana wasn't part of the plan. And I still feel very weird about what she said at her birthday party. Abeer's probably dodging my eyes because she feels guilty. But Rumana's strong-willed; once she decides something, it's hard to argue with her. And now that they're close, Abeer probably didn't want to upset her.

Belatedly, I check my phone and see that Abeer had sent me a text a few minutes ago: **hey girlie. rumana's tagging along too, wanted to lyk!**

I take a deep breath. It's okay. This is fine. It's gonna be fine.

⌒◠

We were supposed to go to the movies after the farm, but I end up making an excuse that my mom needs me home and ask Abeer to drop me off early.

Nothing has happened, per se, but the entire time the three of us hang out, it feels *off*. So much has changed…There are so many conversations I can no longer relate to, and Abeer and Rumana are much closer than they were four months ago.

I can tell Abeer feels horrible and sees right through my lie of my mom needing me. I don't want her to feel like any of this is her fault—it's just that I really would have preferred to spend the day with her alone. All day, I kept wondering—was I the third wheel, or was Rumana? Abeer and I are (used to be?) best friends, but it seems that Rumana has filled a hole in Abeer that I left. And I don't want Abeer to feel torn about who to spend time with.

One of the few things that made the day bearable were Rameez's constant texts: **how's your day going? are you having a good time? what are you eating?** Despite everything, they brought a smile to my face.

When Abeer drops me home in the evening, I hug her extra hard to reassure her that I'm not mad or upset. She gives me a smile that says, *we'll text later.*

As she drives away, I notice that there are four cars parked along our street. *Weird.* Maybe someone's throwing a party—but why block the road?

Wait. Is that…Mikaal's car?

My heart thuds against my chest, and I shake my head and look away quickly. No, why would he be here?

And why does the mere thought of him set my heart racing?

I pull my keys out of my purse and am about to unlock the front door when I hear a rustle and the clang of metal from the backyard. Then someone yelps, "Ow!"

I freeze, keys suspended in my hands.

It's almost 7 P.M., meaning Ihsaan and Papa are home now. So who's outside the house in the cold? Is it Mama? What could she be doing in the backyard right now?

Instinctively, I grip the pepper spray on my keys and slowly trudge along the side of the house to the backyard. My eyes trail over the terrace and then to the chairs spread out across the grass, but it's quiet and there's nobody here.

Weird. The hair on my arms stands on end, the sensation that I'm not alone enveloping me. Maybe it was an animal? But I could've sworn I heard someone—

"Hayat?"

I panic. Without thinking, I whirl around and press the button on my pepper spray. Only after the hiss of the mist fills the air do I realize—if a kidnapper was in my backyard, they a) probably wouldn't know my name and b) wouldn't have a familiar voice.

"AAAH!" the figure shouts.

When the haze of the spray clears, I recognize the all-too-familiar face, now scrunched up in agony.

"Mikaal!" I gasp, covering my mouth with my hands. "Oh, my God, what the hell?"

Mikaal groans, clutching his eyes before frantically fanning his face. He attempts to open his eyes but immediately hisses in pain, squeezing them shut again. His body trembles, overwhelmed by the sting.

"Oh, my God!" I shout again. "I'm so sorry. Are you okay? Oh, my God."

"What the *hell*, Hayat?" he groans, coughing as he inhales.

I stand there helplessly. "Okay, wait," I say frantically. "Is there something I can do? Should I get water? Do you wanna wash your face?"

He coughs profusely, managing to make out a bewildered, "You just *pepper sprayed* me, Hayat."

"I'm sorry!" I wail. "You came out of nowhere, okay? Like, what the hell, Mikaal? What are you *doing*?"

"I could ask you the same thing!" he moans as he sniffs, and for a moment a laugh almost bubbles up my throat at the absurd scene before me: Mikaal's eyes screwed shut as he questions me with dramatic urgency. "What are *you* doing?"

"This is *my* house!" I yell, placing my hands on my hips even though he can't see me. "What are *you* doing here?"

At that moment, the door to the terrace slides open and Ihsaan steps out, eyebrows knitting at the commotion. "Hayat?" he says. "You're home? What's going on?"

I cover my mouth with my hands, unsure how to voice the massive clusterhell I've cooked up. But I'm saved from having to explain myself when Ihsaan walks forward and squints at Mikaal in the glow of the terrace light, widening his eyes.

"Oh, my God, Mikaal," Ihsaan rushes down the terrace stairs, hands hovering in the air. "What happened? Are you okay?"

Mikaal shakes his head, groaning. "Can you please take me to the bathroom so I can wash my face?"

Ihsaan's eyes scan the spray clinging to Mikaal's skin, then flick to the pepper spray that had fallen beside my feet in the chaos. His eyes widen with comprehension, but he moves fast. He shrugs out of his fleece, wrapping it around Mikaal's hand without touching him. He then grabs the cloth-covered hand and guides Mikaal towards the house.

I anxiously trail after them, nerves fizzing, only half-registering the lavish spread laid out on the kitchen table. My mom is standing by the stove and turns at the sound of our footsteps, eyebrows scrunching at Mikaal's state.

Ihsaan turns to me with a bewildered look. "Did you do what I think you did, Hayat?" he whispers.

I freeze.

"I went to—" Mikaal breaks off, wheezing as he attempts to inhale. "I went to get the barbecue tongs from the storage shed like you asked me to. One of them fell on my foot. Your sister thought I was a *murderer* and pepper sprayed me."

"I said I'm sorry!" I wail hysterically, cowering under the weight of Ihsaan's murderous glare.

"Hayat," Mama says, covering her mouth with her hands. "Beta, what did you do?"

"I'm sorry, Mama!" I whisper-shout.

"Ihsaan, beta," my mom says hurriedly as Mikaal begins coughing profusely. "Take Mikaal to the bathroom and have him wash his face with cold water."

Ihsaan nods and leads Mikaal away, and I glance sheepishly at my mom. "I'm sorry," I repeat. "I thought some stranger was in the backyard."

Mama shakes her head solemnly. "Hayat, it could've been any one of us, why would you immediately use your pepper spray? Beta, kitni buri baat hai. Ihsaan invited his friends after such a long time, and look what happened."

"Ihsaan invited his friends?" *That's why there were cars parked along the road.*

Mama nods. "The rest of the boys are in his room—Riaz, Zaroon, and Ali." She shakes her head again and covers her mouth, concern etched between her brows. "Bichaara. Hayat, what were you thinking?"

"Mama!" I hiss. "You're a woman; you know what it's like! The smallest things seem suspicious to us. When I heard noises from the backyard, I got scared. I wasn't thinking when I pushed the button." I press my palms to my hot cheeks. "I hope he's okay," I whimper.

"Beta, you should've been more careful. Seriously, kitni buri baat hai."

I'm too embarrassed to say anything else in my defense, but I would be lying if I said I don't partially enjoy my mom's scolding. She hasn't spoken to me this way for so long—it's weird, but I didn't realize how badly I'd missed it.

My mom paces around the kitchen. "Should we take him to the hospital?"

"Mama, he's a med student," I say hastily. "He probably knows what to do."

She doesn't seem convinced by my answer and continues to pace back and forth.

Twenty minutes later, my dad and Ihsaan's other friends have joined us in the living room, and everyone is hovering around a red-eyed, sniffling Mikaal.

Zaroon and Ali are concerned for their friend but simultaneously attempting to hide their amusement. Riaz—who we used to call Ihsaan's twin due to their tendency to joke and laugh at the most inopportune of times—has unabashedly been cackling at Mikaal's expense. He keeps looking at me and bursting into laughter, which only further increases my desire to melt into the ground.

My parents are constantly asking Mikaal if there's anything

they can do for him, if they should take him to the hospital, if they should call poison control. He shakes his head and thanks them, bloodshot eyes briefly flitting to mine before he looks away.

I am absolutely mortified.

Later, when everything has somewhat settled down and everyone but Mikaal has eaten and left, my parents are fretting about how to tell Mikaal's parents what happened.

"Auntie. Uncle," he says, voice still gravelly from the aftereffects of the spray. "It's okay. You don't need to tell them anything."

"Beta," my dad says. "It wouldn't be right to hide it from them."

Mikaal's gaze flits to my panicked one as he answers my dad, "It's alright, seriously." He turns fully to me. "And Hayat, I'm, um, I'm really sorry for being rude earlier."

For a moment, I'm so stunned by his apology that I'm unsure how to respond. Relief crashes over me in a wave so sudden, I blurt out, "Oh, my God, *no*. Don't apologize. If anything, you had the right to be *more* rude. *I'm* sorry, really. I wasn't thinking and I should have made sure who it was before"—I grimace—"attacking you."

A soft smile spreads across Mikaal's face, and I'm even more confused by the weird fluttering in my chest that takes place as a result of it.

It's only because the last time we spoke, there was bad blood, and I left angry and upset and promised I wouldn't interact with him again. I'm just relieved that the bad blood has been cleared, that's all.

Nothing else.

Once my family's finished falling over themselves apologizing and Mikaal assures my frantic mother that he's fine, he promises updates and agrees to see a doctor if necessary. Then Ihsaan takes Mikaal's car keys and drives him home.

When my brother returns, he exhales deeply, fixes me with an incredulous look, and says, "So if you plan on pepper spraying or attacking any of my other friends, let me know beforehand. I won't invite them over."

"Ihsaan!" I groan, mortified.

Twenty-one

Oleander: Caution

UNDER THE GUISE OF hanging out with Abeer, I'm spending the day with Rameez.

At first I was a little hesitant, Abeer's cautious warnings about my changing personality ringing in my ears. But when I saw the informal itinerary Rameez sent me, a pleased flush bloomed across my cheeks. He remembered the tiniest details from our conversations—how I loved hay rides and cornfields, how I had been craving mochi donuts for days, how I was dying to watch the sunset atop the scenic Washington Rock. He had planned the day out for us with all my activities and interests in mind. Not only would it be super rude of me to reject his offer, but I would be pretty upset not to spend the day with him too.

As I'm heading out, I kiss my mom's forehead. She walks me to the door and furrows her brows. "Where's Abeer's car?"

Shoot. I was not expecting my mom to see me off since she always used to be in her room.

My heart thuds against my chest as I scramble for a response. "Oh, I just asked her to wait down the road so I could get some walking in." I chuckle nervously, a little too loud.

She nods, and guilt crawls up my throat at her immediate and oblivious acceptance of my lie. Then I wave and head down the street to where Rameez's car is waiting, as I'd requested.

"Hi," I say brightly as I open the passenger door.

He looks up from his phone, breaking into a breathtaking smile when our eyes meet. "Hey!" he says as I settle in and lock my seatbelt. "How are you?"

He seems genuinely happy to see me. The realization causes color to rise to my cheeks and dispels any anxiety about spending the day with him. "I'm good!" I chirp. "How are you?"

"Excited," he says breathlessly, switching gears and lightly pressing on the gas.

"Me, too," I admit, nervously playing with my fingers. The exhilaration I'm experiencing is so foreign that I have to take a breath before saying my next words. "I really appreciate this, Rameez," I say quietly. "The way you planned out the whole day, your attention to detail—seriously, I appreciate it so much."

He clicks his tongue. "Stop thanking me. I wanted to spend the day with you. Also, I have a surprise for you."

"A surprise?" I squeal, then blush at the amused expression on his face. "What kind of surprise?"

He quirks his lips and throws me a sidelong glance. "Wouldn't be a surprise if I told you, would it?"

"Sorry, sorry." I mime zipping my lips shut and throwing away the key.

He chuckles, then strategically maneuvers the conversation into different territory in a way I've begun to envy. It seems as effortless as breathing. "We'll grab food first and then head to the sunflower farm. Sound good?" I nod, jittery with excitement.

"Hey," Rameez says softly after a couple moments. "I'm glad you came."

"Me too."

⌒

The day is absolutely, heartbreakingly perfect. Every moment feels straight out of a dream. I eat mochi donuts and drink apple cider to my heart's content, and we take the hayride twice. As we're driving away from the farm, we pass by a seasonal carnival and I squeal when I see the giant Ferris wheel. Rameez chuckles at my childish excitement, then immediately heads to the entrance. We ride the Ferris wheel, eat churros, and I laugh until my cheeks are stained pink.

It's so beautiful I don't want it to end.

And yet. There's a nagging voice at the far back of my mind, constantly whispering that something feels…*wrong*. My exhilaration is accompanied by a spike of fear, my laughter is loud and boisterous but dies down quickly, and a strange sort of unease envelops me.

Now we're at Washington Rock. The view is breathtaking—sun dripping behind the trees, air crisp with October. We sit on a ledge, arms looped around our knees, swallowed by stillness. I sigh, content, and lean my head against my arm.

"Rameez," I whisper, afraid to disturb the stillness and the peace surrounding us. "Thank you."

"For what?"

"For everything. For today. I…" I lift my head to look at him shyly, pushing the growing unease away. "I couldn't ask for a better way to spend the day."

His eyes twinkle as the last few rays of the sun are setting. He cocks his head to the side, gauging something from my expression. He must find what he's seeking, because suddenly he's leaning forward.

I stop breathing.

Rameez places a gentle kiss on my forehead. My eyes flutter closed, pleasure and shock warring under my skin. When I open them again, he's watching me, a shy smile curling across his lips.

For some reason, I'm unable to form words. The feeling of his lips on my forehead lingers, and I resist the urge to touch the spot and savor it. I break into a soft smile, and he grins back at me.

Then, in a moment of sudden panic, the smile vanishes from my face and I quickly get off the ledge. "Oh, my God."

"What?" Rameez immediately stands with me, concern etching between his brows.

"Oh, my God, we missed Asr," I gasp, my heart beginning to thump frantically.

For a moment, there's a relieved expression on Rameez's face, as if he was afraid I would say something about the kiss. Then he blinks. "Oh. Yeah, you're right."

I look around, trying to find a suitable place to pray. "Do you have a prayer mat? It's almost Maghrib now, we should pray both."

He shrugs out of his fleece and places it on the ground. "Here, we can pray on this."

I stand there clutching a hand against my heart, too disturbed by our missing a prayer to move. I haven't missed a prayer in years. I'm definitely not the most religious person and I have a hell of a long way to go, but I've always made it a point to keep my prayers consistent, especially since Arafat passed away.

"Hayat?" Rameez's voice breaks me out of my distressed thoughts. "You okay?"

"Yeah, I just…" I take a deep breath. "Can't believe we forgot." I glance at the fleece. "Won't this get dirty?"

He shakes his head. "It's okay. Let me get another one from my car, and we'll pray together?"

I nod wordlessly, pulling the scarf wrapped around my neck over my head. As he jogs back to the car, I inhale deeply and watch the sunset, trying to calm myself down. It's breathtaking, orange and pink hues decorating the sky in vibrant colors. I've always been fascinated by how sunrises are usually more pink, and sunsets more orange. As if the sky knows we need a softer hue to begin the day, and a darker one to complete it.

I sigh, my heart still rapidly beating, and I squeeze my eyes shut. I can't believe I was having such a good time with Rameez that I missed a prayer. The thought upsets me more than I expect it to, and suddenly Abeer's words about how I've changed are nagging at me again. It feels like this is a culmination of the unease I've been tamping down all day.

Rameez returns with another hoodie and spreads it on the floor behind and to the right of the fleece. We take our places and he begins leading the prayer. I'm so distressed that I'm unable to focus properly, and suddenly I want nothing more than to go home.

On the drive back home, I'm quieter. Rameez notices, because he attempts conversation at first but we lapse into silence when I become unresponsive.

When we're a street down from my house, I turn to him. "Thank you," I say quietly. "For today. I really enjoyed it."

I turn to go before he grabs my hand. "Hayat," he murmurs. "Are you okay? Did something happen or—"

"No." I shake my head, eyeing our entwined hands. "I'm just a little tired, that's all."

"Okay." He nods, but I can tell he doesn't believe me. After hesitating, he reaches into the backseat and grabs a gift bag, handing it to me. "Your surprise," he murmurs, avoiding my eyes.

I take it and slowly remove the gift paper from the top, pulling out the item inside. I spread it out on my lap and gasp when I realize what it is.

"You got me a floral printed lab coat?" I whisper, running my fingers over the material in awe.

He ducks his head and rubs the back of his neck, sheepish. "I just…wanted to give you something small for when you go to college and med school. And…you love flowers, so—"

I cut him off by leaning forward and embracing him impulsively. Rameez is frozen for a moment before he wraps his arms tightly around me, burying his face in my hair.

"Thank you," I say quietly, voice thick with emotion even as my heart is warring with itself to physically let go of him.

He rubs a soothing hand against my back. "You're welcome."

I pull back and smile, the anxiety from earlier abruptly resurfacing. "I should go now," I say. He nods and I wave goodbye as I exit the car.

I walk down the street and trudge up the driveway to my front door, taking a deep breath before turning to wave at Rameez. He waves back as I unlock the door, then drives away once I'm inside.

I have no time to process the past couple of hours because as soon as I enter, my mom rushes up to me and shakes my shoulders. Her eyes are bloodshot and her nose is puffy, as if she's spent the past hour crying.

My heart quickly begins thumping against my chest.

"Hayat!" she says frantically, continuing to shake my shoulders. "Have you spoken to Ihsaan? Where is he?"

"Ihsaan?" I say, my body registering the tension in the air before my mind is able to. My teeth begin to chatter as terror spreads throughout me from the expression on her face. "No, I haven't s-spoken to him. W-Why, what happened?"

I know my mom is still treading dangerous emotional waters, so I had been texting and giving her updates all day so she wouldn't worry about me. But I haven't spoken to Ihsaan.

"He was supposed to be back three hours ago and he's still not here. I called him so many times and he's not picking up. Hayat," my mom's voice breaks and fresh tears roll down her face. "Hayat, what if something happened?"

I feel as if someone has just dumped cold water all over me. My eyes widen at her words, breath beginning to come in sporadic bursts. "W-What?"

Mama begins to sob, frail hands letting go of me as she presses them against her temples. She shakes her head back and forth, managing to let out a stream of barely comprehensible words before she collapses on the floor.

For a moment, I'm too stunned to move. I stare down at my mom with growing horror, filled with a dread so cold I feel as if I'm turning to ice.

Then I remember Arafat's words from what feels like a lifetime ago. He had returned home after a particularly nerve-wracking lecture and simulation on emergency medicine, and as he relayed the day's events to me, I marveled over the levelheaded way he spoke about it.

"How do you guys do it?" I asked him, baffled.

He brushed his hands through his hair and blew out an exhausted sigh. "We have to remain clinical and focused, always. You know when you're on a flight and there's really bad turbulence or other technical issues, but you see the calm smiles of the air hostesses and you become relaxed again, even if something's potentially wrong? Medicine as a profession is the same. People trust us to put them at ease. We're the air hostesses, they're the travelers. We have to remain calm at all times."

I break out of my trance and place Rameez's gift bag on the foyer table. I bend down, taking a shaky breath as I grasp my mom's shoulder. "Mama," I whisper. She doesn't seem to hear me and continues to sob, wrapping her arms around herself.

"Mama," I repeat, sharper this time as I gain my bearings. My teeth are still chattering, but I slip into the facade of the brave daughter.

I've gotten pretty good at that over the past few months.

"Mama, *nothing* happened to Ihsaan, okay? He's fine. He's *fine*." I'm not sure if the words are more for myself than for her, but I have to say them. I squeeze her shoulder and retrieve my phone from my purse with trembling hands. "Where's Papa?"

"At a company d-dinner."

"Did you call him?"

She shakes her head, breath hitching as she cries. "I didn't…I didn't want anyone to worry if it was nothing. And your dad is always worrying about me anyway…"

"Mama," I say quietly, heart thumping against my chest. "We're family. We have to take care of each other." I unlock my phone and press Ihsaan's number.

It goes straight to voicemail. All three times.

I try looking up Ihsaan's company's page so I can find something in the staff directory, but my hands are shaking so badly I can't type.

So I call my dad. He picks up on the third ring. "Shehzaadi?" he says, inserting cheer into his weary voice. "How are you?"

I swallow, losing my nerve at the glimpse of happiness in his voice and the hubbub of voices in the background. "I'm good, Papa, how are you?"

"Good, beti. I'm sorry about being late today. There was a team dinner, you know how it is. Everything okay? Are you back home? Did you have a good time with Abeer today?"

And just like that, I suddenly feel wracked with guilt. I place a hand against my throat, unable to voice the purpose of my call.

"Shehzaadi?" Papa says, concern lacing his voice. "Hello? Everything okay?"

"Yes!" I chirp, heading to the living room so Papa can't hear Mama crying. "Yes, sorry. I was wondering…do you have Ihsaan's company phone number, by any chance? I think I forgot to save it because I can't find it."

There's shuffling at the other end of the line, and the hubbub of voices dies down. "Ihsaan's company number? Yes, I have it. Why, is everything okay?"

"Yes!" I exclaim a little too quickly. "Yes, everything's fine. Actually…I wanted to surprise him with something at his office one of these days, and I wanted to ask his coworkers something." I'm momentarily fascinated by how easily the lie rolls off my tongue.

"Oh, acha. That's so sweet of you, beta. I'll send you the number right now."

When Papa disconnects the call, I dial the office number. It's way after work hours, so I don't expect anyone to pick up, but I try nonetheless.

Dread coils my insides with each ring of the phone. I try Ihsaan's landline next. I avoid my mom's eyes, which are piercing me from the foyer area as she mutely waits for me to provide her with the reassurance I don't have.

As soon as I end the call I knew wouldn't be answered, my mom rushes towards me and grabs my hand. Her grip is so strong that I resist flinching. "Did anyone answer? Is Ihsaan at work?"

I shake my head mutely and she sags against the sofa. "Oh Allah," she cries, agony lacing her words. "Something happened to him, I just know it."

"*Nothing* happened." My voice is razor sharp. "Nothing, okay?" I grab a bottle of water from the kitchen and open it with trembling hands, holding it out in front of my mom. "Please calm down, Mama. I'm sure he'll be coming home soon."

My mom thrusts the bottle away and places her head in her hands, shoulders shaking with sobs.

I pace around the living room, frantically thinking of what to do next. If I tell my dad, he'll leave work immediately and rush home, and I don't want him to drive recklessly as a result.

Maybe I can tell Abeer? Or Rameez? But what would they do? I would succeed in nothing but making them worried as well.

My mom's sobs intensify, and I bite my lower lip.

Before I can overthink and go back on my decision, I'm grabbing my phone and calling the only person I can think of.

He picks up on the second ring.

"Mikaal?" I say hurriedly. "Are you home?"

"Yes, I am. What's wrong with your voice? Is everything okay, Hayat?"

"No, nothing is okay." My voice breaks, the composure I've been carefully constructing since I came home crumbling. I press a hand to my forehead, taking a deep breath before relaying the story to Mikaal.

"Oh, no," he says when I'm finished. "Okay, you guys don't worry, alright? I'm going to figure this out."

"Wait!" I cry, panic clawing its way up my throat when I realize he's going to disconnect. "What are you going to do?"

"I'll figure it out, Hayat, don't worry. My mom and I will be over in a few minutes, okay?"

The call ends, and my teeth begin to chatter again. I edge closer to my mom and take her hands, placing them in my lap—trying to anchor myself even as the floor beneath me feels like it might give way into a bottomless void.

Memories from four months ago flash in spurts in my mind: the joy of nearly surprising my family with the Princeton news, shattered by that gutting call from the police; the frantic dash to the hospital, only to be directed not to the ICU but the morgue; the deafening numbness when I lifted the white sheet and looked into my brother's dead eyes.

I shiver as the memory of that night grips me, and despite her own descent into sorrow, my mom turns and wraps her arms around me.

"It'll be okay," I whisper against her temple. "Mikaal and his mom are coming. It'll be fine. It'll be fine." I continuously repeat the words like a mantra until the doorbell rings.

As soon as I open the door, Mikaal's mom rushes forward and embraces me tightly. "Don't worry, Hayat." She smoothes my hair. "Ihsaan will be fine, Insha Allah."

Those are all the words I need. I sag against her, throat clogging with the tears I've been holding back. Mikaal enters behind her and throws me a reassuring smile.

Auntie heads to my mom, and Mikaal nods to the side, a couple feet away from our moms but still in plain sight. I approach him with shaky legs, and for a stupid, distracted moment, I fumble over my appearance.

Mikaal turns to me. "Okay, I called Riaz and the others to ask if they knew where Ihsaan might be. They didn't, but Riaz has his location." His voice is comforting in a clinical sort of way. I figure this is how he must be talking to patients. "Ihsaan's phone is probably dead, but Riaz said that around 5:30 he called Ihsaan to ask him something, and he was on 287 then. There's a massive slowdown on the highway because of traffic. Riaz is heading there right now and will update me soon, okay?"

I can't form a reply. His voice seems to be coming from very far away, as if my ears are blocked and his words are attempting to wriggle through. The expression on my face must concern him because he waves a hand in front of my face and ducks his head to look in my eyes. "Hayat? You okay?"

I blink, nodding quickly. Then I fumble with my hands, suddenly remembering the last time Mikaal and I met. We were in my house, and he was sitting at the kitchen table with red eyes and a puffy nose as everyone surrounded him. I was standing at the far corner of the kitchen, wanting to melt into the ground from having pepper sprayed him.

I tug a strand of my hair as I mumble, "I'm really sorry again about last time. I really didn't know it was you, and I panicked, and—"

"Hayat." Mikaal huffs out a surprised laugh as he runs a hand through his hair. "Are you serious? Stop apologizing. That's not a concern right now, and I already forgot about it."

My cheeks heat, embarrassment crawling through me again. "I know, I just—I still feel horrible about it. And I…" I trail off at the exasperated look in his eyes, then clear my throat. "I'm sorry, I forgot to ask if you wanted water or something—"

"Hayat," he says. An odd sort of pressure builds in my chest as I watch his eyes light up with something like amusement. "Calm down. There's no need to be hospitable right now. Just relax, okay? Breathe."

Nodding wordlessly, I make my way to the couch. Auntie is soothingly rubbing my mom's hands between hers and constantly throwing me reassuring smiles. The four of us sit in agonizing silence for a couple minutes, eyes constantly darting to Mikaal's phone in hopes of an update from Riaz.

Until we hear the sound of a car pulling into the driveway, then the jingle of keys as someone opens the front door. Seconds later, a weary-looking Ihsaan steps inside.

The relief that envelops me is suffocating in its intensity. My mom cries out and rushes towards him, wrapping him in a hug and sobbing against him. His eyes are wide with confusion as he slowly returns the embrace.

"Ihsaan," my mom sobs. "Thank God, thank God. Where were you, beta?"

My brother's eyes dart to mine, then trail to Mikaal and his mom. His brows furrow.

The sight of him standing in our foyer, weary after a long day of work, is one my horrified subconscious had begun to convince me I would never see again. I'm so relieved by it that my knees crumple, and I sag against the sofa. Mikaal's mom squeezes my shoulder reassuringly.

"There were three accidents on the highway," Ihsaan says in a voice of bewilderment. "So much traffic it was impossible to drive. I left you a voice note when I got on the highway—did you not get it? My phone must have died before it sent, and I haven't been able to find my charger for days—Mama, why are you crying?"

My mom shakes her head back and forth against Ihsaan's chest, tears streaming down her face. My brother's baffled expression morphs into one of guilt as he wraps her more tightly in his embrace. "Okay. It's alright, Mama. I'm sorry," he whispers against her temple. "I'm so sorry, Mama."

Slowly, I muster the strength to walk towards Ihsaan, tears blurring my vision. Without a word, he reaches for me and pulls me into his arms with Mama.

"You're trembling," Ihsaan whispers in my ear.

"You…you scared the *hell* out of me, Ihsaan," I whisper back.

"I'm sorry," he repeats, rubbing my back soothingly. "Won't happen again."

Later, when Ihsaan has profusely apologized to Mama and she's stopped crying, and Mikaal has notified Riaz that Ihsaan has safely returned home, he and his mom stand to leave.

"We should get going, Layla," Auntie says to my mom. She turns a stern glance to Ihsaan. "Beta, your mom was very worried about you. Be careful next time, okay? May Allah always protect you."

"Ameen, Auntie. I'm sorry to have troubled you," Ihsaan says sheepishly, ducking his head.

She shakes her head and smiles. "It was no trouble. I'm glad Hayat called us."

Before they leave, Mikaal pulls Ihsaan to the side and murmurs something in a low voice. I strain to hear him over Mama and Auntie's voices.

"Look, man, you gotta be really careful," Mikaal says with folded arms. "Don't let anything like this happen again. Your family is still really vulnerable; anything could send them over the edge."

"I know, I know." Ihsaan blows out a sigh and shoves a hand through his hair. "I just—I lost my charger and my phone was dead and there were so many accidents on the highway and the traffic was *insane*—"

"I know. Believe me, I understand. But Hayat and your mom—they're in a delicate place right now, so you need to be *really* careful. Take extra precautions. Do everything you can to keep them posted so they don't worry." Mikaal pats Ihsaan's shoulder and my brother nods.

Watching the two of them, an odd sensation blooms in my chest—a soft warmth, as if a light has been switched on in a once-dark room, spilling gently into every hidden corner.

A sensation I'm becoming increasingly familiar with every time Mikaal Zaman is near.

Twenty-two

Daffodil: Unrequited love

My gardening gloves are covered in mud when Aneela replies to my text.

> Salaam! Sure, I would love to look over your scholarship applications. When do you wanna meet?

I dust my gloves off and hurriedly pull them off my hands. whenever you're free!

She responds immediately: I'm free today! If you're okay with that.

I bite my lip. Even though Ihsaan claims he isn't affected by Aneela's presence, I don't want to do anything that may trigger his anxiety. Then again, she'll probably be gone by the time he gets back from work, so it should be okay.

I text her a thumbs-up and a time to meet, then busy myself with gardening again.

I asked Abeer if she could run to the store and pick up some sunflower seeds for me. I'd been reading a chapter on sunflowers in one of my gardening books, and even though the ideal time to grow them isn't during fall, I found all the pictures mesmerizing. There's something about their vibrancy, timelessness, and cheerfulness that feels like exactly what my family needs right now.

Plus, I know they're secretly Ihsaan's favorite flowers. He acts all manly and responsible now, but sometimes I think a man just needs to be given flowers. He'll never admit it, but I used to see the way he would happily tag along with me to the sunflower farms around this time of year, asking the workers all sorts of interesting questions about them.

I'm so busy working that I lose all track of time and am momentarily thrown off by the sound of the doorbell.

"Hayat, beta," my mom calls. "It's Aneela."

"Coming!" I shout, shoving my gloves off and hurriedly placing my flowerpot to the side.

When I step inside the house, my mom has already seated Aneela and is asking her if she'd like something to drink. The way my mom watches her—all starry-eyed and creased cheeks—is adorable. It brings a pang to my chest.

I wish I could see Arafat like this—settled on the sofa, his arms wrapped around the woman who might have been his wife, chatting easily with her and Mama. I wonder if Aneela would have made him shy, if being loved by a woman would have softened something in him, opened up a version of himself the rest of us never got to meet.

My reverie breaks when Aneela stands to greet me.

"Sorry!" I say sheepishly, dusting myself off. "I'm a bit of a mess right now. Would you mind just giving me five minutes to clean myself up?"

"Of course!" she says brightly. "Auntie is such wonderful company."

My mom positively glows at the compliment, and I rush upstairs to change out of my gardening clothes, splashing cold water on my face to get rid of the grime. By the time I'm back downstairs, Aneela and my mom are at the dining table drinking apple cider juice and eating donuts.

I furrow my brows. "Did you…order donuts, Mama?"

My mom shakes her head and gestures to Aneela. "Aneela beti

brought them. I told her she really shouldn't have gone through the trouble."

"Oh, no, no, it's no big deal!" Aneela waves her off. "I didn't want to come empty-handed."

I join them at the table, securing my too-long hair in a low bun with a claw clip. "I will be annoying you even more now that I've decided to go the pre-med track, which means you will probably be here more often. So please don't feel like you need to bring something every time."

She smiles and pinches my nose lightly. "You're not annoying at all."

God, I wish Arafat were here.

My mom leaves the two of us to our work after a bit, and Aneela reviews my scholarship applications with me. A couple times while she's speaking, my eyes glaze over and I begin to zone out. I snap back to attention when she asks me a question, sheepishly requesting she repeat herself. Aneela closes my laptop and turns to me after the third time this happens. She raises her brows. "Hayat, are you okay?"

My cheeks heat with embarrassment. "Oh, God, I'm so sorry, Aneela. I'm being rude as hell. You came all the way to my house to help me and I'm—"

She shakes her head, cutting me off. "Hey, don't apologize. I'm just worried about you. You seem distracted. Is everything okay?"

My gaze tracks her fingers as they drum my laptop lid. She has such pretty, slender fingers. My eyes hone in on her bare ring finger.

"Hayat?"

I blink and refocus on Aneela's worried gaze. "I'm sorry," I murmur.

"Stop saying sorry, please. What's wrong? I'm worried about you."

I blow out a sigh and shrug. "I'm missing Arafat a little extra these days, I think."

Aneela quiets immediately, and I risk darting a glance at her face. A pained expression has taken over her features, and her eyes have taken on a faraway look.

Shaking my head, I grasp her hand. "I'm sorry," I whisper. "I always talk about how hard it is for me, but ever since I found out about you guys...I don't think I've ever asked you how you're doing."

She smiles as tears well in her eyes. "You know..." Her voice cracks as she speaks after a few moments. "It's kind of surprising that we were attending the same college for undergrad and then the same med school and were a part of the same community. I mean, it's not impossible, but it's kind of surprising." My thumb traces her palm soothingly as she speaks. "I was always fascinated by how Arafat and I ended up in relatively the same circles for the past few years. I think I've always had a special place in my heart for him. It's like I always knew he would be the one."

She sniffs and clears her throat. "When we met under Ihsaan's supervision, Arafat kept saying this phrase that my heart always comes back to. It reaffirms my faith and makes me believe anything is possible."

"'It's the qadr of Allah,'" we both whisper in unison. Our eyes meet, and by now we're both silently crying. Aneela's lips are trembling, and a teardrop slides down her cheek as she takes a deep breath.

"As difficult as this is," she says. "It's the qadr of Allah. Even on nights when I cry myself to sleep and days where his absence feels like a physical ache, I try to remind myself of what Arafat would always say: this is Allah's will. And there is khair and hikmah in it." She quiets and drops her head, watching our clasped hands with a forlorn expression.

I wrap her in a hug I think we both desperately need. She returns the embrace, squeezing me tightly and stroking my hair.

When we pull back, she shakes her head and laughs sheepishly. "I didn't mean to get emotional. Sorry about that. We were talking about you."

I furrow my brows. "Who's saying sorry now? Listen, you can talk to me whenever you need to. I'm always here for you."

Aneela smiles, grabbing a tissue and dabbing her face with it. "I know. Thank you, Hayat. Now will you tell me what else is bothering you? Because I know it's not just Arafat."

Fingering the table's lace cover, I glance up at her through my lashes. "You really are too perceptive for your own good."

She chuckles. "So I've been told."

I sigh, then hesitantly ask, "Have you ever done something that feels good but may not be good for you?"

She doesn't hesitate. "Yes."

"When did you know it wasn't good for you?"

"When I started to dislike the person I was becoming as a result of it."

I freeze, feeling oddly attacked by her words. "But is change bad if it makes you feel good while you're doing it?"

She cocks her head to the side. "If you feel good temporarily, then you've answered your own question."

I quiet, continuing to finger the table cover.

"Hayat," Aneela starts slowly. "Is something going on? Do you wanna talk about it?"

I take a deep breath and shake my head. "No, nothing specific. I'm just…curious."

She gives me a dubious look but doesn't press further. We continue working on the scholarship applications until the doorbell rings.

"I'll get it!" Aneela chirps. "You finish up that question."

My hands freeze on the keyboard as I glance at the time.

Oh, shoot. I completely lost track of time and now Ihsaan is home.

"Salaam!" I hear Aneela say. "Sorry for the shock, Hayat is a little occupied right now."

"I, uh—Wa 'Alaikum Salaam." Ihsaan's voice has an odd tremble to it.

I finish up the question I was working on and hurriedly stand to greet my brother.

He walks into the kitchen with two bags of food in his hand.

The color has visibly drained from his face and his hands are shaking.

"Hey," I murmur, avoiding his eyes.

"Hi," he says, a little breathless.

Aneela enters and stands to the side as Ihsaan sets the food on the kitchen island. "How are you doing, Ihsaan?"

His shoulders tense, and his voice comes out shaky as he replies, "I'm, uh, I'm good, Alhamdulillah. How are you?"

"Good, Alhamdulillah. Hayat and I were having a good time."

"Oh, yeah?"

"Yeah, she's amazing. I wish we had met earlier."

Tension descends in the kitchen as the implication of her words hits us. She seems to realize the same thing as she shakes her head and looks at her watch. "Anyway, I won't intrude on your evening now. I should get going. We'll talk soon, Hayat, okay?"

I nod as she begins to gather her things. "Thank you so much, Aneela. I appreciate it so much. I know you're busy, so you taking out the time means so much to me—"

"Oh, hush," she murmurs as she pulls me in for a hug. "What are friends for?"

"Friends" feels a little too minuscule to describe what she has begun to mean to me, but I smile nonetheless and walk her to the door.

Aneela turns to Ihsaan before heading out of the kitchen. "Have a good night, Ihsaan. Salaam!"

"Yeah," he responds, a little too late and a little too quietly. "You too."

Once she's gone, I'm oddly wary to return to the kitchen. Having Ihsaan and Aneela in the same vicinity feels strange. I can physically feel the tension rolling off of my brother in waves, tension he won't give a name to and won't allow me to understand. I don't understand why he seems so uneasy around her—or even at the mere mention of her name.

When I reluctantly trudge back into the kitchen, Ihsaan is lost in thought, a faraway look in his eyes. He startles at the sound of my footsteps and hurriedly turns away from me, but not before I see the pained expression on his face.

"Ihsaan," I say exasperatedly, throwing my hands up in the air. "Will you *please,* for the *love of God,* tell me what's wrong?"

He shakes his head and hastily uses the corner of his shirt to wipe his eyes. My eyes widen. "Ihsaan!" I whisper-shout. "Are you crying?"

I haven't seen my brother cry since Arafat's funeral.

"What the hell? No, of course not," he says vehemently, but he's angling his body away from me and discreetly trying to rush out of the kitchen.

I grab his arm as he's halfway up the stairs. "*Not* today, Ihsaan," I hiss lowly so as not to disturb our mom while she's reading in her room. "You need to tell me what's going on."

Ihsaan is visibly trembling now, and the sight brings a pang to my chest. My expression softens. "Okay. Relax, Ihsaan. Do you need to take your meds?"

He nods, and I follow him to his room, shaking a pill out of his medication bottle and handing him a bottle of water. Once he downs the pill, he places his head in his hands.

I really should've been more careful about the timing of Aneela's visit. My heart hurts seeing my brother like this.

"God, Hayat," he says hoarsely a few moments later. Venom laces his words as he glances up at me. "I keep telling you *not* to invite her or be close to her or anything. It's like you *purposely* do it to drive me crazy!"

I hesitate, confused by the terror in his eyes. "But you said it didn't matter to you and…why would my hanging out with Aneela drive you crazy?"

He stands abruptly and shouts, "Because I'm in love with her!"

Silence descends on us. Thick, heavy, and suffocating. Ihsaan's eyes are wide, his chest heaving with the pressure of breathing. My hand is on my chest, and I just stare at my brother as his confession echoes in my ears—one I've been desperate to hear but unprepared for.

After a moment, Ihsaan turns away and shoves a hand through his hair, shaking his head back and forth.

"You're…in love with Aneela?" I whisper, trying to make sense of it, my voice incredibly loud in the silent room.

Arafat's Aneela?

Ihsaan's shoulders are shaking. Instead of responding, he shoves past me and rushes out of the room.

I follow him down the stairs and grab his arm just as he's looping his keys through his fingers and heading out the front door.

"Ihsaan!" I say sharply, yanking him back to face me and shutting the front door. "Stop. Just *stop*. When will you stop running away?"

"Hayat." Ihsaan's voice is trembling. It seems the anti-anxiety meds haven't had their desired effect yet. "Please just let me go."

I move to physically block the front door and fold my arms. "No, Ihsaan. How long will you keep running away from yourself and your feelings? You don't realize it, but every time you do this, you push yourself deeper into quicksand." Slowly, I place a gentle hand on his arm. "Please talk to me. Just let it out. I *promise* you'll feel better."

He hangs his head low, eyes trained to the floor, and I'm once again struck by how fatigue coats every inch of him. Dark, bruised circles frame his tired eyes; his shoulders droop in a permanent hunch, and his steps drag like he's walking through tar. Ihsaan isn't just tired; he's utterly spent. This is the same guy who used to tug at my hair, peel off every Post-It in my terrace garden, and call me a churail every chance he got.

I want to lead him into the living room and have this conversation in a relaxed environment, but I'm afraid he'll run away again if I suggest that, so I rub my hand along his arm soothingly and murmur, "Since when?"

He takes a deep breath and meets my eyes, tentative. "Since Arafat introduced us…so I could supervise them when they wanted to get to know each other."

I suck in a sharp breath and release my hold on his arm. Ihsaan's eyes track my movements, and he steps back with a wounded expression.

"No!" I rush to say. "No, no, I'm not mad or weirded out. I'm just surprised. Please don't stop talking." I squeeze his shoulder as a form of reassurance, then gently continue, "And what were you planning on doing about it then?"

He shrugs, but I detect the hurt behind the casual movement. "I had to tamp it down, obviously. And it became a little easier to ignore my feelings when the two of them so clearly liked each other." Ihsaan fingers a loose thread on his sweater. He's avoiding my gaze, but he's visibly less tense than a couple moments ago, as if blurting the truth has given him room to breathe.

"And now?" I ask quietly.

He furrows his brows. "Now what?"

"How do you feel now?"

The confusion immediately vanishes from his face. He rubs a hand behind his neck and squeezes his eyes shut. When he reopens them, he steps away from my comforting grasp on his arm and shakes his head. "Can we please stop talking about this now?" He turns away and starts heading to his room.

I rush forward and stop him halfway. "Stop," I say exasperatedly. "Just tell me. Let it out. Please. We're finally getting somewhere."

Ihsaan throws his hands up in the air and shouts, "Fine! What do you want me to say? *Yes*, I'm still in love with the woman my brother wanted to marry. *Yes*, I'm a horrible person for it. *Yes*, it eats away at me everyday…And *no*, your constant pestering does not make it easier for me!"

"It doesn't make you a horrible person," I murmur quietly. "It just makes you human."

He laughs in bewilderment, but the sound is jagged, almost desperate. "She was supposed to marry Arafat!" he explodes, eyes wide and incredulous. "How is it right for me to want the woman who was supposed to be his?"

A moment of strained silence stretches between us. I watch the grief flicker in his eyes, and something in me breaks at the way he holds himself—like his very posture is a sacrifice. "He would've wanted you to be happy," I whisper.

Ihsaan scoffs vehemently. "I don't deserve to be happy when my brother is dead."

His words hang in the air between us.

He presses his nose between his thumb and forefinger and shakes his head, letting out a mirthless laugh. "His name was Arafat!" His eyes are two wide pools of grief as he turns to me and gestures a mountain. "Arafat!" Then, quieter, "How am I supposed to top that?"

"You don't have to top it," I say softly. "You just have to be Ihsaan."

Another scoff and a shake of his head. "That will never be enough."

I watch speechlessly as he turns and trudges back to his room. Only when he's vanished from sight do I notice what I missed before. A flicker of movement. A breath held too long.

My mom—standing at the far corner of the hallway, one hand clutched to her chest, eyes as wide and round as saucers. And she's staring straight at me.

Twenty-three

Ivy: Attachment

I TAKE A DEEP breath and steal a quick glance at my mom. She's sitting at the dining table, hands folded neatly in front of her, gaze fixed somewhere far away.

"Look, Mama," I say with a sigh. "You know I only told you because you overheard most of it, right? It was very difficult to get Ihsaan to open up. Who knows how long he's been holding this in?" I place a hand atop hers. "So don't mention this to him until you feel like he's ready to talk about it."

She blinks, refocusing her gaze on me. "Of course, Hayat. This is an amanah. But…" She rubs a hand against her forehead. "You know, I think he saw me when he was going back to his room. I'm sure he knows I heard everything. Knowing Ihsaan, I think he will just avoid it and pretend the conversation never happened unless I bring it up with him."

"Will you?" I raise my brows. "Bring it up with him?"

She blows out a sigh. "Eventually, yes."

"How do you think that will go?"

Mama shakes her head. "I don't know, to be honest." She drops her head and presses her palms to her eyelids. "Bichaara. Who knows how much he's been suffering? Who knows how much *both* of you have been suffering? This is all my fault. If I had been more present—"

"No, Mama," I interrupt softly. "None of this is your fault. Please don't blame yourself."

Mama lifts her head and looks at me with a stricken expression. "Can you imagine how he must be feeling? He loved her when she might have been…his brother's…and he still loves her. Imagine the guilt he must be feeling."

"I know, Mama. And I feel so bad—I kept telling her to come here…But the important thing is for us to let him know we're here for him and to reassure him that he's not a bad person for feeling the way he does."

Mama squeezes my hand, to comfort herself or comfort me, I'm not sure. But it feels good all the same. "I'm going to talk to your dad tonight and see what he says. Then we'll talk to Ihsaan together."

I nod. "That sounds good."

We stay sitting like that for a couple more minutes until my phone lights up with a text. I extract my hand from my mom's as I unlock my phone, and she busies herself with getting dinner ready.

It's Rameez. Immediately my heart rate spikes, cheeks flushed in anticipation.

And yet, the thrill is shadowed by something quieter. A strange wariness that's lingered ever since I returned from our day together. I try to name it, pin it down, but it slips past me every time.

Objectively, everything is fine. Rameez is kind and sweet and we've been texting for days (although I think my texts have been a bit drier than usual, for reasons I can't explain). Every time I walk into my room and see the lab coat he gifted me, my heart flutters. He's always checking in, encouraging me to take care of myself, asking about my hobbies, my mood, whether I've eaten, how my family's doing.

Rameez Khan makes me feel all the ways a teenage crush should: spirited, alive, carefree, and special.

So why is this quiet wariness tugging at the edges of my heart? Why does something feel slightly off? I'm not just confused—I'm frustrated with myself for feeling this at all.

I shake the disturbing thoughts out of my head and open his text.

these reminded me of you.

It's a picture of a cluster of yellow roses, each bloom kissed with raindrops that glimmer like fallen stars. My lips tug up at the corners as I type out a response.

awww. do they really remind you of me or is this an excuse to text me? ;)

I bite my lip in anticipation of his response.

guilty. both. :)

A smile blooms on my face, accompanied by the racing of my heart.

Then he asks, **did you eat dinner yet?**

I try wiping the stupid smile off my face before my mom thinks I'm acting suspicious.

about to. you?

just ate. abeer attempted a pasta recipe. let's just say i won't be looking at pasta the same ever again.

A laugh bubbles out of me before I can contain it. My mom turns to me with a quizzical brow, and I rush to say, "Abeer sent me something funny."

The wariness briefly returns, just before I turn back to my screen to respond. I don't know what possesses me to type it, but suddenly I've sent him a text that reads, **don't worry. i'll make sure you love pasta again :)**

I slap a hand over my mouth as soon as my demonic fingers send the text. *Why did I say that? Oh my God, that was so flirtatious.*

I scramble to unsend the message, fingers fumbling, mind

racing. But before I can, the dreaded dots appear. He's typing. Too late. I've shoved myself into quicksand.

it's a date :)

The next morning, Ihsaan trudges downstairs with barely a glance my way. He murmurs an incomprehensible "Morning" before pulling eggs from the fridge.

I had been expecting him to avoid me in classic Ihsaan fashion, but his coldness still stings. "Morning," I chirp, falsely cheerful. "What are you making?"

"Eggs," he mumbles. His under-eyes look less bruised today, as if shedding the weight of his secret has finally lightened something inside him.

"I can see that," I say sarcastically. "What kind of eggs?"

"Omelet."

I bite my lip. I've dealt with crackhead Ihsaan, feisty Ihsaan, upset Ihsaan, angry Ihsaan—but this version, embarrassed and quiet—I'm unaccustomed to.

"Want me to make it?" I offer, but he just shakes his head.

This is going to be fun.

I close the book I'm reading and take a deep breath. "I'm not going to talk about it unless you want to, but I just think you should know that I'm always here to listen. And I think you're being too hard on yourself."

He adds salt and paprika powder to a splash of water in a bowl. Then he grabs a tomato and an onion and begins chopping them, preparing an omelet with his weird Ihsaan method. "I thought you weren't going to talk to me unless I wanted to, but you're blabbing as usual."

My jaw drops. He's going straight to insults? Fine, two can play at this game. "That's rich, coming from a guy who gets scared of a girl's *name*."

He flinches, and for a moment I feel guilty, until he says, "You're like twelve years old. Stop acting like a miss-know-it-all."

I lean back, a smile tugging at the corners of my lips. So this is his tactic—avoid the matter at hand and tread lighthearted waters. "You woke up on the wrong side of the bed today, huh?"

Ihsaan places the knife down and finally looks me in the eyes, scrunching his brows. "I've always hated that statement. There are way better ways to insult someone."

"You're right," I challenge. "You would know. You're a pro at insults."

He returns to his tomato, cubing it painfully slow. "I'm a pro at a lot of things."

I choke on a laugh, coughing profusely. Ihsaan throws me a dry look. "Like what?" I tease.

"Many things."

"Name these 'many things.'"

He sighs, setting the knife down again. "I didn't wanna tell you this yet because you're being annoying, but I think this is time sensitive, so I have to do it now."

My brows furrow. "What are you talking about?"

Ihsaan lifts a finger as an indication to wait, then steps out of the kitchen. I wait in confusion for a couple seconds before he returns with his laptop and sets it in front of me, quietly returning to the kitchen island.

I lean in to read the email on the screen.

from: uaoffice@princeton.edu
to: ihsaan.amanullah@granthr.com
date: November 2, 2023, 8:19 AM
subject: Approval of Deferral Request Due to Bereavement

Dear Ihsaan,

I hope this email finds you well during this difficult time.

Thank you for reaching out on behalf of your sister, Hayat Amanullah. I'm writing to express my deepest condolences for your family's recent loss and to inform you that your request to defer Hayat Amanullah's enrollment at Princeton University has been approved by the admissions committee.

Please find important details regarding the deferral below:

Hayat's place in the Environmental Studies program is secured for the Spring 2024 semester (please note that she is free to alter her program of study later if desired). She will receive updated instructions closer to the start of the academic term regarding registration and orientation.

If there are any additional ways we can assist you during this time or if you have any questions, please do not hesitate to reach out to our admissions office at uaoffice@princeton.edu.

Please take all the time you need to grieve and take care of yourself and your loved ones. We look forward to welcoming Hayat to our university community when she is ready.

Warm regards,

Director of Admissions
Admissions Office
Princeton University
uaoffice@princeton.edu

Plink. Plink. Plink.

The soft sound of my tears plopping against the laptop keys is the only thing that pulls me out of my stunned state. I must have read the email a dozen times. I lift my blurry gaze to Ihsaan, who's casually whisking eggs in a bowl as if he hasn't just changed my entire future.

"Ihsaan?" I whisper.

He pauses and looks up, inhaling sharply at the expression on my face.

"You did this for me?" My voice barely survives the sentence.

Ihsaan avoids my gaze, turning the stove on under the frying pan. "Don't get too excited. I still don't like you and don't feel like talking to you right now—"

I cut him off by standing and rushing to him, embracing him from the side and burying my face in his hoodie. Tears burn my throat and stain his clothes as I warble, "Thank you, thank you, thank you so much, Ihsaan."

He's still for a moment before he reluctantly pats the top of my head and murmurs, "It was your hard work, so don't thank me."

I shake my head against him, sobbing. "No, Ihsaan. Thank you for everything. Thank you for always being there for me and for taking care of me even when you were grieving yourself. I've been really ungrateful and I haven't appreciated you enough."

He's been saying *I love you and I care about you* ever since Arafat died. In the quiet car rides he gives his licensed sister after long days of work. In the worries he swallows so no one else has to. In the packets of seeds and gardening tools he leaves scattered across the terrace. In the steady refrain of *don't worry, I got it,* spoken like a vow. He's been telling me he loves me every single day.

And I didn't see it. Didn't say it back. Not nearly enough.

Ihsaan tenses, wrapping a single arm around me and setting his chin on my head. His voice rumbles through his chest when he says, "Okay, now that's not true—"

"It is," I whimper. "It is, and I'm so sorry for not being a better sister. I've been blaming you all this time and accusing you of ignoring me, but you've been battling your own demons, and you've *still* been taking care of me. I'm sorry, I'm *so*—"

"Hey," Ihsaan says sharply, pulling back to look at me. All traces of annoyance or fatigue have left his features, replaced by concern instead. "Will you stop saying that? What am I here for if not to take care of you?" He hesitates, then wipes my tears with his thumbs. It's such an Arafat move that for a moment I'm stunned as my heart thumps painfully against my chest. "You have nothing to be sorry for. We've all been struggling."

I sniff, wiping my nose with the sleeve of my shirt.

Ihsaan scrunches his face, breaking the tension with, "And stop crying. Did you know you look really ugly when you cry?"

I shove him away, letting out a sound somewhere between a laugh and a sob. A moment later, a thought that has been nagging at me resurfaces. "Ihsaan," I say. "How will I attend Princeton, though? I got a full ride, housing included."

He turns back to the frying pan. "Yeah, you're gonna dorm."

I suck in a sharp breath. "But what about Mama? And everything at home—"

"That's not for you to worry about," he says, flipping the omelet to cook the other side. "I'm here, I will take care of everything."

"But how will you—"

"Again, not for you to worry about. I already talked to Mama and Papa. They're both in full agreement."

I finger a chipped edge on the kitchen island. "I appreciate it, Ihsaan, but...I don't want to leave Mama. It's too soon and I..."

Ihsaan sets his omelet on a plate along with two pieces of toast and turns to me with raised brows. "If you got a full ride, you *should* dorm, and I'm pretty sure you have to for the first two years. It'll be good for you in more ways than one. Otherwise, are you willing to use public transport to commute every day? I won't be able to chauffeur your sorry self an hour back and forth," he teases.

Biting my lip, I train my eyes to the kitchen's tile floor. Words bubble to my lips, ones I've been contemplating for a long time but haven't had the courage to voice.

Now is finally the time.

"I, uh…" I look up through my lashes. "I want to start driving again."

Twenty-four

Dandelion: Resilience

I'M IN A GARDEN *full of dandelions. Strange, since it's November, but this is a dream, and anything is possible.*

Rays of sunlight dance across my vision as I shield my eyes and squint across the field. A lone figure is sitting at the far end, and something propels my feet towards them.

As I approach, the sound of rushing water greets me, and I realize the field stretches to the edge of a cliff. I turn in a slow circle, absorbing the view—sunlight glittering across the landscape, dandelions swaying in the breeze, and the soft roar of water far below. For a moment, peace settles into my chest.

When I turn back to the cliff face, I stop short, heart thumping rapidly against my chest. Because the figure sitting at the edge of the cliff is as familiar as the reflection I see in the mirror every day.

He's wearing a clean white shirt and trousers and gazing into the rushing water below, but I can see his side profile. Brown waves fall softly against the back of his neck, his face sports a neatly trimmed beard, and the hint of a smile tugs at the corners of his lips.

"Arafat?" I whisper breathlessly, my voice carrying.

He turns and my breath catches in my throat, tears immediately welling in my eyes. His face blooms into a grin, and my heart aches so bad that for a moment it all feels too real.

"Hi," I say shakily.

"Hey, yourself," he replies. The sound of his voice is the most comforting thing ever. His eyes—his familiar, beautiful brown eyes—twinkle as he pats the space next to him. "Come sit."

With trembling limbs, I settle down next to him, barely daring to breathe—afraid that the slightest movement or word might make him vanish.

"You're so quiet," he murmurs conversationally.

I turn to him, inhaling sharply when our eyes lock. "I've missed you so much, you have no idea." My voice breaks as I whisper, "I need you so much. We need you so much."

Arafat shakes his head, a strange smile on his face. "You don't need me anymore. You just miss me."

"That's not true. I—"

"It is," he insists, and for a moment I think he's upset until I see the content expression on his face. "You're all grown up, Hayat."

I shake my head profusely. "I'm not."

He laughs, loud and boisterous. I miss the sound so much that fresh tears prick at my eyes. "You don't give yourself enough credit. You're stronger than you know."

I shake my head. "I'm not strong at all."

"That's the farthest thing from the truth." He reaches over and squeezes my hand. "You're doing so well on your own."

"On her own?" a voice scoffs from behind us. We turn to see Ihsaan walking towards us, folding his arms once he reaches us. "Taking care of this churail is a workout in and of itself. She's a handful. You know, she pepper sprayed Mikaal?"

"I apologized!" I practically scream.

Arafat chuckles as I gape at Ihsaan. For a moment it feels like old times, the three of us bantering and arguing as siblings.

Ihsaan settles down next to me and raises his brows. "What?" he says indignantly. "Did I lie?"

"Yes!" I hiss. "I'm a handful? Have you tried having a conversation with Ihsaan Amanullah? It's a headache!"

Ihsaan mocks me in a high-pitched voice, then locks me in a dramatic headlock. I shriek for him to let me go, laughter spilling out in gasps between each breath.

"Guys, guys," Arafat says in a placatory tone. We straighten and turn to him as he sighs. "Cut it out."

The three of us sit in silence, listening to the rush of water below. Ihsaan swings his legs over the edge of the cliff, carefree, while Arafat rests with his hands at his sides, eyes closed and face tilted towards the sun.

"Hayat and Ihsaan," Arafat murmurs. We turn to him, but he doesn't seem to be speaking to us. He seems to be lost in thought as he continues, "Hayat and Ihsaan. Our parents knew exactly what they were doing when they named you guys."

My brows furrow. "What do you mean?"

Arafat opens his eyes and locks gazes with me. His eyes are sparkling as he says, "Hayat: Life. Allah put it in you to bring life to this family over the past few months. You took care of everyone and pulled everyone out of a dark place even though you were in a dark place yourself."

A shiver runs through me despite the warm breeze. His words echo painfully against the walls of my mind. I focus on the sound of the water to reorient myself.

"Ihsaan," he continues, smiling as he stares off into the distance. "The pursuit of excellence." He swivels his head towards Ihsaan, who has gone very still beside me. "You've been striving towards excellence for months. You strive to be excellent for our parents, for Hayat, for yourself. To be honest, you're too hard on yourself; you're trying to achieve perfection in everything that you do. Sometimes a little too much."

Arafat is quiet for a moment. Then he begins to dust himself off as he stands. "Hayat and Ihsaan," he murmurs again, smiling wistfully down at us. "Life and the pursuit of excellence. The perfect complements to one another."

He turns and begins to walk away. My eyes follow him as I cry out in a panicked voice, "Where are you going?"

Arafat turns slowly, eyes locking on Ihsaan's arm still draped around my shoulders from the playful headlock earlier. He smiles a mysterious smile. "It's time for me to go. You don't need Arafat anymore."

The words aren't tinged with pain or nostalgia. Instead, they're full of satisfaction as he continues to watch us.

Then his smile blooms into a real one as he turns and begins walking. A couple seconds later, he disappears in the twinkle of the sun's rays and the rustling of the dandelions, almost as if he was never there.

I'm left feeling disoriented and deeply saddened by my dream, so when Abeer asks me to hang out later that day, I don't say no.

Initially, when I open her text message, I'm a little shocked by the amount of time it's been since I last texted her. I scroll through our conversation and notice that over the past week or two, she has been initiating almost every conversation. At first it was pretty frequent—every day or every other day—but later, as my texts became less frequent, so did hers. The last message I received from her before today was three days ago.

This realization unsettles me in a way I can't explain—not just because of this weird distance between us, but because I'm embarrassed I didn't notice it sooner. I was so focused on staying connected with her brother that I forgot to stay connected with my best friend. It reminds me of the days right after Arafat died, when Abeer kept reaching out—texts, calls, meetups—until she quietly gave me space, sensing I didn't have the energy to maintain any friendships. But this time feels different. Her message to hang out lacks its usual enthusiasm, as if she expects me to say no. Still, I find the strength to say yes, even though I'm not in the mood for anything today.

I bid my mom goodbye and make my way down the block. Ihsaan promised he would practice driving with me over the weekend, so Abeer is picking me up today. I asked her to meet me at the entrance of the neighborhood so I could get some steps in—

ironically, the same as the excuse I'd used the last time Rameez picked me up.

I don't know if it's a coincidence or if, subconsciously, my body was propelling me in this direction, but I've taken the longer route and somehow ended up outside Mikaal Zaman's house.

I freeze on the sidewalk beside his front yard, stunned by the sight of him. It's always so strange seeing him out of his lab coat or professional attire. Today, he's dressed in a hoodie and sweatpants, knee deep in the grass, sleeves rolled up at the elbows as he tends to the garden.

Somehow, amidst all the chaos in his busy life, he still has the time to nurture his garden.

I watch as Mikaal shovels soil into a large plant pot, patting it down with his bare hands. Gardening gloves lie haphazardly nearby, as if he had attempted to make use of them but decided he preferred getting his hands dirty.

Before I know what I'm doing, I'm walking towards him, wiping my clammy hands on my coat despite the cold November air. I stop a couple feet away, rooted in place by an unnamed force.

I'm suddenly strangled by the sense that if he were to turn around and look at me, I would burst into tears. I don't know why I feel this way every time I'm around him, as if I'm an abyss of vulnerability, and his presence is like a torch in the dark.

He hasn't noticed my arrival yet. As he wipes the sweat on his forehead with the back of his arm, a strange feeling tugs at my heartstrings.

All this time, I've been telling myself that Mikaal Zaman's presence brings me comfort because he reminds me of a time when Arafat was alive. But I don't think that's true anymore, and I think I've been doing myself a disservice by lying to myself. I can no longer avoid the truth, can no longer ignore the way my heart thumps in a peculiar way when he's near, or the quiet calm that settles over me when we speak.

Some part of my heart feels something for Mikaal Zaman, and I can no longer hide that part from myself.

The moment the thought surfaces, I'm met with a relief so great it feels as if a boulder has been lifted from my chest. It seems I've been hiding from the truth for far too long.

I'm beginning to understand all the thoughts I used to shove away before they could fully form. Like all the times I found Mikaal Zaman's kohl-lined eyes mesmerizing. Or the way my breath would catch at the mention of his name. Or how I felt an urgent need to make a good impression every time we crossed paths. And always, the mantra: *he's my brother's best friend he's my brother's best friend*—repeating in my head like a warning every time he laughed or his eyes sparkled. Because it would be irrational to think of him as anything *but* my brother's best friend. So I buried those dangerous moments, locked them away in a box my heart didn't dare approach.

Now, this discovery both terrifies and confuses me. Terrifies, because I don't know how to deal with it. Confuses, because I also feel drawn to Rameez Khan—infatuated, even. How can I harbor feelings for two guys at the same time?

But my feelings for Rameez have always felt…lighthearted. Youthful. Blissful in a carefree sort of way. Whatever's stirring for Mikaal Zaman feels different—heavier. More intense. As if my connection to him carries a kind of gravity that wraps itself around my heart, tangling it in a web of emotions I don't understand.

"Hayat?" Mikaal's voice breaks me out of my epiphany. I blink, registering his widened eyes and stiff posture. "Hey. You scared the hell out of me. Everything okay?"

My heart is racing like it's in a race and it's determined to win. I swallow, squeezing my eyes shut and reopening them in an attempt to bring myself back to normalcy.

Mikaal is watching me expectantly.

I desperately reach for a topic of conversation that won't make me look like a dumb fool. My eyes zero in on the plant seed packet next to the plant pot. Without thinking, I blurt, "You should use a smaller pot for petunias. When they start growing, you can transfer them to a bigger pot."

A cleft appears between his brows, his expression morphing

from surprised to baffled. His eyes dart back and forth between the large pot he had been adding soil to and the packet of petunia seeds. Finally, he says, "Thank you. I'm not a pro so I just do this when I get the time, but you just saved me from a lot of trial and error. Although I should probably have done better research."

An awkward silence hangs in the chilly air between us. I'm distantly aware of my phone buzzing in my pocket, but I pay it no heed. Instead, I'm mesmerized by Mikaal's lightly kohl-lined eyes.

"Did…you come here to tell me that?" Mikaal's lips are turned up at one corner, but the line has reappeared between his brows.

Having no other excuse that won't make me look even stupider than I already do, I nod quietly.

His lips quirk because we both know there's no way I saw the packet of petunia seeds from the sidewalk, but thankfully, he simply nods. "Well, thank you again, Hayat."

Hayat.

My heart jolts, and suddenly I remember Arafat's words from my dream: *Hayat: Life.*

My phone begins buzzing again, and Mikaal's eyes zero in on my pocket. "I think someone's calling you," he murmurs.

My throat tightens, the strange urge to cry resurfacing. I take a deep breath and hold it in, pressing my lips together tightly.

But Mikaal makes the mistake of gently asking, "Are you okay?"

My eyes burn with the promise of tears, and my chin wobbles. I'm suddenly overcome with the desire to blurt out everything I'm feeling to him.

Thankfully, some rational part of me forces me to swallow my words. I nod tightly and spin on my heel, quite literally running away from him.

I don't look back. Not once, even though everything in me aches to see the expression on his face. I keep running until I see Abeer's car idling by the curb. I rush up to the passenger side and open the door but am met with an unpleasant surprise.

Rumana looks up, amusement flickering in her eyes. "Hi, Hayat."

I shoot a furious glance at Abeer, but she simply smiles—one of those polite, practiced ones.

It doesn't reach her eyes.

She didn't mention that Rumana was coming. If she had, I wouldn't have agreed to hang out. Or maybe she had mentioned it, but I wasn't paying attention. I was already in a weird mood from my dream, but I thought that since Abeer knew me like the back of her hand, it wouldn't be a problem spending time with her.

I didn't factor Rumana into the equation.

"Sorry, I already claimed shotgun," Rumana says playfully.

I slam the door with a little more force than necessary and settle in the backseat.

"Where were you?" Abeer asks. "I called a bunch of times—"

"Sorry," I say in a clipped tone. "I ran into a neighbor."

Abeer looks as if she wants to say more, especially regarding my sour mood, but thinks better of it and begins driving.

We chat for a few minutes—well, *they* chat. I offer minimal responses, feeling like a third wheel. Objectively, there's nothing about Rumana that should irritate me. But ever since her comment at her birthday party—about it being strange that I cook for my brother—everything she says feels laced with judgment. Or maybe I'm imagining it. Maybe I just can't look at her the same way anymore.

It's crazy how one remark can shift your entire perspective of someone.

When we arrive at Dave's, I'm relieved for the opportunity to escape this car. Abeer comes over to my side and links arms with me, and for a moment I feel infinitesimally better until she loops her other arm through Rumana's.

This is going to be *so* much fun.

⁓

I slam the car door and storm up the driveway towards my house.

"Hayat!" Abeer shouts, chasing after me. "Hayat, stop!"

I ignore her and keep walking until she grabs my arm and spins me around.

"Hayat!" she says exasperatedly. "Will you stop? Please tell me what's wrong."

I fold my arms, my gaze lingering on my best friend's tense features. The curls peeking out from under her beanie frame her face, and for a moment I'm distracted by the split ends. Abeer always complains that each season brings a new set of problems for her hair—frizz in the heat, dryness in the cold.

"Will you tell me what's wrong? Abeer repeats. "Or are you just going to stand there?"

Her unyielding tone is like a spark to a flame. My face twists in disgust as anger surges up, and I spit, "Are you really asking me that?"

Abeer turns her head towards the sky and closes her eyes. "*Yes*, Hayat, I'm really asking you that."

"If I need to explain it to you, then you don't really understand me," I murmur, beginning to turn away once more.

She opens her eyes and grabs my arm again, her grip like a vise. "Can you stop doing that? I'm trying to understand what the problem is. Can we just talk?"

"Fine!" I shout. "You don't see the way Rumana talks about me, as if I'm throwing my life away? Sure, *Harvard-bound* Hayat isn't going to college right now like the rest of you are, but I kinda have"—I laugh bitterly—"extenuating circumstances. And it's no one's business what I do, or whether I go to college or not, *especially* not Rumana's."

Abeer releases her hold on me and trains her eyes on the ground. "I don't think she meant it like that," she says quietly. "She was just worried about you—"

I scoff. "Rumana, worried about *me*? Since when does she give a damn about me?"

Abeer's surprised eyes meet mine—whether from my question or my rare use of profanity, I'm not sure.

"Don't say that, Hayat. She's always been a friend to you before…before your brother passed away."

"Why are you taking her side?" I hiss venomously.

Abeer stiffens, eyes hardening. "I'm not taking sides. I'm just trying to figure out the problem and diffuse the tension."

I shake my head. "Right, and this has nothing to do with your sudden love for your new bestie."

Abeer steps back, eyes wounded. "That's not fair, Hayat. Rumana has always been my friend, but I've never treated either of you differently. You're both important to me."

"Yeah, except *she's* more important to you now." I turn away, trudging up the walkway to my porch.

"What did you think would happen?" Abeer's voice rings out, rooting me in place. I slowly turn and lock eyes with her furious gaze. "You were grieving after Arafat bhai and you didn't wanna talk to anyone no matter how much I tried. I understood, and I wanted to give you your space because…" Her voice cracks, and my resolve quivers. "I knew you would come back when you were ready. But things changed, Hayat." She blows a curl out of her face exasperatedly. "Rumana… Rumana was there for me when you couldn't be. And I know sometimes she can have strong opinions and be a little blunt, but… she's become a really dear friend.

"But that doesn't mean I've ever differentiated between you two. You're equally important to me." Abeer shakes her head and laughs mirthlessly. "But now…even when you and I finally reconnected, you're becoming distant again. It gets exhausting being the only one trying, you know that? Always being the first to text and make plans and see how you're doing. I mean, you blamed me because of Rumana today but if you told me you didn't want her there, I would have understood. You just…" Her eyes grow sad and weary. "You talk to my brother all the time but it's like you don't care about me anymore unless you need me."

My chin wobbles, her words striking me somewhere deep. I step forward and open my mouth to counter her words but realize I have no defense. She's barreled all my walls down, leaving me exposed and vulnerable as the truth hits me.

"You know what the saddest part is, though?" Abeer scoffs. "When you need me again, I'll still be here. I'll always be here for you."

She turns and heads back to her car, and I'm left feeling as if the ground has crumbled beneath my feet.

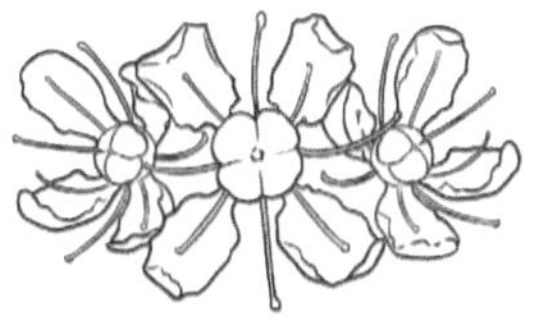

Twenty-five

Rue: Regret

I'M RESTLESS THE ENTIRE night, tossing and turning and constantly checking my phone to see if Abeer has texted.

I don't expect her to—not after the spitfire in my front yard—but it still hurts. I open our chat again and again, trying to draft a message, but I lose my nerve every time and backspace everything.

Abeer and I have never fought like this. We would occasionally have playful arguments, but nowhere near as serious as this. Ihsaan would often joke that we were like disgusting inseparable twin fetuses.

After an uneasy and sleepless night, I pray Fajr and trudge downstairs like a zombie. I spend the morning frantically cleaning the house and tending to my garden. Papa took the day off from work, and he's reading a newspaper and occasionally asking me questions like, "Shehzaadi, what are you up to?" and "Shehzaadi, how's the garden going?"

When I'm completely spent and can no longer find a poor chore to release all my frustration on, I settle on the couch next to him and lean my head back.

Immediately he puts his newspaper down and wraps an arm around me, tucking me into his chest. I melt into him, closing my eyes and focusing on the sound of his heartbeat. Distantly I'm aware of the dishes clinking in the kitchen as my mom makes chai, and for a moment everything feels fine.

Ever since Arafat passed away, I feel like I've been thirsty for any form of love. Having been the laadli, carefree child of the family, adjusting to a cold, quiet life afterward was painful and miserable. And even though things have improved over the past couple of weeks, there's still a distance between us. One I'm not sure will ever fully disappear.

As I snuggle deeper into my dad's embrace, he kisses the top of my head and murmurs, "You okay, Shehzaadi? You've been on autopilot all morning."

I just nod, lacking the energy to even formulate a coherent sentence.

He sighs after a moment. "I know I haven't been here for you enough. For you, for Ihsaan, for Layla. I haven't been the father or the husband I should have been."

My eyes crack open. "What are you talking about?" I croak. "Don't say things like that."

"It's true. We had to stick together, but I left you all to fend for yourselves. I wasn't there for you. I thought that if I went to work as usual every day and forced a laugh here and there and pretended everything was fine…then maybe everything *would* eventually be fine." He tenses. "I was wrong."

I lift my head so that I'm facing my dad. Grabbing his other hand, I rub soothing circles on his palm. There's a rare vulnerability on his face, one he has tactfully kept hidden for so long. "That's not true, Papa. You tried everything you could to hold this family together. You've always been here for us. Everyone's just been…" I shrug lightly. "Dealing in their own ways."

He's quiet for a moment, staring blankly into space as I continue to rub his palm. Then a fissure appears between his brows as he turns to me. "We talked to Ihsaan last night about Aneela."

I straighten. No wonder Ihsaan barely spared me a glance before he holed himself up in his home office. "Really? What did he say?"

Papa sighs and places his hand over mine. At that moment, Mama enters the living room with a tray of chai and sets it on the table in front of us. She settles down on my other side and gently picks up my other hand.

"He said no," my mom says softly.

"What?" My brows knit. "No to what?"

"He says he won't do that to his brother," Papa continues. "We told him there's no pressure, but to think about whether he wants to talk to Aneela and see if she may be interested in getting to know each other for the purpose of marriage. But he was very firm about it. Kept saying he would never do that to Arafat."

"Wow," I breathe. I don't know why I'm surprised; I should've expected this from Ihsaan given how harshly he spoke about himself the day he confessed. "But…he really, really likes her. He's just gonna keep suffering?"

Mama rubs a hand along the length of her face and sighs. "Beta, we *really* tried. We obviously understand his feelings and we're not saying that his decision is wrong, but we really don't know what else we can do." She sets her chin in her hands and gazes somewhere far away. "Bichaara Ihsaan. My poor bacha. He's doing what he thinks is best for Aneela and for himself, but it breaks my heart to see him so helpless and heartbroken. I just pray that Allah grants him sabr and rewards him for his sacrifice."

"Ameen," my dad murmurs. "Sometimes the most noble thing to do is to let them go, even if you love them. Especially if you love them."

I'm too distraught by Ihsaan's decision and my parents' words to respond.

How does someone so easily let go of the person they love?

I thought—after all the AP English classes, all the classics I devoured—that love was *the* thing worth dying for. Shakespeare, Austen, Dickens, Brontë—they taught me that love is what you chase across oceans, what you cling to with both hands, what you never, ever let slip away.

So how is it possible to let go of the person who makes your heart race? To ask your heart to quiet its longing, to convince it that what it yearns for might not be what's best for it?

Does that make a person stronger, then, or weaker?

Is letting go an act of courage, a choice rooted in selflessness? Or is it a sign that you're too afraid to fight for a different ending?

I know my brother is anything but weak, but having witnessed the grief and heartbreak in his eyes when he speaks about Aneela, and then hearing about how he's going to let her go and continue to possibly suffer, makes me wonder.

Is he strong enough to place a stone on his heart and bid his love goodbye? Or is he too afraid to fight for the one thing that might make him whole again?

True to my promise, I make plans to meet up with Rameez for our pasta date on Friday.

He keeps calling it a "date" and while I don't correct him (because what the hell, that's exactly what it is), the word makes me really uncomfortable.

When he picks me up, I regurgitate my all-too-familiar lie of meeting Abeer by the neighborhood entrance to my mom. This time, however, it feels even worse, considering Abeer and I haven't been speaking for the past couple of days.

I thought it might be strange to hang out with Rameez when his sister and I are currently not on good terms, but surprisingly he hasn't broached the topic with me. And honestly, he seems to be one of the few people bringing a smile to my face these days.

That, and I need to be in his presence to remind myself that *he's* the one I like. That whatever strange feelings I have for Mikaal Zaman are just a combination of grief and vulnerability. Of him being there when I was falling apart.

But then a thought burrows through all others—nagging, persistent. That if I need to distract myself from Mikaal…maybe I've underestimated the depth of my feelings.

I shove the thought away.

When Rameez picks me up, I slide into the passenger seat. Before I know what I'm doing, I lean forward and embrace him tightly, burying my face in his chest. His arms wrap around me instinctively, and he strokes my hair. "You okay?" he murmurs.

I nod, pulling back. For a moment, a terrible discomfort suffocates me at my need for his physical comfort. But, like always, I shove the feeling away and smile, holding up the little bag I brought with me. "World's best pasta," I singsong.

A corner of his lips turns up. "I can't wait to try it."

While he's driving, I tell him about Princeton, my wish to drive again, and the situation with Ihsaan and Aneela. I'm very careful not to mention Abeer—even though I'm burning with curiosity as to whether she's spoken to him about me—and he doesn't bring her up either. He listens to me rant, occasionally throwing in a word of advice or a follow-up question, and when we reach Washington Rock, I laugh nervously.

"I'm sorry, I talked so much."

His brows knit as he chuckles. "Why are you saying sorry? I like listening to you."

A blush coats my cheeks as I duck my head to retrieve the bag of pasta. Rameez grabs blankets from the backseat along with snacks he packed for the occasion—including strawberry cheesecake, my favorite.

We spread one blanket on the ground and lay the food out like a makeshift picnic. The other two blankets we wrap around ourselves.

We spend the next hour conversing and laughing and eating good food. He compliments my pasta so many times that my cheeks stay warm the entire time I'm with him. There's something about being around him that loosens the tension in my body, like all the tight places I didn't know were there are slowly unknotting.

But at the same time, new knots form. Knots of discomfort. Of guilt. I can't put a finger on it, but being with Rameez feels like sitting too close to a fire—comforting, yes, but always on the edge of getting burned.

To distract from the disturbing thoughts, I ask him something I've been meaning to ask for a while.

"Do you remember Abeer's birthday party? When I was leaving, you approached me and asked me how I was doing. We started talking sometime after that. Can I ask…we've known each other for years; how come you were suddenly interested in me then?"

Rameez tilts his face towards the sun, closing his eyes. For a stupid, distracted moment, I remember how Mikaal's kohl-lined eyes looked under the sun the other day.

"It may have seemed sudden, but I think I've always thought you were amazing," Rameez murmurs, opening his eyes to look at me. He fingers the edge of his blanket as he speaks. "Powerhouse, Harvard-bound Hayat. You're kind and intelligent and thoughtful and funny. And…freaking gorgeous. But you got so quiet and subdued after your brother passed away. It physically hurt seeing you like that. And…I was never sure how Abeer would feel about it, and I was always hesitant to bring it up with her. But by then we had graduated high school and I figured we were old enough to choose what we wanted for ourselves."

Choose what we wanted for ourselves. My heart jolts and an involuntary smile blooms on my face. I shyly train my eyes to the ground, focusing on the sound of the rustling leaves to stabilize my heartbeat. "So…you've always liked me?"

In response, he gently lifts my hand and brings it to his lips, pressing a tender kiss to my knuckles. His lips curve up as he gazes at me.

My heart is warring with itself. On the one hand, nothing feels more tempting than letting him keep holding my hand, kissing it like it's something sacred. On the other, that terrible discomfort creeps back in—like I've stepped too close to the fire and finally felt the sting. Warmth and pain, tangled together.

Luckily I'm spared from having to pull my hand back when Rameez lets go to grab his phone. He opens the front camera and extends his arm so both of us are in the frame. Scooting a little closer, he grins, "We have to capture this moment."

He snaps the picture and opens it to inspect it. We're both smiling, bathed in the muted mid-November sunlight, golden streaks threading through our hair. "Perfect," he whispers. He opens Instagram, adds the picture to his story, and captions it *good day*, tagging me underneath.

Panic, quick and hot, flares in me. The knots have returned, tightly winding themselves in my chest. I open my mouth to request him to delete it but realize I don't have a reason that won't make me sound stupid. And worse—I can't even pinpoint why it's bothering me so much.

"Will Abeer see that?" I blurt out.

He looks up from his phone, and the smile on his face is so genuine that I feel a pang of guilt for disrupting his happiness.

"Is that okay?" he asks.

I hesitate. Asking him to delete it just for Abeer won't untangle the discomfort. Plus, I haven't really told him what happened between us—I don't want to make things awkward. Sure, I don't want her to see the story and get upset. But I also don't want to dim his happiness. He looks so proud to share this moment, even if I'm uneasy about what it might imply.

I smile tightly. "That's fine."

"Are you sure? I can take it down or hide my story from her if—"

"No, no!" I quickly interrupt. God, I don't want to be the reason he lies to his sister or hides the truth from her.

"Okay." He tilts his head. "You wanna go get some ice cream?"

I squeal, and his eyes light up. One of his adorable quirks is his love for ice cream in cold weather (but only from a very specific place), and I've found that I've started to love it, too.

"I should probably say no since I just ate strawberry cheesecake *and* it's freezing, but I'm going to bury myself in quicksand and say yes."

"Oh, stop," he jokes, beginning to wrap up our supplies. "You only live once."

We head to Surreal Creamery. Rameez pays, and we settle in

the back with our sundaes. Surreal's pretty close to home, and I find myself glancing around nervously, hoping no one familiar walks in.

We swap sundaes and rate which one's better. I'm mid-giggle, recovering from a brutal brain freeze, when the bell above the door jingles.

Rumana walks in with a friend. *Oh, shoot.*

I duck instinctively to hide myself from view. Rameez furrows his brows and reaches for my hand.

"Are you okay? Is the ice cream too cold?"

Oh, you sweet, adorable guy. I shake my head. "No, no, I'm fine."

"Are you sure?" And then he does exactly what I *don't* need him to do right now: he slides over from across the table and settles beside me, wrapping an arm around my shoulders and twining his fingers through mine. He rubs soothing circles on the back of my hand.

"You're freezing," he says.

"What?" My voice comes out too high, too sharp, eyes zeroed in on Rumana and her friend as they order at the counter. We're sitting in the worst possible spot, too; if she turns her head, I'll be directly in her line of vision.

"Your hands are really cold." Rameez continues to rub them.

I laugh nervously. "No, I'm fine, really. Can we go? I think I'm just tired."

If Rameez finds my behavior odd, he doesn't comment on it. He nods and stands, pulling me along with him. He doesn't remove his arm from around me or let go of my hand. Normally, I might find it sweet, but right now I really just wish he'd let go.

To my dismay, however, we aren't quick enough. Rumana and her friend finish placing their order and turn in our direction. Her eyes immediately find mine. For a moment her expression flickers with shock as her gaze travels from me to Rameez, then traces the way his arm is wrapped around me and our fingers are entwined. Her brows lift. And then, of course, she walks over with her friend.

Shoot, shoot, shoot.

"Hi, guys!" she chirps, and maybe I just hate her a little bit right now. She was the reason Abeer and I fought, after all.

"Hi," I huff. "We were just heading out. See you!"

I try tugging Rameez away, but he gives me a bewildered look. I know I'm acting strange, but can't deal with Rumana and her inevitable speculations right now.

Her friend breaks the ice with, "Hi, I'm Sana. You're Hayat, right?"

I nod, forcing a weak smile.

Rumana's eyes continue to dart back and forth between me and Rameez. A slow smile spreads across her face. "So are you guys, like, a thing?"

Oh, my God.

New knots twist in my chest, and I let out an embarrassing titter. "Oh, shoot, my mom's calling me. We have to go. It was nice seeing you guys!" I ignore the dubious look on Rumana's face and tug Rameez away.

Only when we're safely in his car and driving away do I finally breathe again.

"Are you okay?" Rameez asks after a few minutes. He gives me a perplexed look. "You were acting kind of strange back there."

I nod quickly. "Yup, fine. I just didn't want to talk to Rumana right now because of this whole thing with Abeer..." I trail off, sensing he doesn't believe me and unsure how to convince him otherwise. Also unsure how much he knows about what happened between me and Abeer.

After a couple more moments of silence, he pulls into my neighborhood and remarks casually, "Are you sure it has nothing to do with not wanting to be seen with me in public?"

Oh, shoot.

"What?" I let out a high-pitched laugh. "No, of course not."

Rameez parks down the street from my house and turns to me. He seems to be contemplating something before he says quietly, "Hayat, I don't want whatever is between us to be a secret."

My body tenses. We've been skirting around *whatever is*

between us for a while. I've been simultaneously dreading and preparing for this very conversation.

I've been thinking about this for an embarrassingly long time. At random moments throughout the day, at night before sleeping. We're both only eighteen-year-old Muslims, but the past couple of months have made me feel so much older.

I know it's too early for any kind of official commitment. But I've never been the type to casually date or just be someone's girlfriend. And from what I know of Rameez, marriage isn't a priority for him—it's not even on the horizon. To be honest, it's not something I envision for myself right now either.

Which means whatever this is—whatever *we* are—will be labeled something I'm sure to be deeply uncomfortable with.

He covers my hand with his and watches me with a smoldering gaze. I feel as if I've gotten too close to the fire again.

"Are you embarrassed about being with me?" he asks

"No, um…" My eyes lock on his hand wrapped around mine. "I just…I'm not ready for…"

He removes his hand and sighs. "You're not sure about me."

I shake my head. "Um…that's not true, Rameez. I just…"

How do I even begin to explain the realization I've started to come to? That whatever exists between us—this blissful, carefree thing—feels fleeting. Ephemeral. That the wariness I used to carry like a dull ache in his presence has sharpened into something more persistent. A throbbing discomfort. And I can barely look at myself in the mirror anymore, because deep down I *know* what we're doing is wrong. And it needs to stop.

"It's fine," he says, fingering the steering wheel. "You can think about it."

"Rameez," I say in a placatory tone. "I really like you. I'm just…" The words feel almost true. No matter how intense my feelings have been for Mikaal lately, the warmth I feel with Rameez is unmistakable.

But that doesn't mean it's right.

He turns to me with a wounded expression. "Then what's bothering you?"

I bite my lip.

The truth is…I'm lying to myself. Convincing myself that my biggest concern is being involved in something premarital instead of…something else.

I think of one of Arafat's mantras: *Kuch bhi karo, lekin kisi ka dil kabhi na dukhao.*

Whatever you do, never hurt someone's heart.

I don't want to be strung along or string Rameez along, pretending whatever *this* is will become something real someday. The knots in my chest multiply every time we're together. My brain knows what my heart refuses to admit—that this arrangement is making me restless. Uneasy. That I've been pushing my own boundaries and my faith for a fleeting kind of happiness.

I keep remembering something he said seemingly a lifetime ago, when we were talking about college majors: *I'm trying to be less sporadic and indecisive. I can never figure out what I want.*

I don't want to be someone's uncertainty.

But that's not it, Hayat, is it? a voice in my head whispers. *That's not really why you're conflicted.*

Rameez clears his throat, sparing me from having to respond. "It's okay, Hayat." His voice is uncharacteristically cold. "Get some rest and think on it. I don't want to pressure you into anything."

Only when I step inside my house do I realize I missed a prayer yet again.

Twenty-six

Gladiolus: Strength

RAMEEZ HAS BEEN AWFULLY quiet for the past couple of hours.

I know he said he'd give me space to think about our conversation, but his tone had been off. And I didn't realize how attached I've become to his constant texts and check-ins.

Restlessness consumes me the next morning. I scroll through our old conversations, searching for comfort in the familiarity of his words. But it doesn't really work.

It feels as if a storm is brewing around me. Rameez is giving me space, his twin and I still aren't speaking, Ihsaan and Aneela's situation is troubling me, and on top of it all, my heart has decided it feels some kind of way about Mikaal Zaman.

That last one has been bothering me more than I want to admit. Normally, I'd turn to Abeer for things like this, but since I can't do that, I ended up confiding in Aneela—desperately, embarrassingly. I was even crazy enough to ask her to find out what Mikaal thinks of me, if he feels any way about me. Which is insane, because I was never this desperate to know what Rameez felt.

And even though Aneela's the sweetest person ever and talked to me at length about it, it wasn't the same as ranting to Abeer. No one can replace what I have with her.

I have the strongest urge to sit in the middle of this storm, wrap my arms around my legs, and simply rock back and forth like a baby. All the fight has left me; I don't have the energy to do anything.

But Ihsaan said he would practice driving with me today. And if I cancel, he'll know something's up.

I knock on his door after Dhuhr prayer. A loud "Damn it!" startles me, and I hurriedly open his door to see what's wrong.

He removes his headset and sets his Xbox controller aside, and I let out a sigh of relief. Yells and PG-13 curses were commonly heard from Ihsaan's room before, but it's been so long that I'm unused to the youthful spark in his eyes as he turns from his screen to me.

"You killed me, Hayat," he grumbles.

I raise my brows. "Maybe you're just out of practice."

He rolls his eyes. "Ha ha."

I watch him carefully, tracing his carefree expression and relaxed posture. He doesn't seem to be faking nonchalance, but with Ihsaan nothing is ever as it seems. He's become too good at pretending everything is alright.

We both have.

I fold my arms and lean against the doorframe. "You owe me something."

His eyes flick to the clock on his table. "Oh, shoot, you're right. I lost track of time. Let me pray Dhuhr and then we'll head out, okay?"

I nod and head downstairs. Ihsaan arrives fifteen minutes later, eyes oddly red and puffy as he throws me a lighthearted smile. I don't comment on how he very obviously just cried, and together we don our coats and bid our parents goodbye.

The Volkswagen Bug sits parked at the far end of the driveway. Ihsaan tells me to wait while he pulls his car out and parks it behind Papa's, then jogs back to me.

Once we're in the Bug, I take a deep breath and turn to Ihsaan.

His brows incline. "Ready?"

"Shouldn't you, like, test my knowledge before we go?"

Ihsaan's lips turn up at one corner. "Driving's like breathing; you never forget how to do it. Now stop making excuses and start the car."

I fill my cheeks with air before blowing out a loud sigh. My heart is beating like helicopter blades against my chest. Despite the November cold, sweat begins to bead at my hairline and on top of my lip.

And then Ihsaan's hand is on top of mine, and he squeezes once before letting go. "You can do it," he whispers. "You're Hayat freaking Amanullah. You got this."

I let out a breathless chuckle, raising a trembling hand to fit the key in the ignition.

Then I start the car.

The engine rumbles to life, the seat slightly vibrating underneath me. A bewildered laugh bubbles out of me, accompanied by the racing of my heart.

"Good job," Ihsaan says. "Now shift gears."

"Wait!" I say hurriedly. "I need a second."

Ihsaan quiets, waiting for me to gain my bearings. A few moments later, I place a foot on the brake pedal and a shaky hand on the gear shift before shifting to drive.

"Awesome," Ihsaan murmurs, lightly bumping our elbows in encouragement. He's not one to constantly give positive affirmation or physical affection, so his behavior is warming my heart and making this significantly easier. "Now slowly take your foot off the brake pedal and move to the gas pedal."

I do as he says and the car begins idling forward, trekking down the driveway. As if on cue, my breath heaves out, but I muster the courage to turn the corner and lightly press on the gas.

"You're doing great," Ihsaan says quietly. I feel his eyes honing in on my hands clenched tightly around the steering wheel. "Everything's fine, see? Just think of how excited you were when you first got your license in junior year."

I smile softly as we drive through the neighborhood. A minute or so later, my hands relax on the steering wheel and my breathing begins to return to normal.

"Hey, wanna hear a joke?" Ihsaan says brightly. "I was driving home from work the other day and this lady was driving in front of me. She put on her left indicator and guess what?"

"What?"

"She actually turned left!"

I huff out a laugh and roll my eyes, braking at a stop sign. "Not the sexist driving jokes."

Ihsaan shrugs. "I mean, come on, look at the way you're sitting." He mocks me and hunches forward all the way against the dashboard, lifting his hands over an imaginary steering wheel and squinting extra hard at the road.

Boisterous laughter bursts from me as I press on the gas again. "Oh, shut up. At least we don't drive like it's a competition to see who can honk the most and the fastest in two seconds."

"Touché."

As we're trekking down the block, we pass Mikaal's house. A weight lodges in my throat as my eyes rove over the little garden in the front yard—the one I had been standing in just a few days ago. The inexplicable ache that has accompanied every thought of him for the past few days resurfaces, and I find myself fighting the sharp prick of oncoming tears.

"Uh, Hayat?" I blink as Ihsaan waves a hand in front of my face. "Not that you're not a *spectacular* driver, but eyes on the road, okay?"

"Right, sorry," I say hurriedly.

As I'm driving, Ihsaan starts randomly rummaging through the car like a man on a mission. He opens the glove compartment, shuffles through the insurance papers, then reaches his hands into the seat-back pockets before feeling around under his chair.

"What are you *doing*? You're supposed to be watching me, remember?" I say, trying to focus on the road.

"Checking to see if my long-lost charger is here; I came to check the insurance paperwork the other day. And I told you driving's like breathing—you're a pro at this; you don't even need me. Wait—what's this?" He pulls something from underneath the chair and sits back up. He dusts off the item and twists it around to inspect it.

Judging by the way he has gone still, it's probably something of value. I sneak a peek at him and clock the widening of his eyes as he grips the item in his hand. It's a perfume bottle.

"What's wrong? Are you okay?" I say, alternating between glancing at my brother and the road.

"This was Arafat's," Ihsaan mumbles, uncapping the perfume bottle. "He must have left it here by accident." He hesitates, then presses the bottle against the inside of his wrist and sprays it once.

In a couple seconds, the entire car fills with the familiar, comforting scent of our older brother. And as if on cue, the tears I had been holding back since Mikaal's house surge forward.

It's astonishing how quickly my body reacts to the scent. I remember learning that smell is the only sense that bypasses the thalamus and goes straight to the primary olfactory cortex of the brain. That's why it hits differently—why it's so tightly bound to memory.

It also explains why, as soon as Ihsaan sprays the perfume, I'm so overcome with emotion that I barely make it to the curb and shift the gear to park, turning the car off. Taking a deep, shuddering breath, I wipe my eyes of the tears that have accumulated.

"God, I'm sorry, Hayat," Ihsaan whispers to me, but his eyes are glazed over too as he hugs the bottle against his chest.

It's strange, how one moment we're bantering like any normal siblings, and the next grief suddenly overpowers us, reminding us that we had gone too long without it. I've often felt guilty when I've laughed or cracked a joke or tried to have a good day because my brother is *dead* and that's an undeniable fact. But recently, I've somewhat begun to make peace with it. Chasing the *what-ifs* left me restless and anxious. Acceptance, however quiet, has slowly settled in.

But sometimes—sometimes a single moment changes

everything. Like when I'm driving with my brother and remember how the last time I sat behind the wheel, I had two brothers. Or how I used to be the kind of girl who would burst into tears in a situation like this, but right now I feel strangely patient. Composed.

Especially when I think of Arafat's words from my dream: *You're stronger than you know.*

I take a deep breath, inhaling the scent that has taken up space in the car and in our hearts. "Ihsaan, can I ask you something?" He nods for me to continue. "What was the last thing you talked to him about?"

He sucks in a sharp breath, turning to me with wounded eyes. "You tell me first."

"I said good night to him," I murmur. "The next morning he was asleep when I went to school, and we got the call later that evening and…that was the last time I ever spoke to him."

Ihsaan cradles the perfume bottle in his hands like it's the most precious thing he owns. "I…I told him I could never be like him. That I'd always be trying and trying and trying but I would never be able to come close to the man he was: the future doctor, the better brother, the pride of our parents, the better person in every way." He laughs bitterly. "It's terrifying, not knowing what your last words to someone are."

His words are laced with so much agony that I want nothing more than to reach forward and wrap him in the warmest, tightest hug. But I know that's not what he wants or needs.

It hits me suddenly—no wonder Ihsaan has looked so haunted over the past few months. We both lost our brother and have been grieving, but Ihsaan is drowning in the guilt of their last conversation.

Dream Arafat's words about Ihsaan flit through my mind again. *You've been striving towards excellence for months. To be honest, you're too hard on yourself.*

"Ihsaan…" I whisper. "I saw Arafat in my dream the other day."

His head snaps towards me, eyes alight with hunger. "Really? I never see him in my dreams. It's like he's mad at me or something."

This statement is so absurd that I reach forward and squeeze his shoulder. "Stop, Ihsaan. You know that's crazy, right? Why would he be mad at you? Don't do that to yourself, please."

He's quiet for a moment before he says, "What did you see in your dream?"

I relay the dream to him, describing at length what Arafat said about Ihsaan and the meaning of his name. As I'm speaking, Ihsaan's posture goes from rigid to sagging. All the fight leaves him, and a cleft appears between his brows. His eyes, in a rare moment of vulnerability, fill with tears.

I can't help it; I entwine my fingers with his.

"Ihsaan," I say quietly. "Arafat was right, even if it was a dream. You're too hard on yourself. There's absolutely nothing wrong with who you are; stop trying to be someone else or achieve perfection. Ihsaan means the *pursuit* of excellence, not excellence itself. Try every day to be a better man than you were yesterday, but not because you feel like you aren't enough. And not because you're trying to be Arafat, but because you want to be a better *Ihsaan*. You are, and will always be, enough."

He catches me totally off guard by crushing me against his chest, burying his face in my hair. I quickly return the embrace, rubbing a soothing palm over his back.

"You scare me, did you know that?" he mumbles against my hair. "When you talk like a grown up. It freaks me out. And it makes it hard for me to keep roasting you and calling you a churail."

I huff out a laugh and pull back, lightly shoving his shoulder. "Leave it to you to ruin the moment."

He grins, but it doesn't reach his eyes.

I tilt my head. "There's something else."

"Oh, no. I don't know how much more of therapist Hayat Amanullah I can handle."

"Don't worry, our session is almost over," I joke. I turn so my body is angled towards him and fold my arms across my chest. "Aneela?"

"Ugh," he groans, covering his face with a hand. "I've had enough from Mama and Papa. Can we not, please?"

I tug at his hand. "We have to. You can't run away from me forever."

He peeks at me through his fingers. "This is really damn awkward, okay? Let's just not do this."

I pull the hand off his face and lock both in an iron grip. "Do you want to marry her?"

He doesn't respond, just struggles against my grip. But his silence is answer enough.

"Then fight for her, Ihsaan. Adding on to everything I just said, you don't deserve to suffer." Ihsaan struggles against my hold but gives up when I relentlessly pin his hands down. "Our brother was an amazing person. He always cared about us and *always* wanted the best for us. For *all* of us. If he was here right now, do you know what he would say?"

"If Arafat was here, things would be different," Ihsaan mumbles, casting his eyes downward. "He would be marrying Aneela."

I huff. "Metaphorically, I mean. If he was here with us in this moment, he would say it's the qadr of Allah. That God's plan works in wonderful, mysterious ways. And that above everything else, Arafat cared about your *happiness*." I let go of Ihsaan's hands and duck to look into his eyes. "Don't do this to yourself, please. You've been unnecessarily drowning in guilt for so long, blaming yourself because you think you aren't enough and because of the last words you said to him."

For a moment, the car is silent, echoing with the force of my words. Then I give his hands a comforting squeeze. "Let it go, Ihsaan. Let the guilt go. It's bogging you down and it isn't letting you move forward. And moving forward doesn't mean you're forgetting your brother or dishonoring his memory; on the contrary, it means you're honoring his memory by living your life the way he would have wanted: happily."

Ihsaan is silent, but he stares at our entwined hands, as if the sight of them is the only thing grounding him.

We don't speak about it again, but the next evening, my mom

rushes into my room with twinkling eyes and a bright smile. She settles at the edge of my bed and grabs my hand. "Hayat," she says hurriedly, voice alight with excitement. "He said yes!"

"Who said yes, Mama?" I touch her cheek gently. "What are you talking about?"

"I don't know what changed his mind, but Ihsaan said we can talk to Aneela's parents to see what she thinks and how she's feeling." She covers her mouth with trembling fingers, eyes glittering with happiness. "And if Aneela agrees, we can arrange a meeting for her and Ihsaan!"

It takes me a moment to process her words. Then a slow grin spreads across my face.

Twenty-seven

Begonia: A warning

MY PARENTS WASTE NO time in calling Aneela's parents. They have a lengthy conversation over the phone, which I unabashedly eavesdrop on, and when my mom is ending the call, I rush quickly away from their bedroom door.

Only to find Ihsaan not far from where I had been standing, huddled in a corner of the hallway and trying to make himself invisible.

I fold my arms and smirk. "I can see you, you know."

He squeezes his eyes shut and presses himself against the wall. "No. Nothing to see here. This is just another part of the wall."

A burst of giggles escapes me. I walk up to my brother and poke his shoulder. He opens one eye and gives me a sheepish look. "Ihsaan, were you *eavesdropping*?"

His other eye opens and he sighs, rubbing the spot where I poked him. "Why do your fingers feel like knives?"

"Why are you avoiding the question?"

"Well, *you* were eavesdropping too," he shoots back defensively.

A slow, mischievous smile spreads across my face. "Dear, dear, Ihsaan Amanullah. *This* excited to hear what Aneela's parents have to say, are we?"

He opens his mouth to retaliate but at that moment my parents exit their room. Immediately Ihsaan and I straighten, wiping the smiles off our faces and standing shoulder to shoulder with our arms behind our backs.

Papa's eyes are glittering as his gaze darts between the two of us. "Do I need to ask what you two are doing here?"

My mom tsks. "Sharam karo. Listening to your parents' conversations." Then her face breaks into a smile as she fixes her attention on Ihsaan. "Beta, her parents were very happy. Aneela happened to be home, and they spoke to her before calling us back. She seemed a bit shocked, understandably, but she has asked for some time to think about it and pray istikhara, as you did."

I snap my head towards Ihsaan, barely contained excitement roiling through me. He tries to play the news off as nonchalant, but I don't miss the spark of happiness in his eyes. He squeezes his eyes shut for a moment as if in contentment, then reopens them and nods to my parents.

I nudge him playfully. "We can see right through your act."

"Oh, shut up." He lightly shoves my shoulder and dashes downstairs, leaving the three of us exchanging overjoyed glances.

"I hope she really considers it and gives it some thought," Mama murmurs.

Papa wraps an arm around her shoulder. "She will, Insha Allah. And Allah will grant both of them what is best for them."

A week later, my mom receives a phone call from Aneela's mom. I wait with bated breath as she picks it up in front of me, then squeal as soon as she turns it off a few minutes later.

Aneela has agreed to a meeting.

Maybe it's the excitement of our home finally being showered with happiness, or maybe the thought has been marinating in my head for the past two weeks anyway, but the first person I want to share the news with is Abeer. I rush to my room and grab my phone, prepared to text her a footlong apology and urge her to meet me.

I stop short when I see a text from Rameez, received thirty-two minutes ago.

how are you?

Guilt immediately seizes me. I've been thinking of him periodically over the past few days but haven't had the courage to reach out. Every time I would open our chat, something stopped me from typing out a request to meet and talk. I felt as if I was having an out-of-body experience.

He probably thinks I don't give a damn about him, especially after our last conversation and the radio silence on my end.

I sigh, my fingers hovering over the screen as I mull over an appropriate response.

Maybe it's the adrenaline from hearing about Aneela's decision, but a couple seconds and a spur of the moment decision later, I've sent Rameez a text that reads: **do you wanna meet today?**

This is it. Maybe today I can tell him how I really feel, what I'm comfortable with, and what's been making me uneasy. Maybe we can finally come to some sort of understanding—one we can both be content with.

An hour later, once I've changed and am heading downstairs, Mama asks, "Where are you going, Hayat?"

I hesitate, eyes roving over her sweater dress, her cheeks suffused with a pretty blush. "Just meeting some friends."

Her face falls. "Oh. Your dad and Ihsaan are leaving work early today, so we were making plans to go out. Ihsaan wanted to try the halal Korean barbecue place in Mahwah."

"Oh." I'm rooted in place by her words. We haven't gone out as a family since Arafat passed away.

But…if I go back on my plan to meet Rameez, I might further reinforce the idea that I don't care about him. The image of his crestfallen face from our last meeting flashes in my mind.

Once again, Arafat's words echo: *Kuch bhi karo, lekin kisi ka dil kabhi na dukhao.*

I don't want to intentionally hurt anyone—or break anyone's heart.

Mama must sense my hesitation because she quickly adds, "It's okay, though. You go ahead and have fun."

Uneasiness crawls through me. Why do I feel like I'm standing at a crossroads, and a step in any direction will be costly? We haven't gone out as a family in months. But I've already said yes to Rameez.

Sighing, I kiss my mom's forehead and bid her goodbye. Every step out of the house feels like trudging through water. When I finally make it to Rameez's car at the end of the block, I've been fisting my hands so tight that there are half-moon indentations in my palms.

When Rameez sees me, his face breaks into a guarded smile. Just the sight of it causes my worries to momentarily melt away. I shove everything but him to the back of my mind—a habit I've allowed myself to become dangerously accustomed to—as I settle in the passenger seat.

"How are you?" he asks.

I nod. "I'm well, thank you. How are you?"

This feels strangely formal. But what does one say to someone they haven't spoken to in over a week?

"Good. Where to?" Rameez's voice breaks me out of my thoughts. I turn to him, gaze roving over the expectant look on his face.

"You pick," I murmur, then rush to add, "just not anywhere near that halal Korean spot in Mahwah."

He gives me a skeptical look. "That's a drive anyway. But you don't like the food there?"

"No, it's just…my family's gonna be there."

Immediately his expression shutters. For a moment guilt takes a hold of me, but then Rameez nods and begins driving.

The entire ride, he chatters nonstop, a forced smile stretched across his face—like he's trying too hard to pretend everything's fine between us.

I play along.

All the while, dread begins to consume me. Slow and painful. I feel like I've gotten too close to the fire, and instead of nursing my burns, I don't move away from it.

Why have I begun to feel this way in Rameez's presence? When we began…whatever this is, I'd been wary since day one. But over time, as I became more lenient with breaking my boundaries, it became easier to shove my anxieties to the back of my mind.

Recently, however, it's been increasingly difficult to just live in the moment and put a pin in my worries. I don't know if it's because my poorly made decisions are finally catching up to me, or if it's because something's changed.

I take a deep breath as we pull into the parking lot of a Turkish restaurant—a popular spot in New Brunswick and one of my mom's favorites—and plaster on a smile. I just have to get through this evening. Whatever comes next can wait.

Inside, we slide into a booth by the window. The waiter takes our orders, and once he walks away, Rameez begins drumming his fingers against the tabletop. I scramble for something to say, but he spares me the effort.

"So are you excited about attending Princeton?"

It takes me a second to process the question before a strange sadness settles over me. A fleeting thought flashes through my mind: how do you stop communicating with someone who knows so much about your dreams and desires?

"I am," I reply. "But also nervous and anxious, to be honest. I don't want to leave my family, especially my mom."

Speaking of, I wonder if they've reached the restaurant yet. A pang of guilt stirs in my chest at the thought of not being there with them.

"I know what you mean." Rameez reaches forward and caresses my fingers. His eyes are guarded as he observes my reaction, but when I don't pull away he continues to rub soothing circles on my skin.

How do you go back to a time before you knew what this felt like? And why am I already imagining a time when I won't have it?

"You okay?" His voice is soft, breaking down my already crumbling walls. I smile weakly and nod, grateful when our appetizers arrive and I can remove my hand from under his.

We dig in, eating in near silence save for the occasional "Wow, this is good." When our main courses arrive, we pick at each other's plates, exchanging small talk between bites.

I don't know if it's the unspoken tension between us, or the familiarity of sharing food like we always have—or maybe it's everything all at once—but suddenly my throat tightens with tears. I can't bring myself to meet his eyes.

The bell above the door jingles, and the sound breaks me out of my trance. I barely make out an "excuse me" before rushing to the back exit, tears blurring my vision. Rameez calls my name several times, but I ignore him and keep running.

I stumble outside, the cold air whipping sharply against my face. My tears halt momentarily, and I feel infinitesimally better.

Then the door swings open behind me.

"Hayat," Rameez says breathlessly. "Are you okay? What's wrong?

Having left my jacket inside, I wrap my arms around myself, rapid tears pooling in my eyes at the concern in his voice. I shake my head in response, afraid that if I try to speak, I'll burst into tears.

He takes a step, and suddenly I feel the warmth of his body right behind mine. He's not touching me, but he's close—so close that even a breath would bridge the distance.

"Hayat," he murmurs. "You've been distant all week and quiet all evening and now…please tell me what's wrong."

The softness of his voice breaks something in me. I slowly turn, raising my teary-eyed gaze to his.

His face falls. He raises a tentative hand and cups my cheek, rubbing his thumb against it. "Please talk to me."

As if on instinct, my hand goes up and wraps around his. We gaze deeply into one another's eyes, and I feel as if we've been suspended in time.

"I'm sorry," I whisper, impulsively tucking a strand of hair behind his ear. Why do I always reach for touch to soothe myself with him? And why does this fleeting comfort leave me feeling even worse afterward?

Something shifts in Rameez's tender gaze. Resolve? Before I can make sense of it—before I know what's happening, he's bending his face towards mine.

Oh, no. I think I've given the wrong signals. I'm so *stupid*. Oh God, oh God. How do I stop this?

My heart beats rapidly against my chest. Just as Rameez's lips hover an inch from mine, the door swings open behind him.

We spring apart instantly, but my relief is short-lived.

"Ihsaan?" I gasp.

My brother is standing in the doorway, eyes wide with shock and something else…disappointment? Guilt and panic flare within me, and I step further away from Rameez.

Moments ago, I felt as if I was suspended in time. As if I was existing inside a snow globe. Now, the glass feels shattered. And I'm left blinking at the shards, disoriented and exposed.

Ihsaan casts Rameez a pained look, then says in a voice of dead calm, "Let's go, Hayat."

I dare a glance at Rameez, whose shoulders are hunched and eyes are apologetic. "Ihsaan," he starts. "We weren't—"

"Please," Ihsaan cuts him off. "Let me talk to my sister."

"Ihsaan!" I shout as he turns and rushes inside the restaurant. I throw Rameez a wounded look, which he mirrors with a quiet, "I'm sorry, Hayat."

Then I rush after my brother.

I run straight into him as he halts abruptly in front of the bathrooms. He grabs my arm and pulls me aside, shielding us from the view of our parents, who are seated at a booth and looking down at the menus.

There are so many things I want to say. Apologies, explanations, questions. But what comes out of my mouth is an absurd "I thought you guys were going to the Korean place?"

Ihsaan's nostrils flare as he folds his arms. "There was an hour and a half wait time. And unlucky for you, Mama loves it here, so we ended up right where you were having your…adventure." He pinches the bridge of his nose between his thumb and forefinger and closes his eyes, inhaling a sharp breath. "You wanna tell me what's going on?"

My heart is still pulsating furiously against my chest from what almost happened—and what Ihsaan saw. But the tone of his voice jars me out of my shock, leaving room only for anger. "*Adventure?*" I hiss. Ihsaan's eyes open, and he pins with an austere gaze. "That's it? You're just gonna assume you know what's going on? You're not even gonna give me a chance to explain?"

"I *am* giving you a chance to explain," he snaps.

I flinch, ignoring his statement and laughing bitterly as hurt roils throughout me. "Wow. I thought we were finally getting somewhere, Ihsaan. I thought trust was finally building between us. I guess I was wrong." I'm about to stomp away from him when he grabs my arm and holds me in place.

His gaze softens. "Look…I'm sorry. You're right. But what am I supposed to think when you lie about where you're going and I find you with a guy an inch away from you?"

Some of my anger ebbs away at the confusion in his voice. He's reacting the way any brother would. I extract my arm from his grasp and sigh. "I'm…I was trying to…" I slump against the wall, raising my gaze to the miniature chandelier above us. "I don't know, honestly," I whisper. "I don't know, Ihsaan."

My brother stays silent, giving me space to gather myself. Moments later, the truth spills out of me like an unraveling spool.

"I was trying to figure out what to do about our situation."

"Situation?"

Blinking back tears, I shove off the wall and take a deep breath. "This is not the time and place. I promise I will tell you, but not now. Mama and Papa are waiting."

The intense cut of his shoulders signals he's not ready to end this conversation. But to his credit, he nods tightly and follows me to our parents' table.

"Sorry, guys. Important call," Ihsaan says cheerfully as we approach the table.

"It's okay—oh, Shehzaadi!" Papa's face breaks into a million-dollar smile when he sees me. "I thought you were with your friends?"

I plaster on a bright smile, clearing my throat so as not to sound like I've been crying. "I was! Right here, actually. But I wanted to spend time with you guys, too. So here I am!"

Mama kisses my temple as I slide in next to her. "We're glad you're here, beta. We just ordered appetizers, so everyone decide what you want for the main course."

As my family happily converses, my heart drips with sorrow. I wish I could join in, wish I could force laughs like Ihsaan and pretend everything's fine. But as Rameez discreetly pays at the counter and heads outside, I make the mistake of locking eyes with him.

His are two wide pools of sadness and apology.

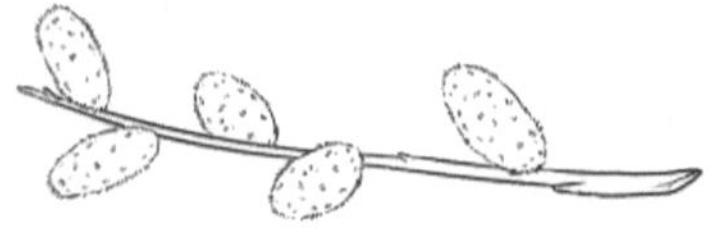

Twenty-eight

Willow: Goodbye

ONCE WE'RE HOME, MY parents kiss us goodnight and head upstairs, making plans to watch a movie before sleeping. My mom's laughter permeates throughout the house, my dad's arms wrapped around her shoulders as they whisper in one another's ears like star-crossed teens.

My eyes fill with happy tears as I watch them disappear. Too long has their relationship been quiet and strained—ever since they lost their oldest child. They deserve this happiness.

When I head to the terrace, Ihsaan follows close behind. I switch on the light and make a show of monitoring the condition of my sunflowers, and to Ihsaan's credit, he doesn't bombard me with questions.

I knew I took a risk when I decided to plant sunflowers in *fall*, but I'm still holding my breath and praying for them to grow.

When Ihsaan finally speaks, his voice is a quiet thrum in the space between us. "You okay?"

I nod, my back still turned to him.

"Do you wanna talk about it? It's okay if you're not ready right now and…I'm sorry for cornering you at the restaurant." I hear him sigh. "It's just…Walking in on you like that…"

He trails off, and I suck in a sharp breath, whirling around. Since Ihsaan stumbled on me and Rameez, discomfort has been plaguing me. He's not really the macho man type—he's overprotective at times, like any brother would be. Still, I don't want him to get the wrong idea.

But the entire car ride home, I kept thinking: What *is* the wrong idea? There's no denying what I've been doing with Rameez for the past couple of months—or what I had been about to do tonight. The thought terrifies me even now. So why am I ashamed to speak about it?

I'm tired of holding all this in. I'm tired of constantly playing tug of war in my mind—is this right, is this wrong? Is it wrong if it makes me feel good temporarily? Why does Abeer's observation about how I've changed keep haunting me? Why do I keep thinking of Aneela's words about how change is problematic when you start disliking who you've become?

Whatever decisions I've made, it's time to own them.

"You might wanna sit down." I gesture to the wicker chairs.

Ihsaan rubs his shoulders, teeth chattering slightly. "Okay, but let me start the fire."

I settle in the chair next to my brother's as he prepares the fire pit. Once the flames are licking the air and the scent of crisp winter smoke surrounds us, Ihsaan grabs two blankets from inside and hands me one before settling down.

We snuggle into our blankets, gazing at the fire in silence. Then I take a deep breath and tell him everything.

How I've been drawn to Rameez. How I never imagined he'd be interested in me. How his attention made me feel special—less isolated—and was a relief from our silent house. How we started seeing each other a few months ago. And how, despite the happiness, I've felt morally conflicted ever since.

Ihsaan listens quietly, occasionally stoking the fire when the flames begin to die down. His silence allows me to ramble comfortably, and I find myself able to relay things I've been concealing even from myself. When I finish telling him my story right down to tonight's events, he's quiet for so long that I begin to think he's angry or upset.

But when he speaks, he turns to me with a softness in his gaze that I'm entirely unprepared for. "I'm only going to say two things," he murmurs. "First of all, I want you to ask yourself something." Ihsaan places a hand over his heart. "Do you think that being with Rameez makes you a better person? Does he push you to be a better version of yourself and a better Muslim?" His voice lowers, as if he's afraid of the effect his words might have on me. "Do you find yourself wanting to become a better person when you're in his presence?"

His words strike me somewhere deep. My breath hitches, and I turn away from the force of his gaze, focusing on the flames in the fire pit curling against the cold air.

Ihsaan continues in the same gentle voice. "Second, every relationship gives us something we're missing in our lives. For some, it's love. For others, it's comfort, security, or stability. And a lot of times, it's ideally a combination of things. Whatever the return may be, we invest in relationships because they fill a void in us. And as a result, we either gain or lose something from them—sometimes both."

He pauses, letting me absorb his words. "Hayat, you need to ask yourself: What does your relationship with Rameez give you, and what do you lose because of it?"

A shiver passes through me, unrelated to the cold. I wrap the blanket tighter around myself, Ihsaan's words echoing in my mind.

My brother stands, folds his blanket, and places it on his chair. Before heading inside, he places a hand against my shoulder and squeezes reassuringly. "And then ask yourself if the gain or loss in the relationship is worth it.'"

Long after my brother has headed inside, I remain wrapped in my blanket, staring deep into the fire's embers. As if the answers to all the questions plaguing me may be found within the dying flames.

The week passes in a blur. Each day feels more mechanical than the last—wake up, do chores, tend to the garden, go to sleep, repeat. Nights are restless, filled with tossing and turning. Days are spent drowning in uneasy thoughts.

The stress clawing at my insides has left its mark: ghost-like shadows under my eyes. My parents keep asking if I'm okay, and I offer them the same rehearsed reassurances.

Only Ihsaan sees through my lies. He watches me like a hawk every day, his gaze heavy and unrelenting. More than once, he looks as if he wants to say something, then pretends to busy himself in a task.

By the time Friday rolls around, I feel as if I've been on autopilot all week and every emotion I've been trying to shove away is threatening to consume me. I can't even bring myself to be excited for Ihsaan, who is meeting Aneela with both our parents this evening.

My parents are sitting in the living room and having breakfast. I pour their chai into cups, arrange them on a tray, and head towards the table. But I'm so troubled by the thoughts that have been swimming in my head for the past week that I don't pay attention to where I'm headed. My elbow knocks against the doorway of the kitchen and I stumble forward, sending the tray of chai flying.

The crash of porcelain snaps me out of my daze. Shards scatter across the floor, chai bleeding into the marble tiles. I stand frozen, eyes widening at the mess.

"Shehzaadi?" My dad's frantic voice sounds strangely warbled, as if I'm hearing it through a glass. "Are you okay?"

Mama's grip on my arm jars me out of my shock. I turn my widened eyes to her concerned ones as she shakes me and asks, "Hayat, baby, are you hurt?"

Slowly I shake my head, my eyes flicking back to the shattered porcelain strewn across the floor. My parents have stepped around the mess to reach me, abandoning their breakfast as their voices rise with concern.

I don't know if the spilled chai is a culmination of the stress and anxiety that has kept me restless this entire week, or if the worried eyes of my parents are the last straw, but suddenly every emotion I've been holding back comes rushing forth.

My shoulders shake as I break out into sobs. My parents exchange worried glances and bombard me with question after question about where I'm hurt. The distress in their voices only makes me cry harder as I wrap my arms around myself and slide to the floor.

"Shehzaadi, you're worrying us," my dad says in a panic-stricken voice as he and Mama join me on the floor. "Please tell us where it hurts. Did you get cut? Are you bleeding anywhere?"

"Beta," Mama says worriedly as she pushes the hair back from my face. "Kaha lagi hai, meri jaan? Where are you hurt?"

"*Everywhere*," I manage between sobs, curling tighter into myself until my forehead rests against my knees.

I'm tired of being strong. I'm tired of holding everything in and pretending it isn't poisoning me from the inside out. I'm tired of carefully curating expressions, slipping on masks just so no one else has to worry.

For once, I want to stop caring about who I might worry. For once, I want to be taken care of.

My parents wrap their arms around me and hold me close, whispering words of comfort in my ears. Mama smoothes my hair down my back and Papa kisses the top of my head. I melt in their arms as my breath hitches with sobs, their voices grounding me here—to this moment.

Even after the tears subside, they don't let go. They stay beside me, telling silly jokes and lighthearted stories. Weak laughter bubbles out of me—fragile but real. They don't ask me what's wrong. They don't push me to explain. They simply surround me with warmth, their presence soothing everything aching inside.

Once the mess is cleaned and I've assured my parents that I'm okay, my dad heads off to work. I'm about to wash the dishes when my mom grabs my elbow and gestures for me to sit with her at the kitchen table.

"Hayat," she begins, tucking strands of hair away from my face.

Her chin wobbles. "My love, I don't *ever* want you to cry. The sight of your tears does something to my heart."

I squeeze her hand reassuringly. "I'm fine now, Mama."

She shakes her head, tears pooling in her eyes. "No, you're not. And it's all my fault."

"Mama, what are you talking about?"

She places her head in her hands, quiet for a moment before she murmurs, "I think I've been seeing you, my daughter, as an extension of myself this whole time. As long as you were okay, I would be okay. I've been…worrying about Ihsaan and your dad but I never stopped to ask you how you were doing. Or see how much you've been sacrificing." She raises her tear-stained gaze to mine. "I'm your mother. *I* should have been taking care of you. You've been doing absolutely everything possible for this family. But you're just a *kid*, Hayat. Baby, you're just a kid." Mama gathers me in her arms and crushes me to her chest, rocking us back and forth.

The force of her words and the sound of her erratic breathing causes tightness to spread through my chest. I wrap my arms around her and bury my face in her neck, inhaling the sweet, familiar scent of my mother.

I didn't realize how much I've missed this—how much I needed it.

"I'm sorry!" Mama hiccups through tears, grasping me tighter with every breath.

"It's okay, Mama, it's okay. We've all been grieving—"

"*You* haven't!" she mumbles against my hair. "You've been forced to push everything down so you could put a smile on all of our faces. I'm sorry. I'm so sorry, meri jaan. I'm sorry for not being there for you."

I huff out a laugh. "Stop it. Stop saying sorry. I don't wanna hear you say any of this stuff again, okay? I love you guys. You're *everything* to me, and *nothing* is more important than the three of you anymore."

I halt at my own words, something clicking into place in my heart. Something I feel I've been wrestling with for far too long.

Once I've calmed my mother down and she's retired upstairs to take a shower, I take a deep breath and grab my phone.

Then I do what I've been avoiding all week.

I open my messages with Rameez, scrolling through the few texts he sent over the past several days. My fingers tremble as I type three blunt words: **can we meet***?*

I know what I have to do. I think, deep down, I've known for weeks—maybe since the very beginning. But Ihsaan's questions, echoing through every corner of my mind, have finally burrowed deep enough to unlock the last piece of the puzzle I've been trying to solve.

Rameez responds a couple minutes later. **sure. when & where?**

My heart thuds painfully against my chest, as if protesting what I'm about to do.

washington rock at 6?

He responds with a thumbs-up emoji. Tears sting the corners of my eyes. His quiet willingness—his care—makes this even harder.

But later that evening, once Ihsaan and my parents have left to meet Aneela and her parents, I find myself standing behind the ledge at Washington Rock. The New York skyline glimmers in the distance. The air is sharp and cold. The last few migrating ducks call out overhead, their cries echoing through the frosty stillness. I wrap an arm around myself and burrow deeper into my jacket, my breath rising in soft, puffy clouds.

I hear Rameez before I see him.

The engine of his car dies down in the distance, followed by the sound of his quiet footsteps. I squeeze my eyes shut painfully.

I recognize the sound of his *footsteps*, for God's sake.

When I open my eyes, he's standing quietly next to me, gazing at the soft rays of sun dancing across the frost-laced treetops.

A sharp ache pricks at my chest as I come to a realization. This is the last time we'll be standing here together. The last time we'll be Hayat Amanullah and Rameez Khan at *our* Washington Rock.

Even though I know with absolute certainty that what I'm

about to do is for the best—for both of us—it doesn't make it hurt any less.

Rameez takes a shuddering breath, a puff of air curling in the sky. "I've been really worried, and you haven't been responding to any of my texts—"

"Rameez," I interrupt. "We can't do this anymore." I squeeze my eyes shut, unwilling to see the look on his face. But he's quiet for so long that I'm forced to open them.

He's staring at me, eyes guarded, unreadable. The faded winter sun dances across his curls and glimmers against his skin, and for a moment I want to remain suspended in time.

He shatters my illusion by saying, "What?"

I shake my head. "We can't do"—I gesture vaguely between us—"this. Us. Whatever this is…anymore."

A crease forms between his brows. "If this is about what happened at the restaurant last week, I'm so sorry Hayat. I shouldn't have—"

"It's not just that." I cut him off, sharper than I mean to. "I just…we can't, Rameez."

The line between his brows deepens, eyes marred by panic. "Um…what's wrong? Did I do something to upset you or—"

"*Please*," I make out desperately. "Please don't make this harder than it already is."

He's quiet as I attempt to gain my bearings, but I don't miss the tense set of his shoulders.

"Rameez, the past couple of months with you have been… unquestionably amazing. You came into my life when I was drowning. Back in August, I was so vulnerable and in such a dark place." I laugh, bitter and soft. "You helped pull me out of it." I pause, the memories pressing against my chest like ice. "After Arafat died, no one in my family really talked to me. My dad tried to busy himself with work, my mom never left her room, and Ihsaan became so distant. I was so damn lonely, Rameez."

I wrap my arms around myself, watching my breath curl into the air like smoke.

"And then you came along and…You brought light to my life. You filled a void in me, Rameez. One I had been desperate to fill."

As Rameez watches me with guarded eyes, Ihsaan's words filter through my mind. *Every relationship gives us something we're missing in our lives. What does your relationship with Rameez give you?*

I've spent the better part of this week haunted by this question. Every toss and turn in bed, every waking moment riddled with restlessness, has brought me back to this.

Rameez happened upon me when I was vulnerable—sick with loneliness and starved for affection. He didn't just offer comfort, he gave me something I hadn't realized I needed. *Care.* And because of that care, I grew stronger. Arafat's words from my dream were no lie—I *have* grown up. And Rameez has been a significant part of the reason why.

I take a shuddering breath. "But…I've realized that I've become emotionally and physically dependent on you to continue filling that void in me. I've started to crave your presence because it allows me to forget everything for the moments we're together."

I pause, the truth pressing against my chest.

"But then? Then what? I come crashing back from cloud nine and realize what sacrifices I've been making." I swallow thickly. "Rameez, I've been compromising too much for this relationship. I haven't been…" I rub a hand along the length of my face. "I haven't been quite myself."

His voice is shaky when he responds. "I never…I never noticed you were uncomfortable. Have I been forcing you to do something you're not okay with?"

I blow out a sigh and meet his wounded gaze. "I hate to say this because it's so damn cliché, but it's not you, Rameez. It's me. I never verbally voiced my concerns, and I shouldn't have expected you to magically understand them." I toe a patch of frozen grass and laugh bitterly. "I never went to mixed gatherings, never hung out with guys—heck, I never even saved a *guy's number* if it wasn't related to school. I've been indulging in things I'm not necessarily comfortable with, and it's not fair to blame you for them. I'm a human with free will; you didn't force me into anything. But it's like I've been playing tug of war with myself for the past couple of months now, and…it isn't fair to you. None of this is fair to you, or to myself. I can't continue to depend on you for affection and comfort."

Ihsaan's questions continue to filter through my mind.

Do you think that being with Rameez makes you a better person?

Ask yourself if the gain or loss in the relationship is worth it.

What have I gained? Temporary happiness and affection in Rameez's presence. But has it been worth the sleepless nights, the dread-filled waking hours, the moral unease that gnaws at me? Has every date filled with laughter and smiles been worth the anxiety that claws at my throat afterward—the feeling that I've been doing something wrong, that I've been losing Hayat Amanullah while indulging Rameez Khan?

Suddenly Abeer's words flash through my mind. *Just…be sure you're coming back to* you. *To Hayat.*

I suck in a sharp breath, realization striking me hard and deep. I've been losing myself; I've been losing Hayat. I've been compromising my morals for a temporary laugh or two with Rameez. I've been putting my scruples on the chopping block in exchange for sweet nothings.

Ask yourself if the gain or loss in the relationship is worth it.

I raise my tear-filled gaze to Rameez's perplexed one, and suddenly everything clicks into place. The time I've spent with him, the questions that have troubled me afterward, the crossroads I've come to.

And then, Papa's words from seemingly a lifetime ago: *Sometimes the most noble thing to do is to let them go, even if you love them. Especially if you love them.*

At the time, I had been shocked by his statement and Ihsaan's decision to let go of Aneela. I kept asking myself how it was possible to convince the heart to give up what it yearned for, to convince the heart that what it desired may not be what was best for it. I battled with the question of whether it made a person stronger or weaker to let someone go.

I don't think my feelings for Rameez can be equated with something as powerful as *love*, but I finally understand the magnitude of my father's words.

"I've lost so much; I don't want to lose myself or my family. I want to be better. I want to be a better person and a better Muslim. A better Hayat. A true Hayat," I whisper through trembling lips. "I'm sorry, Rameez. I'm so sorry."

He's been oddly quiet as I've spoken, but as we lock gazes, something in his eyes gives me pause.

He's been anticipating this. However shocked and upset he is, something in his eyes tells me he's been expecting this to happen, one way or another. Maybe he's sensed it from my words, or maybe he's known all along that I've been battling myself by being with him. Or perhaps he never intended for this to last. Either way, I watch as the fight drains from him, as his shoulders sag, as the light dims in his eyes. My heart aches.

He isn't fighting back. Or trying to convince me to change my mind.

Maybe deep down, we both know this has to happen.

"Well...*I'm* sorry, Hayat," he says quietly, lowering his gaze. "For not being the right man for you. For making you feel like you had to choose between me or yourself."

Something shatters in my chest, splintering my insides. I take a tentative step forward, and his head snaps up, sadness in his gaze. "Don't say sorry," I say. "This is already hard enough."

Rameez exhales shakily. His face contorts into a weak smile as he murmurs, "I've enjoyed all the time I've spent with you. Thank you for the best memories."

My throat thickens with tears and unsaid words. Rameez opens his arms and raises tentative brows. "One last time?" he whispers.

Everything in me tells me I shouldn't. That doing this now will only make it hurt even worse later. But the problem is I've always been impulsive in his presence. I can't bring myself to care about later.

I step forward and fall against Rameez's chest one last time as he crushes me in his arms. I squeeze my eyes shut as he places a tender kiss against my hair.

"Thank you," I whisper in his ear. "Thank you for everything. And I'm so sorry."

When I pull back, Rameez smiles weakly and raises a hand to thumb my tears away. But halfway to my face, his hand pauses midair and I take a step back as he clears his throat.

The warmth we shared disappears as we pull apart. I mirror his forced smile and take a deep breath. "Goodbye, Rameez."

His lips turn up at one corner as he forces a bravado I know we both don't feel. "Goodbye, Hayat."

Having driven to Washington Rock myself, I only make it halfway home before tears clog my throat and blur my vision and I'm forced to pull over. Raucous sobs shake throughout my body as I press my forehead against the steering wheel, Rameez's sorrowful expression branded into my mind's eye.

Kuch bhi karo, lekin kisi ka dil kabhi na dukhao.

I know I did the right thing. I saved both Rameez and myself from a greater heartbreak, but that doesn't mean I haven't still hurt him.

I sniffle, swiping my tears away, battling with the thought that has begun to circle through my mind. Of the only person I want to see right now.

In the end, selfishness wins.

When Abeer enters the boba place, the mere sight of her brings fresh tears to my eyes. She takes one look at me, concern etched into her face, and pulls me into a breathless hug.

Crushed against my best friend with a wounded heart, I cry for the third time that day. Shoulders shaking, tears streaming endlessly down my face. When my breath starts to hitch, Abeer pulls back, her eyes wide with concern as she gently instructs me to breathe.

She goes to purchase my favorite boba—taro with tapioca balls—and sets it in front of me, her brows furrowed in concern.

She refuses to sit, placing her hand on her hips as she stands in front of me.

"I love my brother, but if Rameez did something, say the word. I'll teach him a lesson."

I've missed her so much over the past month that instead of prompting more tears, her words draw something between a sob and a laugh from me. I wrap my arms around her and bury my face in her chest, and she smoothes my hair against my head. "I'm sorry, Abeer. I've been such a bad friend, and I've been meaning to apologize forever but—"

"Shut up," she huffs, her body tensing. "Let's just get over this, okay? Let's pretend it never happened. I'm sorry, too. I shouldn't have exploded like that."

I laugh, the sound muffled by her sweater. "I love you."

"I love you too, bozo. Now stop crying." Abeer continues to caress my hair, and my eyelids flutter shut. Moments later, she whispers, "I will always support you, and I will always be here for you."

My arms tighten around my best friend. "Me, too. I promise."

We simply embrace each other for a few quiet moments. Then I pull back and Abeer thumbs my tears away. I grasp her hands and clutch them to my chest. "I'm sorry—"

Faux anger flickers across her face. "I said let's not—"

"No, please," I murmur, guiding her to sit beside me, still keeping a firm grasp on her hands in my lap. "I need to say this."

I focus on our entwined hands, slowly rubbing my thumbs across her skin.

I inhale a sharp breath. "You've always been there for me. Since day one. Unconditionally. You've been my safety net for years. I knew I could always fall back and you'd always be there. I didn't realize..." My breath hitches. "I didn't realize how easily I pushed you into the background of my life." I raise my teary gaze to her earnest one. "I've always been in your foreground, and I'm sorry for not putting you in mine. I'm sorry for not loving you as unconditionally as you've loved me."

She shakes her head gently, slipping one hand free and placing it against my cheek to swipe away a fallen tear.

"That's the thing about love," she says softly, a quiet smile blooming across her face. "It's unconditional."

I lean forward and embrace her again.

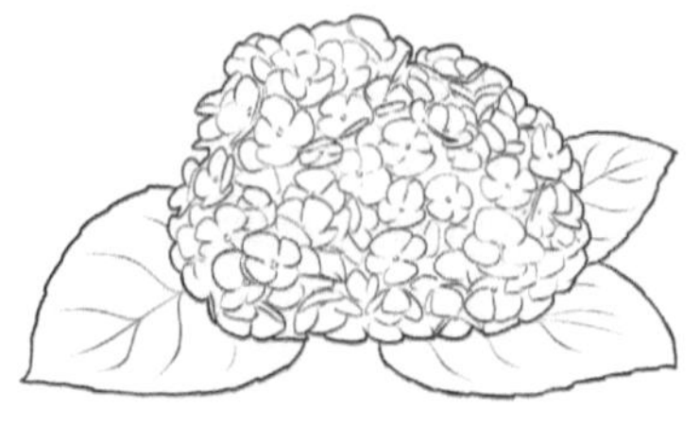

Twenty-nine

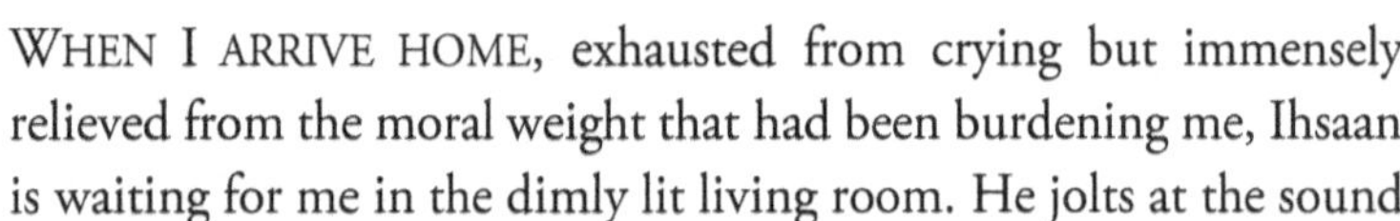

Green hydrangea: New beginnings

WHEN I ARRIVE HOME, exhausted from crying but immensely relieved from the moral weight that had been burdening me, Ihsaan is waiting for me in the dimly lit living room. He jolts at the sound of my keys and rushes towards me.

"You're still up?" I mumble, rubbing my eyes. "I texted in the family chat that I would be late—"

"She said yes!" Ihsaan blurts out, grabbing my shoulders and shaking me back and forth.

I blink at him, standing in the dark foyer and trying to process his words. He must sense my disorientation because he laughs breathlessly, shaking me again like he can't believe it himself. "Aneela said yes!"

After the clusterhell I've been through today, I had almost forgotten where Ihsaan and my parents went. His words throw me for a loop before my eyes spark with comprehension, a bout of happiness consuming me.

My response is too delayed, however, because Ihsaan squints his brows and cocks his head to the side. He pulls me into the light and examines me. "Hayat, what the hell happened to you? You look horrible. Are you okay?"

"Yeah, I'm fine." My voice comes out too high, and I plaster on a wide smile. "I'm so, so happy to hear that, Ihsaan. Genuinely. You guys will make the most beautiful couple."

He knits his brows, giving me a worried look. "What's up with you? You're not teasing me or making snarky jokes." He tugs at my hand and leads me to the living room, setting me on the sofa. Folding his arms, he stands in front of me, blocking any possibility of an exit.

"I'm okay, Ihsaan," I say reassuringly, massaging my temples. "Just tired."

A spark of understanding flashes in his eyes. "Does this have something to do with Rameez?"

My chest tightens at his name. "Can we just not talk about it, please?"

Ihsaan's expression softens. The lamp light casts a warm glow over his face, and for the first time in months, the tension in his shoulders seems to have melted. His dark circles have faded, and I think he hasn't needed his meds for a few days now.

"Whatever decision you made, it's probably for the best, Hayat," he murmurs. "You wouldn't do anything without thinking it through."

I want to believe him. I want to smile and be happy for him. But for the hundredth time today, tears sting my eyes. I turn away, but Ihsaan crouches down and meets my gaze.

"I know it's for the best and I know I did the right thing. I have no regrets. But God, if it's for the best," I whisper, chin wobbling. "Why does it hurt?"

Ihsaan laughs softly. "Sometimes pain is good. It reminds us to come back to ourselves." He grasps my hands gently, and I'm too upset to be shocked by the uncharacteristic touch. "It helps us grow. It keeps us human. Years down the line you'll look back and be thankful for every experience that led you to where you are. Be brave, Hayat." He rubs a soothing circle on my knuckles. "I know you're brave."

I give him a weak, watery smile.

We sit like that for a while—brother and sister. Wrapped in silence and a touch that says everything words can't.

Early in the morning, I wake up for tahajjud.

I've probably prayed tahajjud only a handful of times in my life, but the need this time is so strong that I don't even set an alarm. When I pray, I sit on the mat for a long time, so lost in crying and making du'aas that I'm startled when I hear the Fajr adhaan.

For the first time since Arafat passed away, a peculiar sense of sukoon blankets me.

Later that day, to distract myself by talking to someone whose presence always calms me down, I decide to surprise Aneela with a visit at the hospital.

She had sent me her schedule a while ago in case I ever needed anything. I check it and see that she has a shift later in the afternoon. After eating a late breakfast with my mom, I kiss her goodbye, explaining that I want to congratulate Aneela in person.

Once I reach the hospital and have gone through all the necessary formalities, I'm making my way towards the cafeteria. I'm in the middle of texting Aneela to see if she could meet me here from the pediatrics unit when a sight causes me to stop short.

The hospital cafeteria is relatively empty, save for a couple at one table and a family with a squabbling baby at another. But at a third table are Aneela and Mikaal, both donned in white coats. Although they sit across from one another, they maintain a respectful distance. Aneela is earnestly saying something to him, her hand movements indicating it's a serious conversation. A frown grazes Mikaal's face as he trains his eyes to the tabletop.

Normally, I'm not the kind of person who would eavesdrop on a conversation like this, but the tension in the air is almost palpable and piques my curiosity.

Discreetly I make my way towards them, making sure to remain out of their sight. I quickly settle at a table nearby and turn my back to them, pretending to be on my phone. Straining my ears to listen,

I catch the tail end of Aneela's sentence: "…didn't realize, but do you know what you want to do moving forward?"

"I'm not…I didn't…" Mikaal's voice is strained, and I shift my head slightly to hear him better. "I didn't realize she felt that way."

My heart jolts. *Oh, God. Please tell me I didn't just walk into this conversation.*

"Can I ask you something?" Aneela says. "Do you feel anything for her?"

Oh, God. I *did* walk into this conversation. When Abeer and I weren't talking, I had ranted to Aneela about the whole Mikaal situation. In my panicked and frustrated state, I asked her to do whatever was needed to find out how he felt about me—if anything. At the time, I felt like the not knowing was killing me.

Now I'm not so sure that was the best idea.

There are a few tense moments of silence as I hold my breath before Mikaal says, "To be honest, I don't think I've ever…I'm not sure I've ever thought of her that way."

I think deep down, I had always been aware of this. But hearing it aloud feels like being dunked in ice cold water. My body shivers involuntarily, and I blink to keep the sudden tears at bay.

"But you care about her," Aneela says matter-of-factly.

Again, silence. I wish I could turn around and see the expression on his face.

"Well…yes."

I inhale a sharp breath.

"In what way?" Aneela prompts.

"She's…my late best friend's sister. I've known her for years." Silence stretches between them, thick and heavy. Aneela and I both wait for him to continue.

But he doesn't.

"So you feel responsible for her?"

Mikaal exhales deeply. I risk turning my head slightly. His head is bowed, hands wringing behind his neck.

"Mikaal, look," Aneela's voice is gentle but firm. "If you're not willing to give this responsibility a name, don't give the girl any hope or expectations."

Sharp tears prick at my eyes. I turn away from them and swipe roughly at my face, angered by my out of control emotions.

Mikaal must have lifted his head because his voice is clearer when he asks, "Do you really think she has feelings for me?"

Aneela's response is immediate. "Is that a rhetorical question?"

When Mikaal speaks again after a long pause, his voice is tinged with sorrow. "A few weeks ago, I felt like things were getting…risky. Hayat and I were on shaky ground, and I felt it was best to keep my distance. I respect her—not just as my best friend's sister, but as a woman as well. So I told her we should keep our distance. I don't have any regrets on that front, but I really didn't mean to hurt her. She seemed to be in a vulnerable place and it was almost as if…" He takes a deep breath. "As if she was relying on me as a source of comfort?" His sentence comes out a question. "Like a remnant of the life she had when her brother was alive. And I would never want to be the kind of guy who would take advantage of her vulnerability, especially while she was still grieving."

"And you thought that since she was already hurting, you didn't want her to get emotionally attached or cause any emotional damage to herself," Aneela concludes quietly.

Mikaal's silence is answer enough.

Aneela's voice is conciliatory when she speaks. "You're a good man, Mikaal." Pause. "All of what you said may be true, but so are Hayat's feelings. Nothing on her end is insincere."

Suddenly, I no longer have the strength or the desire to listen to this conversation.

God, what am I doing?

Things are finally going well at home. I'm going to Princeton in about two months. I really don't have the energy to keep chasing answers or holding onto things that aren't mine. I just want to let go. I want to focus on my family. On myself.

I swipe at the tears that have been rapidly streaming down my face and quietly stand, making my way to the cafeteria's exit.

"Hayat?" Aneela's voice rings out, stopping me in my tracks.

Oh, God. My heart beats rapidly against my chest. I wipe my face with my sleeve and plaster on a bright smile before turning around.

Aneela scrutinizes me with narrowed eyes, honing in on my reddened nose and dampened eyelashes even from a couple feet away.

Mikaal's head snaps towards me before he immediately looks away, a remorseful look passing over his features.

"Salaam, guys!" I chirp, my voice dripping with false cheer. "What a surprise. I was just…passing by and…meeting a friend."

Mikaal throws me a look of disbelief, but it's only halfhearted as his eyes are still marred by guilt.

Aneela glances between the two of us, then clears her throat. "Oh, I see!" she says, attempting to dissolve any tension. "Wanna grab a coffee and sit for a bit? I have a few minutes."

Mikaal takes that as his cue to stand. "I'll leave you guys to it," he murmurs. "I gotta get back. Salaam." He nods at both of us before turning and exiting the cafeteria, disappearing from view.

An ache sears through my chest.

"Hayat?" Aneela's voice brings me back to earth. She walks over and wraps me in a breathless hug. The familiar scent of her surrounds me—lavender and lilies—and I cling to her fiercely.

"You okay?" she whispers as she pulls back, tracing my blotched features.

I muster the courage to smile. "Yes."

Either she doesn't think now is an appropriate time to extend the conversation, or she senses I have no desire to dwell on it. Whatever the reason is, I'm grateful when she simply nods and leads me to a table.

After she buys me a coffee and settles across from me, I finally voice the real reason for my visit. "I wanted to congratulate you in person."

A pleased flush creeps up Aneela's cheeks as she beams. The

sight brings a smile to my face as well, the dried tears creasing on my cheeks. "Thank you, Hayat."

I ask the question that's been lingering in my mind since Ihsaan broke the news last night. "If you don't mind, I'm curious to know…what made you say yes?"

She settles her chin in her hands and gazes thoughtfully into the distance. "It's the qadr of Allah." Pause. "Ihsaan is a good person. A good man, a good son, a good brother. I have no reason to say no. I trust that he'll be a good husband as well."

I watch her, quietly marveling at how life has brought me here—witnessing two people choosing to lay down their grief and give each other a chance.

Aneela's eyes glaze with contemplation as she continues, "I felt guilty at first, felt like I was…betraying Arafat. But after praying istikhara and thinking about it for a bit, I came to a decision. As much as it hurts, he's gone, Hayat." Her lips tremble slightly, but she takes a deep breath to gain her bearings. I reach forward and grasp her hand in mine. "Life…has to go on. And it isn't fair to myself or to his memory to live any less than to the fullest. To keep turning people away."

I startle. "Keep turning people away? Have you been getting a lot of proposals?"

"A few," she admits humbly.

My lips lift in a smirk. "And Ihsaan is the one you said yes to."

Aneela ducks her head, but I don't miss the smile inching across her face. "Like I said, Ihsaan is a good man. And it feels as if…our destinies are connected. He's written in my qadr, and I'm written in his." She locks gazes with me and squeezes my hand, eyes sparkling with an indecipherable emotion. "So yes, I choose him."

***

December dawns frosty and bitter cold. Snow blankets every surface and holiday decorations adorn the entire neighborhood, casting a peaceful glow on the shimmering white. In a little over a month, I'll be leaving for Princeton University. And with most people on holiday break by mid-December, our families saw no reason to delay Ihsaan and Aneela's nikah.

They both wanted to keep it small, saving the larger walima for when Aneela graduates med school. So we're hosting the nikah at our house. But being Pakistani, "small" still means extravagant decorations and over-the-top arrangements. My brother and his fiancée have tasked me with taking care of the floral decorations, a duty I am both overwhelmingly excited and nervous for.

When the day of the nikah arrives, everyone is frantically running around the house and making sure all arrangements are taken care of. Papa is gesturing to the caterers while Mama is drilling a list of orders to someone on the phone. Ihsaan's friends are helping him get ready in his room, and Abeer and I are tending to the floral arrangements, tangled in garlands and petals.

"Okay," my best friend huffs. "I got this. You go do any last minute touch ups."

"Are you sure?" I say hastily.

"Yes, of course, girlie." She winks at me. "Don't worry, help is arriving."

Right on cue, the doorbell rings. I rush to open it and smile at the person standing on the porch. "Salaam, Rumana."

"Wa 'Alaikum Salaam, Hayat." Her eyes rove over me as she pulls me in for a hug. "You look stunning."

"Thank you," I reply breathlessly. After much contemplation—and a sort-of tense conversation—I decided to invite Rumana to the nikah too. It was about time to accept that while Abeer is still my best friend, we have evolved into a trio. It will take some time and adjustment, but I figured this is as good a time as any to mend any fissures in my relationship with Rumana.

She beelines to a struggling Abeer, who's wrestling with a fallen floral garland around the staircase. "Go, Hayat," Rumana says. "We got this."

I nod gratefully and head upstairs to check my appearance. As per the floral arrangements, the color scheme of the nikah is green and white. All my family members are wearing green, while all of

Aneela's family members are wearing white. I smooth my kameez over my gharara and adjust my dupatta to fall neatly over my neck and chest. Abeer curled my hair and did my makeup, and I turn this way and that in the mirror, inspecting the final look.

Last night, something compelled me to line my eyes with kohl—a rare choice for me. I didn't dwell on the reason, just buried myself in today's preparations.

After a spritz of some subtle hair glitter and a quick lipstick touch-up, I head back downstairs to see that everything is under control.

Guests begin arriving an hour later. Despite our intentions to keep it small, there are still somehow fifty people filling the house (which is also somehow still small by Pakistani standards). As I scan the crowd, the twinkling lights, the lush decorations, a lightness blooms in my chest.

When Abeer's family arrives, I catch Rameez's eye and tense, unsure what to expect. We haven't spoken since parting ways about a month ago, and although it hurt a lot at first, the ache considerably lessened and has almost disappeared altogether. At the end of the day, I know I made the right decision. And I've honestly been too busy with Ihsaan's nikah and prepping for Princeton to dwell on anything.

But then, Rameez surprises me by throwing me a tentative smile and a little wave. My shoulders relax and I smile back, nodding in greeting. It feels as if another weight has been lifted off my chest.

When my parents walk Ihsaan into the living room, the crowd erupts in cheers. I clap so hard and grin so brightly that my hands and cheeks hurt. It takes all of my willpower to keep my gaze trained on my brother and not on a certain med student tugging him in for a hug, whom I have been religiously avoiding for the past two weeks.

When Aneela walks into the living room, accompanied by her mother and sister, all the women gasp and *ooh* and *aah*. She looks positively regal in a white and golden gharara set, a white hijab, and an embroidered veil with *Ihsaan ki dulhan* written across it. I grasp her hand as she walks by and she squeezes it softly, as if I'm the one who needs reassurance.

I cry when Ihsaan and Aneela say "Yes, I do." I cry when the imam makes a collective du'aa for them. I cry when they exchange rings. I cry when both our parents place floral necklaces around their necks. I cry when Ihsaan's eyes shine with adoration as he looks at Aneela and gives her a hug. Abeer keeps chiding me that I will ruin my makeup, but she wraps a comforting arm around me and rests her head against mine all the same.

When the food is being served, Mama asks me to go around and make sure all the guests are helping themselves to dinner. I do as she asks, flitting around the living room, the family room, and towards the few brave souls who have ventured to the terrace despite the bitter cold.

As I'm heading back inside, I turn the corner into the living room and almost slam straight into Mikaal Zaman.

Mayday mayday!

I'd been so focused on the guests that I forgot I was trying to avoid him. Panic flares. I spin around to retreat, but his voice rings out, rooting me in place.

"Hayat, can we talk? If you're not busy."

I squeeze my eyes shut, debating whether to pretend I didn't hear him. But I must linger in indecision too long because he coughs and says, "Hayat, I know you heard me."

My eyes fly open and I turn around slowly, wiping any sheepishness off my face. I plaster on a huge smile as I say, "Mikaal! Did you have something to eat?"

His lips quirk as if he knows I'm trying to throw him off my tracks. But he remains, as always, polite as he nods. "Yes, I did. Thank you for asking."

"Great!" I chirp, grabbing the ends of my dupatta and playing with the ornaments. "Please take some more food! There's plenty."

I turn to go, but once more his voice freezes me in my tracks. "Can we talk, please? I know you've been trying to avoid me, but I promise it'll just be for a few minutes." He gestures to the hallway, where we will still be visible but won't have to fear any eavesdroppers.

I laugh, and it comes out too high and too breathless. "Avoid you?" I squeak. "Nonsense. I'm just busy."

He sighs and steps into the hallway, and I'm forced to follow despite wanting to flee. Mikaal runs a hand through his hair. I hate how endearing I find the motion and immediately shift my gaze.

His next words do enough to distract me. "I know you overheard me and Aneela at the hospital that day."

My body tenses, triggering my fight-or-flight response. If I choose fight, I'll probably walk away from this conversation with my dignity and self-esteem in tatters. But if I choose flight, my chances of maintaining any dignity or self-respect at all are also pretty slim.

The odds are not in my favor today.

"I'm sorry," Mikaal says, his voice low. "I don't mean to embarrass you or make you feel weird. I know this must be awkward."

He averts his gaze, tugging on the sleeve of his royal blue kurta. Something about the motion—so unsure, so human—softens something in me. My eyes lose their edge as I look at him.

"I've honestly been wanting to talk about this for a while but didn't know how to approach you."

"It's okay," I murmur, looking away to quiet the ache that has begun to form in my heart.

I make the mistake of locking eyes with my brother from across the living room, whose gaze darts between Mikaal and me. He frowns, then raises his brows in question, as if to ask: *Everything okay?*

I give a slight nod, and his shoulders relax. He turns back to Aneela, a softness appearing in his eyes as he listens to her speak.

Mikaal's voice jars me back to attention. "Look, I just"—He shoves a hand through his hair again—"I wanted to apologize."

My brows fly. "Apologize? For what?"

He rubs a hand behind his neck. "I'm sorry that I've—I'm sorry if I've ever"—he presses his lips together as a frustrated blush creeps up his neck.

My heart thuds painfully against my chest. I take a deep breath and raise my gaze to the ceiling, blowing out a sigh. "Stop, Mikaal. You don't have to apologize for anything."

"I do—"

"No." I straighten my head, locking gazes with him as a sudden bout of surety consumes me. I don't know where I muster the courage to form my next words. "Look, I have no control over my feelings. But there's no reason for you to feel weirdly indebted to or responsible for me. You have no obligation towards me, Mikaal Zaman."

Even though it hurts, I can see some of the tension easing from his face. He shakes his head, the familiar crease reappearing between his brows. "I've made some mistakes. I—"

"Stop." I hold up a hand and inhale a sharp breath. "Yes, I have some…complicated feelings for you. Yes, they confuse me and I wasn't sure how to deal with them, which is why I asked Aneela to speak to you. Yes, I've been restless ever since I started feeling this way. But…"

My gaze lingers on his five o'clock shadow, his neatly combed hair, the crisp lines of his ironed kurta—and suddenly everything clicks into place.

The way he was so careful around me. The way he gently suggested we keep our distance. I was furious at first, convinced he was pushing me away when I needed someone most. But now I see it clearly.

He didn't want to cloud my judgment while I was grieving. And though it hurts, I'm grateful.

He did the right thing because he cares about me, in whatever way it may be.

"It's okay, Mikaal," I say gently, the truth coming to me hard and fast. "We're both at very different junctures in our lives. I'm heading to college for my Bachelor's; you're going to be finishing up med school. We should focus on that."

An emotion I can't place shines in his eyes. Surprise? Pride? Whatever it is, the force of it causes me to shift my gaze and swallow.

"You don't have to feel responsible for me anymore, Mikaal," I say quietly.

Silence stretches between us as the seconds tick by, long and heavy. I dare to glance at him after a few moments and find him fidgeting with the sleeve of his kurta again. Finally, he speaks.

"I still want to apologize. I'm sorry if I ever…led you on or gave you any sort of expectations. That genuinely was never my intention, and I'm truly sorry if that's the case. I don't want to hurt you. Not now, not ever."

I smile softly, a strange lightness spreading throughout my body despite the dull ache at his words. At the realization that I'm yet again coming to the end of something. "It's okay, Mikaal. Don't burden yourself with thoughts like that. You're not responsible for how I felt or thought."

For a moment, it seems as if he wants to argue before he shakes his head. The ghost of a smile flits across his face. "I'll be making du'aa for you. For your happiness, your success, your well being."

I swallow the lump that has formed in my throat and continue to smile, although it feels too forced now. "Likewise."

After a moment, Mikaal gives me a nod. "Take care of yourself, okay, Hayat?" He turns to go.

"Wait," I call out. He angles his body towards me and furrows his brows. "There's…a flower stuck to the bottom of your kurta."

He looks down at where I'm pointing and chuckles softly, shaking his head. I ignore the ache that forms in my chest as he plucks the tiny green flower between his fingers.

"Must have caught on from the decorations." Mikaal sweeps his gaze across the arrangements, pausing on my terrace garden in the distance. He looks back at the flower and murmurs, "I'm assuming you know which one this is?"

A corner of my lips turns up. "Hydrangea."

"Mm." He nods thoughtfully, twirling it around in his fingers. For some reason, as my eyes track the bright flower, something compels me to tell him what this particular green one symbolizes.

This time when I smile, it's real.

"For new beginnings."

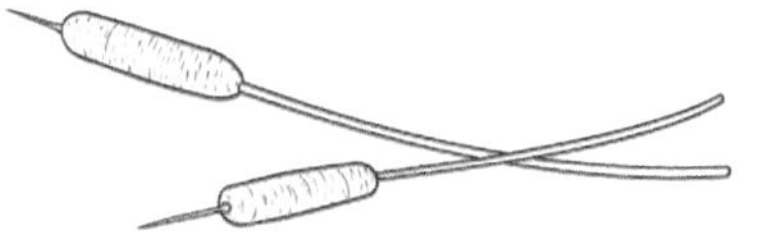

Thirty

Cattail: Peace

WE TRUDGE ACROSS THE frozen grass, my parents holding hands and Ihsaan holding one of Aneela's hands and one of mine.

There has always been a strange, unexpected sort of peace in this place. The Marlboro Muslim Memorial Cemetery, one of the largest Muslim graveyards in the tristate area, is surrounded by trees on all sides. The bare branches are coated with snow, occasionally shedding flakes when a light breeze drifts across the graveyard. Visitors all share brief greetings and sad smiles as we pass by one another.

In summer it was even more peaceful. Ducks waddled around, scattering every time we got too close. The scent of fresh flowers lingered in the air. Trees swayed gently, our clothes rippling with the wind. If you needed water to pour over the graves, you'd dash to the little cabin nearby and fill a jug from the hose. If you needed a chair, there were always a few stacked nearby.

There's a quiet communion among the visitors here—a shared sorrow, a shared reverence. It's oddly comforting.

The graveyard feels like a strange, melancholy garden. But instead of just planting flowers, we plant tears and memories in the soil as well.

I'm carrying a bouquet of peonies—Arafat's favorite flowers, symbolic for healing. Once we arrive at his grave, I grab two chairs and gesture for my parents to sit.

I take a deep breath, removing the peonies from the bouquet and pressing them gently into the mud atop the grave. I brush the snow off the headstone and rest my hand against it.

OUR BELOVED

ARAFAT AMANULLAH

LOVING SON AND BROTHER

ALWAYS REMEMBERED, ALWAYS IN OUR HEARTS

"EVERY SOUL WILL TASTE DEATH." (QUR'AN 3:185)

DOB: 4/7/1999. DOD: 6/3/2023

Every visit since Arafat's death has brought tears the moment we pulled into the graveyard. But today feels different. Today I feel almost…at peace as I rub my hand gently along the gravestone.

Aneela joins me, resting one hand next to mine and squeezing the other around my arm reassuringly.

Or perhaps she needs comfort as well.

We all hold our hands up in du'aa, our combined voices a warm thrum in the bitter January cold.

Once we're done, I settle down on the ground, ignoring the sludge of snow and mud. Ihsaan and Aneela join me while our parents remain in their chairs behind us.

Tomorrow, I'm leaving for Princeton University. The semester begins in a few days, and move-in week begins tomorrow. My belongings are all packed and ready at home, and I'm a bundle of nerves.

The past seven months have been challenging and heartbreaking, to say the least. Arafat's death rattled my family so hard that we became unrecognizable, to ourselves and to each other. My dad buried his grief in his work, my mom seldom left her room, and my brother became distant and wary. It seemed we would never be able to resume life as before.

Things have obviously changed since then. We're definitely not the same happy family as before, but we're finally coming to a good place. Arafat's absence has ripped a hole through our hearts, but we were able to find our way back to each other to mend it. Despite the challenges and the ache that accompanied us every day, we managed to take a deep breath and pull through until the next day. And then the next day. And then the next day. Day by day, breath by breath. Until we stopped surviving and started living—for each other, for ourselves.

Hearing his name still stings. We still pause and have to reorient ourselves when we receive mail with his name on it. Laughter sometimes falters when it feels like someone is missing.

But.

Tentative smiles have morphed into soft jokes and laughter. Sadness and tears have become fond memories. Agony has shifted into steady, painful healing.

I rub my hand along Arafat's name on the gravestone, letting out a deep sigh.

I'm anxious about leaving. About attending Princeton. About stepping away from my fragile, healing family. But I also feel something else—something like hope. My parents sat me down and told me it was time to turn the page, to focus on my education. They reassured me that they'd be okay. Ihsaan mussed my hair and joked that he'd finally be rid of the churail in his house. Aneela held my hands and murmured soothing words.

If Arafat were here, he would've been over the moon with happiness. I hold onto that thought, letting it steady my heart.

I look at my four family members, my gaze drifting behind me to Papa's arm around Mama's shoulders and then beside me to Aneela's hands grasped in mine and Ihsaan's.

Dream Arafat's words come back to me. *Hayat: Life.*

My eyes drift to Ihsaan, his lips moving in du'aa, his five o'clock shadow catching the light. *Ihsaan. The pursuit of excellence.*

Hayat and Ihsaan. Life and the pursuit of excellence. The perfect complements to one another.

As if he feels my eyes on him, Ihsaan turns to me. Grief shines in his eyes, but he cracks a tentative smile when we lock gazes.

And despite the anxiety, despite the ache, his smile—and the sight of my family huddled close—eases my troubled heart.

I take a deep breath, smiling back at my brother.

We'll be okay. I know we'll be okay.

"Boohoo," Abeer teases Ihsaan as he and Papa unload the car and set the boxes on the sidewalk of the dorm building.

"Yeah, yeah, wait till we take these to the dorm," Ihsaan huffs. "I'm gonna make you carry all the heavy ones."

"Joke's on you, Ihsaan bhai," Abeer says, looping her arms through mine and Aneela's. She pouts dramatically, chin trembling and worry lines creasing her forehead as she blinks rapidly. "We're just girls."

"I find it deeply unsettling when you do that," I comment, eyeing my best friend's exaggerated expression.

She breaks into a grin as my parents chuckle.

"Ihsaan," Aneela says gently, extracting her arm from Abeer's. "Let me help you. They're not even that heavy."

Ihsaan holds out an arm to stop Aneela from getting close to the boxes. "How about," his lips curve in a teasing smile, "you just stand there and look pretty."

Aneela rolls her eyes, but a blush spreads across her face as she grins at him.

He blinks in a disoriented fashion, reaching up to place a hand over his chest. "Actually," his voice comes out breathless, "don't do that. I'm suddenly weak in the knees."

Abeer squeals, clapping her hands together and pressing them against her cheeks. "They're *soooo* cute," she whisper-shouts. "Masha Allah."

Two hours later, after all the boxes have been lugged upstairs and my dorm room is officially settled, we return to the car. Mama's eyes are shining with tears as she recites a prayer. Papa has his arms around her shoulders and he gives me a watery smile. Aneela and Abeer beam at me encouragingly. And Ihsaan wears a poorly disguised expression of heartbreak.

I take turns hugging each of them, my own eyes shining with tears. My parents whisper words of comfort and encouragement in my ears, telling me how proud they are of me. Aneela and Abeer do the same, throwing in a joke or two to coax a giggle out of me. When I get to Ihsaan, he takes a deep breath and lifts his head towards the sky.

"I hate goodbyes," he groans.

"Me too." Before I can say anything else, he pulls me into a fierce hug, arms tightening around me like the ground beneath us might give way. I bury my face in his chest with equal enthusiasm, eyes closed, heart full.

"You're gonna be the greatest academic weapon history has ever seen—even greater than high school Hayat Amanullah. It's time for Princeton Hayat Amanullah," he murmurs against my hair.

I laugh hoarsely. "Let's not get ahead of ourselves."

Ihsaan pulls back and places his hands on my shoulders. He stares intently at me as he says, "Don't stress about anything, focus on your education, and make good friends. If anyone makes you cry, give me a phone call and I'll break their face, even if it's your professor—"

"Ihsaan!"

"Just kidding. Sort of. But you got this, okay? Don't worry about anything at home. I'm here, I will take care of everything." He tucks a strand of hair behind my ear and smiles. "You need this. This will be so good for you. It's the qadr of Allah."

I startle at the words, emotion crawling up my throat. I swallow thickly, reaching up to press a hand against my chest.

Both my brothers have come to say goodbye.

"Group hug!" Abeer says, clapping her hands together. Then her gaze darts to Papa and Ihsaan. "Actually, uhhh, family group hug first, and then Abeer hug."

Everyone laughs as my family huddles together one last time. Then I give Abeer a final squeeze before waving to everyone. For a moment I pause, imprinting the image in my mind: Mama's head resting on Papa's shoulder as she blows me a kiss, Ihsaan and Aneela's arms around each other, and Abeer waving like she'll never stop.

When Arafat died, it seemed as if our life came to a sudden halt. Like our happiness was a pendulum, and it was struck by a sudden force that made it stop oscillating back and forth altogether.

As I turn around and make my way back to the dorm building entrance, a content smile blooms on my lips.

I know he's here with me.

And our pendulum has finally begun to swing again.

Epilogue

Sunflower: Timelessness

FOUR YEARS LATER

STUDENTS SPILL OUT OF the lab, chattering amongst themselves about the first round of simulated patient encounters and feedback sessions we just observed. I nod at my new friends to head to the dining hall without me, idling by the entrance to the lab room as the instructors and residents filter out.

My phone lights up with a text. I open it to see that Mama's sent a picture of my thriving terrace garden, sunflowers in full bloom, to the family group chat. Underneath it, she's put a thumbs-up emoji and the caption: Lookin goooooood.

Papa's reply follows. Tell Shehzaadi how much I help too.

A laugh bubbles out of me, accompanied by a searing homesickness. I take a deep breath and shove it away, focusing on the door to the lab again.

When the resident I'm waiting for steps out, he does a double take before his face breaks out into a smile.

"Salaam, Dr. Zaman," I say with a little wave.

Mikaal hasn't changed much. There's more stubble along his

jaw now, and faint shadows under his eyes—probably the toll of residency—but still the same gentle eyes and radiant smile.

I assume I've changed in his eyes, too. Shorter hair, a more confident gait, and happier eyes, to say the least.

"Hayat Amanullah," Mikaal pronounces my name as if he's revealing something grand. We pause, locked in a gaze full of unspoken words, before breaking eye contact. "Wa 'Alaikum Salaam. It was a pleasant surprise seeing you in lab. How are you?"

I laugh nervously, unsure how to summarize the whirlwind of the past four years. When I was at Princeton, I made it a point to come home as often as possible, but I seldom saw Mikaal Zaman. His last two years of med school and first two years of residency seemed to become more gruesome and time-consuming, just as Aneela's did, and he was barely ever home. Not that I was bothered (much); I needed to clear my head of any romantic notions regarding the male species and focus completely on my family and my education.

And the past four years honestly did me so good.

"I'm good, Alhamdulillah," I settle for, ignoring the buzzing of my phone. "I saw you in there and just wanted to say Salaam and see how everything's going. How are you?"

"Awesome, Alhamdulillah." He adjusts the file in his hands, eyes flicking briefly to my fingers as I turn the call off. It's Abeer; I'll just call her back. "The last time I talked to Ihsaan, he mentioned you were coming to Harvard. It's an *amazing* achievement, and you're gonna thrive here. Congratulations, Hayat."

I bloom like a flower at his words. "Thank you so much. When I saw you with the instructors, I had to do a double take. I'd heard you matched with Harvard, but of all med schools, of all programs, we've ended up in the same place yet again, huh? Small world, Subhan Allah."

Mikaal chuckles, eyes crinkling at the motion. I discover that I find this as endearing as I found it four years ago, yet it's not accompanied by an ache as before. "Honestly, I thought the same when I saw you in there." He pauses, shifting the file to his other hand and tapping his fingers against it, staccato. A surprising realization dawns.

Mikaal Zamaan is nervous.

I try to hide the smile tugging at the corners of my lips.

"So you mentioned you're doing residency in emergency medicine, right?" I say.

"Yes!" Mikaal replies, launching into stories from residency. His passion is magnetic—his eyes light up, his gestures animated, his smile constant. The way he speaks of his profession is, quite frankly, breathtaking.

"Wow," I breathe. "That sounds like a dream."

He huffs out a surprised laugh. "I think you're the first person I've heard say medicine sounds like a dream. It must be the first-year-of-med-school charm."

A smile grazes my lips. "Hey, I mean, you sounded pretty passionate yourself." Pause. "I know I've just gotten started, but I didn't expect to love it as much as I do. It's obviously still difficult and quite different from APs in high school and rigorous two-hour lectures in undergrad. On the first day, when I saw that the *syllabus* had chapters, I called my parents in tears and asked them why I thought this was a good idea"—Mikaal chuckles, and I press on—"but then I remembered why I'm here, why I'm doing this and"—I shrug—"everything feels worth it. There'll be ups and downs, but I'm enjoying it and I'll be okay, Insha Allah."

Mikaal studies me, eyes full of something intense and unreadable. Finally he says, "Arafat would be so proud of you."

I grin, happiness radiating through me. "I hope so."

"I know so."

"By the way," I add, "I'm interested in pursuing emergency medicine too, whenever I get to residency—*if* I get to residency."

Mikaal shakes his head, eyes alight with laughter. "You will, Insha Allah. Don't let the terrifying syllabi get to you."

"Insha Allah. Sooo…" My phone begins buzzing again, and this time it's a FaceTime call from Ihsaan. I send a quick text that

I'll call back soon before turning back to Mikaal. "Can I keep you in mind when I want to shadow residents or doctors?"

His eyebrows fly in surprise. "Oh. Yeah, of course. I'd be honored."

"Thank you!"

"Yeah, no problem. And if there's anything you need with your academics or anything else to make your time here easier, reach out whenever you need."

My breath catches, even though he's making a courteous, professional offer. "I appreciate that so much. Thank you."

"No problem." There's a loaded pause between us before Mikaal says, in a tone of suspiciously forced nonchalance, "So I guess we'll be seeing more of each other now."

I nod. "I guess so."

He trains his eyes to the ground, fingers resuming their tapping motion against his file. "Well, it was nice seeing you. Take care and...I'll see you soon, Insha Allah." He looks back up at me as he murmurs, "Salaam."

"Wa 'Alaikum Salaam," I respond with a wave as he walks away.

A couple seconds later, I realize I have a stupid smile on my face and quickly wipe it off.

As I walk to the dining hall, I return Ihsaan's FaceTime call and wait as it rings. Ihsaan and Aneela's faces fill the screen, sunlight shining against their skin and the sound of rushing water nearby.

"Salaam!" Aneela chirps.

"Dr. Amanullah!" Ihsaan hollers.

I frantically lower the volume of my phone and chuckle. "Not yet, Ihsaan. Hi, Aneela!"

"Potayto potaato." Ihsaan waves me off. I squint at the screen and study the scene behind them: ocean waves, glittering sand, and rays of sunlight dancing across the water.

"Plan finally made it out the group chat, huh?" I say happily as Ihsaan swivels his camera around. "Bora Bora must be nice."

"It's *this* one," Ihsaan says in mock frustration, tilting his head towards Aneela. "Do you know how impossible it is for Dr. Arshad to get any time off?"

Aneela playfully shoves his shoulder. "Says Mr. HR Specialist."

"Ihsaan," I cluck my tongue disapprovingly. "She's in her third year of residency. She probably doesn't even get any time to breathe."

Ihsaan sticks his tongue out at both of us but wraps his arm around Aneela's shoulders. "Now you two med people are gonna gang up against me, huh? I'm not sure how much of this I can take. My face is too pretty to handle all these stress lines."

Aneela giggles as I roll my eyes. I'm entering the dining hall now and signal to my friends that I'm on my way.

"Stop bickering and focus on having a good time," I reprimand my brother.

He fake gasps, clutching a hand against his chest. "Who's bickering? I'm not bickering. Are we bickering?" he asks Aneela, who continues to giggle at his antics. Ihsaan turns back to me and smirks. "You're just jealous you're cooped up in a depressing lab surrounded by half-crazy people instead of sitting at a beach in Bora Boraaaaaaa," he singsongs.

I shake my head, a smile blooming on my lips. "Oh, hush. I have to go eat dinner now but keep sending pictures in the chat! Have a great time, you guys. And Ihsaan"—I narrow my eyes at my brother and tease—"don't bother Aneela. She's older than you, so listen to her."

His eyes soften, gazing at his wife. "She doesn't need to be older than me for me to listen to her."

My face blossoms into a smile as I bid them goodbye and end the call. I decide to call Abeer back quickly before I get busy again.

"Hello, human!" she says enthusiastically when she picks up. "Before you tell me all about your first week as a big girlboss med student, please let me rant about this guy."

"She's been going on about this nonstop," Rumana adds from outside the screen's view.

Laughter bubbles out of me as I head to the buffet tables. I balance my phone against the counter as I grab a plate. "What did he do now? Did he ask for your dad's number, Abeer?"

"Ugh!" she groans. "Yes! And I'm panicking! I'm panicking! Like, thinking of going for a swim in the Atlantic ocean panicking! Please come back and knock some sense into me!"

"Isn't this exactly what you've been wanting?" I say as I fill my plate with food.

"Yes! But now that's it's happened I'm"—she stops abruptly, eyes narrowing on something behind me.

"What?" I ask, confused.

Her eyes widen. "Oh, my God," she whisper-shouts, covering her mouth and squealing as she throws me a meaningful look. "Is that Mikaal Zaman?"

Shoot.

I turn around slowly and see Mikaal a couple feet away, talking to someone. His eyes flick to me for a moment before he turns back to the student, a smile tugging at the corners of his lips.

He definitely heard Abeer and her loud mouth.

Despite my mission to focus solely on my education and my family over the past four years...I'm human. And there were moments of weakness.

Flashes of memory flicker through my mind—late-night rants and squeals with Abeer about Mikaal Zaman, the rare glimpses of him over the years, the tidbits of news I pretended to be indifferent about. The way Abeer would tease me relentlessly once she realized his name alone could bring a blush to my cheeks.

I turn back to my best friend, frantically sending a please-shut-your-loud-mouth SOS with my eyes.

But then, against my better judgment, a slow smile spreads across my face.

"Yes. Yes, it is."

Acknowledgements

There's always a family and a village behind a work.

First and foremost, Alhamdulillah. All praise and thanks be to God, for providing me with the strength to pull myself and my writing out of a dark place and shed the world's light on it. Without Your guidance and mercy, nothing is possible.

A sincere and heartfelt thanks to my wonderful developmental editor Allison Lau, who embraced my vision as her own and helped reignite my creative spark. Thank you for believing in me and my work; I'm so glad my story found you.

To my lovely copy/line editor Abigail Willis, who was dedicated to making *Pendulum* shine. Thank you for developing a deeply intimate relationship with the characters and ensuring their voices would resonate with readers.

To my amazing book cover designer Maryna Arsenieva, who spectacularly delivered my vision for this book. Thank you for understanding just what I needed visually.

To my sweet interior book designer Lorna Reid, who once again brought my words to life on the page. Thank you for aligning my vision with your superb design experience.

To my illustrator Melisa Labra, who poured passion into the flowers at the beginning of each chapter. Thank you for understanding how sacred that space was.

To my beta readers Noholi Ongshi and Sarah Quraishi: Noholi, thank you for being one of the first sets of eyes to read and give feedback on *Pendulum*. Sarah, thank you for providing your keen med student eye to ensure everything was consistent to the med school experience.

To my proofreaders Ikram Akin and Jennath RK: Ikram, thank

you for being a wonderful friend and an avid reader with an eye for detail. Jennath, thank you for being the last set of eyes to read *Pendulum* and ensure nothing was amiss.

To my friends and cousins Mariam, Duaa, Hafsah, Muskan, Ammarah, Nabihah, Heba, Khadeeja, Noor, and Fakhar, for the girlhood and support. Thank you for keeping me sane and for believing in me.

And most importantly, my family:

To Mama, for your unconditional love, support, and encouragement always. God blessed me with an absolutely amazing mother and no amount of gratitude will ever be enough. Thank you for always believing in me even when I didn't, for encouraging me even when I was at the peak of exhaustion, and for being a constant source of warmth. May God reward you for your big, beautiful heart. Love you.

To Papa, for being the bridge I crossed to get to where I am today. You show your love in different, less overt ways, but in meaningful ways nonetheless. I want you to know that all of your sacrifices mean something, and I hope you're proud of your daughter. Love you.

To Rimsha, for always inspiring me. Through your resilience, your strength, and your courage. Some of Arafat's oldest sibling tendencies were drawn from you, and I don't think I could've written a story about siblings without having a sister like you to look up to.

To Fasiih, for being the source of so much of Ihsaan's crackhead goofiness. Every time I struggled to write lighthearted banter between Ihsaan and Hayat, I thought "What would Fasiih say here?" Thanks for showing support in your own weird brotherly way (much like Ihsaan).

To Fatima, for being a mirror to Hayat. For your sleepless nights and AP classes and plethora of involvements that you think no one sees—I see you, crazy little sister. Thank you for listening to me every time I tied my hair back, sat down, and said "Wanna hear my dilemma?"

To Ujala, my precious little baby cousin. Thank you for coming into my life and spreading ujala (light) in the darkest corners. Love you with all my heart, meri jaan.

And to you, wonderful reader. Thank you for picking up this book. I hope something—anything—in these pages has touched your heart.

About the Author

Kainat Azhar is a Pakistani-American Muslim author who cherishes stories. She writes about brown Muslim women with messy feelings and big hearts chasing happy endings, charming heroes with dynamic personalities, and the experiences of faith, culture, and identity from a Pakistani-American Muslim perspective. She tends to avoid reading books that will make her cry, but has no problem writing them. When not immersed in a book or frantically typing on her laptop, Kainat can probably be found slurping noodles or watching Turkish dramas (often simultaneously).

You can find her at **kainatazharchughtai.com**, on Instagram @author.kainatazhar, and by email at **kainatcazhar@gmail.com**.